Shields and Ramparts

Havoc in Wyoming

Part 4: Shields and Ramparts

Millie Copper

This is a work of fiction. All characters, places, and incidents are products of the author's imagination or are used fictitiously. Any resemblance to actual people, places, or events is entirely coincidental.

Technical information in the book is included to convey realism. The author shall assume no liability or responsibility to any person or entity with respond to any loss or damage caused, or allegedly caused, directly or indirectly by information contained in this book of fiction. Any reference to registered or trademarked brands is used simply to convey familiarity. This manuscript is in no way sponsored or endorsed by any brand mentioned.

Copyright © 2019 CU Publishing
ISBN-13: 978-1-7327482-7-9

All rights reserved.

No part of this publication may be reproduced, stored in a retrieval system, or transmitted in any form or by any means without the prior written permission of the author, except by a reviewer who may quote short passages in a review.

Written by Millie Copper

Edited by Ameryn Tucker

Proofread by Light Hand Proofreading

Cover design by Kesandra Adams

Also by Millie Copper

Now Available

Havoc in Wyoming: Part 1, Caldwell's Homestead

Havoc in Wyoming: Part 2, Katie's Journey

Havoc in Wyoming: Part 3, Mollie's Quest

Havoc in Wyoming: Part 4, Shields and Ramparts

Havoc Begins: A Havoc in Wyoming Story

Havoc in Wyoming: Part 5, Fowler's Snare

Havoc Rises: A Havoc in Wyoming Story

Havoc in Wyoming: Part 6, Pestilence in the Darkness

Christmas on the Mountain: A Havoc in Wyoming Novella

Havoc Peaks: A Havoc in Wyoming Story

Havoc in Wyoming: Part 7, My Refuge and Fortress

Stretchy Beans: Nutritious, Economical Meals the Easy Way

Stock the Real Food Pantry: A Handbook for Making the Most of Your Pantry

Design a Dish: Save Your Food Dollars

Real Food Hits the Road: Budget Friendly Tips, Ideas, and Recipes for Enjoying Real Food Away from Home

Join My Reader's Club!

Receive a complimentary copy of *Wyoming Refuge: A Havoc in Wyoming Prequel*. As part of my reader's club, you'll be the first to know about new releases and specials. I also share info on books I'm reading, preparedness tips, and more. Please sign up on my website:

MillieCopper.com

Who's Who

Jake and Mollie Caldwell: A bachelor until age thirty-seven, Jake married Mollie and suddenly became a dad to four girls. A couple of years later they added a son. They've sacrificed for years to build a safe retreat for their children, sons-in-law, grandson, extended family, and close friends. Many times, they thought they were crazy. Now, in a new world full of danger and heartache, they wonder if their plans were enough.

Sarah and Tate Garrett: Sarah is Mollie's oldest daughter. She and Tate are expecting their first child. Tate's parents, Keith and Lois, and his sister, Karen, were visiting from out of state when the attacks started. They're now stranded in Wyoming.

Angela and Tim Carpenter: Angela is Mollie's second oldest. She and Tim are parents to Gavin, age two. Angela was injured when she and neighbor Doris Snyder were assaulted while on a supply run. Tim's dad, Art, reluctantly joined Tim and Angela at the Caldwell homestead. To everyone's surprise, farm life seems to agree with Art.

Calista "Calley" and Mike Curtis: Calley is Mollie's third born. She married Mike, the boy next door, two years ago. Calley has long thought her mom and Jake had some strange ideas, not just with their prepper lifestyle but with their belief in God. Lately, she's begun to think maybe they aren't so strange after all. Mike's parents, Roy and Deanne, along with Mike's recently single sister, Sheila Stapleton, escaped Casper for the Caldwell homestead with Calley and Mike. Out of everyone, Sheila has had the hardest time adjusting to the new world they find themselves in.

Katrina "Katie" Andrews: Katie is Mollie's youngest daughter. Before the attacks, she was living away from home while finishing college. After her college town was overrun by people escaping the city, Katie and her boyfriend Leo made their way to Bakerville. Katie was severely injured when a Bakerville neighbor tried to kidnap Katie, Sarah, Calley, and Mollie. Her injuries are still life-threatening.

Malcolm Caldwell: Jake and Mollie's youngest child. He's *almost* eleven and is Jake's right-hand man. Before the attacks, he was the only child still living at home.

Leo Burnett: Katie's boyfriend and a former K-State business major, construction worker, and Marine. He has skills but doesn't want to overstep his perceived boundaries.

Alvin and Dodie Caldwell: Jake's parents. They're both in their seventies and fiercely independent. Before the attacks, they lived in nearby Prospect. Prospect has experienced many challenges, including the hospital burning to the ground. Happy to be in Bakerville, Alvin and Dodie now worry about Jake's brother, Robert, and his wife and children living in California. Have they been severely affected by these tragedies?

Bill Shane, Aaron Ogden, and Laurie Esplin: Grandmaster Bill Shane teaches martial arts to Jake, Mollie, and Malcolm in nearby Wesley, Wyoming. Jake invited him to join them at the homestead if the situation deteriorated in Wesley. Bill brought Black Belt and secondary instructor Aaron Ogden as well as Aaron's girlfriend, also a Taekwondo Black Belt, when they escaped Wesley.

Doris and Evan Snyder: Neighbors and good friends of the Caldwells. Evan is a retired deputy sheriff, having been part of the county's Specialized Services Division. Doris is retired from both the Navy and a government job. She insists she wasn't a spy or anything, but she doesn't talk about the work she used to do. Doris, along with Angela, was injured when assaulted on a supply run. Doris's oldest daughter lives in Germany and is assumed safe. Her youngest daughter, Lindsey, and her husband Logan live in San Jose. Evan was able to talk to them when the cell phones started working. But they have no idea where, or how, they are now.

Phil and Kelley Hudson: Community members. Mollie considers Kelley one of her closest friends. Phil, retired Coast Guard, is a leader of the community. Kelley is a psychiatric nurse practitioner, retired from Commissioned Corps. Kelley's children, Sylvia and Sabrina, were packing up to leave Arizona at last contact. They have no idea where they are now.

Belinda and TJ Bosco: Belinda, a nurse practitioner, is fourth generation Bakerville and related to the founders of the community. TJ is friends with Malcolm. Belinda and her mom, Tammy, a retired labor and delivery nurse, are core members of the Bakerville medical team. The family has recently experienced heartache with the death of Belinda's husband and her dad—Tammy's husband—Tom.

David and Betty Hammer: Neighbors and friends of the Caldwells. The Hammers are Texas natives recently transplanted to Wyoming. Their sons Noah and Andrew Hammer lived in Bakerville when the attacks began. Two additional children, spouses, and grandson barely made it to Bakerville with their lives. Their oldest son lives back east. They haven't heard from him since the cyberattacks. David has become the spiritual leader of the local neighborhood.

Chapter 1

Lindsey Maverick

Tuesday, Day 6
San Jose, California

The pain in my neck is instant and excruciating. I'm face down, kissing the sidewalk. He's on top of me, pulling my hair, pawing at me. The smell is unbearable. Ammonia. Sweat. Booze.

He grunts as he gives a yank on my utility belt. I'm lying with my weapon pinned. Useless.

He reaches under my right side, trying to spin me on to my back. I dig into the concrete, resisting his efforts. I turn my head to the side, flattening my body. A pockmarked face and greasy hair greet me. His scrawny forearm pushes on my cheek.

"Fight me, baby. Fight me," he slurs. "We're having a good time now."

From the size of his arm and the hollowness of his cheek bones, I assume he's gaunt and sickly from continual drug abuse. And maybe a drunk. This could play in my favor.

I'm in excellent condition and not a small woman by any means. I'm tall, just shy of six feet. My daily workouts and training should give me an advantage over a scrawny, decrepit drunk. At least that's my hope—that he's on the booze and not a PCP or meth high where his strength is pharmaceutically enhanced, along with providing a sense of invulnerability.

I dig my feet into the ground and start to crawl away—I need a little distance between us. He lets go of me just long enough to pick up a piece of broken concrete and slam it into my hamstring.

"Argh!" I cry out. Did he break my leg? I keep scooting, dragging my injured limb.

"Now, baby, don't be like that. I don't want to hurt you . . . too much. This can be good for both of us."

There's finally space between us, several feet.

I flip to my butt and pull my service weapon. "Stop. Now."

His eyes—glazed and unfocused . . . dead looking—drop slightly, eyeballing my Glock. One side of his lip curls up. He opens his mouth, releasing a guttural roar, then bends his knees and springs toward me.

I squeeze the trigger. The first shot catches him square in the chest. The second shot, immediately following, catches his shoulder. He's knocked back, landing on the ground.

I keep my Glock trained on him, watching for movement. He sucks in a breath, then lets out a loud rattle. His chest shakes several times as blood flows freely. His left arm twitches, moving toward the discarded concrete. The movement stops.

"Hey," a course whisper says. "Hey, Officer, are you okay? Can I get you some help?"

Glock at the ready, I spin my torso.

"Wait, wait," the lady says. "We can help you." Hands in the air, she gestures with her head to the man standing next to her. Eyes wide, his hands are also up.

I let the Glock sag to my thigh.

A few days ago, I would've had a partner to help, to back me up. But everything changed when the power went out.

San Jose, where I work for the police department, had its share of violence when the power was on. I've been with SJPD for about eighteen months. I'm part of The Bureau of Field Operations, or BFO, what many would refer to as a "beat cop."

This has been a big change from my first position after the academy. I was one of sixty-eight commissioned officers in a small city of a hundred thousand people, south of Seattle. With the SJPD, there's just under a thousand of us serving the city of over a million. It can get crazy on a normal day . . . what we've experienced recently is anything but normal.

I work out of the Southern Division, and for the most part, it's been business as usual since the planes crashed Thursday night.

Well, mostly business as usual. Until Sunday, when things started to get a little bit hinky. By the time my shift ended, we'd gone from hinky to bad—very bad.

I showed for my regular shift on Monday to discover we'd lost half of our force overnight. Some had quit, some were just missing, and a few had been killed. To say we were distraught would be an understatement.

My regular partner is one of the missing. I wanted to go by his place and check on him, but we were ordered to conserve fuel. I considered going on my own time after work, but knew conserving my personal fuel was also necessary.

As of yesterday, we're no longer driving, but rather doing walking beats—alone. Fortunately, I'm assigned an area pretty close to the division headquarters. Yesterday was fine.

But today, I guess I wasn't paying enough attention. Head on a swivel is something I've always tried to practice. Why not today? Seems with everything happening, I'd be more alert than ever.

"Can we help you get up?" the lady asks.

"I'm . . . I'm not sure. He hit me with the block." I reach up to wipe my face. Blood. And likely tears.

I straighten my back to pull myself together. What must these two think of me? *Tears at times have the weight of speech* . . . Yeah, thanks, Ovid. But not now. I represent SJPD. I pick up my service cap and place it back on my head. Hats are no longer part of our daily uniform, at least they weren't when we were driving. It was decided we'd wear them now that we are on foot, to give us more of a presence. Didn't help me much.

"Yeah, we saw him hit you," the man says. "We were just down the sidewalk. We wanted to help, but . . . " His voice fades off as he gives a small, embarrassed shrug.

I put my weapon away as they help me stand. The pain is intense, not just in my leg but in my neck and my back too. There's blood dripping from my arm.

I try my radio but can't get it to work. It must have been damaged in the struggle.

"What should we do with . . . with him?" the woman asks.

I take a deep breath and momentarily close my eyes. *What should we do with him?*

"I'm not sure I can move him," the guy says with a small shudder.

"No, probably not," I agree.

I take a look around. We're at the edge of an alleyway—a well-cluttered alleyway with the stink of garbage beginning to take over.

Like the SJPD, other city services—fire trucks, ambulances, libraries, schools, and sanitation—are limited or fully shut down. No garbage trucks are running, and the smell of the city is bordering on offensive. The worst part, it's only been four days since the lights went out and everything shut down.

What's it going to be like in a week? Two weeks? The stench will be unbearable.

Unzipping a small pocket on my utility belt, I pull out an emergency thermal blanket, the cheap space-age kind. They're handy to have on hand to help prevent people from going into shock before an ambulance arrives. It'll also work to cover the dead man.

I killed him.

I'm shaking so badly I can't manage the sealed package. The Good Samaritan offers to help. He uses his teeth to open the package, then struggles with unfolding the sticky mylar as it crinkles its objection. I watch as the woman helps him.

"Wait. Let me get his identification before you cover him."

A chunky, blood-splattered silver chain hangs limply from his right hip, the large clasp hooked around a belt loop. Following the chain, I lift his hip slightly and slide a large black wallet out of his back pocket. The wallet has fancy tooling and stitching with a silver skull in the center. The skull, like the rest of the wallet, is bejeweled in blood. I quickly look for his driver's license.

Stanley James Parker. I compare the photo on the license to the dead guy. *The guy I killed.*

It's him, but definitely a picture from better times. He had more weight on him and better skin. His hair is clean and styled in the photo. And he's smiling. A nice, wholesome, guy next door type of smile. The guy on the concrete looks considerably different. And not just because he's dead.

I step away from Stanley James Parker as the couple covers him with the blanket. The man grabs a couple of small pieces of concrete to hold down each corner. Then they help me limp back to headquarters.

The reception room is overly crowded, with people spilling outside on to the steps. I thank the couple and assure them I'll be fine from here. Using the building as a crutch, I make my way to a side door. Usually, we use an electronic code to open the door, but with the power out, the keypad isn't functioning. Someone is supposed to be nearby to let us in, after verifying who's at the door.

I knock the code—three short, pause, two long. After a good minute, a female voice calls out.

"Yes?"

"Lindsey Maverick, alone and injured," I respond.

"What?"

I clear my throat and try again, louder this time. The door cracks open, and a civilian aid peeks out.

"Oh no," she gasps, reaching out for me and helping me inside to a nearby chair.

"Don't move. I'll get help." She runs down the hall.

In less than a minute, she returns with Sergeant Cunningham. He was a medic in the Army and is likely the most qualified in the building to evaluate me.

His initial expression tells me I look about how I feel. He quickly puts on a mask of professionalism and barks, "Maverick, report."

"I . . . I don't know, sir. I was attacked from behind. I had to . . . he's dead, sir." I'm struggling to keep it together. It wouldn't do any good for me to burst into tears.

"Where?"

"Next block. A couple helped me. Afterward. They helped me get back. I grabbed the guy's identification." I pull his license from my pocket.

Sarge spends several minutes looking me over. "You're going to hurt even more tomorrow. You'll have a nice shiner also. The good news, it doesn't seem you've broken anything. You lose consciousness at all?"

"No."

It wasn't said, but I knew going to the hospital would be reserved as a final option. The hospital's gone to heck in a handbasket and is fully overloaded.

My mom reads a lot of books about the "end of the world," and she's always sharing parts of what she reads. Sometimes I halfway listen. She talks about avoiding hospitals, if at all possible, when things go bad.

We're in our own end-of-the-world situation right now. Not as bad as some of those crazy books, but it's not looking too good. I wish the phones were working so I could call her. She and her husband, Evan, are probably freaking out over my safety.

I'm acutely aware how close I came to dying. If Stanley James Parker would've been armed with anything more than a fortuitous chunk of concrete, I'd be dead.

Would Sarge have sent someone out looking for me if I didn't show up at the end of my shift? If not, would my husband ever know what happened? Would Mom always wonder?

"Well, Maverick, you'll live." He hands me a wet wipe from the medical kit and motions to my face. I gently dab under my nose, bringing back blood.

"Probably want to go into the locker room, do a proper cleanup job. Do you need someone to assist you?"

"No, sir. I'll be fine."

"Good enough, then."

"Thanks, Sarge. What now? Report to IA?"

"Not at this time. Complete an incident report, and we'll address this later."

Things have changed so much in such a short time. Only fill out an incident report after killing a man? We have very strict guidelines to follow when there is an officer-involved shooting. Transparency is big with SJPD, and "Incident Investigations" have extremely precise steps, which are followed to the letter.

"Just be sure to give the address of where you left the body."

"Sure, Sarge." I nod. The lack of paperwork, and not even an interview with Homicide, has me terribly freaked out.

"Rest up a bit. Make sure you have your wits about you, then call it a day. We don't have anyone to drive you home, so be sure you're capable before taking off."

Even though I work in the Southern Division, I live farther north, in the Foothills Division, not too far from Alum Rock Park. Logan and I have a one-bedroom condo with a garage and pay a small fortune for it. We'd pay even more if we lived closer to my district.

I head to the locker room. The water in the station is no longer working on demand. There are now water stations set up in certain areas that people can go and fill their jugs. Someone has provided a few jugs for washing and buckets for flushing. There's considerable concern about how much longer the sewer system will work, something about the pumps being electric powered. They're on generator right now, but we all know it's only a short-term solution. The garbage smell will be minor if the sewer backs up. At least the water's still working at home. I'm super glad about that.

I glance in the mirror. Yikes. *Lindsey Maverick, you are a mess.*

There's a cut above my eyebrow, both eyes are puffy, and one is no doubt going to turn black. My jaw is bruised. My hair, usually worn in a bun at the nape of my neck, is partially undone. Several blond lanks hang down past my shoulders. The collar of my uniform is torn, hanging loose with the top two buttons missing, and my white tank top's peeking out. The shirt is half untucked. My pants have a slit at the knee. I bend over to inspect it, revealing a well-scraped knee compacted with bits of gravel. Lovely.

I set the plug in the sink and put in a little water, washing my hands first. The water quickly turns a muddy red—blood and dirt. Draining the sink, I reset the plug and add fresh water, then gently wash my face. Next, I take care of my knee. Everything stings as the water touches it. Once I'm somewhat clean, I fix my hair. The bun, while not as tidy as I'd like, looks better. I retuck my uniform, knowing there isn't anything I can do about the cuts and tears until I'm home with a sewing kit.

After I deem myself presentable, I head to the squad room to take care of the paperwork. While I'm finishing my incident report, Sarge spreads the word we are done.

Fully and completely done.

Chapter 2

Lindsey

Tuesday, Day 6
San Jose, California

SJPD is finished until the crisis passes. Besides my incident, two officers are missing and assumed dead. Dozens have been injured. Things have gone crazy, and without vehicles, we're pretty much sitting ducks. We're told to go home, stay safe, and protect our families and neighborhoods as best as we can.

While we all see the wisdom in stepping down, I don't think many of us like it. I figure, the ones who would really be okay with it are likely in the group that stopped showing up for work.

"Maverick, can I see you for a moment?" Sergeant Cunningham bellows.

My married name, Maverick, brought me a bit of grief when I was in the academy and early on the job. At first, I tried to encourage people to call me Lindsey, but that's just not done. I know many thought I'd fit my name, and maybe once I'm seasoned it'll be okay to be a Maverick, but as a rookie . . . nope. I've endeavored to prove myself as someone who's by the book and dependable.

"Yes, Sergeant?" I respond, while limping toward him.

He lowers his voice. "You feeling well enough to get on that bike of yours?"

"Yes, I can make it home."

"Stop by the arms room. Winchester will have a package for you."

"A package?" I ask dumbly.

"Yes. When things stop being a crap sandwich, bring back what you can. In the meantime, stay safe. I seem to remember you have family in the Midwest? You might want to head there. Less people might mean less violence. 'Course, getting there . . . " He shakes his head and says nothing more.

"Wyoming. My mom and stepdad live in Wyoming."

"Yeah, I remember meeting them when they visited you. Your stepdad's a retired deputy, right? And your mom was Army or something?"

"Navy, she was active duty, then retired from reserves. And, yes, Evan's a retired deputy sheriff."

"Lois, right? Your mom's name is Lois?"

"Doris."

He shrugs. "Well, I'd be heading to Wyoming if it was me. Go down and get your package. Best to clean out your locker too. Do you have a backpack here?"

"Yes, my usual one for commuting."

"That tiny little thing? I think we have some saddlebags that were given to us for something. Ask Winchester. He'll know where they are. And see if he has a bigger backpack you can use to get your gear home." I'm always amused our armory guy is named Winchester.

There are several people ahead of me, waiting for their own package. When it's my turn, he take me back and, as with everyone else, we speak privately. I wonder, do we all end up with the same things, or does he customize our packages based on individual needs?

"Hey, Maverick. You on your bike today?"

"Absolutely. Sarge said you might have some saddlebags I can use?"

"Yep. Sure do. Have a few specialty items you might like also. Wait here."

He's back in a few minutes with two rifles—neither are department issued.

My eyes go wide as he begins to tear one of them down, separating the barrel from the action.

"It's only a .22, and I don't have much ammo for it. But it'll fit in a backpack, maybe help you not be such a target on your trip home. And this one," he says, motioning to the second, larger rifle, "it's a beauty. The forend separates, giving you a bipod. There are two extra magazines stored in the stock. It's a 5.56, so the size you're used to."

"Wow. Nice. Uh, but these aren't . . . "

"Maverick, don't ask, don't tell. Okay? Let's find you a backpack too."

By the time Winchester's finished with me, I have a decent amount of ammo for the 5.56, a small amount for the .22, a few tear gas grenades, several flashbangs, and a non-department issued 9-millimeter. Another don't ask, don't tell situation. After I'm outfitted, he has an officer help me carry the goods to my bike.

Getting the saddlebags in place around my little tail bag, which I keep on the passenger seat for hauling things, takes some doing, but it works. I'm loaded a little more than I'm comfortable with, but not terribly so.

The trip home is mostly uneventful. I do have one guy try to stop me, and think I may hear a shot, but no real issues.

Are they shooting at me or someone else? Who knows.

I'm later getting home than I should be, and Logan, my husband of five years, is near frantic when I arrive.

"Lindsey! I was just thinking I should go look for you."

"I'm here. I'm okay," I answer, taking off my helmet.

He looks at my face, showing evidence of the earlier attack, and quickly pulls me into his arms. "What happened?"

In the safety of Logan's arms, I breakdown sobbing. Several minutes pass before I can gulp out the story of the attack and how I had to kill the guy, Stanley James Parker. I know his name will stick with me forever. The dead look in his eyes and his smell . . . that smell . . .

Through my tears, I let him know the department is done, shut down until this—whatever it is—is over. Logan says little but makes appropriate soothing responses while stroking my hair. When I'm done, I carefully step away.

I take a large breath. "Now what? Sarge said we should head for Mom and Evan's place. What do you think?"

Logan starts to talk, then stops. I suspect he's thinking of his folks in upstate New York and wishing we could go there. The idea of trying to make it to Wyoming right now is hard enough. I can't even imagine getting to New York.

He gives me a sad look. "Probably not a bad idea. Seems less people might be smart. I know it's one of the reasons your folks live there."

"How will we get there? I don't think we have enough gas to make it that far, do you?"

Logan contorts his mouth slightly to chew on the inside of his lip. He does this when he's thinking. I find it to be adorable and irritating at the same time. The contortion of his mouth gives his slightly round face an entirely different look. It's cute but isn't the Logan I love.

Of course, the stress from the last few days has also given him a different look. He looks tired. And like he needs a shave, not just his face but also his usual silky, hairless head.

He took to a clean shave a year or two back when his hairline began to recede. He was faced with buying Rogaine in bulk or embracing the baldness. I'll be the first to say, I wasn't in favor of him shaving his head. But now, what I affectionately refer to as his "chrome dome" is amazingly sexy and fits him perfectly.

"You know, your mom insisted on us filling up the bikes after the bridges were hit."

Logan and I both switched to motorcycles last year to help save on fuel costs. We had a small car until last month—we sold it since we drove it so rarely. Besides, Logan's filled up our garage with bikes.

In addition to our commuter bikes, my Honda and Logan's Kawasaki, the garage also houses Logan's old kick-start bikes. Somehow, he developed a fascination with these crazy bikes. He currently owns a 1984 Harley Davidson FXST Softail in candy red and a mostly white '92 Suzuki DR 650. He refers to them as "old-school bikes."

"I filled up the Harley and the Zuki and haven't driven them since," Logan says. "I took my Kawa to the grocery store, what, three times?"

I nod. "And I've been driving my bike back and forth to work after topping it off on Saturday afternoon."

"Your mom also told me to buy and fill a few gas cans. We already had one to fill up our fuel bottle holders. I bought another two-gallon can. 'Course, I think that may have been a dumb move since we don't have a good way to haul gas cans."

"Winchester set me up with saddlebags for my trip home. They're somewhat like ours, each with a fuel bottle in a holder. That will help some. And we can figure out something else—maybe zip tie a can on each of the pillion pads?"

"Did he give you fuel for them?"

"Nope, just the empty bottles in the little holders. He asked me if I wanted to take them, so I did."

"Maybe . . . I know you aren't going to like this, Linds, but I think we should take the kick-starts."

"Ugh. No."

He gives me a sweet smile. "It would really be best. There's less to go wrong with them. Plus, when I redid them, I swapped out the stock fuel tanks for larger ones. The Harley has a five gallon, and the Zuki has a 4.2."

"But the commuters do better on fuel," I whine.

"Yes, they do, but I can work on the Harley and Zuki. You know that. I can't do much on the newer bikes with the systems they have. The Harley still isn't terrible."

I know he's right about this. We took the kick-starters on a road trip to Sacramento, about 120 miles, last summer. We easily made it there without needing to stop and refuel. But it was far from a comfortable ride. Plus, starting the bikes using the kick-starter . . . blech. Logan has tried to show me some of the tricks for getting it to "top dead center" before trying to start it. I always forget, so he has to walk me through it.

"You just don't want to leave your babies behind," I say, attempting to tease, but I know I sound pretty snotty.

He has the decency to look contrite as he quietly says, "There is that too."

"When?" I ask.

He looks me over. "Let's see how you are tomorrow, then we can start making a plan."

Chapter 3

Lindsey

Wednesday, Day 7
San Jose, California

I slept on the couch last night. It was the only place I could get even partway comfortable. My leg hurt so much, even the slightest movement was almost unbearable. Combined with the pain was the noise from outside. We've been hearing shots in the distance the past few nights. But last night, everything sounded closer—much closer.

Logan, as always, was wonderful to me. Our marriage is truly a love story. From our first date, he's gone out of his way to make me feel appreciated and special. Life with him is fun and easy. I have to admit, he spoils me terribly. Moving to San Jose was not something he wanted. We did it for me, for my career.

California and SJPD is just a pit stop, a way to gain experience for my true desire, my ideal career, my dream job—Special Agent with the Federal Bureau of Investigations. The FBI.

With the way the world is falling apart, I wonder what will become of my dream? Is the FBI still functioning, or were they sent home like the SJPD?

"You want some coffee, babe?" Logan asks, walking in from our small balcony.

"You made coffee?"

"Sure. It's not too bad either."

He sets two hot, steamy mugs on the breakfast bar separating the kitchen from the rest of the living space. We don't have an actual dining room, just a decent-sized living room and dining room combination. Instead of a table, we have a desk for Logan's freelance work and gaming. We use the breakfast bar for our meals or just sit on the sofa.

I try to sit up.

"Here, let me help. There's no reason to get off the couch. I'll bring the coffee to you."

"Help me to the bathroom?"

I make the mistake of looking in the bathroom mirror. I'm a scary sight! Not only do I sport a blackened right eye, the left one is puffy and bruised. The small cut above my eyebrow is showing new blood; I must have scratched the scab off in the night. My nose is swollen and puffy. I thought my voice sounded funny; it makes sense now. I do my best to make myself presentable.

Once that task is complete, Logan helps me back to the couch. He moves a small ottoman under my injured leg, gives me my mug, and sits next to me.

I take a small sip. It's good. Strong, but good. "How'd you make the coffee?" Our electric coffeemaker stopped working when the power went out.

"I saw Felix Turner yesterday. I happened to tell him how much I was missing coffee. He suggested boiling water on the gas grill, using a small strainer or colander lined with a coffee filter, and then slowly pouring the water through it. Turned out pretty good, if I do say so myself."

"It turned out great."

We sip in silence for several minutes. My mind keeps going back to yesterday. I know I did what I had to do, but I still hate that I did it.

"I think I'll start packing us up," Logan says.

"When do you think we should leave?"

"A few days. Let's wait until you're well enough to travel and when you think it's safe to leave. Sounds pretty bad out there right now."

I nod my response and take another sip.

"Felix said several people in his neighborhood have left. He and Anna are planning to stay put. They don't really have anywhere to go. Her parents live on the East Coast. I saw your friend Amy yesterday also. She and her husband . . . what's his name?"

"Chris," I answer.

"Mm-hmm. Right. They're going to leave, heading to Texas where his family is. She said they're waiting a few more days, thinking the craziness might calm down a bit."

"It might," I agree. "Or it could get even worse. Some of the guys at the station were talking about a lull in the violence. They think a lot of people will die in the next several days, then it'll calm down a bit until a second wave hits."

"So we should leave in the lull?"

"Ideally. But I'm not sure we'd know when the lull happens. We're kind of protected here. It's not the same as it is out there." I take a deep breath. "Home is different."

I rest on the couch while Logan starts organizing things. Taking the old bikes does make the most sense. He's right; there's less stuff to go wrong with them.

I hate the idea of leaving our home and so much of our stuff behind. Because we're traveling on the bikes, we're truly taking only what we need to survive.

We each have a tail bag on our commuter bikes. Logan moved those over to the Harley and the Suzuki, along with setting up the saddlebags on each bike. Each saddlebag has two thirty-ounce fuel bottles tucked into a little holder. Along with the two fuel holders Winchester provided in the saddlebags, and our two eleven-ounce MSR liquid fuel canisters, we are able to carry just over one and a half gallons pretty safely. We still have a little under half a gallon in one of the two-gallon gas cans, plus a full two-gallon can from the fuel Logan bought at my mom's suggestion.

Logan topped off the tanks with the almost-empty can, then siphoned from our commuter bikes to refill it. He strapped one can on top of each of our filled tail bags.

Once he had it all put together, he helped me out to the garage so I could check out his handiwork.

I'll be riding on a motorcycle bomb.

That much gas doesn't seem safe at all. On the other hand, getting stuck somewhere because we can't refuel doesn't sound much better. Sadly, even with what he's done, we'll only be able to get out of California—we hope. We'll have to find more along the way, or we'll be walking.

"I know what you're thinking," Logan says. "And I agree, but we'll be careful. Besides, it beats walking."

"True. But I think we should plan to end up on foot. We'll need to pack light."

He looks at me, taking in my injuries and how I hobbled out here.

"I just need a day or two. If we can start on the bikes, I should be fine to walk if we have to."

"Want to go back into the house? Or can I get you a chair and you can supervise while I start getting gear together?"

"You know, I'm an excellent supervisor." I chuckle.

"That you are, babe. So, you know we'll be camping."

I nod my agreement. The problem is, we don't camp. Camping is not my idea of fun. I went a few times with Evan after he and Mom were married, but it wasn't something I enjoyed. The bugs and dirt—not my cup of tea.

They no longer tent camp but have a nice fifth wheel. That's a little bit better, but I prefer a Holiday Inn. Logan used to camp with his family in New York and even went a few times in college. He has a few miscellaneous things in our garage, stuff I've often referred to as "crapola," but there isn't much.

After grabbing me a folding chair, he pulls a dust-covered tote over. He takes off the lid, scattering the tiny particles everywhere, causing us both to sneeze.

Once we recover from our sneezing fit, he says, "Okay, Linds, let's see what we've got."

"I hope the inside's in better shape than the outside."

"Yeah . . . looks a little better." He starts pulling things out. "Okay, this is good. We have a few things we can use. I thought there might be a sleeping bag, but it doesn't look like it. Do you remember what happened to my sleeping bag?"

"No, sorry." I shrug, though I have a vague recollection of it going to the Salvation Army when we moved from our last house into this place.

"Okay, well, I have a small tarp. I camped with a guy once who used a tarp and a walking stick as a tent. We have ski poles. We could do the same thing."

"Ski poles . . . you want to carry those on our bikes?"

"Uh, right. That might not work too well. We'll take the tarp anyway. We can find a limb or a branch or something."

"What's this?" I ask, poking at a small dusty box.

Logan shrugs and picks it up. He starts to blow off the dust, then changes his mind. He opens it up, but I still have no idea what it is—some sort of small metal box with holes in it.

"Oh, hey. I completely forgot about this. That guy from school, what was his name? Eddie? He was one of the guys I camped with. He gave me this. It's a cook stove."

"That's a cook stove? No way."

"Sure, look. See? It unfolds. The top flips up and the fire goes in here— " he motions to a little space within the metal box " —with the top opened. That's where the cooking pan goes."

"It's going to have to be an awfully small cooking pan. And what do you build the fire out of? Wood?"

"Yeah, I think so. Sticks, anyway. Look. Here's an instruction manual. Why don't you read it while I figure out what else we have?"

He hands me a slick piece of paper. "Um, babe, this isn't much of an instruction manual. Basically, it says it can be used outdoors with any wood or similar fuel alternative such as sticks, alcohol burner, Sterno, charcoal, or solid fuel tablets. The box stove can be used in multiple different positions to accommodate different needs, such as cooking fast or slow, or cooking on a large pot or small cup."

"Okay, then, it'll be great. Eddie made a stove out of a soda can. I think he burned some kind of alcohol in it. I suppose the alcohol burner refers to that. Wish I could remember what he did. I'll think about it."

"We have briquettes we can use. And I have a can of Sterno, maybe even two, leftover from that baby shower I helped host." I put the stove back in its box and set it on top of the tarp. "You find anything else interesting? Or helpful?"

"Yep, a hatchet, a headlamp, a small lantern thing—it's kind of neat, rechargeable—a bigger tarp, a multitool, and a metal coffee mug."

"So do you have anything else out here we can use?"

"Bungee cords. I have a new package and some zip ties. Let me grab those. Then let's go in the house and see what we can find."

Back in the house, we roll up a couple of light blankets and secure them with the bungee cords so they'll travel well.

When visiting Mom last fall during hunting season, I ended up bringing home a few things she'd given me in case we got stuck. Zipped up in the inside pocket of my coat were three emergency blankets—not the mylar kind I use for work, but the higher-quality Heatsheet brand—three disposable hand warmers, two toe warmers, a small box of matches, and a few packets of water purification tablets. I stashed these in my vanity drawer, forgotten, until we started rummaging for things we might need.

Instead of packing up, we're laying things out on the bed so we can see what we have. Then we'll figure out how best to load everything up.

Next, we go through our hunting gear. In addition to firearms, we have various other essentials: two small pairs of binoculars, paracord, knives, and a range finder. I also add a dozen of my cheap mylar blankets.

We'll go light on clothes, bringing only one extra set each plus something to sleep in. I choose yoga pants and a tank top. Logan picks shorts and a T-shirt. We both pull out several pairs of underclothes and socks, along with a light hoody. On the bike, we'll wear boots and our riding leathers, but we'll both bring a pair of athletic shoes too. We also pack our swimsuits, just in case we need to bathe in rivers or lakes.

"Let me grab my toiletries kit. I don't think I have room for the whole thing, but I at least want to get a few things out," Logan says.

"Same here. Guess I don't need a bunch of makeup, but a tube of mascara won't take up too much room. And we both need deodorant. I'll bring some soap and shampoo we can share. I have a couple of travel-sized containers."

We finish gathering essentials from the bathroom and tuck in a few more items from the bedroom. We move to the kitchen next.

"Why don't you sit down, rest a bit." Logan motions me to the couch. "You can supervise from there."

"Sounds like a plan. I'm feeling pretty rough."

Logan starts to empty our cabinets, scrounging for food. With our schedules, neither of us spends much time cooking, so we have lots of easy-to-prepare items. When Mom suggested we fill up the gas tanks, she also recommended food purchases. Things like small packages of mashed potatoes, pasta, and rice sides and packages and cans of tuna, chicken, and other meats—you know, the kind of food that's super easy to cook and haul around, which isn't much different than our normal fare, just packaged differently.

We were also ahead of the crowd when we bought a container of plain bleach on the first day the news came out about the food and water poisonings. We've been using that, along with boiling, since everyone was told to drink only treated or filtered water due to the threat of E. Coli and typhoid fever.

When was that? Saturday, I think. The days all kind of blend together.

I have a small glass bottle that'll work for taking the bleach. Not much is needed for purifying, so I hope it'll be enough. We'll use the bleach first and save the tablets for an emergency.

Once Logan has the food we want to take laid out on the breakfast bar, I move to a bar stool so we can evaluate everything.

"So I think we can still wear our commuter backpacks. We can fill up the saddlebags and attach a second backpack above the tail bags."

"You already have the gas cans strapped to the tail bags," I remind him.

"Yeah. I'll take them off, add the backpacks, then reattach the gas cans."

"Sounds even more dangerous and crazy."

Logan gives me a shrug. I don't think he likes it either, but what can we do?

"We'll keep the second packs light. I don't want to mess up our weight distribution. We'll utilize the saddlebags first, making sure the heavier stuff is in those. I think we'll be fine, Linds. We really need larger backpacks in case we end up on foot. Our commuters just don't hold enough."

I nod my agreement. "I can use the one Winchester gave me. What will you use?"

"I found an old backpack in the closet, one from college. It's smaller than the one you have but larger than my commuter bag. If we end up on foot, we'll really have to pare down our supplies."

"Maybe we'll be able to find larger backpacks along the way."

"You look tired, babe. Why don't you stretch out on the couch and rest? I'll start filling the bags."

"I'd appreciate it. Yesterday is really catching up with me."

Chapter 4

Sylvia Eriksen

Friday, Day 9
Outside of Shoshoni, Wyoming

I turn my head, gasping for breath, as I try to shake off the hand covering my mouth. "Don't move," the husky voice orders. Fetid breath accompanies the command, causing me to curl my nose in an attempt to avoid the stench.

I nod my agreement as the sides of the tent shake slightly.

A bear?

Grizzly bears aren't in this area, are they? I heard a rumor about grizzlies moving into the Wind River Mountain Range but I don't know if it's true. Besides, we're well away from the range, in the flatlands. We made last night's camp in a nice, level field.

I turn my head slightly to try to remove the hand from my mouth. Sabrina and her stinky breath move closer, whispering, "I'm not sure what's going on."

"Hey!" a loud, booming male voice yells from outside the tent. "You in there, what do you think you're doing?"

With wide eyes, Sabrina motions to me, pursing her lips and jabbing her finger into my left bicep.

I mouth "ow" while rubbing my arm. That hurt.

She narrows her eyes and then points toward the shadow on the nylon wall of the tent. The human outline includes either a rifle or a shotgun. I watch as Sabrina silently pulls her sidearm out of the holster, resting it on the floor of our tent.

Sabrina and I talked about this last night—about the fact we were likely camping in someone's field, not on one of the numerous patches of public land checker boarded across Wyoming.

Sabrina packed a Wyoming Gazetteer, an incredibly detailed map book, that indicates state and federal land along with private land and many other things. When we were driving, she had the book intact. When we switched to walking, she tore out the relevant pages to reach Bakerville. We've been using it along the way. Problem is, we aren't always exactly sure where we are.

Sabrina didn't want to stop. She thought there was a good chance we weren't on a block of state land—which is where I tried to convince her we were—but on a private section. I was done, dog-tired and not going another step. She conceded and made it clear, if we ran into trouble, I'd better talk us out of it.

I shrug and roll my eyes. "Fine," I mouth.

She grabs my arm and bows her head, no doubt sending a petition to her God for help. We're better off relying on my linguistic skills and charm than her useless prayers.

I square up my shoulders, and in my sweetest, most polite voice say, "So sorry. It's my fault, sir. I was so tired last night. We thought we might be on public land."

"Well, you're not," he bellows back. "I don't know where you come from, but around these parts, we make sure we know where we are before we go setting up tents. Now, you come on out here and let's get you on your way."

"Please, Lord, help us," Sabrina whispers. While she doesn't have her gun at the ready, I can tell it won't take much. It's lying next to her thigh, finger indexed properly—well away from the trigger but ready for action.

"Okay, yes. Sure. I'm coming out. I'm unarmed."

"Unarmed? What are you, some kind of hippy?" he asks incredulously. "Only a hippy or a nitwit would be out here without some way to defend himself . . . uh, herself."

Sabrina and I share a look.

"I don't think I'm a hippy or a nitwit, sir. I just don't want to get shot stepping out of my tent."

"Gah. I'm not going to shoot you. What gives you a fool idea like that? I just want to get you on your way before my cows come over here and start licking your tent or some such thing. Who knows what they could catch from you vagrants?"

Sabrina suppresses a smile. She motions for me to unzip the tent. She'll still try to provide some sort of cover in case he isn't being truthful. Immediately, I realize we're at his mercy. Opening the tent flap will leave me fully exposed. Of course, it's only a tent. Not like he couldn't just start blasting away if he wanted to. Nylon isn't exactly bulletproof.

Within a few seconds, I'm out of the tent. He's standing completely nonchalant, cradling the shotgun in his arm. The quintessential farmer, wearing overalls, a floppy straw hat, and scuffed boots—all of which have seen better days.

He lets loose a large stream of brown tobacco juice. "How about your friend? He coming out too?"

"Yes, sir," Sabrina says from the tent. "I'm right behind her."

He has a strange look on his face, as I clarify with a wave of my hand, "My younger sister. We're traveling to our mom's house."

Sabrina steps out next to me.

He shrugs. "Why don't you two get your stuff packed up, then follow me up to the house. My misses said I should invite you for breakfast if you seem like decent folks."

"Thank you. That's extremely kind of you," Sabrina says with a large smile.

"Yeah, well. My wife's that way. Always putting up a fuss over people. Me, I think you spending the night in our field is more than enough hospitality." The kindness on his face belays the gruffness of his words. "Get yourselves pulled together, then head on up to the house." He motions toward the east, where the sun is just peeking over the horizon. "I'll wait until you're away from this field 'fore I let the cows out."

An hour later, after one of the biggest and most fat-laden breakfasts I've ever eaten, we're back on the road. Well, not really a road. We've been skirting the river, making our way toward a large reservoir on the way to our mom and stepdad's house.

I light a cigarette, inhaling deeply. Dessert after my breakfast feast. Also, my first smoke of the day. I'll allow myself two more; I'm rationing them, trying to make them last. *Two more.* Who am I kidding? Every morning since we've been on the road, I make a pact with myself to smoke only three per day. I've failed each day.

Sabrina and I have been on foot since Monday afternoon. While the breakfast was a welcome treat, I wish we could have stayed at the farmhouse awhile and rested, maybe taken a bath.

I can't even begin to tell you how much I need a hot bath. Washing in the river just isn't cutting it. And my hair—gross. I can't do anything with it except pull it up.

Wistfully, I wish for the lovely and complicated braided style I used to wear, known as Havana Twists. Those ended when one of the partners at my new firm dubbed them "too ethnic" and asked me to "tone things down a bit." Oh, she did it in a completely PC way, making it clear it wasn't about my race but rather about company dress code. Sure, whatever.

My "work hair" is now a low, sleek bun, very classic. The bun I'm wearing today, there's nothing sleek or classic about it. I self-consciously run my hand over my hair. Today's bun crudely resembles one of the cow droppings we've been deftly dodging on our way out of the farmer's field. A cow patty bun. Maybe I can start a new end-of-the-world trend.

"What are you thinking about?" Sabrina interrupts my reflecting. I take a quick glance at her hair—not in a cow patty bun. Her hair is in a stylish messy bun with just the right amount of tension and locks hanging loose. *Of course.*

At twenty-five, two years younger than me, Sabrina still has an especially youthful look about her. She looks so young, sometimes people think she's still in high school. Bright, soft brown eyes, high cheekbones, perfectly pouty lips, and a very toned and athletic body. *Miss Perfect.*

On the contrary, I look every bit of my age—and then some. My eyes are hard and cold, giving me a "don't mess with me" look, which I'm not opposed to having. My cheekbones are barely noticeable and my lips are usually drawn in a hard line. We won't even talk about my lack of athleticism.

"Why?" I grumble back at her.

"Just thought . . . " She shakes her head. "I was just thinking we could talk."

"Humph. We've been talking enough."

"Sylvia, I know you blame me for this." She gestures to encompass the world we find ourselves in. "But I still completely believe we made the correct choice."

"You've told me that over and over. I'm pretty much sick of hearing it. You thought you had such a great plan to get out of Arizona, to get us to Mom and Phil's place. I seem to remember you making a big deal about how we had to take your car instead of mine. Seems you were concerned we'd end up walking if we took my car. Well, dear sister, what are we doing?"

I'm doing my best to control myself, to not yell. I suck in a breath, glancing at Sabrina. She's staring at the ground, chewing on her thumb. I shake my head.

"You don't even know if we would've had trouble. We could've stayed home, stayed in our apartment. Instead, here we are." I slap at a mosquito, one of a hundred feasting on me during this walk or hike or whatever you want to call it.

"Mom was right, Sylvia. I'm sure of it. She was right to tell us to pack up and go to their place. Peoria is too close to Phoenix. We'd have trouble."

"You're as paranoid as she is," I snap. "She and Phil with their stupid prepping. You and your stupid prepping. You're all nuts." I light up another cigarette. Listening to Sabrina yap doesn't help my rationing.

Besides, maybe I don't even really need to ration. Maybe the next town we get to will be just fine and dandy. Okay, so far that hasn't been the case. Pretty much every town but one, a small town in Colorado, has been without power. We were able to add in a little fuel there, even though they did limit how much. Without it, we'd be walking even farther. They didn't have cigarettes. Every mini-mart was out—or so they said. I bought a fresh carton the day the power went out. I haven't broken into it yet, but I'm on my last single pack, so I'll be opening it up soon.

I inhale deeply, filling my lungs with smoke. My life in Peoria is pretty great. I recently started a new paralegal position at a larger law firm. Well, sort of.

The small firm I used to work for merged with the larger firm, and I was part of the deal. Now, instead of just working for one attorney, I work for four. I got a nice pay bump and better benefits, including money to go back to school. The downside: my duties more than quadrupled.

And, of course, I had to change my hairstyle and make a few other provisions. None were big deals, but I did have a few growing pains. I'm finally starting to get into my groove. I've even signed up to go back to college in the fall. I only need a few credits to turn my associate degree into a bachelor's degree. Then I'll go to law school. That's when my life will really change.

I'll finally be able to afford my own apartment instead of sharing with Sabrina. In fact, I've been thinking, maybe I can find a small studio close to work sooner rather than later? I might be able to handle the rent and live on my own. Yeah, sounds pretty good.

But now, here we are, walking the remaining 150 or so miles to reach Mom's place in Bakerville. I smack another mosquito and silently curse Sabrina for putting us here.

"Do you want some salve for the mosquito bites?" Sabrina asks me quietly.

Of course, she has to be nice to me when she knows I'm mad at her. She's always doing stuff like that. The thing is, I know she's truly just *nice*. Nice to me, nice to strangers, nice to pretty much everyone. Oh, she can be antagonistic when necessary, though it's not her natural instinct. It didn't used to be mine either. These last few years, I tend to choose hostility over friendliness in most instances.

Ignoring her, I scratch at my arm.

"Sylvia, please," she begs. "Don't be like this. Let me put some spray on you to help stop the biting and some salve to soothe it. You'll feel better."

"Okay," I hiss, dropping my messenger bag. I put the handle down on the roller bag and shimmy out of my backpack. Sabrina's backpack, really. Her old one she used when taking off to the hills, or wherever it is she goes with her nature-loving friends.

Even though I try to be angry with her, I'm secretly thankful for the things she packed. I'll mutter, "I wish we had . . . " whatever, and she'll be like, "Oh, yeah, I packed that," or, "I don't have exactly so-and-so, but how about . . . " It's possible she's a packing genius.

The fact we're carrying way too much junk, though, does grate on me. I think about how much quicker we could move if we weren't so laden down. She also has a backpack, slightly larger than the one I wear; a medium-sized crossbody messenger bag, identical to mine except the color, both gifts from our mom last Christmas; and is dragging the shopping cart thing we use when we walk to the grocery store.

Sabrina assures me, even though we're moving slowly because of the supplies, it'll be helpful in the long run. I argued, if we traveled light, we could get to Bakerville sooner.

To her credit, she seemed to consider my suggestion by nodding a few times and chewing on her thumb. Finally, she said, "There's some merit to your suggestion. But I just can't shake the feeling we need everything we have. Plus, traveling slow is smart while we're starting out. Do you need me to rearrange your things? Is something uncomfortable?"

I glared at her, not wanting to give in so easily. I did consider her question. Even though we're heavily loaded, I'm not terribly uncomfortable. My backpack isn't overly heavy, the messenger bag hangs fine, and the roller bag is an inconvenience, but that's all. I do have to wonder how well the suitcase and the shopping cart will hold up if we don't start walking on a road again.

"Fine. We'll do it your way," I said and tromped off.

When Sabrina's SUV sputtered and coasted to a stop a few miles outside of Riverton, Wyoming, I started crying. Sabrina gave me a "seriously?" look, then started preparing us for walking.

I took a good ten minutes to mourn our loss of a vehicle. By the time I was done, Sabrina had made good headway.

"If you're done blubbering, you can make us something to eat," she said to me, not completely unkindly.

While my first instinct was to provide a witty retort, I reluctantly agreed.

After lunch, we hit the trail. Sabrina did a great job at packing us up, moving as much as she could from the SUV to our traveling gear. Even so, we left behind several gallons of water and two totes of food. She left the car unlocked so someone could use what we couldn't carry. See what I mean—she's nice. *Too nice.*

We heard some noises from the direction of Riverton so decided to avoid it. We've been following the river and now skirting the reservoir. What a mess. The first day, we probably only made two or three miles.

We found nice, out-of-the-way places to camp those first few nights and were not woken up by a farmer with a shotgun.

"Close your eyes," Sabrina says, holding up a spray bottle of some concoction.

I oblige, as she gives me several squirts. It smells good, like lavender, lemon, and a few other things I can't identify. And it's nice and cool, a welcome in the heat of the morning.

"That should help keep them off you. Remember to let me know if they start bothering you again." She smiles at me. I scowl in return. With a shake of her head, she hands me a small tube. "Rub this on the bites, just like yesterday."

"Yes, boss," I grumble.

Chapter 5

Lindsey

Friday, Day 9
San Jose, California

"Lindsey! Hey, Linds! Where are you?"

"Bathroom," I say around the toothpaste in my mouth. Our tap water stopped working yesterday. We filled up the tub, empty bottles, and every pot in our kitchen before it went out. Pouring water from a jug over the toothbrush isn't quite as easy as turning on the faucet, but it's working fine.

"Huh?" He comes into the bedroom. I turn to face him full on so he can see me brushing my teeth.

"Oh, hey. You look good."

I spit and say, "I still look pretty terrible. Worse even since some of my bruising is now various shades of yellow and green."

"Yeah, but you combed your hair and even did whatever with it."

"You mean braids?"

"I like it. You look very wholesome, like a Scandinavian girl running down a hillside."

"You're very strange, Logan Maverick."

He gives me a huge smile. "Well, I have good news. At least hopeful news. The guy in the condo next to us, you know, the one with the crazy beard?"

I nod.

"Right. Anyway, he said he heard from someone else, who spoke with another guy, who said the phones were working—not reliably but a few people were successful calling and even getting calls. I thought we should try our folks."

"Really? That's great! Why were you wasting time talking about my hair? I can't believe you don't already have your phone out dialing!"

"I would be, but my phone's completely dead. I thought I shut it off, but I guess not. I'm not sure where yours is."

"Oh . . . good question. Try the junk drawer in the kitchen."

"Already did."

We spend several minutes and finally find my phone in my jewelry box. I don't even remember putting it there but must have when we were packing our bags. We discussed not needing to take the phones since they didn't work, but now . . . if the phones are working, maybe the lights will come back on. Maybe things will return to normal and we won't even need to leave our home.

"Go ahead, Logan. Try your parents first."

"You sure?" he asks, swiping the screen with a huge smile on his face. "Let me put it on speaker."

After waiting several minutes for it to start ringing, we realize the call has failed. He tries again. It rings once and drops. Logan's smile is gone. "Let me try my dad's phone and then their home number."

When those also fail, he says, "Your mom is next."

My mom's and Evan's phones go straight to voicemail. We leave a message on both. Without being able to reach anyone, I'm feeling less hopeful about things returning to normal than I was just a few short minutes ago.

"Leave your phone on, Linds. I'm going to charge mine on your commuter bike's USB charger. Once it's charged, I'll give your phone a full charge."

"Maybe we should rethink taking my commuter bike," I say hopefully. "Now that the phones are starting to work, it'd be good to have a charger."

"Way ahead of you. I'm already thinking about how I can remove the USB charger from your commuter and wire it to the battery on the Suzuki."

I close my eyes and envision the bike. With the gas can strapped to the back, it already resembles a motorcycle bomb. Adding the charger . . . yeah, that's really going to add to the effect. I shake my head.

"Uh, Linds. You know, you are doing better. Maybe we should think about going. Things seemed a little calmer last night."

"Yeah. I think Thursday night was definitely the peak." I hesitate as I remember how we both huddled together most of the night, often being jarred awake by screams, shots, and once by what sounded like a bomb going off. Yesterday morning, Logan ventured out of the neighborhood and found a couple of burned-out cars.

"But if the phones are coming back on, maybe everything else will too. We might not need to leave."

Several times throughout the day, we try our parents, but we're not able to connect with any of our family. Finally, shortly before dinner, my phone sings out, *"Dodadodaloo, Wah, Wah, Wah."* The theme song from *The Good, the Bad and the Ugly* proudly plays, Evan's distinctive ringtone.

"Evan! Oh my goodness! I'm so happy to hear from you. Where's Mom? You guys okay?" I ramble, while putting him on speaker so Logan can listen also.

"Hey, Lindsey. I'm glad I got through. Your mom, she's . . . yeah, she's okay."

"Evan? What's going on?"

"There was an incident. She was injured . . . shot, actually . . . on Wednesday."

I cry out, wondering what is going on.

Evan quickly says, "She's doing okay. We have a nurse . . . um, Belinda Bosco. Have you met her?"

"A nurse? Evan, if Mom was shot, she needs more than a nurse."

"Belinda is more than a nurse. She's a surgical nurse practitioner. She has her own practice, even assisted her doctor with surgeries. Your mom is in good hands. And there's a doctor here. He was . . . uh, visiting, when things went down. He's also caring for your mom."

"So she has a doctor. That's good. But why not just take her to the hospital in Prospect?"

"It's gone, Lindsey." Evan says it so softly I'm not sure I heard him.

"Gone?"

"Yeah, gone. Things are not good here—around here, anyway. We seem to be safe in Bakerville. And your mom will be okay. The bullet broke her leg, and she'll have a long recovery, but she's doing okay . . . and asking about you. Are you safe?"

"I'm no longer working. They told us to stay home. Sarge said I should head your way, but we're not sure. It's a bit of a war zone here and getting out might be hard. We're waiting for now, but we're ready to go at a moment's notice. Maybe, if the power comes back, we can just stay here. I'll let you know if we do leave."

We spend a few more minutes on the phone before the call drops. I try to call back but am unsuccessful. Logan tries his parents again. It rings once and then goes dead. His second and third tries are also unsuccessful.

He lets out a big sigh. "At least you talked to Evan. And it sounds like your mom's in good hands. Why didn't you tell him about your injuries?"

I shrug. "He has enough on his plate. He doesn't need to worry about me, and Mom definitely doesn't need to be worrying. Besides, I'm pretty much fine now."

Chapter 6

Lindsey

Saturday, Day 10
San Jose, California

"Lindsey, wake up. Linds, you need to get up."

"What's going on?" I ask, sitting up quickly. Big mistake—both my head and leg rebel.

"Smoke. There's a fire somewhere."

"Our condo?" I exclaim, while quickly and carefully moving from the bed. It's just turning to dawn and the room has a slight glow to it. I can see Logan is already dressed—fully dressed, including his leathers.

"No, I don't think so. It seems like a grassland fire, but I don't think we should stick around."

Grassland fires in the foothills around San Jose are pretty common, but not usually in June when things are still greenish. We'll often have small fires in the fall, which are quickly put out. The last few years have been rough for fires, with many areas in California burning—even the small town of Paradise, about an hour and a half from Sacramento, was devastated. We had a couple of small brush fires, too, but nothing like they experienced. It'll be years before Paradise makes a full recovery.

I can't imagine our fire department is in any shape to battle this fire.

"I'll get dressed. You really think we need to leave?"

"Let's get ready, just in case. If we don't need to go today, we'll be ready for tomorrow, giving you one more day of rest. But, Lindsey, I think it's getting time we head to Wyoming."

"But the phones . . . maybe the power will come back."

"We'll see."

I get dressed in my leathers while Logan finishes our packing. The sun is trying to come up, but the sky is darkening from smoke. Within the hour, we know without a doubt it's time to leave.

We finish our last-minute preparations, which takes less than half an hour, then lock the house and go to the garage. From here, we can see flames only a few blocks away. I start crying as I realize we'll likely never be able to return to our home. Then I see people running, carrying whatever they can, in an effort to retreat from the fire.

"Lindsey, we need to go. The fire's coming fast," Logan says, while putting on his helmet.

I nod and buckle the strap on my helmet. I climb on the bike and begin the process of trying to start the stupid thing using the kick.

I hear Logan in my ear via the communicator in my helmet. "Calm down, Linds. Take a deep breath. Leave the kill switch and key in the off position. Now turn on the choke and switch the fuel to the prime position."

I catch his eye and motion to the little fuel knob on the side.

"Yes, that's it. Now hold the decompression lever and prime it with your foot six times. That puts a little fuel in the system."

I use my right foot and count to six while pushing down.

"Perfect, Linds. Now turn the key on. Switch the fuel back to the normal position."

I'm starting to remember this process now. I move the kick-starter down and press it until it won't move—the top dead center position. Now there is something with the decompression lever . . . what is it?

"The decompression lever?"

"Yep, pull it back and release it, then just let it go. Now push it down to start and get it back to top dead center. Perfect. Okay, pull the decompression lever again and start her up."

I'm shocked when it works.

"Great, Lindsey. Give me a second to get going and we'll head out. Let's head toward Piedmont."

Over the past few days, we've looked over our maps to find the best way out of town. We think Piedmont will likely be crazy, but we want to check it out. If it's bad, we'll skirt around on side streets. With fuel being a big concern, we don't want to have to do too much extra driving or backtracking. We have a plan for getting more fuel—or I should say, Logan has a plan. I don't like his idea. Not at all.

The fire is moving fast. We keep having to change our course to avoid not only flames and smoke but people. There are so many people on the roads, trying to get away from the fire.

People in their cars, likely using the last of their gas, are blaring their horns to clear the path. Many people are on foot, some trying to stop the cars. Trying to stop us. There are bicycles and a few other motorcycles. My heart nearly breaks as I watch complete families fleeing for their lives. There's a man and woman, with the man carrying a small pink bundle and the woman holding the hand of a little boy, maybe four years old, tears streaming down their faces from smoke and fear.

Logan sees me looking, watching them. Very softly, he says, "I know it's terrible, but we have to keep going. There isn't anything we can do for them."

The wind blasts around us with debris, embers, and ash. People are gathering in the parking lots of shopping centers, trying to find a place to be safe from the flames and smoke, covering themselves with whatever they can find. There are screams and cries all around us.

Explosions are going off as combustibles ignite. The ground shakes. The air shakes. I'm shaking. My bike wobbles and I almost go down. I correct a little too much and almost lose it again. I'm not sure how my tires are still on the ground.

"That was a close one, Lindsey. You need to stay focused. Getting out of here is all that matters right now."

I try to take a deep breath but stop as smoke fills my lungs. "I'm good," I say, after choking out a cough.

Then, suddenly, we're out of it. Out of the worst of it, anyway, and racing toward fresh, clean air. Once we clear the smoke and the main throng of people, we start making better time.

Logan and I avoid the main roads—interstates and highways—and try for smaller, local roads. We're pretty familiar with the area, having taken many bike rides just for fun and to see the sights, which helps. Even so, we still end up backtracking more than we want.

"I need a break," I tell Logan into the headset.

"Yeah, me too. Let's stop for a bit. I could use something to eat."

We take a half hour off the bikes, snacking and drinking sodas. My leg aches from the injury and riding. My bottom isn't feeling too great either.

"You holding up okay?" Logan asks, while hugging me tight. "Are you ready to ride some more?"

"Not really. This bike is even more uncomfortable than I remember."

"Discomfort is very much part of my master plan." He rings his hands together, looking like a mad scientist.

"Who said that? Dr. Jekyll?" The game of quotes is something Logan and I spend too much time on. We make a point of searching out obscure sayings and adages to try and stump each other.

"Maybe." He shrugs. "Can't remember for sure. But by the time we get to your folks' place, you'll feel just fine."

"Ha. I highly doubt that!"

Back on the bikes, everything's quiet until just outside of Stockton. We find a way around the main part of the city but still have trouble with four guys yelling and chasing us. We lay on the gas and manage to hightail it out of there.

After we're several miles away, Logan says, "Let's call it a day. Find some place to hole up, then start again tonight. What do you think?"

"Where?" I ask.

"Lodi, the nice park by the lake? We can refill our water."

"The nice park that is always crazy busy and has the boat tours down the river?"

He gives me a long look, then very patiently says, "Honey, I am pretty sure the boat tours aren't running right now."

"Well, maybe," I stutter. "But there could still be tons of people there."

"We'll check it out, and if it's too busy, we'll find someplace else."

He was right. No boat tours and no people to speak of, other than a few we determined to be area homeless and a few people like us, trying to get someplace else.

"You can rest first," Logan says. "You should stretch out. It'll probably help your leg."

He puts a tarp on the ground, a small blanket on top of it, and then spreads a blue full-sized sheet—one we use on our fold-out sofa, which is now part of my bedroll—for me to cover up with. I'm glad it's June and warm. Even so, I do wish I wouldn't have disposed of his ratty old sleeping bag.

It takes me very little time to fall asleep. Logan wakes me up at 7:00 so he can sleep. He doesn't bother spreading out his own blanket and sheet, just hops into my setup. I have strict instructions to wake him up at 11:00 so we can hit the road. Our plan is to ride all night and sleep during the day, thinking it might be safer.

At 11:30, we're back on the bikes. This time, we decide to stay on main roads.

Chapter 7

Sylvia

Saturday, Day 10
Between Shoshoni and Thermopolis, Wyoming

Tents of various sizes and conditions dot the landscape. I'm reminded of a photo of a New Mexico tent city. The difference: that tent city housed about fifty. This tent city, in a Wyoming state park, consists of several hundred—more people than in many Wyoming towns.

The official camping spots are filled and people are, essentially, dispersed camping—setting up tents wherever it looks good. Even though this is a developed campground, I find it hard to imagine people would want to camp here on purpose. Sure, there's a lake—or more accurately, a reservoir—and the water looks lovely from here, but the rest of the area . . . not as lovely. Barren, dusty, and bone-dry—a lake surrounded by desert.

"Oh, it's beautiful," Sabrina gushes, "like an oasis in the desert. The shimmering blue of the water against the rolling hills—isn't it amazing, Sylvia?"

"Not particularly. Those hills look like giant anthills. Nothing's even growing on them!"

"Not true. I can see the dots of sagebrush."

"Have you noticed the wind?" I ask, squinting as a gust blows cigarette smoke in my eye. My third for today. No, it won't be my last. I really do need to start my rationing efforts. I have half a dozen left in this pack plus the full carton in my suitcase. I'd better be able to find some in Thermopolis, the next town on our journey. Me without my smokes will not be pleasant for anyone.

"Where do you want to set up the tent?"

"Who cares?" I shrug. "It all looks the same."

Sabrina ignores my snide. "Let's try to find a family to camp by. I think that'd be best."

She scans the assorted campsites, finally zeroing in on one with a very colorful small tent, the kind a child might use as a fort in the living room. She points and says, "There. Looks like enough space for us to set up."

She makes a beeline for the spot. The colorful play tent has a small one-person tent inches from it and a larger two-person tent right next to the small tent. I stop walking when I notice the man sitting on the ground.

Even from this distance, he's drop-dead gorgeous—blond hair worn on the longer side, hanging straight from a center part, and well-shaped sideburns leading to a scruffy beard. The stylish kind guys do on purpose to look wonderfully unkempt. Even sitting down, it's obvious he's in shape—amazing shape. I raise a hand to my hair, to my cow patty bun. Is there anything I can do to make it look better in the next five seconds?

No.

I let out a sigh and start walking again, hurrying my pace to catch up with Sabrina.

The exquisite man is holding a young girl on his lap. An older girl, early teens probably, and a boy around the same age are sitting next to them. The children are equally attractive. Obviously, they're his children. *Oh well.* They're talking quietly when we walk up.

"Hi," Sabrina says with a smile and wave. "Okay if we set up our tent over here?" She gestures to the small bare spot next to the colorful play tent.

The man lifts his head, making eye contact. Piercing blue eyes scan us and quickly dismiss us. *Fine, then.*

"Sure. Go ahead," the man responds with a wave.

"Thank you. I'm Sabrina. This is my sister, Sylvia."

He gives a cursory nod and returns to visiting with his children.

Well, then. I guess someone that good looking can get away with being so surly. A quick glance at the older children suggests they may be equally inhospitable. At least the youngest girl gives us a small wave.

Last night we skipped the tent and slept under the stars. Sabrina said she'd felt too vulnerable inside the tent after realizing how easy it was for the farmer to come up on us with his gun.

At the time, I thought it was a good idea, but once the mosquitos discovered me again, I changed my mind. I have even more bumps and itchy bites covering me. I've used so much of her salve and spray, I'm close to an overdose on it. Sabrina's welcome to sleep outside tonight, but I'm sleeping in the tent, and it'll be zipped up. Tight.

It doesn't take long for us to get camp put up. By us, I mainly mean Sabrina. She's much better at setting up and taking down camp than I am.

"There we go." She rubs her hands together. "Getting hungry?"

"Not terribly." I blow my smoke out. "Maybe in a bit."

Sabrina turns toward the family next to us and whispers, "I'm going to try to say hello again."

"Sabrina," I hiss, "he's way too old, even if he is yummy. Besides, he's totally stuck up."

"What? No. The kids just seem really sad."

"Look around. Everyone is sad . . . or scared or mad or something. No one's here to have a good time—especially me. We're all in a terrible situation."

"Even so, maybe I can pray with them."

"Oh, yeah. That's what they need."

"Maybe I can pray with you too." She smiles and pulls me into a hug.

"Watch it. You almost crushed my cigarette." I try to be gruff but fail. As much as Sabrina annoys me, I have no doubt of her love for me. Being roomies is a challenge some days. I think again of a little studio near work. Maybe, once all this settles down . . .

"Hi again," Sabrina says in an overly cheery voice, stepping slightly toward the family's camp.

"Hello," the dad says. "You set up quick."

"Yeah, it's an easy tent." She nods. "Have you been here long?"

"Since Tuesday," the little girl says excitedly.

"No, we haven't, you weirdo," the boy says.

"Dad! Nate called me a weirdo again!"

"Children, enough. Your mom's still sleeping."

Bummer. Even though I told Sabrina he was too old, I only meant for her. Not that I'd really be interested in him with three kids and all, but he might be a fun diversion while we're camped next door. A fun diversion . . . that's pretty much how I view all men these days.

"No, I'm not," a voice tersely answers from inside the one-person tent. "It's next to impossible to sleep with all the noise around here."

"Mommy!" the little girl exclaims. "Will you come out and sit with me?"

"In a moment, Naomi."

"Okay. I'll be waiting."

"Would you like to sit down?" the man asks us. "Can't offer you a chair, but you can pull up some dirt."

The oldest girl rolls her eyes and shakes her head at her dad's quip.

"Smooth, Dad," the boy, Nate, says.

"Thanks," Sabrina says.

I grind out my cigarette and stick it in a partially filled water bottle—my traveling ashtray—before I move over to their camp.

We're barely positioned on the hard ground when the zipper on the tent starts moving. I swear the sun suddenly has an extra sparkle as the woman—the mom—steps out with her smooth blond hair, sparkly blue eyes, and a pert little nose. The perfect match for this hunk of a man. She's dressed in yoga pants and a tank top, showing off her well-toned body. There's a pink tinge to her skin, indicating too much sun.

No way she's had three children. No way. She certainly looks amazing for being in a dusty, overcrowded campground.

I suddenly feel incredibly frumpy with my cow patty bun, capri-length pants, T-shirt, and extra twenty-five pounds I'm carrying around. *Okay, thirty pounds.*

She spares me an obviously fake smile and says, in a perfectly modulated voice, "Hello, I'm Kim Hoffmann. And you are?"

"Oh, hi. I'm Sylvia. Sylvia Eriksen."

"Eriksen? Isn't that Scandinavian?"

If only I had a dollar for every time I went to an appointment and surprised the person I was meeting. Sylvia Eriksen does sound like I should look like a Barbie doll . . . or like Kim Hoffmann. I start to respond when Sabrina jumps in, most likely to keep me from giving a snappy comeback.

"Norwegian, our dad is from Norway. I'm Sabrina. It's very nice to meet you, Kim."

"Oh, yes. Nice to meet you also," she says dismissively. "Now, which one of you has the cigarettes?"

Sabrina yanks her thumb in my direction.

Kim makes eye contact with me and offers me another insincere smile. "That so? Can you spare one?"

"Mom, you quit, remember?" the older girl says quietly.

"Absolutely, Nicole," she answers, her eyes never leaving mine. "One little cigarette isn't going to get me started again."

As much as I'd rather not share my limited supply, I concur, handing her one.

"Have a light?"

I figure I might as well join her and, after lighting her cigarette, get one of my own. I wouldn't want her to have to smoke alone.

Once she's set up and smoking, she says, "So how'd you two end up in this wretched wasteland?"

Chapter 8

Sylvia

Saturday, Day 10
Between Shoshoni and Thermopolis, Wyoming

"We're heading to our mom's house," Sabrina answers.

"Humph. Good you have someplace to go," Kim sneers. "We're doomed to wander in this desert for eternity."

"Now, Kim," the man says quietly, "that's not true."

"Oh, really? You have some spectacular plan to get us to Bozeman?"

He takes a deep breath. "We've discussed this. We'll walk."

"See? Told you we'd be wandering this desert for eternity. Do you know how long it'll take us to walk to Bozeman?"

I look at the ground, attempting to avoid witnessing the marital spat.

Not my sister, she jumps right in. "How'd you end up here?"

"Same way as most of these other fools. We left our perfectly safe home thinking something worse was going to happen. Well, the joke's on us. We're now living the something worse."

"Kim, that's not exactly what happened," the man says.

"There was a big boom," young Naomi says. "So big it shook the windows of our house. It was super scary. I'm glad my dad was home and not in his office when it happened."

"Oh?" Sabrina asks.

"We live in Denver, in a building right by the Speer Boulevard Bridge," the man says. "When the bridge exploded, it shook our windows. We're fortunate our condo is on the backside of the building instead of the bridge side. Kim and I own another smaller condo in

42

our building to use as our office. It didn't fare nearly as well. Those windows blew out."

"But our place was fine, Ray," Kim punctuates her words with the cigarette.

A look of anger passes over Ray's attractive face. He quickly composes himself. Smoothing out his features, he quietly says, "I think we know Denver isn't faring well. You heard the news. Besides, we're together, honey. That's pretty good. I could have been out of town for work. Or one of us could have been in the office when the explosion hit. You saw the glass all over our desks."

Kim says nothing, just shakes her head, tumbling her very blonde, very smooth, almost perfect hair about her shoulders. How in the world does her hair still look so good?

I think again about how Ray and Kim both look so amazing—like movie star attractive. I'm suddenly filled with a vision of Brad Pitt and Jennifer Aniston. Ray and Kim resemble the couple. Oh, not in looks so much, though, Ray is definitely as attractive as Brad, and Kim is nothing short of beautiful. But there's something about them, something almost . . . luminary.

"As soon as we realized what happened, and thought about what could happen based on the airplane crashes and explosions from the night before, we took off," Ray says. "I think we set a record for fastest packing ever. Even so, getting out of the city wasn't easy. We decided we'd make our way to Bozeman, Montana, and stay with some friends. Trying to get around the explosion and back on Interstate 25 took some doing. Then, once we got there, it was stop and go. Seems we weren't the only ones leaving town. And then we found out the same thing was happening in other places. The Speer Boulevard Bridge wasn't the only one to blow up, but I guess you know that."

Sabrina and I both nod. We know. Almost fifty bridges exploded within minutes of each other. Only the one bridge was hit in Denver. Several cities had numerous strikes. And most were large, heavily traveled bridges. The Speer Boulevard Bridge wasn't very big, but it was in a very busy area. Plus, it was one of the few Midwest bridges blown up. Most were on the East and West Coasts.

"Daddy wouldn't even let me stop to go to the bathroom until we were far, far away," Naomi pouts.

"It wasn't that far," her older brother Nate jumps in. "You just don't know how to tell time or judge distance yet, so it seemed like a long way. You probably don't even know how long ago we left our home."

"Do so!"

"Oh yeah? What day did we leave?"

"Um . . . Tuesday?"

"Bzzzzt. Wrong answer, squirt. We left last Friday. Do you know what today is?"

"Um . . . Tuesday?"

"Ha. Nope. Saturday. We've been gone from home for over a week."

"Yeah, a really *loooong* week," Nicole says. The children inherited the parents' good looks with perfect little features and blue eyes of varying shades. Nicole and Nate both look a lot like their dad, while Naomi looks a little more like her mom. But all are so similar, there's no doubt they're a family. I self-consciously reach to smooth my cow patty bun.

"Even though it was slow going, it wasn't terrible," Ray continues. "Well, it wasn't great. We slept in the car the first night, parked at a rest stop with a ton of other people. The next day, we were still jammed up on the interstate, but it was fine. Until we tried to get fuel in Casper, then things got a little dicey. We were waiting in line for over an hour before we finally reached the pump. Then, because of the number of people needing fuel, they were limiting everyone to two gallons. Two gallons. Can you believe that?"

"We encountered the same thing," Sabrina says softly.

I just nod.

"I guess you probably did. Heard it from others here and on the way. We were all in the same situation. Thought I'd try a few more stations since Casper was the largest town we'd be passing through for a while. That turned out to be a mistake. We were in line at the second station—again, only two gallons—when the power went out. We didn't know it was a cyberattack until later."

"I didn't like that, Daddy. I didn't like it when the power went out."

"It was daylight, dork," Nate says. "You didn't even know the power was out."

"Yeah, but . . . the guy *said* it was out and said he couldn't give us gas. *Remember?* And I'm not a dork. Mommy said you can't call me that anymore. Right, Mommy?"

Kim stares into space, taking a final puff of the cigarette, burned to the filter.

"Mommy? Right?"

"Right, sweetie," Ray answers for Kim, while Kim grinds out the smoke, flicking it aside. "Nate, don't call your sister names. The children are a little tense," Ray says by way of apology.

"How old are you, Nate?" Sabrina asks.

"Almost thirteen," he says proudly.

"Really? I thought you were older." Sabrina turns to Naomi. "And you?"

"I'm five. And N'cole is sixteen. She just had a birthday, with cake and everything. But then the planes crashed. But since she had her birthday, she's really old. She's almost as old as our mommy." She beams at her mom, but Kim takes no notice.

"Nicole isn't even as close to as old as Mom." Nate shakes his head. "You just don't know how to count or add or anything like that."

"Nate," Ray warns.

Nate shrugs, as Ray continues his narrative, "Like Naomi said, the attendant turned us away. He went from car to car telling everyone the power was out and they couldn't help us. We were waiting for people to start moving when some guy lost it. He started yelling, completely throwing a fit, and the next thing we knew, *BAM*. He shot the attendant. At that point, the place became a madhouse with all of us trying to get away. We were jammed in and couldn't maneuver. More shots were fired. The car in front of us ended up ramming the car in front of him. That gave us just enough room to get away."

"See. I told you I didn't like it when the power went out," Naomi insists as she sticks her tongue out at Nate, who quickly reciprocates the gesture.

Ray ignores them both, lost in his memories.

"We finally found our way through the town," Nicole says, voice vacant and eyes hollow. "Mom was screaming and crying. Naomi was crying. I was crying. Dad was lost. We ended up by the airport . . . which wasn't the right way to go. We were supposed to stay on the interstate. But Dad said he'd been this way before, so we stayed on the road. Eventually, Mom pulled a map out of the glovebox. The rest stop we stayed at the night before had maps to give away for free. Good thing we picked it up."

"Very good thing," Ray agrees with a nod. "Even though I've been through the Wind River Canyon before, the map has been helpful. Especially now . . . now that we're on foot. I thought we might have enough to make it to the next little town, but we didn't find any gas stations before we ran out. The bumper to bumper along the little highway didn't help. And we weren't the only ones who ran out. The cars along the side of the road just added to the highway troubles. We were about twenty miles from Shoshoni when the car belched and we coasted to a stop."

Kim seems to come around a little, joining the conversation. She now has the same vacant eyes and hollow voice as her daughter Nicole. "At that point, I thought we were done for. We'd been seeing other people walking and knew there was a chance we'd be joining them. But I thought we'd make it into Shoshoni at least and there would be enough gas to get us to the next town—that we'd be able to limp along until we reached Bozeman."

"It's okay, Mama," Naomi says. "We found a nice spot here. And with the lake, we have water and fish. But I'm going to get pretty tired of fish soon."

"Yeah," Nate chimes in. "Fish is getting old fast."

Kim is once again staring into the distance.

"We had no choice but to walk," Ray says. "That stretch of road is pretty desolate. We thought maybe we could walk into Shoshoni and get a tow truck to go back for the car."

"Ha," Kim scoffs. "We were so naive. Or maybe delusional. Something. Definitely not based in reality."

Chapter 9

Sylvia

Saturday, Day 10
Between Shoshoni and Thermopolis, Wyoming

Ray pats his wife's hand, the way a grandmother would comfort a small child. "We spent some time deciding what to take from the car, not that we had much stuff since we'd packed so quickly. We talked about just me walking in and setting everyone else up to wait, but none of us wanted to be separated. So we repacked Kim's roller suitcase. Nicole and Nate each had school backpacks, along with small duffle bags."

"I have my Dora the Explorer suitcase," Naomi says proudly. "It has wheels like Mama's bag, but it's a little smaller."

Kim gives Naomi a sad smile and gently touches her arm, pulling her toward her.

Ray nods. "And I had my suitcase, still packed from returning from a business trip on Wednesday, plus my hiking backpack and gear. I do a Pike's Peak hike every year with some buddies, then get out a few more times a year as my time allows. Unfortunately, the rest of the family doesn't have any good backpacking items. We have a little two-man tent Nate and I use sometimes, and Naomi has the tent for playing in the house. As you can see, these three tents are now our home." Ray motions to their setup.

"When we left the house, we grabbed pretty much every bit of canned food and easy-to-cook dry goods from our pantry. We had a few leftovers in the fridge plus odds and ends, enough to fill a small cooler. When we packed the bags, we focused on the food. We managed to get it all in, leaving extra clothes and other things behind.

We each have the clothes we're wearing, pajamas, and one additional set of clothes.

"Nate's duffel bag holds most of the clothes. I'm glad I had my gear. We were dangerously low on water when we started out, but from where the car stopped, I could see a grove of trees. I thought there might be water there. It was off the highway a bit but made sense to go there and see what we found. It was already late in the day, and we thought we might stay the night there. When I hike, I'm good going ten or fifteen miles a day, sometimes farther. With the kids and our situation . . . " Ray shakes his head.

"The tree grove did have a nice stream where we were able to refill all the empty bottles from the car and my hydration bladder. I have some iodine tincture we used for purifying, and we also boiled water in my small camping pot. We camped there for the night and started out the next day, following a small creek. While we weren't on the highway, it was within sight. We thought staying off the road might be safer. Not that it really mattered, since it's so flat through there anyone on the road could've seen us, just like we could see them. The traffic was as bad as the day before, maybe even a little worse. And we weren't the only ones walking. We met several others in the same predicament.

"We found another camping spot with a water source that night and made it into Shoshoni the next day. I'm glad I didn't strike out on my own. The town was a bust. It had been completely overwhelmed by the deluge of people. They were in such bad shape, they wouldn't even let us stay. Oh, they were nice enough about it. They filled up our water bottles, suggested we camp here at the state park, and even gave us a ride through town. We weren't the only ones. They used a pickup truck to transport us. The bed of the truck was full of people like us . . . transients, I guess."

Kim gives him a hard look; he shrugs.

I wish we would have walked into Shoshoni instead of staying on the lake edge. Would have been nice to have a ride. It would've saved us at least a day.

"As you can see, the place is pretty full up. We're like a small town. This section isn't even part of the actual campground. At least we're able to walk to the lake for water and a little fishing."

"Being able to fish is good," Sabrina says.

"Definitely." Ray nods. "A guy gave me a couple of hooks and some line, along with a couple of weights. He even showed me how to make a pole out of a stick. It's working okay, so overall, this isn't too bad. There's even talk of shooting an antelope, which would be good. I guess we'll stay here a few more days, then decide what to do next. Maybe move on down the road to one of the other campgrounds. The ones on the river might be better . . . " Ray's voice trails off.

Sabrina gives me a look.

I immediately know what she is thinking. I give my head a small shake.

She intensifies her look, staring me down.

My shoulders sag. My baby sister knows how to get to me. Besides, married or not, Ray is some serious eye candy. Could be good for passing the time.

She gives me a big smile and acknowledges our unspoken agreement with a slight nod of her head.

"We'll be leaving in the morning," she says to Ray. "Maybe you should come with us?"

"Why? What's the point?" Kim asks in a quiet, defeated voice.

I wonder where the luminescent woman who came out of the tent a short time ago has gone. This version of her, while still beautiful, seems an empty shell and completely beaten.

"It's a good idea," Ray answers. "Two more people might make things easier, and safer, with the children. How far are you going?"

"We're going to our parents' house in Northern Wyoming," Sabrina answers. "It'll still be quite a ways to your friend's place, but will get you . . . I don't know, over a third of the way, I'd guess."

Ray looks at his wife. Her only response is an aloof shrug. Nate and Naomi both look excited.

"We can't just stay here," Nicole says. "More people arrive every day, and it's scary, especially at night. Plus, we're having a hard time finding fire-making stuff. How will we cook? There aren't many trees here, and the sagebrush has been picked over pretty well. I don't want to walk to Montana, but I guess we don't have a choice. Mom, I think we should go."

Kim lets out a very large sigh. "I guess so. When are you leaving?"

Sabrina quickly says, "We'll leave early, as soon as there's enough light to see. We'll need to start breaking down camp in the dark. It'd be best if you can pack up as much as possible tonight."

Kim shakes her head. "Fine. Ray, you'll need to figure it all out. I'm going to bed. Wake me up at the last possible moment in the morning."

"Is there anything we can help you with, Ray?" Sabrina asks.

"His name isn't Ray," Kim advises.

"Oh! I'm so sorry. I thought you called him Ray."

"It's Rey, R-E-Y. You are saying it wrong. It's Rey." The ways she says his name does sound slightly different than the way Sabrina said it, but not so much as to make such a big deal of it.

Sabrina tries again, making the middle sound more of an *eh* and less of a long *a*.

Kim shakes her head, but Rey laughs. "It's fine. My name's Reynard. Reynard Hoffmann. Rey for short. You know the old adage, 'call me anything you like, just don't call me late for dinner.'"

"Is it dinnertime, Daddy?" Naomi asks with excitement. "I'm ready to eat."

"Yes, munchkin, I think it is."

With that, Sabrina and I excuse ourselves.

"I'll start packing things up at 5:00 in the morning," Rey says. "Sound good?"

We agree it's probably about right.

We eat our own dinner at our next-door camp. "Do you think we should have offered them something?" Sabrina whispers.

"Since you invited them to travel with us, I suspect we'll be feeding them plenty." I'm rethinking the addition of Rey being eye candy. "Seriously, what were you thinking? They're only going to slow us down. And the mom . . . she's something."

"I don't know. There's just something about them. I felt pushed to include them, like God was nudging me."

"Whatever," I say, taking out another cigarette while Sabrina starts cleaning up. I watch as she expertly repacks everything. As always, she'll make sure things are in order to make leaving in the morning as easy as possible.

My body hurts and I'm exhausted. I don't even know how many miles we walked today. Ten? Fifteen? Farther? We were picking our way along the river and then the lake, so it's hard to say. After I finish smoking and Sabrina has us organized, she says, "I'm going to watch the sunset, then turn in."

Of course she is. Even at home, she rarely misses a sunset. Our apartment has a small west-facing balcony. She put two chairs out there, thinking I'd join her. I don't. Boring. She's also fond of watching the sunrise. Usually, she's out for her morning jog just before daylight so she can watch the sun come up. I don't join her for that either. Jogging is not my idea of fun.

"I'm going to skip the sunset," I say. "You sleeping in the tent tonight?"

"Yeah. I think we'll be okay here."

I'm still awake when Sabrina climbs in the tent a short while later.

"You should have stayed out," she whispers. "The sunset was amazing."

"Meh. You've seen one, you've seen them all."

"Not true, Sylvia. Each night is a new show, so magnificent and tranquil. Watching the setting sun reminds me to be thankful for the day, thankful for the blessings God has given us."

"Blessings?" I hiss. "You call what's happened to us—to the United States—a blessing? You think the people here in this wasteland are feeling blessed?"

"I think some of them are. You heard Rey say how fortunate it was they weren't in their office facing the blast. You don't think that's a blessing?"

"Luck, Sabrina. It was luck." I turn over, ending the conversation.

I feel Sabrina settle into her sleeping bag next to mine. Even though it's June, the nights are chilly and our summer-weight sleeping bags and bag liners are welcome. Most nights, like tonight, I start off only in the bag liner, kind of like a sheet for the sleeping bag, but need to move into the full bag within a short time.

My bag and liner were a gift from Mom a few years ago, probably at Sabrina's suggestion so I'd camp with her. They were both still in the packaging when Sabrina started loading us up for this trip. I'm just about to drift off when the camp suddenly comes alive, and not in a good way.

More like the wildest, craziest, seediest nightclub in the most dangerous part of the city just came to life. What starts as revelry and fun with lots of laughter and hooting, soon becomes something more . . . something sinister.

"Was that a woman screaming?" Sabrina whispers.

"Pretty sure it was."

She sits up, moves to the door, and unzips the tent.

"Where are you going?" I murmur.

"To see if I can help, of course," she answers like I'm a brain-dead fool.

"Sabrina. No."

"Shh." She sticks her head out.

"You don't want to come out here," Rey says quietly. "It's best just to stay in your tent and try to sleep."

"You want me to ignore what's going on?" Sabrina stammers.

"Nothing you can do about it. It's a nightly occurrence."

"So you . . . what? Just . . . just ignore it?"

"I figure, if I can watch out for my family, then that'll have to do. You should zip your tent back up. Try and get some rest."

"Try and get some rest? Are you nuts?" she hisses.

"No, I'm not nuts. I'm smart."

"Sabrina," I say quietly, choking back tears. I'm trying not to lose my composure as I'm transported to a different time, a different night. "He's right. From the sounds of it, it's not just one woman in trouble with one person causing the trouble. It's . . . I'm not sure what it is, but you can't stop it. *We* can't stop it."

Chapter 10

Lindsey

Sunday, Day 11
Central California

There are many, many stalled cars along Highway 99—perfect for Logan's refueling plan.

In a section on 99, without people around but with plenty of abandoned cars, he starts punching holes in gas tanks. Even though the cars are mostly stopped due to running out of gas, he still finds a small amount in each.

He planned his procedure out. First, empty all our canisters into the bikes, then use a rechargeable cordless screwdriver with a screw in place. Leave the screw in the newly made hole and set up a funnel with a coffee filter over a Gatorade bottle to filter out any bottom-of-the-tank sediment. Then, take the screw out slightly and let it run slowly into the funnel.

My job is sentry while he's draining the tanks. It takes some time, but the process works well, and we've been able to refill the two small bottles.

"See, Linds. Piece of cake," he says with a huge grin.

"Sure, Logan. People always say stealing is easy," I snipe.

He avoids taking the bait and moves on to the next car.

"Whoa, baby," he says after a few seconds. "This one's a gusher."

"What do you mean?"

"Coming out faster than the others. I don't think it was empty."

With this car, we have enough fuel to finish filling both of our little cans and all but one bottle. The final bottle is over half full before the flow stops.

"Why do you think this car was here?" I ask. "It didn't run out of gas, did it?"

"Doesn't seem so. Not sure why it's here."

I have to admit, I feel pretty bad about our refueling method. I'm sworn to uphold the law, and here I am, not only stealing but causing destruction of property. This, combined with our illegal firearms transfer . . . I guess I'm not the person I've always thought I was.

Even though I don't like the refueling method, we repeat it on a stretch of I-80 before leaving it to take a lesser traveled road to avoid the larger towns. We did pretty well, making it through Sacramento on Highway 99 and then getting on I-80, but Logan wants to avoid Reno. A bad experience during a bachelor party weekend has him convinced it's better stay away from the "Biggest Little City in the World."

On this small state highway, with cars few and far between, we've still managed to fully refill. With the sun starting to rise, we call it a night and find a forest access road of some sort—maybe an old logging road—to set up camp.

I reach into the sky as far as possible, then bend at the waist and sweep my fingers on the ground, feeling a definite pinch in my injured hamstring. *Ouch! Easy, Lindsey.* I'm better but definitely not fully healed.

After traveling all night, it feels amazing to be off of the bike. The last half hour of our ride, in the twilight before dawn, was beautiful, with a pale yellow-orange glow streaming through the trees. Now that it is almost full daylight, we're finished riding and ready to rest.

Removing my rubber band, I shake out my hair. It's good to have it freed from the helmet. I realize I should've washed my hair before we left yesterday.

"Brrrr." Logan rubs his arms. "It's chilly. I'm thinking I should put my leathers back on."

"Bet you wish you would've brought something a little more substantial than shorts and a T-shirt for sleeping."

"You're not kidding." He pulls a hoody over his head. "I totally forgot how cold it can get in these mountains. It should warm up, though, with the sunrise."

"Put your jacket back on at least," I suggest. Our leather jackets aren't lined but will offer some protection. I started getting cold a few hours ago. We had to stop for me then so I could put my hoody on under my jacket. I've yet to take either off. I'm still wearing my chaps too.

He gives me a look.

"At least give it a try," I say. "You may not be able to zip up the jacket, but it could help."

Logan's put on some weight over the last several months. His riding gear has become noticeably smaller—to the point he doesn't even bother with it when commuting, just wears a windbreaker and jeans. He was able to expand the chaps to the largest option, so they somewhat fit. Only the top two buttons on the jacket snap, so he left it open while we rode.

"I'll be fine." He gives a dismissive wave. "Let's get some food, then you can sleep for a while."

Logan uses his little stove with a few twigs. We brought along several charcoal briquettes but decide to save those for places where there aren't many trees.

Our breakfast is a can of soup and a can of peaches. We decided starting with the canned goods would be smart in case we end up walking. We'll want as little weight as possible.

"Good thing you have all this nice camping stuff we never use, honey," I say with a smile.

"You're telling me. I guess I'm glad we didn't trash it after all. I didn't even remember having this stove. Glad Eddie gave it to me."

"Well, I'm enjoying my hot soup, thanks to your top-of-the-line gear. I do kind of wish we had a real tent and sleeping bags. Yesterday was too hot, but up here . . . " I gesture to encompass the entire forest. It's starting to warm up, but not to the point I'm ready to take off any of my clothes.

"I was thinking, it probably won't be too cold once we reach your parents' place, but . . . well, I guess you know we'll probably be there through the winter at least. Hopefully they'll have some warmer clothes we can wear. I can't imagine things getting much better before winter. And now, with the fire back home . . . " His voice fades off as he gives a slight shrug.

A few minutes later, Logan breaks the silence. "You ready? I'll wake you up in a few hours, then I can sleep."

"Maybe we could sleep at the same time? It's so quiet and desolate here. Plus, we're well off the road, and you used brush to scratch out our tire marks. Let's both sleep."

"I'd rather be smart about it. Besides, I'm going to try calling our parents, then look for some water to replenish what we've used."

"Okay. Where are you planning to go?"

"Oh, just up the hill a bit." He gestures farther up the forest service road. "I won't go far."

"Taking the bike?"

"Nope, on foot. I'll keep the camp in view."

"Yeah, good idea. I don't want you getting lost in the woods."

When we slept at the lake yesterday, we spread out the tarp and put our blankets on top. There were a few bugs there, which left their mark, but it wasn't terrible. Up here, it's not only considerably colder but buggier. I'm wishing for a tent we can seal up tight from the elements. Logan spends several minutes turning the larger tarp into a shelter.

While he's working on the shelter, I change into my sleeping clothes, layering my hoody over the top. The rising sun has warmed things up, but it's still on the cool side, with the sharp breeze giving me goosebumps.

"Okay, babe, give it a try. I can't do anything to make it fully mosquito proof, but it should be a little warmer at least. Once you get in, I'll finish it up."

I crawl into the leaning A-frame-like structure. The tarp is perched precariously over an assortment of branches.

"Ready?" he asks.

"Ready."

A full-sized white sheet, also from our fold-out sofa at home and now part of Logan's bedroll, billows through the air. It finally comes to rest over the opening I just crawled into.

"I'll secure it with a few rocks to keep all but the most determined bloodsuckers out."

"You're very good to me, Logan Maverick," I say from inside my refuge, as I gently press my hand to the white sheet.

He presses back from the outside. "You're my best girl, Lindsey Maverick. Don't you ever forget it. Now get some sleep. I'll wake you up in a few hours so I can take over your warm, bug-free abode and you can sit out here swatting and shivering."

"Great. I can't wait."

"Sleep well," he says, as I settle in.

Chapter 11

Sylvia

Sunday, Day 11
Between Shoshoni and Thermopolis, Wyoming

"Sylvia? Sylvia? It's time to get going."

"Not yet," I say with a moan. "Give me five more minutes."

"It's time, Sylvia," Sabrina insists, tapping my shoulder repeatedly.

"Fine," I huff, sitting up, making sure to knock her hand away. I brush the side of the tent in the process, dampening my arm with the overnight condensation. *Thanks, Sabrina.*

"We need to get going," she says, as she crawls out of the tent.

The eastern sky is just beginning to lighten as I stumble out. Sabrina hands me a flashlight, already on the red-light option. She insists the red light is best so we can maintain our night vision. I could care less about night vision on my trek to the bathroom.

I hold my breath as I stagger into the neglected vault toilet. The stench is nearly unbearable. I'm glad Sabrina insisted I keep a few squares of toilet paper in my pocket, because there isn't any in the toilet. *Ick. What a mess.*

Back in camp, Sabrina has the tent down and everything ready. As always, she's even repacked my sleeping mat, bag liner, and sleeping bag, readying my backpack for the day. She gives me a big smile and hands me a warm cup—some kind of tea from her stash. I'd prefer coffee, but she doesn't drink it, so we don't have any.

Rey, looking amazingly wonderful, has most of his camp ready. He doesn't bother with a red light. Instead, he has a very bright LED lantern lighting up his camp. The three children are up. Nate is helping Rey, while Nicole and Naomi huddle together in the predawn chill.

When we're almost ready to go, he wakes Kim. She stumbles out and heads to the malodorous vault toilet. While she's gone, Rey packs the tent she was using. I wonder how well this trek is going to go with the makeshift items they have. The one-man tent looks like a decent quality, and maybe the two-man is sufficient. But the play tent and their luggage, I'm not so sure about. Mostly, I wonder about their attitudes.

We still have about 150 miles to go before we get to Mom's place. At the rate we're going, it'll take us over two weeks. We need to start making better time, but with the addition of the Hoffmann family, we'll be even slower.

Kim returns from the bathroom, and we start our journey. Sabrina gives Rey a headset lantern to wear, asking him to use the red-light version, in hopes of not disturbing the other inhabitants. There's very little conversation as we pick our way out of the camping area.

Once we reach the highway, the sound of Kim's, Naomi's, and my roller bags provide a cadence. After a few minutes, Kim asks, "Spare me a smoke?"

"Mom," Nicole hisses.

I'd been putting off my first for the day, thinking about rationing again. I stifle a sigh as I pull two out. I light hers, then my own. Ah. The first inhale is glorious. I get a slight head rush. Way too soon, I'm down to the filter.

After the sun has come up enough for us to see clearly, Sabrina says, "Let's stop for a minute and look at the map."

We're now well away from the state park and the large group of campers in the new tent city. At the suggestion of stopping, Kim and Nicole find a spot to sit down, then little Naomi joins them.

Sabrina stretches the map across a large boulder on the side of the road, with Nate and Rey looking over her shoulder. I take a long drink of water. Sabrina purchased a new gravity water filtration system last month as an upgrade to her camping gear. She'd always had a small straw filter before but loved the gravity system her friend used on one of their trips last summer, a gallon bag and mini-filter setup.

She was, in my opinion, overly excited about it when it arrived. I faked interest while helping her master working it a few times. Now, I'm super glad for it. Not that I'll admit it to her.

"Okay, so I was thinking, maybe we should go across the dam here." Sabrina points to the map.

"Why?" I ask, not bothering to mask my annoyance at how ridiculous the idea is.

"Following the railroad track on the other side of the river, through the canyon, might give us some better places to camp tonight. Remember how the road is mostly rock on the right side with the river on the left side? I know there are a couple of open spaces, but not many, and I don't want to try and camp so close to the highway."

We've traveled this route before—by car, of course—and I vaguely recall this road through the Wind River Canyon. We still have quite a ways until the series of three tunnels signals the start of the canyon. Seems she's right about it being mostly cliff and rock along the roadside. There's also rock and cliff on the train side. Doesn't sound much better.

"You think the railroad track would be better? Isn't that on the edge of a cliff also?"

"Yes, for the most part. But we know trains aren't running, so we could go ahead and set up on the track if we had to. It's around thirty miles to Thermopolis, so we'll definitely have to camp somewhere tonight and probably tomorrow night. On this side, I wouldn't feel comfortable setting up on the road, since we do still see cars occasionally."

"Yeah, I guess that makes sense." I shrug. "Not just cars but bikes and motorcycles plus people walking, like us. I guess there will probably be people walking on the tracks, too, don't you think?"

"Sure. We'll need to be careful, just like we've been so far." Sabrina turns to Rey. "What do you think?"

"I like the idea. I think you're right about the rock cliffs. Seems smart to try to avoid issues if we can. But with the attacks on the railroads, they might have destroyed it. We could have trouble."

"I can't imagine they'd target these tracks. Did you hear anything about where the incidents happened?"

"Not much. There was a Presidential Address. Someone played it at the camp, and he briefly spoke about the railroad issue. That was the same day Congress was hit, so the assassinations were the focus."

Sabrina and I both nod, as Rey says, "Probably worth trying it. This is such a remote area, why bother?"

"All right. Fine, then. Let's cross the dam and walk the tracks," I agree.

"Okay, good," Sabrina says. "Sylvia, while we're stopped do you want to check your phone? We might be in a good spot for reception."

Our phones stopped working last Saturday during the cyberattacks. We tried them off and on while we were in the car, without success. We made a point of keeping them fully charged, by way of the car charger, just in case. When we ditched the car, we took our phones, but left them off. A couple of days ago, we met up with a couple who said they heard the phones were working intermittently. The Hoffmann family confirmed they'd heard the same thing and even tried using someone's phone in camp to reach Kim's parents. It did ring, but no one answered. Sabrina and I decided we'd try Mom and Phil three times a day on each phone, in hopes of getting through.

I turn my phone on and shake my head. "No good, no signal at all, maybe because of the location. Let's get across the dam and then try again. It might be a little more open on the other side."

Rey gets his family moving again. The small rest seems to have improved Kim's disposition; she's now talking with the children. Crossing the dam, the train track is below us. There's a road along the far side of the dam, so we'll take it until it meets with the track farther in toward the canyon.

About half an hour later, we connect with the railroad track. We've been on a slight downhill slope and making good time. A few minutes later, I'm startled by a loud *beep, beep, beep.*

"What is that? Your phone?" Nate asks.

I reach in my pocket, where I stashed my cell when trying to call out earlier. It's vibrating while beeping. I guess I forgot to shut it off. I'm confused by the beep since that's not a ringtone I've chosen. A quick glance at my phone shows an emergency alert.

BALLISTIC MISSILE THREAT INBOUND TO UNITED STATES. MULTIPLE INBOUND MISSILES DETECTED. SEEK IMMEDIATE SHELTER. THIS IS NOT A DRILL.

Chapter 12

Lindsey

Sunday, Day 11
Tahoe National Forest
Near Sierra City, California

"Lindsey, wake up. You have to wake up. There's no time. Wake up now!"

"What? What are you doing, Logan?" I'm so tired and confused. It takes me a minute to remember I'm in a tent-like shelter in the middle of a forest, on the way to Mom's place in Wyoming. Why is Logan shaking me like this?

"The phone . . . it went off. We have to go."

"Someone called and we have to go?"

"No. Look!" Logan thrusts his phone at me.

BALLISTIC MISSILE THREAT INBOUND TO UNITED STATES. MULTIPLE INBOUND MISSILES DETECTED. SEEK IMMEDIATE SHELTER. THIS IS NOT A DRILL.

All feeling immediately leaves my body as my mouth goes dry. I'm woozy and sick to my stomach. We're in a forest. Where are we going to seek shelter to protect us from a missile?

Missile . . . a nuclear missile?

How can this end but badly? They nuke us and we nuke them back? We're in so much trouble. I start to cry.

"Stop." Logan grabs my shoulder with his left hand and puts his right index finger on my chin, forcing me to look at him. "I know you're scared. I am too. But you have to pull yourself together. We have to go. We need to find a place to . . . hide."

"Hide from a nuke? How's that going to work, Logan?" I say with a sniffle.

He takes a breath and says calmly, much too calmly in my opinion, "We're pretty much in the middle of nowhere. Chances are good we won't get nuked here, but we need protection from the fallout. Remember the class you took in the academy? What did you learn? You told me some, but I'm sure you learned more than you shared. Let's think."

He's right. I did have a short training on nuclear warfare. More of a "what do we do with all of the people afterward" thing, but there was training on blasts and a little about fallout. We may not be where a bomb strikes, but chances are, we'll get fallout. I know large cities on the West Coast—LA, San Francisco, Portland, and Seattle—are considered targets, along with military bases and East Coast cities like DC and New York.

Westward winds would bring any West Coast fallout our way. Would Sacramento be a target? We're not very far from Sac. And how about Reno to the east? Are we close enough to either of those that, if there is a hit, we'll be in the blast zone?

I quickly think about where we are. We're likely not close enough to any possible target to be affected by the immediate blast, but we could definitely receive fallout if San Francisco or Sacramento are hit—maybe even from Reno if the wind shifts and comes from the east. What about LA? I think we're too far north to get fallout, but I don't want to chance it.

"We need to get underground."

Logan's already throwing things in our bags. I didn't even realize he started taking down our camp. "Yep. Get all of this stuff packed up and let's go. I think I remember going over some sort of bridge a mile or so back. We can get under there for now, then maybe figure out something better."

I nod as I begin to put on my leathers.

"Don't bother with those. Let's just go."

I'm wearing yoga pants and a tank top, what I was wearing to sleep in. As my little tent warmed up, I shed the hoody. Logan must have warmed up also. He's in his basketball shorts and a T-shirt. At least he has athletic shoes on; I'm still barefoot.

I shrug and quickly stuff things in my saddlebags and backpack. We tried to unpack only what we'd need, so there is not a lot that needs repacking. I cram things in, not worrying about neatness. Getting my leathers in is a challenge. I quickly shove my boots on my bare feet, not bothering with socks. Logan's doing about the same job with his packing. Within a couple of minutes, I notice him taking a look around.

"We got everything?" he asks, while putting on his helmet.

"Looks like it. You lead and I'll follow." I put on my helmet and hop on my bike. I'm nervous and forget the starting procedure.

"Deep breath, Linds. You need me to talk you through it?"

"No, I've got it." Soon, my bike is running. I follow Logan off the dirt road and back to the main road. We're driving fast, but after a minute, he slows down to navigate around an old clunker of a pickup truck pulling a utility trailer—half off, half on the road. He immediately pulls to the side of the road and stops. Instead of a bridge, it's a large culvert running under the road.

"Walk your bike down. It looks high enough we can take them under. We'll have to stoop a little, but not too bad." What he likely means is, he'll have to stoop a little and I'll have to stoop a little more. At just shy of six foot, he's three inches shorter than I am.

"Do you think we need to worry about water in the culvert?"

"Not right now. There would be water in it if it were a regular use thing, but I think it's just an overflow during heavy rains. Might be a little damp, but we should be fine."

"You mean, unless it starts raining."

Logan chooses to ignore my snark as he starts down the embankment. "You know, it's kind of steep. I'll take your bike down. Should we move the pickup on top of the bridge to provide a little more protection for us?"

"Why?" I ask, not understanding, then remember some of the materials I was given when I had the nuke training. They handed out several old flyers from Civil Defense, and one of them had a picture of people digging a trench and parking their car on top of it. The lead in the car was supposed to help protect them. I thought it sounded terrible—I had visions of the walls of the trench giving way and the car crushing the people in the trench. No thank you.

"You think it'd help with fallout?" I ask. "Cars today aren't made like tanks, like they used to be. I'm not sure it'd be of much benefit."

"You're right, but I think anything we can put between us and the fallout will help. Also, this isn't a new truck. It's from, I don't know, the late '70s or early '80s. Let me get the bikes down and then see if we can move it."

I stand there, thinking how bad things are, while Logan moves the bikes under the bridge. When he's done, he stops and gives me a quick kiss. I grab for him and pull him into a hug. I'm scared and he knows it.

"We're going to be okay, Lindsey. This is just a bump in the road. Maybe it's a false alarm. Let's see if we can move the truck." He gently releases me and walks toward it.

The truck is an old, light blue, single cab Toyota with a ton of rust all over the body. The truck bed is filled with garbage bags and other miscellaneous items, to the point it's mounded over the top and secured with a variety of straps and cargo netting.

Stuffed just as full, and secured in the same haphazard manner, is a small rickety box-style utility trailer. To say it has seen better days would be an understatement. Even so, I'm impressed with the amount of junk crammed in the truck bed and the trailer. Maybe the guy was heading to the dump when he ran out of gas? No idea. We expect it to be locked but are pleasantly surprised when it opens with a gentle tug on the driver's door.

The inside doesn't look any better than the outside. The seats are ripped, the passenger's side floorboard is being used as a trash can, and the accompanying smell is definitely reminiscent of a garbage bin.

I make a face. Logan breaks into a big grin—which I find totally inappropriate for the severity of our situation.

"It's a manual. I thought it might be. That should make things easier. Hop on in, Linds. Put it in neutral, and I'll give you a push."

"Uh . . . no. That thing is disgusting. You hop in."

Logan sighs. "I need to push. Since it's on an incline, it'll start moving once it's in neutral. You need to keep some pressure on the brake while we navigate it back on to the road. If this thing's fully in the ditch, it isn't going to help us any."

"Fine."

It takes only a few minutes to move the truck over the bridge. We position it near the edge so there's still room to get by in case another car comes along. As I step out of the truck, a flash catches my eye. Is it lightning?

"Oh no," Logan whispers. A little louder, he says, "I think it was a detonation. We're pretty far away, but the light . . . it might have been a detonation."

I look toward the west in time to see the beginnings of a cloud formation—a mushroom cloud.

"Lindsey."

I turn to look at Logan as there is another dim flash.

"Will we be affected by the blast?" I exclaim.

"I don't think so. We're pretty far away."

"San Francisco? You think it was San Francisco?"

"Yeah, maybe Sacramento too," he quietly answers.

I involuntarily start to cry and rush into his arms. He takes a minute to hold me before gently saying, "We need to get ready. We might be within the fallout zone."

I nod in agreement. "In the training, we were told we had half an hour after a blast to find shelter. Of course, that was assuming a nearby blast . . . maybe we have a little longer with the distance?"

"Maybe so, but let's not risk it." Logan pulls out his phone. "It's 8:42. Let's make sure we're secure no later than 9:12." He releases me and starts removing the full bags of trash from the back of the pickup.

"What are you doing?" I ask.

"I thought we could use the garbage and stuff in the back of the pickup to seal off the ends of the culvert. There's no doubt now about the bomb, so we need to prepare for fallout."

"Okay, yeah. I don't know if it'll work, but let's try. I think we should put the garbage bags on the far side."

Logan keeps pulling trash out while I move them down the slope to the culvert. I pile the odorous bags up, something like bricks, to try to seal off the entrance to the culvert.

"What about the other side?" I ask as I'm putting the last bag in place. It's not as tight as I think it should be, but it'll have to do.

"We'll use the other junk he has back here and then add in the brush and stuff from the pile over there," Logan answers, while motioning to a small slash pile left behind by someone cutting timber. I'm surprised to see this since logging isn't much of an industry in California forests. Maybe this is part of the new plan to help prevent future fire disasters.

The other trash consists of an old lawn mower, paint cans, and a few cut pieces of plywood. There are also some nonjunk items—a shovel, an ax, and a high-lift jack. We set all of the rubbish on the opposite end of the culvert from the trash bag collection.

"Go ahead and get inside, Lindsey. I'm going to grab some brush."

"No, I'll help. Then we'll both go in."

"Okay, fine. Big pieces first."

There are actual logs in the slash pile. We pull out the ones we can easily retrieve and haul them to the culvert, then we grab small pieces to fill in with. It's soon obvious we need to be inside the culvert to finish filling in the spaces.

With our bikes and supplies, it's a tight fit trying to get things arranged. We put the plywood on the inside of the trash bags and add a few of the logs to secure it all. On the junk end of the culvert, we pull the longer logs as tight up against the culvert as we can, filling everything in with brush and smaller pieces. It's not great, but we're hopeful it'll provide enough protection from the fallout.

"What about space blankets? Would it help at all to put those over the debris? I remember sealing up windows with plastic was one of the recommendations for those without an underground option. Maybe the emergency blankets will work in a similar way?" I suggest.

"Yeah, let's do that. One on each end. I have a roll of duct tape we can use to hold everything together."

It takes us several minutes to get the emergency blankets in place. With the tight space, working so closely together is a challenge. After getting the blankets up, we spread the small tarp on the damp ground, then huddle close together. With the bikes, there isn't a lot of extra room. Lying down might be a challenge.

"Let's turn out the light, Linds. Save the battery for now."

In the darkness, I whisper, "So . . . that's it, I guess?"

"Yeah, I think so," Logan whispers back. "Can you think of anything else that could help?"

"Maybe covering our faces? We have bandanas we can use so we don't breathe in any particles."

"Okay, might be smart."

With our faces covered, we decide we're as set as we can be. I wonder if Mom knows what's happening. Did they get the alert text in Wyoming? Were they able to get to a safe spot?

Chapter 13

Mollie

Sunday, Day 11
Makeshift Hospital
Bakerville, Wyoming

While all the smartphones reverberate with the emergency alert, my flip phone is silent.

We're engulfed in sudden pandemonium.

Ten-year-old Malcolm shrieks, "Mom! Dad! What does it mean? Are we being bombed?"

My daughter Calley pulls Malcolm close to her. "We'll be fine, Buddy. Everything will be okay." Calley then looks expectantly at me and Jake.

Jake immediately says, "We will. But we need to get moving. Phil, you set up at your place?"

"Yep. We're good," Phil answers. "We've made arrangements for our neighborhood to join us in our . . . uh . . . basement. Yesterday, we set up neighborhood contacts. Kelley entered everyone in her phone."

He's barely finished speaking before my phone rings. Almost simultaneously, Jake's phone is ringing. Our friends Kelley and Phil are swiping their phones.

Instead of hello, Jake answers with, "Art, you know what to do?"

I answer my phone with an abrupt hello. I don't recognize the number, other than it's local.

"Mollie Caldwell? Mick Michaelson. Kelley and Phil gave me your number when we set up the neighborhood contacts yesterday. We just got the alert and are going to start calling the other neighborhood contacts. We think anyone without a basement should go to the community center—it has a storage room in the basement. Any chance your husband can drop off the generator?"

Jake is finishing up his call with Art, and I hear him say, "We'll be there shortly," as he disconnects.

"Just a minute," I say to Mick. Covering the mouthpiece, I share with Jake the conversation.

Jake looks flustered for a moment, as my son-in-law Tate says, "I'll take the generator to them. They'll need water. Jake can concentrate on getting everything set at your place."

Sarah has a frantic look about her. She starts to say something, but her husband gives a gentle headshake. She nods, knowing Tate will do what he needs to do.

"Yep. Let's do it." Jake nods.

I go back to my phone call. "Yes, someone will bring it down. We'd best get moving. Stay safe, Mick."

Phil and Kelley finish their calls as Tammy, along with her daughter Belinda, run into the room.

"Jake, I understand you have a basement," Belinda says. "I'm inviting myself, my mom, and my son to join you so we can care for Doris, Madison, and Katie. We need to get going now. Dr. Sam, will you and your family go to the community center? With the basement— "

"Michaelson called, they're organizing people to shelter in the basement," I interrupt.

"We'll go there," Dr. Sam says, quickly leaving the house.

"Kelley, you'll be okay at your shelter?" Belinda asks.

"Yes, of course. It's too bad we can't spread our medical team around a little more, but I don't even really know who all has basements. We'll just have to wait this out and then we can evaluate for any injuries. I pray there will be none."

"Agreed," Belinda says. "I'll take my car, and Katie can lay across the back seat. Mom, you take your car and do the same with Doris. Madison can ride in the front seat. Put Emma in her car seat. Evan, you take her. I assume you're going to Jake's basement?"

Jake says yes, while Evan nods.

"When Hawaii had their false alarm, I read it takes fifteen to thirty minutes for bombs to hit the mainland, once discovered. We're running out of time, people. Leo, you'll take my dad's truck. I want you to load it with as many supplies as possible. You know where everything is. Let's go," Belinda orders.

I'm on crutches and moving terribly slow, so Jake carries me to the truck. Once I'm in, he runs back to help Katie and the others get loaded up. Within a few minutes, we're on the road. It's a ten-minute drive to our house and our basement shelter.

Our truck is full, overflowing even. My husband drives, I'm in the passenger's seat, and my oldest daughter, Sarah, is in the middle front. In the backseat is our son Malcolm and daughters Calley and Angela. Our three sons-in-law—Tate, Tim, and Mike—ride in the bed. Alvin, my father-in-law, is riding with Evan. Katie's boyfriend, Leo, will follow behind.

The cab is filled with cries and sobs. *Are we being bombed? What will happen to us? Will we die?*

Questions that have no answer. I make soothing noises, trying to alleviate my children's fears. Three of them are adults, full-grown women, but they're still my babies.

Can I protect them?

Chapter 14

Sylvia

Sunday, Day 11
Railroad Tracks
Between Shoshoni and Thermopolis, Wyoming

"What is it, Sylvia?"

I shake my head, unable to speak, as I thrust the phone toward Sabrina. She pales as she scans it, then reads aloud.

BALLISTIC MISSILE THREAT INBOUND TO UNITED STATES. MULTIPLE INBOUND MISSILES DETECTED. SEEK IMMEDIATE SHELTER. THIS IS NOT A DRILL.

Kim immediately starts wailing, "Why? Why? Why us?"

Naomi is too young to really know what's going on, but she starts crying along with her mom.

"We should go back across the dam," I say. "There's a series of tunnels into the canyon. We're going to need to run."

Sabrina starts to agree, then says, "There's a tunnel for the train also. Remember? We noticed it once when we were going into the car tunnels."

"Really? You sure?" I ask, trying hard to control my own emotions. Like Kim, I feel like wailing.

"She's right," Rey says. "I remember seeing it when I came through here years ago. Let's go. We need to get to shelter."

Nate starts to run, but his dad says, "Slow down, Nate. We stick together. We'll move quickly but safely. I don't think it's very far."

We've been fast walking for several minutes when Naomi says, "I'm tired. I need to stop."

Sabrina adjusts her load and puts Naomi on her hip. Nate sees what she is doing and offers to handle Sabrina's shopping cart. Maybe we should just drop our gear and run? No, we'll definitely need it if we're stuck in the tunnel for any length of time. But for the umpteenth time, I wonder how much longer we can carry so much stuff.

After a few minutes, when it's obvious Sabrina is tiring, I take Naomi from her. Sabrina grabs my rolling suitcase. "How much farther do you think it is to the tunnel?" Better not be too far; I'm struggling to breathe.

Rey, also well loaded with trying to jostle his family's items, says between haggard breaths, "Not far, I don't think. There's the second campground over there." He gestures ahead a good quarter of a mile. "If I remember correctly, the tunnels on the road begin right after that campground. The train tunnel should be about the same area."

Looking across the river, I see the campground, and like the campground we spent last night in, it's full of people. None of them seem to be moving toward the tunnels. I wonder if they know about the alert. With the roar of the water, yelling across to warn them would be a futile effort.

"Yep. We're close," Sabrina says.

Good, because this kid is heavy.

Nate soon exclaims, "There! There it is."

We all get a second wind.

Naomi asks to be let down, and she hustles behind her brother.

When we're three football fields away from the mouth of the tunnel, Sabrina says, "Hold up a minute. Let's make sure we're not running in on someone else who's holed up in here."

"Good idea," Rey says. "I'll check it out."

"Are you armed?" Sabrina asks.

"Um, no. Do you think I need to be?" He looks around and reaches for a medium-sized rock. "There, now I am."

Sabrina gives a slight eye roll as she carefully removes her pistol from inside her waistband. "Let me check it out. Sylvia, you stay at the mouth of the tunnel and be ready."

Sabrina puts her headlamp back on, again using the red-light option, while I remove my pistol from my hip and pull out my flashlight, leaving it switched off.

With her voice laced with disgust, Kim says, "You two have guns? You have guns around my children? How dare you! You should've told us you're gun nuts. We never would've joined you. Tell them, Rey. Tell them how we feel about guns."

"I don't think I need to, Kim. You've stated your position rather well. And remember, I'm fine with guns." Rey then turns to Sabrina. "I've been around guns. It's fine. I'd back you up if I had one."

Sabrina glances at me; I lift one shoulder. She quickly removes her backpack and opens an outside pocket, removing a small holster containing an 8-shot .22 revolver—a gift from her previous boyfriend. Not something she would have chosen herself for personal protection, but something used for competition.

She could've given him the backup weapon in her bra holster, or the one in my ankle holster, or the little subcompact 9-millimeter holstered inside my messenger bag. Firepower is something we made sure we brought along—well, Sabrina made sure to arm us. While the 9-millimeter Beretta I carry on my hip belongs to me, and is usually in my nightstand collecting dust, the rest of the handguns belong to Sabrina.

And we won't even think to mention the weapons Sabrina managed to stow in the shopping cart she's dragging along. Blankets and tarps do a fine job of concealing long guns.

While she's not a gun nut, as Kim suggested, she does enjoy firearms and shooting for fun. A few years ago, she started getting serious about practicing, even entering several shooting competitions. She's tried to get me to join her, gently prodding, reminding me of . . . things. But I'm just not in that place right now. Even though I agree with her, I just can't.

Kim shoots daggers at Rey as he takes the revolver. He checks to make sure it's loaded, pulls out his flashlight, and moves to the left side of the tunnel mouth, while I move to the right.

"Kim, take the kids and go down on the edge so you're out of harm's way," Rey says quietly.

Kim continues her death stare.

"Kim. Go. Now," Rey says between clenched teeth.

"Fine."

After several murmured expletives, Kim moves the children slightly down the bank toward the river, behind a large boulder.

We quickly cover the remaining distance to the mouth of the train tunnel. Each of us catches our breath, then Sabrina nods as she cautiously enters the tunnel from my side, staying close to the wall. After only a few steps, the only thing visible is a dot of red light, which disappears a few seconds later.

We're silent for many minutes, then Rey whispers, "You think she's okay?"

"Probably," I whisper back, hoping she is. Minutes later, I see a pinprick of red in the distance.

"There she is," Rey says.

"Let's make sure," I respond. "Be ready, just in case."

While I don't have my weapon aimed, I am at the ready and can pull it up if the light bobbing toward us isn't my sister. Rey follows my lead.

From the tunnel, I hear, "It's me. Everything's okay. You can relax."

"Really?" I ask.

"Yes, Bongo, really."

Bongo is the word I was looking for. It's one of the safe words we use—one she insisted on me learning. If she would've called me Charlene, I would've known I couldn't really relax—something would be wrong and she'd be under some sort of duress. But Bongo means all is well.

Sabrina's finally at the mouth of the tunnel. "Rey, get your family inside. Gather all of your water containers and leave them here. Sylvia and I will fill them. We need to be prepared to stay in the tunnel for a few days."

Gee, thanks for volunteering me.

Rey nods, removes two empty containers from his pack—a Mountain Dew and a Smartwater bottle—then hustles back for Kim and the children.

It's way too steep by the mouth of the tunnel to try to get down to the river's edge. Sabrina motions me to walk with her while we look for a better access.

"You doing okay?" she asks quietly.

"Are you crazy? No, I'm far from okay."

"We'll be safe in the tunnel. Here, let's go down here."

It's still steep. She sees the look on my face and says, "I'll go down. You go just to the big rock there. I'll hand the bottles back up to you."

73

"Okay. Be careful. I don't need you falling in the river."

Sabrina winds her way down to the edge of the river. The large rocks are helpful, but it's still nerve wracking. I'm on my perch, when Rey startles me. "Here's a few more bottles."

I throw out my arms, trying to keep my balance. Once stable, I shoot him a look.

"Oops. Sorry. You want me to bring them down to you or just toss them?"

"Can you toss them carefully so we don't lose them?"

"Absolutely."

After sending four bottles down, he waits. Sabrina already has a few filled up. From my perch, it's a stretch for me to get the full ones from her and give her the empties.

I look up to Rey. He's down a few feet below the tracks on a large rock. "Here, I'll take them up," he says.

We finally finish filling all of the bottles. Sabrina also fills the one-gallon bladder of the gravity filter system, knowing we can filter it out when a few of the containers are empty.

Climbing back up the side of the cliff is harder for me than it should be. Rey offers me his hand, which helps. Sabrina has little trouble, scurrying up like a mountain goat.

At the tunnel, the Hoffmann family is a few feet inside from the mouth.

"Let's move farther in," Sabrina says. "The tunnel's about forty feet in length. I think we should go about halfway."

"You think a missile will hit here?" Kim asks with disbelief.

"I don't know," Sabrina answers. "I can't imagine it would, but I'd rather not hang out here and find out. Plus, if it's a nuclear strike, we could get fallout. We'd be better protected deeper inside the tunnel."

Even in the dim lighting of the tunnel, I can see the color fade from Kim's face. She almost trips over her feet as she starts to move farther inside. Sabrina, Rey, and I have our flashlights to help guide the way.

Soon, Sabrina says, "This is probably good. I'd say we're about halfway."

"Did you walk all the way to the end?" I ask.

"I did. I think this is a good place for us to be right now."

"Can you get a signal on your phone?" Rey asks.

I pull it out to see, even though I can't imagine I would deep in the tunnel like this. The phone lights up, still showing the alert I'd left on the screen, but the service indicator is showing as off. "No, sorry."

"What's the time?" Sabrina asks.

"Eight minutes before 10:00. We got the alert at 9:29."

"Okay, so we should probably get comfortable. If everything remains quiet, maybe we'll go to the mouth in a few hours, see what we see."

"What do you mean *see what we see*?" Kim asks.

"Nothing more than that. We may be able to get an idea about what's happening or we might not. Right now, we don't have much info—other than the alert on the phone. We assume it's legit and not a false alarm."

"You mean like Hawaii?" Nicole asks.

"Right, like Hawaii," I answer.

"If it's a false alarm, won't they send out a second alert, letting us know? You should go to service now and wait for it," Kim demands.

I give Kim a hard look and start to reply, but Sabrina jumps in. "No, if it's not a false alarm, then this is the safest place to be. We'll wait until, I don't know, one o'clock? Then check it out."

"I think, if nothing else happens between now and then, 1:00 sounds good," Rey says.

"Fine," Kim huffs. "I guess my opinion counts for nothing. Rey, since we're going to be stuck in here, set up the tents so we can get some sleep. We got up way too early this morning to end up stuck in a tunnel waiting for nothing."

"I'll set up the tents, Kim, but you need to lighten up. We need to stay where it's safe and wait for more information. I'm sorry you don't like it, but that's the way it has to be."

"Whatever, Rey. I'm going to bed. You do what you want. And make sure our kids get something to eat. I think this is all a crock, so you get to deal with it."

Kim physically turns her body away from us. Wow, were we just shunned? If I wasn't freaking out over the possibility of us being nuked, I might laugh at her antics.

Ignoring her, Rey sets up the small tent, then tucks a blanket inside. I can't imagine it's going to be very comfortable, being on the railroad ties without some sort of a mattress. But I'm not offering her my mattress pad.

I glare at Sabrina, silently sending her a message of, *Thanks so much for asking them to join us.*

She smiles sweetly in return.

I shake my head and intensify my glare. Not only do I have Mean Girl Kim, but also Miss Perfect Sabrina. *Great. Just great.*

After Kim's inside her tent, Rey sets up the tent for the children. Naomi has fallen asleep while sitting and waiting. Nicole helps her into the tent, then comes back out.

She plops down next to Sabrina and quietly says, "My mom doesn't really mean to be so nasty. She wasn't very happy about going up to Bozeman. She thought we should go to the Homeland Security office in Centennial or the Emergency Management office by Civic Center Park. She said they'd have FEMA there soon to help us and we should wait. Dad wants nothing to do with those places, so he said no." Nicole meets her dad's eye, and he gives a small nod—whether in agreement or giving her permission to continue, I'm not sure.

Nicole must interpret it as permission to continue. "Mom's just scared. She doesn't like it when things don't go as planned. And none of this— " she gestures widely " —has gone as planned. When we were shot at in Casper, she kind of lost it. Then the car ran out of gas and we were on foot. We can't really plan for anything. We don't even know where our next meal will come from."

Nicole starts to cry, as Rey says, "I cooked all the fish we caught and made a pot of rice last night. Your next meal is in my backpack. We're going to be fine. We're going to get through this and your mom is going to get better. She'll come around and realize she's only making things worse. She'll be fine."

I wonder if he believes this or if he's also trying to convince himself. She's going to need to show a lot more grit . . . and whine a lot less. Part of me would like to just walk away and leave Rey to handle Kim and her moods on his own. I look at Nicole, leaning against her dad, wiping her eyes. I feel a small desire to help the children. Not the calling Sabrina feels, that would be ridiculous. Oh, and the threat of a nuclear attack making the tunnel a much safer option for the time being also makes me want to stay.

Chapter 15

Mollie

Sunday, Day 11
Bakerville, Wyoming

"Mollie?" Jake touches my leg. "Is that okay?"

"What? Sorry. I wasn't . . . I didn't hear you." I sniff, wishing for a tissue.

"I'll help you out of the truck, but can you get inside on your own? I want to get Katie and the others into the basement."

"Yes, of course. I'm fine."

We hope and pray this is nothing more than a false alarm, but we'll prepare for the worst.

As we pull into our driveway, it's evident the plans we have in place, for a variety of scenarios, have been implemented.

Nuclear attack is one of the scenarios.

Battening down the hatches on our small farm is the main focus of preparation: moving the livestock—goats, sheep, pigs, ducks, and chickens—to our overly large garage, covering the garden crops with plastic, putting sandbags in specific places to help cut down on fallout, and several other items combined with getting the humans into the basement shelter. In the few minutes it took us to get home, our family at the homestead has done an amazing job.

Art, along with help from young Tony Hatch, is filling the garage with livestock. Tony's tightly holding a squawking duck to prevent its escape. Its quack of protest is almost a scream. The same kind of scream I'm currently trying to hold inside. *Why? Why?*

The truck is barely stopped as Tate vaults from the bed and dashes toward the pull-start portable generator.

Calley's husband, Mike, is at Tate's side to lend a hand loading the beast into Tate's truck. They soon tear off down the road, gravel spitting from the tires.

There are so many people at my house! Not just those who now live here, but also people who live nearby. Neighbors. All are moving very quickly and have either grim looks, are openly weeping, or both.

Jake made arrangements with our closest neighbors to come to our place in case of a severe emergency. He told them we had a basement. He didn't tell them our basement was more than a normal basement. It has a few secrets. Of course, soon they'll see all of the secrets. While I know I should be a good neighbor and open my home to our community, part of me hates to share our private spaces.

A deep bellow catches my attention. A very pregnant cow is being led into my oversized garage by neighbor David Hammer. We don't own a cow, and to my knowledge, neither does David. Apparently, we're not just providing refuge for our neighbors but for the area livestock.

Jake helps me out of the pickup, and I start to hobble toward the house.

"Mom, let me help you," Calley says.

"Thanks, sweetie. I'm okay on the crutches."

"Go into the house, Mom. I'll be right there to help you to the basement."

"I need to help— "

"No, Mom. You can't." Calley looks around and spies her brother. "Malcolm, take Mom downstairs. Can you get her down there on your own?"

"Yes, I can do it," Malcolm answers. "Are we going to the safe room or the root cellar?"

"The safe room. Don't you think, Mom?"

While we thought we'd made some pretty amazing plans, we didn't plan for any of us to be injured. Especially not with wounds as severe as Katie's.

"I . . . I think so. That should be the best place."

Calley nods decisively. "Yes, everyone injured goes in there. In fact, Malcolm, you run ahead and set the beds up. Then come back up for Mom. Mom, start making your way. I'll be right back."

"Malcolm," I say loud enough to stop him, "I need you to do something before going to the basement."

"What's that, Mom?"

"Grab our eReaders—yours, mine, and your dad's—keep them turned off and put them inside the Faraday cage. Grab our laptops also."

The understanding crosses his face. He's off at close to the speed of sound, declaring, "Good idea, Mom."

Calley hustles to Belinda's car where a foldup stretcher is being opened. Jake's already there to help move Katie to the basement. After a short conversation with Jake, Calley runs—not a jog but a full-out sprint—to the cabin she and her family are occupying. Propped up against the cabin is a solar panel Jake was installing before he was interrupted by recent events. The solar panels . . .

An EMP, or electromagnetic pulse, is a short burst of electromagnetic radiation that goes hand in hand with a nuclear detonation. In fact, they could choose to only cause an EMP by detonating the nuke high in the atmosphere. The solar systems could be ruined if there's an EMP.

I yell to capture Jake's attention. "Jake! Jake! EMP! We need to unhook everything."

I'm surprised when Roy, Mike's dad, responds, "Already done. It was in the *ERG*. I took care of it first thing. I disconnected the solar systems to the main house, the processing room, the pump system, the milking barn, the garage, and the bunkhouse. With the work Jake was doing, our cabin was already offline."

Our Emergency Response Guide, *ERG*, is Jake's brainchild, a large binder with a variety of to-do lists for different events. We laughed when we created it. We thought we were so silly . . . it's not like these things would really happen. When creating our entire retreat, we often thought we might be a little off our rockers. But we kept going, kept trying to make a safe place for our family.

We didn't succeed.

"Thank you, Roy."

"You betcha. Best start heading in, Mollie. You're not moving as fast as usual."

"Let me help you," Lois, Sarah's mother-in-law, says while moving toward me. Her cheeks are wet with tears, but a weak smile attempts to camouflage her emotions.

I know how she feels. All I really want to do is roll up in a ball and cry.

The din of an engine drowns out the clamor of the people. We live on a butte and have a slight hill to pull before reaching our property. This hill means people rarely sneak up on us when we're outside, with the engine working to make the climb and announcing their arrival.

I recognize the vehicle, another neighbor. As they pull into the driveway, I give a small wave, almost dropping my crutch in the process. Lois grabs it, saying, "Hold up a minute, Mollie. It looks like they have Katie on the stretcher. Should we let them go on by and then we'll get you in the house?"

"Absolutely."

The stretcher is close enough for me to see my sweet Katie. She's bundled up very well with a blanket wrapped around her. A surgical bouffant cap covers her long, wavy hair. Most of her face is covered with a surgical mask. She reaches her left arm toward me, a disposable glove covering her hand. Infection is a serious concern, and Belinda isn't taking any chances.

"Mom, you should sit down. You'll wear yourself out," Katie says softly.

"I will. Just stepping aside so they can get you down the stairs without having to wait for me. I'm pretty slow right now," I say, gesturing with one crutch.

"Okay, see you downstairs. I guess we're going to the safe room. You'll be in there, too, right? Since you're hurt?"

"We'll see, might be kind of crowded."

"Gotta go, Mollie," Jake says as they head around the house.

"Lois, I'd like to go in the front door. I want to grab a few things before we head downstairs. I'm pretty sure Malcolm will be waiting to help me also."

"Sure, Mollie. That's probably a good idea, since Jake and them are using the back door and going straight down. We'll be able to stay out of their way. I do think we need to start getting people underground. It's been almost half an hour since we got the alert, and I'm starting to get nervous."

"Yes. By now, there may have been impacts. I don't think we'd be a target here, but we need to be safe. Or it might just be a false alarm."

"Yes, maybe it's nothing, just a glitch of some sort. But with everything that has happened, do you think it's possible it's only a glitch?"

"Sure, maybe. If they're working on bringing systems back online, there could be some sort of error causing the alert to go out. At least, I pray so."

As we continue our hobble toward the door, the sound of another vehicle pulling the hill attracts my attention. The engine noise suddenly stops.

I'm not sure what to think. Did they decide not to continue up the road? It'd be pretty hard to make a wrong turn and get this far up the road before realizing it. Our road, a two-mile washboard gravel private drive, ends about a mile past our house, turning into a two-track mainly suitable for four-wheel drive or ATVs. Other than those of us living back here, the gravel road gets little use.

"Thought I heard a car starting up the hill," Lois says.

"Yeah, me too . . . not sure where they went."

We both shrug and continue our forward motion. Jake and Lois's husband, Keith, are returning with the empty stretcher.

"We're going to take Doris down now," Jake tells me. "Angela, Katie, and Madison are already downstairs. You are to go there also. All you sickies get to be in the same room so Belinda can keep an eye on you." He tries to smile, fails, then gives me a quick kiss before heading off.

There's still a lot going on, with people securing the livestock and doing the finishing things needing to be done. Art hollers at Tony to head on down to the root cellar, saying they have everything together and he needs to be underground helping with his little sister.

"Okay, here we are," Lois says, as we get to the bottom of the porch. "How are you on steps?"

"I'm good. Give me just a second to catch my breath. I can't believe how difficult it is walking with these things."

"Who is that?" Lois gestures toward the road. We see a fast-moving head pop over the rise, then briefly disappear behind one of our taller bushes lining the road. In a lower spot, the head is once again visible.

"Is that Leo?"

"Yeah, I think so," Lois replies. "Why is he running?"

Tim steps out of his tiny cabin, sees Leo, and runs toward the fence line.

"Can you hear them?"

"No, I can't make it out," I tell Lois.

Tim gestures wildly, then turns and darts toward the main house, stopping at his pickup. He hops in but doesn't start it.

"What's he doing?" Lois asks.

"Not sure."

He jumps out and pops the hood.

"Tim, what's going on?" Jake yells.

Tim shakes his head and runs to Jake. The yelling has stopped, so I can't hear the conversation. Jake drops his shoulders and shakes his head, then hands something to Tim, who takes off running again. He stops at our truck, gets in, and tries to start it. Nothing happens.

"Oh no," I whisper.

After a few seconds, Tim jumps out of the pickup truck and goes to our old Jeep. He climbs in and tries to turn it over. He bangs the steering wheel before trying again. There is a slight whir of the engine. Another try and the Jeep coughs, then catches.

Jake and Keith, carrying Doris on the stretcher, are rapidly heading our way.

"What's going on?" I yell when they're within earshot.

"The truck Leo was driving stopped. Ours won't start. The Jeep—it's okay," Jake answers. Are there tears in his eyes?

"So they really did it?" I ask, appalled as I pull my flip phone out. It's off and won't turn on.

"Seems so." Jake gives me a look, the kind that says he doesn't want to say anything more right now. Is he having trouble controlling his emotions? *I know I am.*

Chapter 16

Mollie

Sunday, Day 11
Bakerville, Wyoming

What was somewhat organized chaos is now frantic chaos, with people running and grabbing whatever they can as they make their way to the perceived safety of the basement.

Doris, lying on the stretcher, is incredibly pale and panicked. I try to give her a look of assurance, fail miserably, and ask, "Where's Evan?"

She takes a deep breath. "He dropped off your father-in-law here, then went up to our place to get supplies and things. He'll be back shortly. If his truck doesn't start, he'll get the old International or Betty Boop. You know, the 1959 GMC. Either should run. Your Jeep did, so that's a good sign. Oh, Mollie, we're in it deep."

I nod. "We'll make it, Doris. I'll see you downstairs."

Lois and I quickly—sort of—climb the stairs. In the house, more of our extended family, who are now sheltering here, are grabbing things out of the refrigerator and filling a cooler.

"Mollie, you doing okay? Can you make it down the stairs? Malcolm said he'd help you, but his grandma told him to wait in the basement. She doesn't want him up top. She was almost frantic when Tony insisted on helping with the animals, but he's in the basement now," Deanne, Calley's mother-in-law, rambles almost frantically, pushing her light red hair away from her face.

"I'm good. We're heading down. You close to done?" I say, my voice deliberately calm and controlled, even though I feel anything but calm.

"Yes, yes. We emptied the bunkhouse fridge and took all of the food from there down first. We had a little food in our cabin, and Tim had some in the Tiny House—that's all downstairs. We emptied the small fridge, but it was mostly beverages. I think we'll have one more load from the big fridge. We're not worrying about the basement fridge for now."

"Good, Deanne. I don't think there's much in the basement fridge, other than cheese."

"There's some meat also. We took it out yesterday after processing everything we had thawed. I planned to get it canned today, but now . . . anyway, the downstairs freezer is empty except frozen water bottles. If nothing . . . " She finally pauses and takes a deep breath. "If nothing catastrophic happens, we'll get the meat done. It'll be fine for now."

"Let's move the meat back to the freezer and cover it with a quilt. I have some set aside just for that purpose. Everything should stay cold for several days. We'll cook the meat up as soon as we can."

Deanne nods. "I already covered the freezer in the pantry with quilts. We familiarized ourselves with the *ERG* plans, so we knew what to do. Jake made sure of it shortly after we all arrived here."

"Great. Thanks, Deanne. Um . . . is Sheila already downstairs?"

A cloud passes over Deanne's face. "No, she's still in the cabin. She won't . . . she said she's staying there unless there's proof she needs to go into the basement or cellar. Jake said he'd tell Roy if the fallout thing on his keychain goes off."

"Ah . . . okay. We all hope this is just a precaution anyway. I'm sure she'll be fine." I try to give Deanne a reassuring smile. I fail.

Lois prods me to get a move on it. "What do you need before we head down, Mollie?"

"I want to grab an overnight bag from my closet. Can you help? Then we'll go down."

After grabbing the bag, Lois and I make our way to the top of the stairs. As promised, Malcolm's waiting at the bottom of the staircase and hustles to help. Lois passes my bag to Malcolm, saying she'll leave me in his hands and help Deanne finish packing the fridge.

"I wanted to come back for you, Mom, but Grandma Dodie wouldn't let me. She said my place was downstairs and you would come to me. Sorry I couldn't help you."

"It's no problem, Malcolm. Lois has been helping me. I'm sure she's glad to have you take over. Where is your grandma?"

84

"She has the little kids in Katie's room. She thought it'd be the best place to keep them . . . um, I think she said contained. Yeah, that sounds right."

I give a slight smile. "That does sound right. Is baby Emma in with Grandma too?"

"Yeah, she is. She's asleep in her car seat. Grandma said to just let her keep sleeping for now. Mr. Hammer's grandson is in there too. Tony and TJ are here also. Tony was helping get the animals in, but Art sent him downstairs. They're in the rec room by the foosball table, maybe playing a little while waiting to see if they can help."

"Walk with me down the stairs, then you can join them if you'd like. We don't need to go into the shelters unless . . . " I stop, not wanting to finish and scare him.

"Unless we start having fallout?"

I suppress a sigh. Of course he would know about this.

"Yes, that's right. We're down here as a precaution right now."

"But there was an EMP?" Malcolm asks.

"Possibly."

"An EMP won't produce fallout?"

"We don't know for certain there was an EMP. If there was a high-altitude detonation, we probably won't have fallout from it. But we don't know if there are other blasts, which may have been surface detonations. Those could produce fallout, so we're down here as a precaution."

"Yeah, I understand," he says with a nod as we reach the bottom of the stairs. Then he turns to me and looks me full in the eyes. "I'm scared but am trying hard not to be."

"It's okay to be scared, Buddy. I'm scared too."

"At least we're all here together and Katie is doing better. Did you see how they have Katie, Doris, and your friend dressed? Miss Belinda and her mom are disinfecting the safe room, then they'll take off their . . . she called it 'protective gear.' Angela's sitting in a chair outside the safe room. There's a chair for you too. They'll take you guys in once the room's ready. Miss Belinda said access to the room will be limited. I guess that means I won't see much of you while you're in there. I thought I'd be in there, too, so I can go up and take care of the animals in the garage. Can you ask? Maybe she'll let me if you ask."

"I'll see what I can do, Buddy. I know Belinda's concerned about infection. We should have thought about having a second access to the garage when we put in the safe room and root cellar . . . just never thought we'd have injured people, I guess."

At the base of the stairs, we're now in the rec room section of our basement. Tony, a year older than Malcolm, lifts his head from his foosball game, giving a small wave. Standing by the door from the rec room to the storage section, holding a clipboard, is Lois's daughter, Karen.

"Hey, Mollie," she says wearily. Like almost everyone else, she's struggling with her emotions, holding back the tears. "Glad to see you. Are you staying down in the basement for good? Or going back up?"

"I'm likely down for the duration. The stairs aren't too easy for me right now." I gesture toward my foot.

She nods and writes on the clipboard.

"You doing the check in?" I ask.

"Yes, I'm here and one of your neighbors is in the root cellar, checking people in when they come in the cellar door. How much time do you think we have before everyone needs to be down here? My parents are still going back and forth, and Tate's not even back yet." She bites her lip, clearly concerned.

"I saw Tim and Leo take off in our Jeep. I'm pretty sure they were going after Tate and Mike. They'll be back soon. Where're Sarah and Calley?" I ask.

"Also back and forth." She lets out a large sigh.

"I suspect Jake's rounding everyone up. They'll be downstairs shortly."

Karen nods, as Malcolm holds the door from the rec room into the storage area for me. The basement is full of activity as people move themselves to various locations. Neighbors and extended family members are buzzing about. There are many subdued hellos and how are you doing's offered in my direction, along with several, "I can't believe this," and many tears. I nod and briefly respond as I continue my slow forward motion with Malcolm by my side.

Sitting calmly, almost stoically, by the door to our safe room—now turned hospital room—is Angela, my second born, who was seriously injured in a recent attack while gathering supplies.

She sees me and cries out, losing all composure, "What else are they going to do to us, Mom?"

86

Chapter 17

Mollie

Sunday, Day 11
Bakerville, Wyoming

Angela, eyes full of tears, repeats, "What else are they going to do?"

I reach out my hand. "I don't know, sweetie. Right now, we don't really know what's happening."

"I heard there was an EMP. My husband drug me down here and then left me while he ran off with Leo," she spews. "Is it true?"

I move to the chair beside her and pull her into an awkward hug. "Tim and Leo went to find Tate and Mike. They'll be back soon. We don't know exactly what's happening. The truck Leo was driving stopped working and all of the phones quit—again. This time, they won't even turn on. Our old Jeep did start, so they took it to go after the others. We don't know for sure it was an EMP, but . . ."

"What about your flip phone?"

"Dead."

"I just hope Tim gets back soon. I hate him being gone right now." Angela covers her face with both hands and collapses in tears.

"He will. They'll be back shortly," I croon, as I rub her back.

Malcolm looks at me, helpless. He sits on the floor next to Angela, patting her arm.

"I'm so glad Grandma Dodie has Gavin in with her," she says through her tears. "There are so many people going in and out, he could easily slip away." The thought of this causes her to cry even harder. Understandable. Her two-year-old son Gavin could definitely make a break for it. Angela cries for several minutes before pulling herself together.

"Sorry, Mom." She gives me a small sheepish smile.

"It's fine. I'm upset too. We'll be okay."

She responds with a noncommittal nod.

We sit in silence for several minutes until I ask, "How are you feeling?"

"My head hurts and my back and bottom itch. All of those little scabs from the BBs feel terrible. How about you, Mom? Is your foot okay? You look pretty terrible," Angela says, gesturing at my face.

"Thanks, dear," I answer with mock indignation.

We both smile, barely.

Malcolm comes to my defense. "I think Mom looks great . . . well, not too bad, anyway."

"Thank you, Buddy."

"There's Dad," Malcolm says excitedly.

Jake is stepping out of the tunnel connecting the basement to the root cellar. He sees us and hustles over. Even with everything going on, seeing him almost takes my breath away. At fifty-one, he's still as handsome as ever. He works hard, we both do, to try to prevent the middle-aged spread. He's solidly built, not fat but definitely not skinny. His almost six-foot frame holds his weight well. When he smiles, he displays bilateral cheek dimples. His hair, grown out longer than he usually wears it, looks overly gray. Not gray—silver. *A silver fox.*

Dressed in denim jeans, which have seen better days, and a T-shirt topped with a button-up shirt, I catch a glimpse of the revolver he now carries full time. In fact, almost everyone now living at our retreat carries. We've had too many incidents to take our security lightly.

So much for our refuge.

Jake gives me a quick kiss, then says, "Mollie, I'm sorry I couldn't help you. Are you doing okay?"

"Yes, I'm fine."

"What about Tim?" Angela blurts.

"He's back." Angela lets out a huge sigh, as Jake says, "Mike and Tate were almost to our gravel road when the truck stopped. They should be downstairs shortly. They were unloading the medical supplies from the Jeep. We already have a good portion of it put in the root cellar. I closed up the cellar door, so everyone will be coming through here now. I have the list of people Betty checked in," Jake says, waving a sheet. "I'll give it to you in a bit, if you wouldn't mind making the master list. I'm going to go find the main binder. I think it's still in the kitchen."

"Any fallout?" Malcolm asks.

"No, Buddy. We're good."

"How long has it been since the alert?" Angela asks.

Jake pulls a watch from his pocket. Like most of us, he's come to rely on his phone for the time over the past several years. However, when I first met him, he didn't have a cell phone and wore a watch. When the attacks started, he pulled an old windup watch with a broken band out of my jewelry box and set it.

I have a windup watch in my overnight bag, plus half a dozen others in a box in the basement as part of our preps. We need to get those out, along with windup clocks. People feel better when they can keep track of the time.

"Let's see . . . it's almost 10:30, so about an hour."

"When will we get fallout?" Angela asks quietly.

"Any time, later today, maybe never," Jake answers with a shrug. "Our location isn't near any likely targets. If there was a ground strike, and that's a big if, we might be far enough away from it to not be affected by fallout. We're down here as a precaution."

"Why a big if?"

"We don't know what exactly is happening. We think there was an EMP, since the phones went dead and the newer vehicles aren't running, but we don't know for sure. The good news, if we can call it that, if it was just a high-altitude EMP, there won't be fallout. We'd need a ground detonation in order to produce fallout. And the EMP . . . we don't really know about it either. It could just be some kind of small, localized thing."

"Yeah, Mom taught me about that stuff in one of our homeschool study units," Malcolm says.

"Okay." Angela nods. "So Gavin's still good in the bedroom? He doesn't need to go into the root cellar or the safe room?"

"Sure, he's fine. As long as there isn't fallout, it's nothing more than a normal day."

The look I give Jake tells him I don't believe it's a normal day at all. He lifts one side of his mouth in a cross between a smile and a grimace while shrugging his left shoulder. He knows I'm on to him.

"How long do we need to stay down here?" Malcolm asks.

Jake and I both shake our heads. It's a good question and one without an answer until we have a better idea of what's going on.

"We'll probably want to spend most of our time down here for a few days. We'll at least sleep down here. Once everyone gets settled,

I'll see if one of the radios we put in the trash can is still working. Maybe we can learn more about what's going on," Jake answers.

The trash can is a homemade Faraday cage . . . three of them, in fact. We found plans on the internet—you can find anything on the internet, you know—and we hope the instructions were accurate for protecting some of our electronics. One of these is where I had Malcolm stash our tablets and laptops.

We already had an eReader and small laptop stored in a Faraday cage. I bought a cheap, basic laptop specifically to be able to play the collection of thumb drives I've been putting together for years. The eReader is loaded with fiction and nonfiction books. These, combined with an extensive paperback collection, binders of printed materials, and notebooks full of essential information, are things I thought might come in handy in an end-of-the-world situation.

End of the world.

Have we found ourselves here now? Were the previous attacks, as terrible as they were, just a precursor? Take out the low-hanging fruit and make us even more vulnerable, then bomb us? To what end? I shake my head. I'm so overwhelmed with what's happening, my mind is flying in a million different directions.

We also have several other things we store in the trash cans, like a couple of NOAA alert radios, two small backup solar systems, FRS radios—things we think can make our lives easier.

The slight squeak of our safe room door causes Angela and me to jump. Belinda sticks her head out, motioning to me and Angela. "Glad to see you two sitting there, taking it easy. Thought you might get some hair-brained idea you needed to help with all the hoopla going on."

"No. No hoopla for me," I answer.

"Me, neither," Angela says. "My husband brought me down here and told me to stay put."

"He's a smart man," Belinda says, while moving fully through the door and securing it behind her. She's wearing scrubs, a face mask, and a surgeon's cap over her hair. She removes the mask and says, "Jake, how's everything going? We have any news?"

"You heard about the EMP?"

The look on Belinda's face instantly changes, as she struggles to contain her emotions. "No. No, I didn't. I can't even imagine— "

Jake quickly says, "At least we think it's an EMP. The signs are there. No phones, cars died . . ."

Belinda straightens her shoulders. "Well, we'll make it through. Now, here's the deal. Mom and I sanitized the room as best we could. We're still very concerned about infection, not just for Katie but for Doris and Madison too. Jake, you said the access to the garage, where the animals are, is located through this room. As long as we don't get fallout, you'll still be able to go outside and care for the animals as normal?"

"Yes, that's correct. We put in a tunnel to reach the garage in a fallout situation so we could minimize our exposure. The garage will provide some protection to the animals but won't be like being underground. I'll go up and care for them morning and night. Without fallout, no biggie, I'll just go around."

"Okay, good. Let's hope this is all just a precaution. My understanding is fallout would be unlikely with an EMP, you agree?"

"Yes, that's our understanding," Jake says, while I nod.

"Okay, so . . . don't take this personally, but I'd prefer you not come traipsing in and out of my clean room if it can be avoided. We need to keep the place as sterile as possible, which means we're going to have to limit access. Mollie, you and Angela are well enough I'm not going to bring you in this room. Instead, one of us—my mom, Leo, or I— will be checking you daily, more often if the need arises. That said, if there is fallout, we'll bring you in with us. Mollie, I don't think you can make it through the tunnel on those crutches."

I bristle at the news she has knowledge of our tunnel, *our secret tunnel*. She must have checked things out before she started her safe room cleaning project. I recognize I'm being slightly ridiculous; many people have been in and out of the tunnel in the few minutes I've been sitting here. And, of course, she's right. The tunnel would be a challenge for me in my current condition.

"Normally," Belinda continues, "I'd be impressed with the way you made the cots into a bunk bed style that fold into the wall. It's a great use of space for sure, but not so great for our needs. I *am* glad you did three sets so we have three bottom bunks. We can make do. Madison, Doris, and Katie are each using a bottom bunk. Leo, my mom, and I will each use a top bunk. I'll bring out the extra cots and things we don't need in there so you have them available for the people here. Looks like you're getting quite a group."

I take a quick look around. Belinda's right. There is quite a group. I've been so focused on whatever is happening, I've developed tunnel vision. I'll need to pull myself together and make the rounds, make sure everyone's doing okay. I smother a sigh. Socializing is the last thing I want to do. Maybe Jake can check on everyone for me?

"Yeah," Jake says. "When things started getting . . . tense . . . with the terrorists, I let our immediate neighbors know they should come if there was an event affecting us locally. So, here they are."

"Are you keeping track of who's here?" Belinda asks.

"Yep, got it covered," Jake responds, motioning with the check-in sheet.

"Good. So anyway, can you all keep an eye on my son for me? I don't want him in the room with us."

Jake nods, while I answer, "Of course. TJ's in the rec room right now. He'll be fine."

"Thanks. What about things like food and water? You have those covered?"

"We should be fine on food for several days." Jake's playing down how long we'd really be okay on food. The bulk of our stored items aren't all visible, due to separate rooms, locked cabinets, and such. "Water, we have many gallons of stored fresh water. How many exactly, Mollie?"

"Um, over 150 gallons."

"Plus, we have the rain barrels attached to the house," Jake says. "We covered each of the rain barrels with a tarp and a layer of sandbags, then disconnected them and capped the holes. The barrels nearest the windows can be utilized by feeding a hose inside. It should work okay. We also have a full underground cistern with a pitcher pump. I can go out and get water from there."

"What if we get fallout?" Belinda asks. "Will the water be safe?"

"Yes, I believe so. The cistern should have adequate protection. The pump is covered and protected. With the rain barrels unhooked and the holes capped off, nothing can enter the water. The sandbags and the tarp should add extra protection."

"And you have a way to filter the rainwater?"

"Berkey systems. We have them set up over there. They're also filled. I didn't count those in my numbers before, or the individual gallons of water nearby," I say, motioning to the line of five stainless steel containers in various sizes sitting on a table and a dozen gallon jugs of water underneath. This table and water setup is also detailed in the *ERG*. I'm incredibly impressed with how well these plans have been carried out.

"Huh. I thought those were coffee machines," Belinda says. "Speaking of coffee, do we have a way to heat water?"

"We have a camping stove we'll use," Jake answers.

"Is it safe to use inside?"

"Yes. As long as we use it with ventilation and keep the cooking times to a minimum, it'll be fine. I also grabbed the single-burner alcohol stove we put in the Tiny House, so there's that too. Provided there's no or minimal fallout, we'll use the grill outside. The large propane tanks are unhooked from the house until we know . . ." Jake's voice fades off. He doesn't want to say we are waiting to make sure there aren't any nearby explosions, which could set off our propane tank.

"Oh, sure." Belinda nods, seeming to catch on. "And how about sanitation? You have a regular bathroom over there and the toilet and sink in the . . . what did you call it? Safe room? The little room we're using as our hospital. I'm not sure I feel very good about the sink being part of the toilet."

Jake and I share a look. We know people can be squeamish about things slightly out of the ordinary. She'd probably really freak if she knew we have a couple of compost toilets as backup, just in case. We think compost toilets are a great alternative when water is scarce or plumbing is an issue. But they do have a certain ewww factor.

"The toilet in the safe room functions as a regular toilet. The sink drains into the toilet, filling the tank for flushing. The faucet works without running water, using a basic pump mechanism like you might find on an RV. You probably noticed the water tank in there?"

"Yes, 'thirty-five gallons' is plastered on the side of the container."

"Right. That feeds the toilet. It can also be used for drinking, and there's a few other containers in there with drinking water. I'd still suggest conserving your flushes as best as possible. Oh, and put the lid down before flushing to avoid germ splash."

Belinda makes a face, as Jake says, "The basement bathroom is designed so it's two powder rooms with a shared tub. The water is currently shut off, due to precautions we took before the EMP, but the toilet will still flush if water's added to the tank. We'll use the rain barrel water for this. For handwashing, we can heat water or use sanitizer. For showering . . . well, if we can hold off, we will. Otherwise, we have a few solar camp showers. There are already hooks in place in the tub of the downstairs bathroom and each upstairs bath to hang the solar showers from."

"Okay, that sounds fine. And we can make do with sponge baths and such."

"We have lots of wet wipes," I offer.

"As soon as everyone gets settled," Jake says, "I'm going to boil some water. I have a couple of insulated water jugs I'll fill up. That way, we'll have hot water at the ready."

"How long will that stay warm? A couple of hours?"

"It'll be hot for several hours," I answer. "Then warm for several more."

Without much enthusiasm, she nods her head. "All right, that'll be helpful. Do me a favor and make hot water a priority, don't let us run out. People need to be able to wash their hands. With so many of us in such a small space, we could have a breeding ground for . . . " She shakes her head. "Let's just make handwashing a priority. Now, where's Leo? Did he make it back with our supplies before the EMP?"

Jake briefly shares how Leo ran back, then they took the Jeep to retrieve the supplies and our other sons-in-law. Then he says, "Leo was putting some stuff upstairs, out of the way, then bringing the stuff he thought you'd need immediately down here. They should be done. In fact, I need to go and see who's still up top. I'd feel better knowing where everyone is."

"And we're sure there wasn't a nuke detonated near us?" Angela asks.

Chapter 18

Mollie

Sunday, Day 11
Bakerville, Wyoming

"We don't think there was a nearby detonation. We didn't see a flash, feel the percussion in the ground, or anything to make us think there was. We definitely wouldn't want anything that close," Jake says, shaking his head.

"Agreed," Belinda and I both say.

A visible shiver runs through Angela's body.

Belinda hands us extra cots, one of the card tables, and all but three of the folding chairs we have stowed in the safe room.

Then Jake kisses me and heads toward the doorway, stopping to talk with Karen. They both look over the sheet she's using for checking people in.

I glance around the room and see many of my friends and neighbors. I make eye contact with several, offering what I hope is a promising smile. *We'll be fine,* is what I want my face to say.

I also notice several people still missing who I would expect to be down here—including Doris's husband, Evan. Hopefully he was able to get one of his vehicles running to bring down supplies. If not, he can easily walk here since it's less than a mile between our homes.

Jake's voice reaches my ears, "Hey, glad to see you back . . . " His voice fades and I can't make out anything further.

In a few seconds, Evan's making his way through the doorway, as Jake gestures toward us. I give him a small wave.

"Mollie, Belinda, Angela, good to see you. Malcolm, how you doing?"

"I'm good," Malcolm answers, sounding anything but. Then he turns to me and asks, "Mom, you think I can go over with Tony and TJ? I won't go upstairs."

"Yeah, sure. That'll be just fine."

With a thank you and a nod, he takes off.

"Belinda, can I see Doris for a minute?" Evan asks.

"You mind just sticking your head in? We have the room somewhat sterilized, and I'd like to preserve it as best we can."

Evan frowns but agrees with a curt nod. Not like he's going to argue with Belinda. Belinda opens the main door; heavy curtains are in place on the inside. We put up a curtain rod inside the door, then hung heavy drapes. We added the drapes in case we needed some sort of barrier between the door and the outside, an extra layer of protection. There's just enough room between the door and the curtain to stand. She ushers Evan over and tells him to poke his head through the curtains.

Angela and I make small talk while Evan visits briefly with his wife. We try not to listen but get the gist of the conversation—at least Evan's side of it. We can't hear Doris's responses.

He asks how she is feeling and says he loves her. Then he tells her there's no fallout so far and everything will be fine. "Yes . . . we think there was an EMP. Don't worry, honey, we'll be fine."

I pray he's right.

Leo and my three sons-in-law, along with each of their dads, all make their way to the basement with a few of the neighbors. Men neighbors. I don't see any of the wives. I can only assume they're enjoying the ambiance of the root cellar. *Ha.*

Based on the people I've seen and the ones I know should be here, a quick tally in my head tells me we have somewhere around forty or forty-five people. We planned sleeping space for thirty via beds, camping mattresses, and cots. We figured any excess people could share beds or hot rack it, as the military term goes.

Tim kisses Angela, while Tate and Mike both ask if we know where their wives are.

"The root cellar," Angela answers. "They went in there. I would've gone with them but was told I had to go into the safe room. Belinda says I don't need to, Mom doesn't either, so I'd like to go over to the root cellar. Let's get Gavin and take him with us. Grandma Dodie is probably ready to lose her mind with all those kids."

"I'll grab Gavin—Lily too," Tate says. "I think Jake's getting ready to shut the doors. No fallout, but he thought it'd be good if everyone just stays down here for now. Oh, hey, Mollie, your Sensei is here."

"My what?" I ask, confused.

"The guy teaching you Kung Fu or whatever," Mike answers, while Tate does a karate chop in the air.

"What? Grandmaster Shane? He's here?"

"Yeah, I guess that's his name," Mike answers with a shrug, while the others nod.

"There's two others with him," Leo adds. "A guy about Katie's age, I think his name is Aaron, and his girlfriend. I don't remember her name."

"Aaron . . . Mr. Ogden?"

"Um, I guess?" Leo answers.

Grandmaster Shane—Bill Shane—is our Yongmudo instructor and a retired Prospector County Sheriff. Mr. Ogden is one of the black belts who also trains us. One of the things we learned early on in class was to address upper belts with terms of respect.

Black belts especially are referred to as Mister or Misses and Sir or Ma'am. I have to admit, calling someone the same age as my youngest daughter Mister was a challenge at first. Now, it's second nature.

I'm amazed they're here and wondering how they even know where we live.

I watch as Tim carefully, lovingly, helps Angela through the tunnel entrance. While she's doing so much better after her injuries, it's obvious she's tired. I hope she can use one of the sleeping chambers at the back of the root cellar to take a nap.

Tate, with Gavin in his arms and Lily walking next to him, is also making his way to the tunnel. The way Gavin is rubbing his eyes, he should be joining Angela for a nap.

I feel like I could use a nap myself. I lean back in the straight-back chair, doing my best to find a comfortable position, and close my eyes.

I awaken with a jerk, realizing this chair isn't very good for napping—unless I want to end up on the floor in a heap. I glance around to see if anyone noticed my near plummet.

Jake is walking through the door with Grandmaster Shane, Mr. Ogden, and a twenty-something girl. I assume she's the girlfriend Leo mentioned, but she looks to be several years older than Mr. Ogden. She also looks incredibly stressed out and like she's been roughed up.

There's still evidence of a black eye and several scratches. Mr. Ogden has a scratch on his cheek and is protectively holding to her arm.

I start to rise to greet them, when Master Shane says, "Mollie, please stay seated. Jake told me what happened. I'm so sorry for the difficulties you've encountered since this whole mess began."

"Thank you, sir."

"Mollie, please call me Bill. Aaron, Laurie, and I are very grateful to be able to join you. Thank you for opening your home and . . . well, basement to us."

"Sure. Yes, of course. How did you know where we lived?" I ask dumbly.

Master Shane—Bill—looks at Jake.

"I stopped by the studio when we were over in Wesley gathering supplies. Master—I mean, Bill—was there boarding up the windows. I helped him finish up, and told him, if things got bad, he was welcome to join us here because we'd made some provisions. I gave him directions then."

"Yes, and I hope you don't mind me bringing Aaron and Laurie. Aaron's parents were visiting his sister in Wisconsin when this all started. Laurie Esplin was staying in Wesley during summer break from school. They came to my place when things started going bad in Wesley. When was that? Wednesday? Thursday?"

"Thursday, sir," Aaron answers. Laurie stares blankly, not even trying to participate in the conversation.

Bill nods. "We've had a rough few days. Wesley . . . " He shakes his head. "So, we're here now. How many people are joining you?"

I shrug, and Jake says, "Forty, fifty maybe. I was going to have Mollie put a master list together of everyone who has checked in. You up for that, Mollie?"

"Sure. Have you locked up the house?"

"Yes, the front gate also. I double checked no one was still up top roaming around when Bill and all of us came down. My dad's still out on sentry duty for the moment. Let me get the lists. I gave the root cellar list to Karen to keep with the one she was working on."

Leo is standing nearby. I tilt my head toward him. He nods and steps closer.

"Have you met Leo?" I ask.

"Yes, I believe we did," Bill responds.

"Yes, sir. Would you like me to show you around? I'd also be happy to introduce you to some of the others. I'm not sure I know everyone here, but most. We can meet the ones I don't know together."

"That sounds fine," Bill answers, while Aaron nods. Laurie continues her vacant stare.

A few minutes later, I have the master list put together. I'm surprised to see our number is fifty-four, fifty-five if I count Sheila, who is still in her cabin refusing to come to the basement. The last several days, Sheila has been around less and less, choosing to stay in the cabin the Curtis family is occupying. And now, even with this latest threat, she won't join us.

I shake my head, focusing on the list. There are so many people here! Even though I know them all, my recently rattled brain is challenged to keep everyone straight.

The ages range from ninety-one years old—the mom of a neighbor—to Madison's baby, Emma, at only a few months old. We also have four pint-sized dogs, including our Penny and Scooter, Dodie and Alvin's Buttercup, and our neighbor from over the hill's little poodle. There are also three larger dogs—a Blue Heeler cross; an unidentified mutt, currently crated in the front section of the root cellar, belonging to a different neighbor; and Evan and Doris's dog, Danny. Evan used to work for a large sheriff department on the West Coast. Danny was his K-9; they retired together.

One neighbor brought her cat in his carrier. She assures me he is leash trained and she'll walk him as needed for now, then will set up a box for him if she can't take him outside.

Our three cats are secured in a special box in the garage, which Jake made just for this purpose. It's essentially a small cat house, with a litter box, food, and water, enclosed by several sandbags.

Right now, all the dogs can be walked outside. If fallout starts, we have a kiddie-sized swimming pool we can dump sand in to give them a spot to relieve themselves, in addition to blue piddle pads.

Please, God, please, don't let us have fallout.

Chapter 19

Lindsey

Sunday, Day 11
Underground Culvert, Tahoe National Forest
Near Sierra City, California

I take out my phone and turn it on. Nothing. I try again.

"What's wrong?" Logan asks.

"My phone won't come on. I thought I had a full charge when I shut it off earlier. Can I use yours?"

Logan takes his phone out and hands it to me. The screen won't light up. I try the power button on the side and nothing happens. I start to cry.

"Your phone isn't working either," I gulp out between sobs.

"It's okay, Lindsey. We'll charge them. It's not a problem using the bikes. We can even do it now."

"I . . . I don't think so. It's like my mom was telling us. *One Second After* . . . the bombs made an electromagnetic pulse."

Logan looks at me with disbelief. "You think so? I would think the EMP would be localized to the blast area. Unless . . . *Oh*. You think there might have been a high-altitude detonation in addition to the nukes hitting the cities?"

I shrug. "Maybe? I think an EMP could kill the phones. If we had power and it went out, or we were driving our bikes and they stopped, then we'd know for sure. Our bikes! If we can't drive them, how will we ever get to Wyoming?"

Logan hugs me close. "We'll make it, Lindsey. We'll make it. I'll get you to Wyoming."

We hold each other for many minutes as we both let our tears flow. After a while, I say, "So I guess we should stay in here for seventy-two hours. I think that was the recommendation. Three days."

"You think? I'd think it would be longer, maybe a couple of weeks."

I try to remember what I learned. "I think the length of time we need to shelter depends on how much fallout we're receiving. But we don't know. We don't have any way to measure it. We don't even know for sure if we're getting fallout."

I can feel Logan nod. "True. We'll just need to do the best we can, be as safe as we can."

Since we sealed up both ends of the culvert, it's dark inside. Logan flips on a small flashlight attached to his keychain. A quick look shows this space is more than just a little bit damp. Near the bikes, there's a puddle. The water seems to be seeping up from the ground.

A shiver overtakes my body.

"You cold, Linds?"

"I guess so."

"Let's get you warmed up." He helps me fumble in the dark so I can put on my hoody and pull out my small blanket. I wad up my leather chaps to use as a pillow and stretch out. It's damp and chilly in this tiny hovel.

"Try to sleep, Lindsey." Logan kisses me on the forehead.

"What about you?"

"Yeah, I will. No reason not to, I guess."

Chapter 20

Sylvia

*Sunday, Day 11
Railroad Tunnel
Between Shoshoni and Thermopolis,
Wyoming*

"Sylvia. Sylvia, wake up," Sabrina says, giving my shoulder a shake. After Kim and the children went down for naps, Sabrina suggested I do the same. We didn't set up our tent, or even pull out our sleeping mats or bags. Instead, I found a not-too-rocky spot and used a jacket as a pillow. Not great, but not terrible. Sabrina said she'd stay awake and keep watch. I'm not exactly sure what she was keeping watch for . . . maybe in case Kim freaked out again.

"Yeah, okay. What's going on?"

"My phone won't work."

"So? You probably can't get service in this tunnel. Duh." Why in the world she is waking me up for this?

"No, not that. It won't turn on. I thought it might be about time to check for fallout, but it's not working for me to check the time. Try yours, okay?"

"Jeez, Sabrina. Who cares? You can just walk to the edge of the tunnel. It'll probably work there."

"Are you listening to me at all? It. Won't. Turn. On. It isn't a service issue, it's dead. D-E-A-D. Dead."

"Fine." I put as much sass into that one word as I dare and pull my phone out. It was shut down when we got into the tunnel to conserve the battery. I try several times and nothing happens. The screen won't light up. "No, nothing."

"I was afraid of that," Sabrina says with a tremble in her voice.

"What now?" I ask, wondering if I really want to know the answer.

"A pulse . . . um . . . I can't remember the name but, you know, the kind that wipes things out? It goes along with a nuke being detonated."

"Like in the movie *Red Dawn*? Not the one Mom likes but the remake with the cute Chris guy in it? Wasn't it a pulse that took out the power?"

Rey must have heard us talking because he says, "An electromagnetic pulse, or EMP. There was talk about North Korea using one on us. What's going on?"

"We're not sure," I answer vaguely, while Sabrina says, "I think it's happened."

"What do you mean you think it happened?" Rey asks.

"Well, I don't really know, but our phones won't turn on."

"Okay, so the phones don't turn on. Maybe the batteries are dead."

"My battery was more than half. How about yours, Sylvia?"

"Yeah, pretty close to half also. We've been keeping them off except to check them."

"Not true," Rey says. "Remember, you left yours on and that's how we got the missile alert."

"Yes, but it was still at half charge when I turned it off after we got settled in here. I'm sure of it." *Take that, Mr. Gorgeous.* You might be good looking, but you don't know everything.

"Do you have a phone?" Sabrina asks Rey.

"Not a working one. We didn't leave ours turned off, and they died days ago."

Sabrina turns her flashlight on, shining the bright white light in my eyes.

"Jeez, Sabrina. I'm blind now. Thanks."

"Sorry, I wanted to check and see if the flashlight was still working. Do you think a pulse would fry a flashlight?"

"I don't know," Rey says. "The little I read about the EMP threat led me to believe no one really knows what the full damage would be. Some people think anything with any electronic components, including simple batteries like a flashlight, would be wiped out. Others think only higher electronics—like cars, computers, and such—would be affected. Then, others think it'd be hit and miss, where some electronics would be wiped out and others would be spared."

"I think I'll walk to the mouth of the tunnel. Maybe Sylvia's right and somehow that could make a difference."

Sabrina rummages through her things, pulling out a small paper plate, several cans of food, her cook stove, and her kitchen bag. She repositions everything for easy access. "I'm going to cook some food while I'm there. That is, as long as everything looks okay. I think that'd be better than cooking in the middle of the tunnel."

"What's the paper plate for?" I ask.

"I was thinking about this video I watched with Mom about a guy who had a giant fallout shelter—some kind of experimental thing or something. He was talking about radiation and how you need a special device to measure fallout."

"Like a Geiger counter?"

"Yeah, I guess. Obviously, we don't have one of those, but he said you can use a plate to determine if there *is* fallout. I thought, maybe, I'd put the paper plate out and see. Of course, he used a regular plate and wasn't in such a dusty area. Maybe it's a dumb idea?"

"I don't think an EMP would let off radiation," Rey says thoughtfully. "I don't know for sure, but I think the type they were talking about before, when North Korea was a threat, would be from a very high-altitude blast, then there wouldn't be fallout. I'm not completely sure, but I think the radiation only happens with an actual ground strike. Oh, I guess there could be an EMP from a nearby hit. Wasn't that how EMPs were discovered? They were testing nuke strikes and found out it messed with electronics?"

Sabrina and I both shrug, while Rey goes on, "Anyway, it's probably smart to check. Will it be like ash on the plate?"

"I'm not sure. I remember he said to put a plate outside and then run your fingers over it to see if there's a film. I was thinking I'd just sit it outside while I cook some food."

"You want some help?" Rey asks.

"Sylvia will help me," Sabrina says, making it obvious I have no choice in the matter. "Besides, your family will probably be waking up soon."

Rey barely stifles a sigh. "Yes, of course."

"Do you want us to heat up the food you have?" I ask.

"That'd be great, if you don't mind."

He takes a plastic zip top bag along with a disposable plastic grocery store bag from his backpack.

"We've been reusing our zipper bags. We had a few with food in them from the fridge and pantry. The grocery bag, we've been using for fish. It's getting kind of ripe, but it's the only one I have, so . . . Kim brought a cooking pot and tea kettle along. Are they too large for your cook stove?"

"No, I brought a regular camping stove along with a little backpacker's stove. I planned on using the camp stove. I don't need the tea kettle right now, but the pot will be helpful."

"Smart. I have a backpacking stove, which is too small for our pot. It didn't matter in the camp since we were using a makeshift fire pit. Of course, finding wood wasn't easy. We were having to walk farther and farther to get anything even resembling firewood. We would've had to find a new camp within a few days."

Sabrina and I gather everything, not wanting to leave any of our gear behind, and head to the mouth of the tunnel, not the side we entered but the other side. I'm not even sure why, but both of us seemed to want to head toward our final destination, toward Mom, even if we can't leave to go there right now.

"Um, Sabrina? Sylvia?" Rey asks as we step away. "You're coming back, right?"

Chapter 21

Lindsey

Sunday, Day 11
Underground Culvert, Tahoe National Forest
Near Sierra City, California

We're so tired and stressed that we sleep most of the day. A few minutes ago, Logan peeked out. Looking at the sun, he thinks it's midafternoon. Without our phones, we have no idea of the exact time.

"You think I can step out and go to the bathroom?" I ask.

"No. We don't know if there's fallout, but we need to assume there is. Good news, though, I thought of this earlier and have a solution."

"Okay?"

"Did you notice the coffee can from the back of the truck? We'll use it as a toilet. I grabbed a couple of plastic grocery sacks from the front seat. We can line it and then, when it gets bad, change the liner."

"Uh . . . right. So that's a pretty good idea, but . . . wow, it's not going to be easy using such a small can. Not for me, anyway."

"I know, but how about if we put the can on the short log and set it up lengthwise to add a little height? I think we should put the . . . uh, facilities . . . on the other side of the bikes to give a little privacy. We'll make it work, okay?"

"Yeah, that's fine. No choice really. Much better than just going in a corner. Good thinking, Logan. I have to admit, until this minute, I didn't even consider what we'd do for our bathroom needs."

"Let me get it set up and then you can use it. Just be careful going around the bikes. And try to stay out of the mud puddle."

"Sure, thanks, Logan."

A while later, after both of us have relieved ourselves, Logan says, "So, Linds, I think maybe the mud puddle is a good thing."

"Why? If the puddle weren't there, we could stretch out better. You wouldn't have had to sleep sitting up. You think we should stay in here a few weeks, with you sitting up to sleep the entire time?"

"Well, I was kind of hoping we could swap on who gets to stretch out and who has to sleep sitting up."

I'm glad it's dark as I blush. I didn't even consider we could swap. I assumed I'd be the comfortable one—well, sort of comfortable one—while we were holed up.

"Yes, of course. I didn't think of it, but you're right. We can swap."

He clumsily reaches out to me. Our night vision isn't as good as it could be, so he misses me on his first grab. I move toward him and accept his hug and a kiss on the forehead—which actually lands on my eyeball.

"So, back to the puddle. You're probably not going to be terribly excited about this, but we can use it for water."

"Oh, no. We can't drink out of a mud puddle. *Mud*, Logan. No. Gross."

"Right now, it doesn't sound too appealing, but we can let it settle and filter it. Once it settles, the mud will go to the bottom. Then we can strain it through a T-shirt or something and we'll use the bleach to sanitize it. I wasn't able to find water before the alert. We have some, but it's not enough to last more than a day, two at the most."

I know he's right; water is a necessity. But ewww. I stopped drinking out of mud puddles when I was six. And I only did it then because my sister dared me. I swear I had mud in my mouth for weeks afterward.

I expel a huge breath. Getting rid of my old air feels good. I realize I'm acting like a brat, both earlier with the disgusting pickup cab I didn't want to get into and now with the water. Sure, normal people would be weirded out by those things, but I'm Lindsey Maverick. I'm a tough broad. I need to suck it up. This is our lives we're talking about. It's not the time for me to be squeamish about silly things.

Our lives . . . how many people were killed today? We saw two mushroom clouds so know at least two bombs went off. Something like 100,000 people were killed when the bombs when off in Hiroshima and Nagasaki—just from the bombs, not even counting the people who died afterward from radiation poisoning.

What about my friends? People I worked with?

It's overwhelming to think of the death toll—this on top of what we've already seen since the terrorist attacks started.

Terrorist attacks?

We've always assumed we were being attacked by terrorists, but with the nuclear attack, could we be wrong? I've heard of terrorists having suitcase nukes and dirty bombs, but not ballistic missiles. We think of North Korea, China, and Russia for ICBMs—not terrorists. But now, with this, I'm not sure what to think.

"Let's turn on the light for a few minutes, and I'll see how well it works getting the . . . uh . . . fresh water out," Logan says.

I swipe the flashlight app on my phone. "Oops. I forgot about it being fried," I say with a small laugh. "Will the flashlight on my keychain still work?"

"It should. Mine was working earlier."

He's right. It does work.

"So I think I'll use the extra plastic cup we have to scoop the water from the puddle, then we can put it in a designated bottle. The bottle and cup will be designated only for "dirty water" use. We won't drink from them until after we can sterilize them somehow. I think that'll help cut down on us getting any bugs we don't want," Logan says, while vigorously nodding his head.

I stifle a laugh. I'd forgotten about the bandana covering his face. He looks like an Old West bank robber.

"Okay, sure," I respond with my own, not nearly as vigorous, nod.

Logan takes his time transferring the water from the puddle to the plastic cup, then into a twenty-ounce Dr Pepper bottle. When we left home yesterday, the bottle was full of soda. We decided we should keep all of our empties for now, in case we needed to haul and store more water than we currently had containers for. Of course, we now know, even with California's various green initiatives, there are bottles laying all over the sides of the roads. We can pick up all we need, clean them out, and are good to go.

When the bottle is full, it's a muddy mess. Logan sees the look on my face. "It'll be better after we let it settle and then strain it. Let's give it a while and check it again."

"If you say so."

"I think it'll be fine. Let's turn the light out to save on the battery. I think we should plan on using only your keychain flashlight for as long as we can, then we'll move to a different flashlight when it gives out."

Once the light is off, we automatically revert to whispers. After a couple of exchanges, I burst out laughing.

"What's up, Lindsey?"

"Us. We're alone in a wet underground pipe, with no one around, while—as far as we know—the world is ending, and we're whispering." I'm laughing so hard I can barely sputter out my thoughts. As quickly as the laughter starts, it leaves, and I'm once again sobbing.

Logan scoots close to me and hugs me tight. I feel his body occasionally shudder and his tears drop on my face. We're both hurting and vulnerable.

We cry for those we assume are now lost or may be in the coming days. Were our friends from San Jose close enough to be affected by the initial blast? Will they be affected by the fallout and become sick from radiation? Are Logan's parents okay in upstate New York? And my parents in Wyoming? Are we trying to make our way someplace we have no likelihood of reaching now that the bombs have hit? And how safe are we? Will this culvert protect us from fallout?

So many questions. We have no answers.

We're soon emotionally spent and, once again, fall asleep. This time we're both sitting up, leaning against the wall of the culvert. The position isn't great, and when I do wake up—who knows how much later—I have a crick in my neck. As I'm trying to move to relieve the discomfort, Logan wakes up.

"Hey, beautiful. You doing okay?"

"Yes . . . no. I don't know. I'm not sure if I'll ever be truly okay again. Our world is so different now."

Logan doesn't answer with words but does give me a squeeze. The squeeze turns into a hug, which soon turns into more—not the easiest task in the tight culvert, but very welcome.

Sometime later, Logan says, "Let's filter the water and see how it turned out."

I reluctantly agree. He takes out the small saucepan we brought and positions a clean bandana over the top. "Hold this for me, Linds."

"Why not use the coffee filters, like you have been for the fuel?"

"I think we should save those. Mud washes out easily, so there's no reason not to use one of the bandanas. I wouldn't want to try to wash the gas out."

"Yeah, okay." I wrap my hands around the top of the pot, holding the bandana in place, while he slowly pours some of the water from the bottle through it. He does his best not to disturb the sediment settled on the bottom. Even so, when he's done, there's a considerable amount of mud collected on the bandana. Blech. Logan seems pleased.

"Look at that, Lindsey. Now, we'll carefully pour it from the saucepan into the other soda bottle we saved, add some bleach, and it'll be just fine. Might taste a little muddy, but it'll keep us hydrated. And we can add those little orange packet things if it's too bad."

The orange packets he refers to are Emergen-C. I had a bunch of them at home, and we packed them up, thinking we might have trouble getting enough Vitamin C while on the road. I don't want scurvy or rickets or whatever it is the lack of Vitamin C gives.

"Sure, good idea," I answer, trying to sound more enthused than I am about drinking mud water. I know he's right, but . . . ick.

I suddenly realize I'm doing it again—being a big baby. If we're going to get through this, I need to buck up. I need to remember who I am. I'm the type of person who looks for solutions instead of focusing on the negative. I make things happen. I'm certainly not a whiner.

"Hey, Logan, look . . . I owe you an apology. I've been way . . . uh . . . not cool, about this whole thing. Especially the water situation. It was brilliant of you to realize we could use the water. And look." I point toward the puddle we had almost drained earlier. "It's filling up again. If it keeps filling up, we can stay in here for some time."

"Yeah, I hoped it'd refill. I don't really want to drink muddy water either." He gives a small laugh. "I knew you'd come around. You forget, we've been together almost five years. I know how you are."

"What's that mean?" I ask indignantly.

"You don't like change. This— " he gestures widely " —is complete change. We had to flee our home, we're currently living in a culvert after watching the West Coast get annihilated, and we're drinking from a mud puddle. Big changes for sure."

I don't say anything as I watch Logan add a small amount of bleach to finish making our mud water drinkable. When the water warnings first came out, we googled how much bleach to add. Two drops per quart. I didn't have a dropper, and Logan couldn't find one at the store. We've been doing our best with estimating, using a measuring spoon to pour a small amount in until we think we are at the right dose. Too much and the water tastes terrible and has to sit longer. Too little and we could get bad bugs.

When he's done, I say, "I'm glad you get me. It's not everyone a girl can face the end of the world with."

Chapter 22

Sylvia

Sunday, Day 11
Railroad Tunnel
Between Shoshoni and Thermopolis, Wyoming

"We'll be back, Rey. We'll warm up the food and be back shortly. Promise," Sabrina answers Rey's concern.

Thanks, Sabrina. A golden opportunity to ditch the Hoffmann family, and you ruin it.

We keep quiet, guided by the beam from Sabrina's red light. As we near the tunnel entrance, she whispers, "Let's take it nice and slow, just in case someone's near the entrance. We don't want to spook them. There's a second tunnel beyond this one, so there could be people in there too. Again . . . nice and slow, plus quiet."

"Duh."

She switches off the headlamp as the light from the mouth floods in. Good. At least we know there's still daylight. Would the sky be black and dark if there was a nuke? Seems so, but what do I know?

We're alone. No one's lurking by the tunnel entrance to share our hidey hole, but Sabrina still whispers, "Let me put the plate out. I think we should stay slightly inside the tunnel, just in case there is some sort of fallout. We might have a little protection compared to being fully outside."

"You think so?" I don't know much about radiation, but I do know we should be underground. Mom and Phil have way too much paranoia over the US being attacked by nukes. So much so, they have a bomb shelter. Yeah, a real honest-to-goodness bunker.

It's a prefab unit they ordered, had delivered, and installed shortly after they found their property up in Bakerville. It's designed to sleep thirty people somewhat comfortably. Knowing Mom and Phil, I suspect they're down there now with even more than the recommended number crammed in. I have to admit, I was pretty sure they'd gone fully off the deep end when Mom first told me about it. I mean, really, *who does that?*

And what they spent on the bunker . . . wow. It was like buying a house—and not a cheap house either. Crazy. Of course, if we've really been bombed, maybe they aren't crazy.

"Bet I know what you're thinking," Sabrina whispers.

I give a single shoulder shrug, not really caring to participate.

"You're thinking about Mom's bunker."

"What I'm thinking about is how I wish we were at Mom's bunker instead of in a tunnel on the train tracks with a bunch of whiney— "

"Mom was smart to start prepping all those years ago. I know it seemed odd at the time, but now, I'm glad for it."

"I guess." No way am I going to agree with her—not out loud, anyway.

"Phil and Mom were definitely made for each other. I mean, really, two preppers finding each other like that, what are the odds? Definitely God's plan."

"Whatever, Sabrina." I give her an exaggerated eye roll. She gives me a small smile and steps out of the tunnel.

"Nothing seems any different than when we went in," she says, while setting the plate up in the middle of the track about fifteen feet from the entrance. She takes a few seconds to place some small rocks on the plate so it doesn't blow away, then hustles back inside the tunnel.

I let out a sigh of relief and give a slight nod. I take advantage of Kim not being around and light up a cigarette. Sabrina shakes her head at me and starts setting up her cooking supplies.

"How else could you explain Mom and Phil meeting?"

"Right place, right time," I answer, blowing smoke from my nose.

"So, they just happened to both be at the same gas station and, completely out of the blue, strike up a conversation? Had Mom ever talked to a guy at a gas station before?"

Instead of letting me answer, she continues, "No. Never. But she talked to Phil. Why? And then they run into each other in a grocery store? A grocery store Mom just happened to stop at, one she'd never shopped before. You don't think God had a hand in it?"

"Circumstances, destiny, fate, the universe—would you like me to continue?"

"And the fact they even worked at the same place?"

"Oh, come on. How many people were at that duty station?"

"Yeah, but Mom wasn't even really supposed to be there, remember? She was covering for someone on medical leave. We were supposed to go to— "

"Sabrina, you know, I do know all of this. I was there too."

"And how do you explain they're both preppers?" she asks, while opening a couple of soup cans.

"I don't need to explain it. And I've heard it all before. So the Commissioned Corps assigned Mom to the Coast Guard. It happens. Yeah, she wasn't supposed to be there and wouldn't have been if she weren't filling in for someone on medical leave. Yes, Mom was terribly overqualified. And, yes, Phil wasn't really supposed to be there either. His cutter was supposed to be out to sea. But, hey, stuff happens."

Sabrina gives me a very patient smile, the kind I'd like to wipe right off her face. *Little sisters.*

Growing up, it was the three of us and Grandma Marie. My dad left when we were really young—I was three and Sabrina was only a year old. We saw him one time when I was ten, and he told Mom he wanted to be a part of our lives. That never amounted to anything. I haven't seen him since. He would call or sometimes write, but those stopped when I was fifteen.

My Grandma Marie, Mom's mom, moved in with us after our dad left. Mom had just got this great job working as a nurse practitioner with Indian Health Services as part of the Commissioned Corps when our dad left. Grandma Marie made it possible for Mom to keep the job and move up in rank over the years.

Mom attained a master's degree and took additional schooling to become a psychiatric nurse practitioner, in high demand at United States Public Health Commissioned Corps. This quickly propelled her career forward. We moved around quite a bit, depending on where her next posting was, but it wasn't a bad life.

"Phil and Mom were meant to be together," Sabrina says quietly, while lighting the propane stove. "Right now, you might not believe

God put them together. But you used to, and I'm confident you will again."

"Ha. Don't bet on it." I snub out my cigarette and debate on lighting a second.

"Mom says she felt it when they first met at the gas station. She wanted to ask for his number but couldn't bring herself to be so forward. When they ran into each other again at the grocery store, she came home so happy."

If Sabrina is going to keep yapping about this, I might as well have my second cigarette.

"She had a total crush on him, even before they had dinner."

"Wait a minute, Miss Perfect. You forgot the part where they had drinks first, and that's when Mom discovered he was career Coast Guard and he discovered she was an officer with USPHS. And how they were fraternizing with the enemy."

"Ha, ha. Very funny. You know it was kind of a gray area. Mom wasn't a Coast Guard officer, but since she was assigned to the same duty station where Phil was an enlisted sailor, they were afraid of how it might look. Even though both were only a few years from retirement, they were each planning on one more promotion."

"Yeah, well. Didn't work out too good for old Phil, did it?"

"Do you really have to be so mean? I thought you liked Phil."

"Sure, sure. He's fine. A little pious, but fine."

"He's not pious."

"You're pious, so how would you know?"

"Do you know what pious means?"

"Seriously, Sabrina? You going to wordsmith me?"

"I'm just saying, pious tends to have a negative connotation to it. It makes us sound . . . sanctimonious. Maybe you could say sincere or devout."

"Whatever."

Sabrina's finally quiet for a few moments while she stirs the concoction in the pan. She mixed a couple of different types of soup together. It doesn't look bad, but not great either.

"Phil says, by the end of dinner, he was smitten and seriously thinking about retiring just so they could date. He was already past his twenty but was staying in as long as he could for maximum benefits. You know Mom wasn't planning on going past twenty years."

Yeah, yeah. I know all of this. I kind of zone out while she rambles. Even though I act like I don't enjoy the story, I kind of do. I used to like it more, back in the days when I believed in true love and thought I might find it myself someday. Mom and Phil had a great time at that one dinner, then went their separate ways . . . until about six weeks later when her temporary assignment came to an end.

She made a point of tracking Phil down and letting him know. Since her next duty would not be attached to the Coast Guard, the rules of fraternization changed. She asked if he was interested in staying in touch. His answer was a resounding yes.

Several weeks later, Mom wrote to Phil. She was settled into her new position with the Department of Defense, which included a promotion from Lieutenant Commander to Commander. She'd committed to a final three-year tour and then she would retire.

Written letters soon changed to email, instant messenger, or phone calls whenever Phil was on shore duty. They stayed with snail mail when he was at sea. Leave was soon spent together.

Mom's last duty station started right after I graduated high school. I moved to Texas with Mom, Grandma, and Sabrina, then started taking classes at the community college, heading toward an associate degree in general studies. I had no idea what I wanted to do with my life, so general studies made the most sense.

The same year I finished my degree, Sabrina graduated from high school. Mom still had over a year left before retirement. Sabrina started college, and I got a job as an administrative assistant at a small law firm.

Phil had one year left of his twenty-six-year hitch, and Mom had thirteen months left of her final three-year commitment, when Phil asked her to marry him. The engagement lasted thirteen months and six days.

They had a Jamaican destination wedding with the five of us—Mom, Phil, Grandma, Sabrina, and me—along with one of Phil's longtime friends. We stayed at an all-inclusive resort, and they hired a wedding service to take care of everything. Other than choosing clothes, all we had to do was show up. We all stayed a full week, then flew home. I'd be lying if I didn't admit to the wedding and the week being wonderful.

"Sylvia?"

"Huh?"

"I said, 'they were right.' You see that now?"

"Right about what?"

"This." She makes a grand gesture to encompass everything around us. "Mom and Phil, their preps . . . all of the stuff they've done."

"Yeah, I guess so."

"The soup's hot. I'm going to start warming up their food. I'll add a little olive oil to the fish and the rice. They need the calories."

"So do we," I snort.

"We can spare a little oil for them."

"We may have made a mistake, you know, with bringing the Hoffmann family along."

"I still think it's the right thing to do. Sure, Kim is a bit much, but maybe she's just scared."

I give a one-shoulder shrug, not wanting to fully agree but acknowledging fear can change a person. At the same time, I think when a person is under stress, their true self tends to come through. Kim may seem to be a nice person in her everyday life, but with the situation we now find ourselves in, the mask has come off and her true demeanor is at the surface.

I think back to the last few years and how my own mask has been lowered. Maybe I'm being too hard on her.

As I'm thinking I should cut Kim some slack, we hear an extremely loud screech from inside the tunnel. I see Sabrina's hand move to her sidearm. Within seconds, it's apparent this isn't a threat. Kim's having what I can only describe as a hissy fit.

"You gave them our food?" Kim exclaims in a high-pitched whine. "What if they leave? They took their packs. You don't even know if they plan to come back. They might just leave us here to fend for ourselves. How could you be so stupid?"

There's a murmur of response, likely Rey answering, but we can't make out what he's saying . . . because he isn't shrieking at the top of his lungs.

Sabrina looks sad and shakes her head.

I'm instantly angry. How dare this shrew of a woman throw around accusations about us?

"I'm going back to the camp," I say to Sabrina. "I'll be back in a few minutes to help you handle the food."

"Be nice."

"Yeah . . . I'll follow Kim's lead on that."

Chapter 23

Sylvia

Sunday, Day 11
Railroad Tunnel
Between Shoshoni and Thermopolis, Wyoming

I leave my backpack with Sabrina—no reason to take it along—and turn on my flashlight. I think about something Mom shared with me. She and Phil found their Bakerville home while on a cross-country honeymoon. They were gone over a month, camping and visiting areas they were interested in settling down at. When they returned from their honeymoon trip, excited with the idea of moving to Wyoming, they proceeded to start packing up. Mom figured Grandma Marie would move with her like she'd done for the past twenty years.

At first, Grandma also seemed enthused about the move, but then things changed. She soon became withdrawn and depressed. Mom tried to talk with her about it, but Grandma wouldn't open up to her. Then Grandma took a fall down the stairs, and with her physical injuries, it became apparent the withdrawing wasn't depression but early dementia.

Their moving plans were put on hold during Grandma's recovery. Unfortunately, the injuries from the fall, while not super severe, were enough to cause troubles with healing, and adding in the dementia just made things worse.

When Mom was having such a hard time while Grandma was sick, she told me she used the Serenity Prayer to help her calm down, citing the ease of remembering it working well for her during stressful times. My mom knows lots of scripture and could have used any of it, but the Serenity Prayer was her go-to. The simplicity of it came through in even the most difficult of times.

Unlike Mom, Phil, and Sabrina, I've found little use for prayer in recent years. I used to believe in prayer . . . until the time I prayed like my life depended on it, because it did. While I didn't die, I wasn't fully spared either. Some may say my prayers were answered. I know better. I know, if there really was a God who cared about me, He would've intervened when I asked—*begged*—for help.

I guess, if a person uses prayer as part of meditation or self-reflection, fine. But so often it lulls people into believing they've accomplished something. And really, what's the use? If a person believes God has a plan, why bother with prayer? Oh yes, I've heard it before. It was God's plan for such and such to happen. I don't want any part of a God who has plans for such awful things.

Even though I think prayer is useless, I do remember some of the prayer she relied on, mainly because she had gone into a big spiel about how people in Alcoholics Anonymous often use it to help ground themselves. To me, that sounded more like meditation than petition, so I checked it out.

I'll admit, the melodic rhythm of the saying does sound comforting, and it's also a reminder of healthy boundaries. Even as a nonbeliever, I've found the Serenity Prayer to be helpful in certain instances. I used it often during the early days of my firm's merger with the larger firm. I've used it when the past overwhelmed my thoughts.

"God, grant me the serenity to accept the things I cannot change, the courage to change the things I can, and the wisdom to know the difference."

Reciting this as I stomp toward Kim, eager to give her a piece of my mind, I realize I can change this. As soon as the threat of the missiles has passed, Sabrina and I can move on—on our own. No matter what Sabrina says, Rey can take care of his own family. Sabrina might think she's doing God's will or some such thing, but I can put my foot down and remind her about her first obligation being to family, to me.

With my chin set and my mind determined, I reach the Hoffmann family. Kim's high-pitched shrill is now a low, under her breath grumble.

I take a deep breath and use what I think of as my lawyer voice, the voice I'm perfecting for when I'm an actual lawyer. "Kim, I'm not entirely sure what the problem is. I'd like to give you the benefit of the doubt and assume you are just scared with everything going on. But I'll be honest— "

"Coming with you and your sister was a mistake. You two . . . survivalists . . . are nothing but trouble. People like you are what Rey and I spent years fighting against."

Survivalists? I almost need to suppress a laugh. With his voice full of warning, Rey quickly says, "Kim, that's enough."

Kim fires him a venomous look and truly appears to be biting her tongue. I have no idea what's going on between these two, but it's time to cut and run. But before that happens, I'm going to have my say.

"I don't know, or particularly care, what your problem is with us." I try the lawyer voice again, speaking calmly, measurably. "We thought we could help your family get closer to where you're going— that's all. I'm more than happy to leave you all on your own. As soon as we know this threat is over, we'll move on. You two can do whatever you think is best for your children."

I spin on my heel and head back to the mouth of the tunnel.

When I reach Sabrina, she whispers, "I couldn't hear you, but still heard her. Guess we're survivalists, huh?"

"Guess so. Look, I know you think we're supposed to help them— "

"We are. I'm convinced of it. We need to be with them."

"Why? They seemed to be doing fine without us."

"It's not just that. There's more. I don't know what it is, but we have to stay together, stay with them. I'm sure of it."

"Could we at least put a little space between us? I don't want to be holed up with that . . . that woman. Let's move to the other tunnel. Then, if you still insist we travel with them, after we know there isn't a threat of being bombed, I'll consider it."

Sabrina puts her hand on my shoulder and very quietly says, "Trust."

"Oh, for Pete's sake, Sabrina. You get loonier each day. Next thing I know you're going to tell me the terrorist attacks, the bombs, all of it was done by God for our own good."

"No, Sylvia," she says quietly. "Suffering and death are part of this corrupt world. It's guaranteed for each of us. God uses the trials of this world to prepare us to spend eternity with Him. You used to know these things. Deep down, I think you still do. Remember how close you used to be to God?"

"Whatever. Now I'm closer to reality instead of having some ridiculous supernatural belief."

I pick up my pack and the soup pot and march back to camp, relishing in hearing my feet pound on the railroad ties. Sabrina follows quietly behind.

The meal is a somber affair. Miss Perfect Sabrina offers everyone some of *our* canned soup.

Rey gladly accepts on behalf of the children, topping their rice with a scoop of soup and a few flakes of fish, but passes for himself and Kim. It's obvious he wants to offer us some of the fish, but a scowl from Kim stops him before he does. No matter; I wouldn't eat their fish if I was starving.

We wait until what we determine to be about an hour after we finish eating, then Sabrina, Rey, and I make our way to the mouth of the tunnel. Rey comes along with us, at Kim's suggestion. Yeah, *suggestion*. We'll go with that, even though it was really more of an order.

The plan is to check the plate, and if there isn't any evidence of fallout, we'll walk down to the edge of the river to wash the dishes. Hopefully, there's a better spot on this end of the tunnel to access the river than the edge of the cliff we were getting water on before.

The Hoffmanns are reusing paper plates they brought along, so those will just get a wipe with a washcloth. Sabrina and I have a few of the small paper plates, like we're using for checking for fallout, and a cheap reusable plastic plate each.

"I'll check the plate," Sabrina says.

"No, let me do it. You've already been out, and if there is fallout, you could get sick."

Sabrina agrees, as Rey walks to the plate. He looks at it and then bends over. "There are a couple of large pebbles on it. You put those there?"

"Yes, to keep it from moving around or blowing away. Just take those off and carefully lift up the plate, then swipe your hand over it to see if there's a film."

Rey nods and does as suggested. It's a full minute before he says, "I don't think there's anything. It seems perfectly clean."

I hear an audible sigh of relief from Sabrina as we exit the tunnel. "Okay, great. We'll set it up again to be sure. I think we should leave it out overnight and see what it looks like tomorrow."

"If there isn't any fallout," I quickly add, "Sabrina and I will be leaving. You all can do what you want. In fact, we might move to the next tunnel to give you guys your own space."

"Sylvia," Sabrina whispers, warningly.

"About that . . . " Rey says haltingly. "Kim isn't very diplomatic at times. She'll calm down and realize we're better off staying with you. In fact, I'd expect her to be nice as pie to you when we get back. If she straightens up, will you consider sticking with us?"

"You know, Rey— "

"We don't want to leave you on your own," Sabrina interrupts. "We did what we thought was right, what God called us to do, by offering to help."

I choose not to point out this is all her doing, as she continues, "I'm not sure why, but I truly believe we should stick together for now."

"I appreciate that. We'd probably be fine, but . . . " His voice drifts away.

"You'd for sure be fine," Sabrina says, "as long as you make some good choices. The fish you gave us to warm up looked very nice—no skin or bones. Did you use those for something else?"

"What do you mean?"

"The skin provides fat and calories. You're going to need both with how many miles you'll have to hike."

Rey shakes his head. "Kim won't eat the skin. It's loaded with toxins and stuff."

"Yeah, I've read some people . . . some doctors . . . say to not eat the skin. And if we were in a normal situation, sure, avoid it. But we aren't in a normal situation. You need all the calories you can get. The toxins, while cumulative over time, are an issue for another day. Get where you're going and then worry about that. Same with the organs and bones. You can get quite a bit of nutrition from them.

"Also, you might want to think about finding stuff to make a simple snare so, if you are camped for a few days, you can get a rabbit. Again, nose to tail eating with the rabbits, using all of the edible parts—except the brains. Rabbits are very lean, so you can't exist on them without some serious consequences. Eating the organs helps."

"Oh, yeah, I've heard of that. Rabbit starvation or something, right? One of my camping buddies was telling us about it."

"Yes, exactly. It happens when eating too much of the lean protein rabbit provides as opposed to consuming the entire animal. You'll need to eat the liver, kidneys, and any fat around the kidneys. Preserve as much of the skin as possible and eat it. Roasting the rabbit is good, then cook down the bones to make broth and crack open the bones to get out the marrow."

At the look on Rey's face, I add, "I know it sounds gross, but it's necessary. Just like the fish, the organs and bones can actually make a nice soup."

"Do you two eat like this? The nose to tail way?"

"Not every day," Sabrina answers. "But our mom made sure we knew how. She was an avid camper and took us on a few trips where we existed mainly on what we caught and foraged. It was very eye opening. And, honestly, I couldn't wait to have a cheeseburger and milkshake afterward. But, of course, that's not an option now. Now, it's not just for fun."

She doesn't need to say it's for survival and their lives depend on it. I quickly think about how many calories the Hoffmann family will need each day. Long distance hikers are notorious for consuming several thousand calories each day. There are lots of stories about people hiking long trails, eating four thousand plus calories a day, and still losing weight. While I don't hike anymore, Sabrina has droned on and on about this kind of stuff. I guess some of it has stuck with me.

If the Hoffmanns try to hike a modest ten miles per day, Rey, with his size and amazing build, will need way more than two thousand calories each day. Kim and the children, not much less than Rey. Trout is very low in calories, something like slightly over a hundred calories per serving. It'd take a lot of fish to supply their needs. With Rey's makeshift fishing setup, I'm not sure he can even catch enough.

And at some point, they won't be walking along the river or a lake. Rabbit, with slightly more calories than trout, will likely become their mainstay. They can also forage . . . if they have knowledge of how to do it. I'm not sure Sabrina and I can even forage very well up here. We didn't grow up in Wyoming and aren't familiar with the native plants.

We finish washing the dishes in silence. Sabrina and I fill up the water filter and replenish our fresh water supply in the same manner we used when entering the tunnel earlier today. Earlier today . . . it feels like it's been much longer. Yeah . . . I'm not sure I want to walk 150 miles with Kim in tow. *Ugh. Thanks a lot, Sabrina.*

Chapter 24

Sylvia

Sunday, Day 11
Railroad Tunnel
Between Shoshoni and Thermopolis, Wyoming

As we near the others in the middle of the tunnel, we're greeted with squeals of delight from little Naomi.

"Daddy, Daddy and . . . new friends, look. Look at how cute I am. Mommy brushed my hair, then put it in a nice braid. She did it all by touching me since we didn't want to waste a light. Right, Mommy?"

"That's right, sweetie," Kim answers in the calmest, kindest voice she's had since we left the campground.

Naomi continues, barely taking a breath, "She brushed N'cole's hair, too, but not Nate's. He said he could do his all by himself and Mom could just fuss with us girls. How about you two girls? You want Mom to fuss with you? She's really good at fixing hair."

I almost laugh out loud thinking about Kim brushing and fixing my hair. First, with our rocky relationship, I envision her using the opportunity to rip my hair out by the roots. Second, my hair likely doesn't behave the way her daughter's silky smooth, stick straight locks do. Caucasian hair is way different than biracial hair.

Shoot, even biracial hair differs from person to person. I ended up with more of my mom's hair, with tight, springy curls. Unlike Mom, who likes to keep her hair cut super short and under control, mine's shoulder length. Of course, on this trip, it's been pulled up in my standard cow patty bun. Sabrina has a lot less curl, leaning toward wavy instead of curly. We both have Mom's deep brown eyes combined with light-brown skin, thanks to our dad's Norwegian heritage.

Before Sabrina or I can respond, Kim says, "I'd be happy to help you with your hair. Just let me know."

Huh. I'm not sure what to think about this. She sounds sincere, but it's a little too soon to have her touching me since she was flinging insults my way not too long ago.

"That's very nice of you, Kim," Sabrina says. "I might take you up on it later."

I mumble something noncommittal.

"When Mommy does your hair, I can help," Naomi says breathlessly. "I know what to do. It'll be fun. We'll pretend we're at the . . . beauty place. Oh! Maybe we can even play with makeup. Mommy! Can you do makeup in the dark?"

Kim and Rey both laugh.

"No, you dork. That won't work," Nate says, while Nicole says, "I can only imagine," and starts to laugh with her parents. Naomi, not getting the joke, joins in. I'm struck by the realization they seem to be a normal, loving family. Maybe Rey's right; we were seeing the worst of Kim.

A short while later, Kim says, "So . . . the plate thing . . . it worked?"

Sabrina and I both hesitate in our response, allowing Rey to take the lead.

"We think it worked fine. The plate was clear. For safety's sake, we left it out, and we'll check it again tomorrow. Then we can talk about how to proceed."

"Okay, sounds good," Kim answers kindly.

Okay . . . who is this woman, and what has she done with that shrew Kim?

To say the rest of day was incredibly boring would be an understatement. Kim continues to be on her best behavior—almost enjoyable, in fact. To save the batteries, we avoid using the flashlights, so we spend time napping, chatting, and even telling stories. Kim and Rey are very good at the storytelling, almost like improvisation with voices and everything. Sabrina and I shared a few stories of our mom and Phil, plus our life in Arizona. Our stories were boring compared to Kim's and Rey's tales.

When the three children were napping, Kim scooted over near Sabrina and me, quietly saying, "I've made a fool of myself and treated you both very poorly. I hope you can forgive me. I have no excuse . . . just, please accept my apology."

She sounds so sincere; I want to readily agree. Instead, I take time to form my thoughts. I'm okay with accepting her apology for what is done, but there needs to be an understanding going forward.

Before I can voice this, Sabrina says, "I do accept your apology. That said, I would hope to see a change in your behavior from here on out. Sylvia and I felt led to offer our assistance. If our assistance isn't needed, we can calmly part ways, as adults, without additional drama."

Sabrina isn't even finished speaking before Kim says, "Absolutely. I'm all drama'd out."

"Okay— " Sabrina starts to say, when Kim says, "I'm so glad you accept my apology. Sylvia? You?"

"Uh . . . yes . . . but what Sabrina says goes for me too. No more drama."

"Yes, yes. Agreed," Kim says excitedly, then crushes us both in a hug, which is terribly clumsy and her head bonks me in the lip. It doesn't really hurt, but part of me wonders if it was entirely on accident. Sure, it's dark in here, but without any illumination for hours, my night vision is pretty good. Kim's should be also . . .

When Naomi starts to complain about being hungry, Rey pulls out two packages of mashed potatoes. I'm pleased to see they're in a foil-type container, which will work for rehydrating the meal. He also produces a single tin of tuna.

"Rey, how about Sylvia and I handle dinner tonight," Sabrina says. "We still have a few heavy cans, and I'd like to lighten our load a bit to make things easier once we're hiking again."

Sabrina pokes me, as I reluctantly agree. "Probably smart, handling the suitcase and the little grocery cart isn't too easy."

Even in the dark of the tunnel, I can see the look of thankfulness on Rey's face and possibly a sheen of tears. He nods his thanks, while Kim says, "That's wonderful. Thank you."

Naomi, once again full of excitement, says, "Oh, yay! What are we having? Can we have hamburgers?"

This gets another "dork" comment from big brother Nate, while Sabrina says, "Sorry, honey. I don't have any hamburgers. I have mostly soup and chili. But I do have a couple of special things, so I'll give you all a choice."

Sabrina keeps her light down so the cans aren't revealed as she sets things up. After a minute or two, while shining the light toward the cans, she says, "Okay, we have your choice of Mexican food, Chinese food, or New England style food."

Illuminated are three cans of tamales and a large can of chili, which I guess represents Mexican; a very large chicken Chow Mein meal thing, Chinese; and two large cans of baked beans, two small Vienna sausage, and a can of brown bread, New England.

Mom, always big on food storage, introduced us to these easy heat-and-eat items. In our normal everyday life, we ate very little processed foods. Mom preferred us eating whole—boring—foods like meat, grains, and vegetables. Even her food storage mainly consisted of whole grains, beans, and other low-processed dry goods. She did, however, feel these easy meals had a place. She kept some canned goods in food storage and for quick meals in our day-to-day life so we didn't eat out as much. Naturally, a diet based solely on these canned meals wouldn't be good, but once in a while, she felt they were fine.

The reaction from the children, and even Kim and Rey to a lesser degree, was surprising. You would've thought each option was a five-course meal at a Michelin-rated restaurant. Even Nicole, who I would've expected to turn up her nose at the idea of Chinese food in a can, is fervent.

With a big smile on her face, Nicole says, "You have bread in a can?"

Oh, so it's not the Chinese food, it's the bread. Makes sense.

"We do," Sabrina says. "Peanut butter, too, if that sounds good."

"And jelly?" Naomi shrieks, nearly piercing my eardrum.

"A little bit of jelly, plus some honey."

"Yes, yes, yes!" Naomi continues her cadence.

"Okay," I say, trying to calm Naomi. "I think we have one vote for bread, beans, and sausage."

"Two votes," Nate says.

"Three, and can we add the peanut butter and jelly?" Nicole asks.

"Yes, we can," Sabrina says. "Rey? Kim? That sound okay to you?"

"Wonderful," Kim responds, while Rey says, "You betcha."

The children want to go with us to the mouth of the tunnel, but since we're not sure if we've started to receive fallout since the last check, they stay behind. Kim asks if she can help us prepare the dinner and Rey will stay with the children. I reluctantly agree.

The difference in Kim's demeanor is night and day. I like it, but something seems very off about it. I truly don't see how she can go from being a coldhearted basket case to someone who seems happy and kind.

I check the plate this time. It's still clear.

While we heat up the beans, Kim talks and jokes. She tells us stories about her life growing up in Florida. "Sometimes I really miss the ocean. We lived outside of Tampa and spent a good portion of our free time at the beach. My mom said it was like being on vacation every weekend. Have you been to Florida?"

"Not Tampa, but we've gone to Disney World."

"Yeah, well, that's not really Florida. I guess it's a fun place to go if you don't mind dropping some serious bucks to visit an old swampland. Anyway, Tampa and the Gulf, that's amazing. Oh, and the Keys. Have you been to the Keys? No . . . I don't suppose you have. The Keys are something. They have the cutest little deer there, endangered species with their own preserve. Of course, they keep getting ran over by cars, so it's not going too well for them."

I pretty much tune her out as she drones on about Florida and how much she misses it. When the beans and sausage are about warm, she says, "Don't get me wrong. I love living in Denver. We have many wonderful things to do and so much sunshine. Rey really likes being near the mountains so he can become one with nature, or some such thing. Me . . . I like the shopping, concerts, restaurants, nightlife, and the airport. We're pretty much smack dab in the middle of the country, so we can jet off to anywhere. A definite plus since Rey's gone so much for work. I don't travel much for our business now—you know, with the kids—but it's still convenient."

As we walk back to the camp, I realize Sabrina and I barely spoke at all. Kim pretty much carried the entire conversation on her own. I do like this version of Kim better than the other version, but she's exhausting. I feel like I need a nap.

The baked beans were good, but only Rey liked the sausage. Vienna sausage is one of those odd foods. I question whether it's really a food or some strange overly processed food-like item. Sabrina likes them, even eating them as an occasional snack in addition to keeping them on hand for emergency meals. Me—no.

The slices of canned brown bread were a huge hit. We put thin smears of peanut butter and jam on the bread for the Hoffmann children. Sabrina and I both skipped the PB&J.

The first several days we were on the road, we mostly ate peanut butter and jelly sandwiches or PB&J on bagels or in a tortilla wrap. We had a loaf of bread, a sleeve of bagels, and a package of tortillas plus two jars of peanut butter and a jar of jam. When we were in the car, we didn't even stop. Whoever was in the passenger seat would pull out the fixings and make a sandwich on the fly.

Thankfully, we finished up one jar of peanut butter and all the bread products the afternoon before we met up with the Hoffmanns. I'm okay with not eating peanut butter again any time soon.

But the children . . . the children made all sorts of appreciative noises. Naomi declared the bread "the best I've ever had." Nate said it was sweeter than most bread, but he liked it. Nicole asked her parents why they'd never bought bread in a can. Both Kim and Rey said they had no idea it even existed. We know about it from our grandma. She learned about it from a friend.

One day, she was visiting her friend and it came on to suppertime. The friend hadn't planned anything, so she pulled out a can of baked beans and a can of brown bread—no Vienna sausage, though. Grandma was hooked. When she lived with us, she called it "canned dinner night" and made it an almost festive event.

My mom didn't care much for canned dinner night, so it was usually reserved for nights she had a work shift. Grandma would pull out the good dishes and fancy tablecloth, and light the candles on the table. She'd give us juice or milk in wine glasses, and we'd pretend we were in a fancy restaurant. It sounds kind of silly to give canned beans and canned bread such a lofty setting, but we loved it. I miss my grandma.

After dinner, Sabrina offers to read a few Psalms from her pocket Bible.

"Don't you think we should conserve the light?" I ask.

"I think a few more minutes will be fine," she answers with a smile, while looking to Rey and Kim.

Rey and Kim share a look.

"I don't think I know that book," Naomi says. "Does it have a princess in it?"

"Well, it does have a few princesses. And a King—the greatest King of all. Is it okay, Kim and Rey? I don't want to overstep."

"Uh, yeah, sure. I guess that'd be fine," Rey answers. "Kim, is it okay?"

"Why not? We don't have much else to do."

Sabrina asks if I'll hold the flashlight for her while she reads. She turns to Psalm 91, one of the passages she's been working on memorizing while we've been walking. She's told me many times over the last few days how fitting this scripture is. I tune her out as she babbles about God's protection. *Yeah, right.*

When she finishes the passage, she immediately bows her head. "Our Father in Heaven, we ask You continue to watch over us. We're so grateful for the protection You've provided so far. Please keep us safe from the fallout, if there is any. And please, dear Lord, be with those tonight who are not as fortunate as us. Please comfort the hearts of those who are hurting. We pray these things in Jesus' name, amen."

She is the sole amen. Amen is an expression of agreement. I don't agree, so I stay quiet. Sabrina doesn't seem at all upset by the lack of consensus.

After a brief silence, Kim says, "Well, Sabrina, that was very . . . interesting."

"Nice. It was very nice," Rey corrects.

"Yes, of course. Nice," Kim says. "Nice is a much better word."

I fight rolling my eyes at the hypocrisy.

Sabrina chooses to ignore it, as Naomi says, "It sounded so pretty . . . like a song. It needed music with it."

Sabrina nods in agreement. "The Psalms were songs. They would sing them while walking from place to place. The Psalms are now often referred to as religious poems. I think they're beautiful."

Nicole quickly agrees. "I had no idea anything from the Bible could sound so nice. I thought it was all about . . . Oh, well, never mind."

"You thought it might be full of hate and anger?" Sabrina gently asks.

"I guess so. I've heard people talk about how the Bible wants to rule our life and it's nothing but a fairytale—an evil fairytale that hates anyone who isn't white, and that it promotes things like slavery. But you're not white. Weren't your ancestors slaves?"

Kim lets out a gasp, while Rey softly says, "Nicole."

I laugh out loud, and Sabrina says with a slight chuckle, "I'm of mixed ancestry, I suspect like most of the people living in the United States. My dad was born in Norway. My mom's family was originally from Africa and did come over on slave ships."

Nicole nods confidently. "And do you think your slave ancestors were fans of a book promoting slavery?"

"That's a great question, one my Grandma Marie—my mom's mom—and I talked about many times. I'd be happy to share more of what I believe the Bible says about slavery, but I need to pull out my full Bible and get the correct scriptures for you. This here," she says, lifting up her pocket Bible, "only has Psalms, Proverbs, and the New Testament. A good number of the things you're asking about are in the Old Testament. My Bible's packed away pretty good, and I don't want to drag it out tonight. If it's okay with your folks, we can read another time."

Nicole shrugs one shoulder. "Sure, yeah, that's fine."

I have no doubt Sabrina is sincere in her offer. But from the looks Rey and Kim exchange, I doubt this conversation will go any further. I'm okay with that. While I may have believed the same as Sabrina at one time, I now find Biblical discussions to be a complete waste of time, and often insulting.

Chapter 25

Mollie

Sunday, Day 11
Bakerville, Wyoming

While tallying up all the people from the check-in sheets, baby Emma makes herself known, and Dodie brings her to the safe room for food.

Madison is exclusively breastfeeding Emma, even with the injuries she sustained when the bandits killed her husband, sending the bullet through him and into Madison's shoulder. When Belinda and Dr. Sam operated on the shoulder, they used a local anesthetic, allowing no interruption in her feeding schedule. Madison's taking painkillers, but they've been keeping the doses as light as possible and trying to time them around Emma's needs.

I don't think Belinda was too terribly happy to introduce Emma into the semi sterile room. Belinda made a point of using a wet wipe followed by a few alcohol swabs on Emma's exposed skin, even gently cleansing her face. She also asked someone to stay nearby in case of Emma needing a diaper change, which would happen outside of the safe room.

"Hey, Mollie," Jake says. "Since you don't have to go into the safe room, how about we move to the rec room? One of the chairs in there or a futon might be a little more comfortable for you. You look like you could use a rest."

"Do we have a plan for sleeping arrangements?" I ask. "There's more people here than we planned on, and I can't see some of them sleeping on mattress pads on the floor."

"We'll figure it out. As long as there isn't fallout, we can use the bedroom and futons for additional sleeping space. Some might even want to sleep upstairs, knowing they can get down here quickly if need be."

He's right. A healthy person can be exposed to a small amount of fallout without needing medical care—of course, zero exposure is much better.

"True. I guess it'll be fine. I just wish we would've thought things through a little more. Especially thought about injuries."

"We did what we could." Jake kisses me on the nose. "Now, let's move you someplace more comfortable. Then we'll sort out the sleeping arrangements. Most people brought sleeping bags and other gear of their own also."

"What about . . . everyone? How's everyone doing?"

"As well as can be expected, I suppose."

"Do they know? Does everyone know what is—what we *think*—is happening?"

"Yes, everyone knows. David Hammer said he'd like to have a prayer service tonight. We thought we could discuss it then, let everyone rest and regroup for now. When we get together, we can have a good discussion."

David lives across the creek from us and leads a neighborhood Bible study. "Okay, but I'll be surprised if the discussion can wait until evening."

I make myself comfortable in the easy chair in the rec room. Malcolm, Tony, and TJ have moved on from foosball to a sedate game of UNO. None seem to be paying much attention to the cards. There are several other people in the room—reading, playing checkers, or quietly talking.

Like the boys, the attention levels are lacking. There are many tears and sad, distracted looks. The storage area of the basement also has a few card tables set up. Jake, after checking on the root cellar occupants, says the same thing is happening in there—games, reading, even arts and crafts. All half-hearted attempts to distract from the situation.

Meals for the day will be a smorgasbord of items brought by everyone. It seems when Jake told people they could join us in the basement, he also asked them to bring their own food and personal supplies. For some families and groups, this isn't much, but others have graciously agreed to share.

Grandmaster Bill Shane, Aaron, and Laurie were ones without much. They were driving Bill's truck, loaded with as much stuff as possible, and towing a trailer with a quad and dirt bike when the EMP hit. The truck shut off immediately.

They were able to use the pull starter on both the quad and dirt bike to get them going. Each wore a book bag style backpack, then used bungee cords to attach as much as they could to the back of the quad. Aaron and Laurie rode the dirt bike, while Bill drove the quad. The rest of their stuff is on a side road at the edge of Bakerville.

"So, Mollie," Jake says hesitantly, "I think we need to go and get Master Shane's things. They made it pretty close, almost to the highway, so it won't take too long. Figured— "

"No, Jake. We have an agreement."

"Honey, I know we have an agreement."

"Jake," I hiss, "I hate it when you know I'm irritated with you and you still call me honey."

"*Mollie*, with the way things are, we can't afford not to get their things. They brought food, bicycles, dirt bikes, and more things we all need."

"Let's at least see if we can get some information on the radio. Maybe the NOAA will be working? The Faraday cages should've protected the radios, right?"

"Maybe? We'd like to think the cages worked, but we don't really know. And we don't know if anyone will be broadcasting."

"Humor me, Jake."

"Okay, but let's move to the bedroom. If it is working, I want to limit what little ears hear," Jake whispers, while gesturing toward Malcolm.

After passing off the youngest children to their parents or other guardians, Dodie moved from the bedroom and is sitting on the futon with Jake's dad, Alvin. They're deep in conversation with Evan and a few others. The topic, of course, is the nukes and what will happen next. They're trying to keep the conversation from going too far with the young boys in the room, but a few times Evan has had to remind them.

I agree with Jake and lift my hand for him to help me up. "Wait a bit, honey. Let me see if it's even working first. If it is, I'll come and get you. No sense in you moving around on your foot if you don't have to."

I don't like it but comply. Jake goes to grab the NOAA and then disappears into the bedroom. About five minutes later, the door opens again and he gives me a thumbs up.

Secreted away in the bedroom, we turn the volume on low and with trepidation, we scan the channels.

Chapter 26

Mollie

Sunday, Day 11
Bakerville, Wyoming

"No, Jake. You can't," I state with more authority than I feel.

"Honey . . . *Mollie* . . . we need to. We need to get the things they brought. Otherwise, someone else will. You know we need the resources with the additional people. It's a blessing Bill and Aaron made it as close as they did. You've heard the stories of how bad the road between here and Wesley has become."

"But we don't have any new information. We don't know if this attack is over. The NOAA gave us only static. You and I made a plan, long ago. We decided we'd stay put during a threat. As far as we know, the threat still exists. We need to stay here, where we're safe, and not be out gallivanting around." I'm trying hard to keep my voice even but failing miserably.

"Mollie, I'm going. I'll hook the utility trailer to the Jeep, and we'll get what we can. Won't take much more than an hour. And I promise you, the first sign of fallout, we'll head back. I have the keychain radiation alert thing, which should go off if there's a problem."

"And what if there's another strike? What if the missile's off target and ends up near us? Or what if they've decided to start for secondary targets? We don't— "

"Stop. Just stop. You're ranting. I know it's because you've been through a lot lately. You're injured, you're tired, you're scared. I'm scared, too, but Bill has supplies he needs—things we can all use. They each brought a backpack with clothes, and he was able to stow some of his armory on the back of his quad. But there's more, a few more weapons, food, camping stuff. We don't know how long this will go on, and supplies are a commodity. We can't afford to waste anything. You know this."

I give him a hard look, probably harder than I should, especially since I know he's right. He gives me the same look back.

"Fine," I snap. "You're going to do what you want to do anyway, so why even bother asking me?"

The hurt crossing his face makes my heart fall. Why did I use such venom?

He gives me a small nod and heads for the bedroom door. Hand on the knob, he turns to me slightly and says, "Let me tell Bill, then I'll be back to help you into the rec room."

I wait until he leaves, then get myself up, almost losing my balance and crashing to the floor. It's just like him to respond with kindness. Well, I won't give Jake the satisfaction of helping me to the room. As I start toward the door, I realize how ridiculous I'm being. Things like this are what caused Jake and me heartache in the past. So much heartache, not long ago we were on the edge of divorce.

Over the last several months, we've worked hard on our marriage, on learning to communicate better, on being honest and loving with each other.

For the most part, things are good. Once in a while, we still revert to our old style of noncommunication, as evidence by my rant. Jake is right, I'm scared and things have sucked lately. Things are not looking much better for the near future. None of it is helping me make good decisions. He's also right; we need the supplies.

Lord, help me. Help me to be strong, to not have fear. Help me to put my hope, my trust in You and You alone. You are my refuge, my fortress. Thank you. Your faithfulness is my shield, my rampart. Please, Lord, please. Please. Oh, and amen.

I wipe the tears from my eyes. I suddenly think about being honest with Jake. Is a lie by omission still a lie?

Of course it is.

Biblically and morally, I know keeping secrets isn't right, especially a big secret. At first, I couldn't find the right time. Then it didn't seem to matter. Recently, as I've returned to my faith in God, I started to think it was time to come clean. A verse from the Book of James keeps going through my head.

If any man among you seem to be religious, and bridleth not his tongue, but deceiveth his own heart, this man's religion is vain.

While I don't think of myself as religious, per se, I am a believer—a follower of Christ. As such, I should strive to be more like Him. This is definitely something I struggle with. Wanting to do everything on my own, in my own way, is a serious weakness of the flesh. Learning to trust and believe . . . I stifle a sigh.

Truthfully, though, I haven't had any real desire to share my secret. The can of worms it would open up . . . I just don't want to deal with it. Then, before all of this started, something happened and I felt I might be forced into revealing all.

My secret is safe once again, but my heart tells me I need to come clean. Earlier today, before the missile alert, I told Jake I wanted to talk with him. Today was to be the day.

Can it still be today? *Should* it be today?

I take a deep breath and swallow my pride as the door opens. Jake spares me a small smile, which I return as I carefully reach my crutch in his direction. My attempt at trying to draw him near. He takes the hint and gently takes me in his arms.

"Sorry, Jake," I say sheepishly. "I know you're right and going after the supplies is important. Your safety is also important."

"We'll be careful. First sign of fallout and we'll stop what we're doing and head back. I know the statistics. We don't want to be out in it for any length of time. I'll have the radiation alert keychain."

"Jake, you know being inside a vehicle won't really protect you, so you have to hustle back if you see anything suspicious. Don't wait for the keychain to go off, use your instincts. Do you think it'll look like a storm cloud or maybe the way snow looks in the distance before it reaches us? If you see anything . . . and be careful of everything. People might use this opportunity to . . . I don't know, cause trouble? Steal? Who knows?"

"Yeah, it's possible. Bill and Aaron know it too. We decided we're going to take three vehicles. Evan's old truck—what's he call that thing?"

"Betty Boop," I offer. Betty Boop is a mostly restored 1959 GMC pickup in cherry red. They rarely drive it but keep it around for the nostalgia of it.

Jake nods. "Yeah, okay. We're taking that thing so we can hook on Bill's trailer to bring it here. We're also taking Evan's International

Scout to hook up Aaron's trailer. And I'll take our Jeep along with the small utility trailer, so we can be sure we can get everything out of both truck beds. Leo's going too. He'll ride shotgun with Evan. Bill will ride with me. Aaron and Aaron's girlfriend will be in the Scout. She said she isn't comfortable staying here without knowing anyone. And, Mollie, we'll all be on alert."

I nod my understanding. "I can't imagine Belinda's happy about Leo going along. Didn't she make a big deal about the medical team not putting themselves in danger?"

"Yep. She did. Things have changed." Jake shrugs. "And both Leo and Dr. Sam told her that having someone medically trained on outings might be more of a benefit. Anyway, we'll be careful. And at Evan's suggestion, we're leaving a couple of sentries out for as long as we can. Keith and Tate are standing watch outside right now, while Roy and Mike are using the upstairs windows to keep an eye out."

"Really? Why? Now that Morse is no longer a threat . . ." I don't finish what I'm thinking—*because I killed him*—but my eyes fill with tears. Even though he needed to die, I still feel icky about it. I blink quickly to remove the moisture.

"Like you said, people could try to take advantage of the situation. The world isn't what it used to be, and we have to be safe." Jake gives a sad shake of his head.

He doesn't like it any more than I do, but it's the way things are. "I've given both Keith and Roy one of the keychain nuke alert things. Roy's pretty upset about Sheila and her refusal to come downstairs. I guess I can't really blame her. As long as there isn't fallout, she's perfectly fine in the cabin."

"That's true. Really, as long as the children and those who can't move very fast— "

"Like you." He gives me a smile and a kiss.

"Yep, like me. As long as we're down here and the livestock is secured, those who are healthy can be out of the basement unless fallout starts. Oh. I guess I pretty much just made your point about going after the supplies."

"You did and you didn't. I totally understand Sheila staying in the cabin. Three hundred yards away from the security of the basement is different than being several miles away if fallout starts. I'll be careful, I promise. Now, you want to go back out to the rec room? Angela, Sarah, and Calley are in there now. Angela had a nap, and Sarah decided it was safe to come out of the cellar for now. She's ready to run back at a moment's notice."

"Oh, I'm sure she is." I can't help but smile. "Sarah and Tate are so excited about the baby. I wish we could've done something special to celebrate their announcement. Maybe when things settle down?"

"Sure, when things settle down. Plus, I don't think they want to make a super big deal about it yet . . . you know, after losing the last one. Tate said they're cautiously optimistic. Did you know they'd started fertility treatments?"

"What? No, what kind of treatments? I knew they were talking about it after they were settled, but I didn't know they started."

"I don't know." Jake shrugs. "Tate said some kind of pill. She only just started taking it, and they got pregnant right away. Guess it worked."

"Huh. I guess it did. Of course, with the way things are now . . . "

"She'll be fine, Mollie. We have Belinda and her mom. Wasn't her mom the kind of nurse that helps deliver babies? And Dr. Sam . . . it'll be fine."

"Dr. Sam was a Navy doctor. You think he delivered a lot of babies in the Navy?"

"Maybe not, but don't they learn how to in medical school? Besides, it's still a long time until the baby will be born. You don't need to worry yet—plenty of time for you to worry in nine months or so."

"Ha. Aren't you funny?" I give him a slight jab in the arm. "And you do know it's going to be less than nine months, right? She's probably at least six weeks, so . . . "

"Sure, honey."

"Are they playing cards?"

"You know it," Jake answers with a cheesy grin.

I allow Jake to help me to the rec room and he gets me situated at the table, where there is one spot open. My beautiful girls—Sarah, Angela, and Calley—along with Lois, Deanne, and two neighborhood ladies, are just starting a game of Nines.

"Hey, Mom. We're ready for you," Calley says, motioning to a spot saved for me at the table.

Calley and Angela, along with Katie, share the same naturally curly medium-brown hair, full lips, and a perfect nose—compliments of their dad—and my green eyes. I know I'm biased, but they're seriously adorable, in the girl next door kind of way.

Sarah has more of a regal beauty about her, elegant and classy, with my aquiline nose and slightly thin lips. She knows just how to do her makeup to make the most of her classic features. Her dark brown hair is usually styled in a sleek pageboy, similar to Rosemary Clooney in *White Christmas*, but today it's pulled back in a low bun. All three are dressed casually in yoga pants or something similar.

Jake gives me a rather ambitious goodbye kiss, causing me to blush slightly, considering our audience.

As he starts to pull away, I hold on to him and whisper, "Be careful. More careful than you've ever been. You see anything that doesn't seem right, come straight home to me. You're more important than any stuff."

He kisses me again, this time on the nose. "I will. I'll see you soon."

I try to focus on the game, to help with passing the time, not that any of us do a great job paying attention. Even so, I often check my watch.

I'm usually fairly competitive, and while I don't mind if I lose, I'd prefer not to. Today, I'm beaten soundly.

Angela, still feeling the effects of getting hit in the head a few days earlier, begs off after the first game to rest on the futon. On the second game, we switch to Crazy Eights, and I'm the first person out. We all spend more time staring at our cards than actively playing.

Jake's been gone an hour and twenty minutes. I suspected his estimate of an hour was a little short, so I'm trying not to be concerned.

Somehow, I do slightly better in the next game of Crazy Eights. We're down to three remaining players, and I'm holding on at ninety-eight points. One hundred is the target to be eliminated. I've had ninety-eight for the last three hands, managing to win each one, when I hear noise on the stairs.

We all look toward the noise, as Leo's head pops down. He's walking backwards, which makes no sense, until it's clear he's carrying a stretcher.

"Oh no!" I gasp. Another one of us is injured.

Chapter 27

Mollie

Sunday, Day 11
Bakerville, Wyoming

"We found her. We found her and the children," Leo says, in answer to our looks of panic.

Aaron's carrying the other end of the stretcher. I breathe a sigh of relief. I don't know the woman on the stretcher. Does being happy it's not one of us make me a bad person? *Maybe so.*

Sarah rushes to the door accessing the storage area of the basement, opening it wide for them to go through. I want to help but know, with my limited mobility, I'm likely to be more of a hindrance than an asset.

Jake is at the bottom of the stairs, holding a young child, three or four years old.

I think it's a girl, but I'm not completely sure. Her hair is shoulder length and matted. She's wearing shorts and a shirt, which may have been pastel pink at one time. It's apparent she's in need of a bath.

Behind him is Bill, holding a younger, and possibly even filthier, version of the child Jake's carrying. Aaron's girlfriend, Laurie, is next, holding the hand of a boy who looks to be six or seven. He's in the same condition as the other two, but his dirty face shows streaks of clean skin from crying.

Jake catches my eye, and I ask, "Are you okay?"

"We're fine. We found Marc here," Jake says, motion to the boy holding Laurie's hand, "when we were heading back. He flagged us down and told us his mom is sick."

Marc starts crying again, burying his face into Laurie's leg. She gently pats his head. I can tell she's trying but doesn't seem to be very comfortable. Then I catch a whiff and suspect the close proximity to the children isn't very pleasant.

Jake continues, "Marc says she's been sleeping a lot. This morning he couldn't wake her up. Leo checked her out and decided we needed to bring them all here. Marc, his brother, and their sister haven't had much to eat or drink lately. So we gave them a few snacks and they shared a soda on the way back here. We told them you'd help them take a bath, then we'll get them a nice, hot meal."

The little one Jake is holding says, "I wanna bath. I love baths."

The smaller one chimes in excitedly, "Me too. Me too. I wanna bath wit' Sissy." His toddler-level language is muddled and hard to understand.

"I guess I could take a bath too," Marc says. "It's been a while since our water stopped working. Uncle Brandon was bringing us water from the river, but he hasn't been around for a few days. Mom's friend John was over yesterday and said he heard someone hurt Uncle and he won't be coming back. John told Mom we're on our own. He's going to hide out in the wilderness so he doesn't get hurt too. Uncle Brandon probably did some bad things." Marc dissolves into tears.

Sarah, always my tenderhearted child, goes to him and immediately pulls him toward her. Laurie looks grateful to have Sarah take over providing comfort.

"You think we could use the master bathroom? Since there's no fallout, it would be fine?" I ask Jake.

"Yeah, the two younger ones at least. I bet Marc would like to use the solar shower in the main bathroom."

Marc perks up and says, "I don't know what that is."

"Let me show you."

"I'll do it, Mom," Sarah says. "You stay off your foot."

"You sure, Sarah?"

"Yes. Jake, you mind if I use the keychain thing? If it goes off while I'm up there, I'll know to get right back down."

"Sure. Bill, you mind if I give Sarah the one you have? Roy and Keith are both using one also. And whoever helps bathe the other children can have mine."

"I'll get the bathtub set up for the younger ones," Deanne says. "The water in the dark gray rain barrel should be warm enough. You think there would be any problem with them bathing in it?"

144

Jake and I look at each other. It looks like they haven't bathed since way before the lights went out. I don't think rainwater will hurt them one bit. Bill is the one who says, "Should be just fine."

Calley helps Deanne, while Sarah asks Laurie if she can grab one of the solar showers. "They're hanging from hooks on the wall in the tub room. The water from the barrel should be warm enough for it also. Can you fill it up and then hang it from the hook in the master bathroom? I think let's take all three into the master bath and we'll put the young ones in the tub while Marc uses the separate shower. Sound good?"

Laurie shrugs. "Fine by me."

"Great. Let's use one of the larger five-gallon shower bags."

Within a few minutes, the three children are set up for a shower and bath. Aaron Ogden is back in the rec room after helping get the children's mom situated.

They decided not to take her into the semi sterile room Katie, Madison, and Doris are in. Instead, she's on a cot outside the door, in the same area Angela and I had been sitting in when we were first brought down to the basement.

Evan, who I just realized didn't reappear with everyone else, returns and quietly says, "Jake, Mollie, I think we should have a little meeting. I'd like to check with Belinda first, get an update on Doris. Maybe we could chat in the bedroom? I think you should invite Bill too. I'll see if Leo's available. Say, ten minutes?"

Ten minutes later, the five of us are in the basement bedroom.

Evan starts with, "Leo, what's the status of the children's mom?"

"She's stable. Looks like she overdosed, likely a combination of alcohol and drugs of some sort. My guess is she's a heavy drinker. There were quite a few bottles of booze in her house. From what the older boy says, though, it sounds like she has a brother who was keeping her supplied and possibly some sort of boyfriend."

"Which brings me to what I wanted to talk about," Evan says. "I don't know this woman or her kids. I thought the house they're living in was abandoned. I just spoke with Pete Fairbanks, and he said no one was living in it over the winter. He had permission from the owner to trap coyotes and such there. Pete said he doesn't even know how someone could live there. The place is barely standing. When we found her, it was full of all sorts of things. It reminds me a lot of how

Phil described Dan Morse's house. I wonder if we might have a second gang operating out of Bakerville."

"What? How?" I ask with disbelief.

"I'm not sure, and I could be wrong," Evan answers with a shrug.

"I'm with you on this, Evan," Bill speaks up. "I don't think they've been there long. Kind of reminded me of a stash house. Marc seemed to be happy to share information. Maybe, after he gets cleaned up and fed, we can learn a little more."

Evan nods and Leo says, "You think whoever they're with will come looking for them?"

No one says anything, but I see the way Jake, Evan, and Bill's eyes are darting around.

"Yep, I guess you do," I say.

"It's possible," Evan agrees with a sigh. "As far as I know, we weren't followed. After everyone was dropped off, I took my truck and went back up the road, then took it up the side road up—that spot makes a great lookout, giving me views in just about every direction. I didn't see anyone. If someone were looking for them, I don't think they'd have any idea to look here."

"I suppose it's too dangerous to go back and empty out the house?" Leo asks.

"Why would you want to do that? Most of the stuff I saw was electronics, probably all fried," Evan says.

"I grabbed the couple of bottles of liquor laying around. I'd like to see if there's more. Medications also. We could use both for our medical supplies," Leo answers.

Evan and Bill both nod.

"Maybe," Jake says. "We can discuss it, but not today. Not until we know the situation with the nukes. We've pushed our luck as it is and need to stay put." I shoot him a grateful look as he says, "We also need to keep our guard up. Evan and Bill, can you take charge of setting up a rotation schedule for guards? Not just the men, but any women comfortable with it—except Mollie and any who have been injured recently. They need to rest up."

"Hold on, Jake," I say. "Aren't Mike and his dad taking watch from the upstairs windows? Why couldn't I do that?"

"Well, babe, because you're kind of terrible at walking up and down stairs right now," Jake says with a straight face.

I have no comeback. He's right, I am. "Okay . . . but as soon as I'm able to, I want to be added in.

"You've got it," Bill says. "Any chance we could find a notebook or something to get started with the schedule?"

"Sure, let me grab one for you," Jake says.

With that, our little meeting is concluded.

The three children are back, and they look and smell so much better. Sissy, hair untangled and put in a ponytail, is all smiles. Sarah found old clothes of Malcolm's for all of them to wear. It's wonderful to see them looking so happy and content, the way children should be.

Chapter 28

Mollie

Sunday, Day 11
Bakerville, Wyoming

The children's mom—Marc says her name is Lydia—has vomited several times. She's still pretty much out of it but is expected to recover. Leo says she's going to have quite the hangover when she wakes up. He's in charge of Lydia, staying out of the sick room, while Belinda and Tammy care for our original injured.

Sarah—through talking with Marc, Sissy, and baby Andy—has learned the family moved to the house after the lights went out in their other house. Marc isn't exactly sure where the other house was, but he thinks it was in Montana. He doesn't know if they moved because of the cyberattack or if the lights went out for a different reason. He doesn't know anything about the plane crashes or other attacks. He also doesn't have much of a concept of time and can't say how long they've been staying in the Bakerville hovel.

He did say their mom made a big deal about not wanting to live in Wyoming and hated the dump they were living in. Their uncle told them it would only be a few more days, then they'd be moving to a much nicer house, with lights and water.

When Belinda was checking on Lydia, she updated us on Katie's condition. "She's really doing quite well. I was concerned she'd have a set back with moving her here, but so far, she's stable."

"Wonderful," Jake says. I'm near tears so only smile and nod. He continues, "So she's out of the woods?"

"Not completely. She's holding her own, and that's encouraging. She has a drain in, and everything looks good there. With an abdomen wound . . . well, lots of things can go wrong. As you know, we worry about infection, so we're taking protective measures. She's starting to ask for food, but we're not to that point yet. Keep a good thought."

"We're praying," Jake says.

Belinda replies with a shrug and, "Whatever works for you."

"And Madison?" I ask, feeling a protectiveness over her.

"Yep. She's doing well. I would've sent her home today so she could recover . . . well, here, I guess. You'll be housing her, right?"

"That's right."

"Yeah, but with so many people here and the tight space . . . for now, I'd like to keep both Madison and Doris in the room with us. It's the most sterile choice. Especially now, since we've added Lydia and her vomiting to the mix. I'm glad you cleaned up the children. Leo checked them over and says they seem in good health. I'll check in with you next time I come out. TJ—he's doing okay?"

"He seems to be doing fine," I answer. "Tony, Malcolm, and him are doing well together. Lydia's older boy, Marc, is with them. They've been very kind to him."

"That's good. Our children have been through a lot lately." Belinda gives a sad shake of her head as she excuses herself to return to the safe room. TJ and Belinda have both been through a lot.

One definite struggle today has been the bathroom situation. With just under sixty people utilizing our basement and root cellar, the two toilets aren't enough. Since we're not receiving fallout, thankfully, the two bathrooms on the main floor plus the additional upstairs bathroom are all in use. Our family members who are living here often return to their personal space for bathroom use and a few minutes of privacy.

People are settling in for the night. With our new number of fifty-eight people, we're full up. Every cot, mattress, bed, and couch we have in the basement is spoken for. Fortunately, others brought their own cots and air mattresses, and four people are on guard duty. Sheila's still in her cabin, but everyone else chooses to sleep in the basement or root cellar. While we've yet to have any type of fallout, we're all a little leery. We know fallout could start at any time.

Jake, Malcolm, and I, along with Tony, TJ, and Lily, set up our sleeping area within our food storage room. While most people are sleeping in open spaces without privacy, Jake pulled the homeownership card and found us a private space. Tomorrow night might be different since Jake has guard duty from midnight to 4:00.

Because the storage room is wall-to-wall shelving with shelves also in the middle, there isn't a ton of space for setting up camp. Jake gets me a cot, the full-size type we used for car camping, while he sleeps on a backpacker's blowup mattress, and each of the children has a backpacker's sleeping pad.

When we're settling in, Malcolm starts crying.

"What's going on, Buddy?" Jake gently asks.

Through his tears, he quietly says, "I don't know. I'm just really sad."

Tony, TJ, and Lily are soon joining Malcolm in tears.

We completely understand; they're not the only ones who've started crying out of the blue today. Today, they were able to stay busy with each other and remain somewhat distracted. They weren't focusing on the events we find ourselves in. Earlier, we included all of the adults, except Dodie and those in the hospital room, in a group meeting. Dodie took the children into the root cellar while we met.

There were many questions and tears during the meeting. None of us really know what's happening, not with any certainty. Maybe we should've let the older children join the meeting.

We spend many minutes talking with the children about what we know: most cars won't run, phones won't work, and the lights may or may not come back on. We think there was an electromagnetic pulse, but we're not sure. If it was a pulse, we don't know if our solar systems survived.

While Jake and I don't share this with the children, we have things in place that will allow us to still have a good quality of life whether the solar works or not. People thrived without electricity for years, and just under a billion people live without power worldwide, even in these modern times—well, considerably more than that since the cyberattacks last week.

But still, at least some electricity will make our lives easier and give us the ability to put other things into practice that, up to now, have been strictly theoretical. Sure, we've made lots of plans and gathered lots of information, but at this point, it is all theoretical. We've never had to actually survive without electricity before.

Malcolm soon asks, "Do you think there are lots of other people who made plans like we did?"

Neither Jake nor I are sure how to answer, as three pairs of eyes look at us expectantly. Lily has settled somewhat and appears to be ready to fall asleep.

We know preppers are a minority. Most people think crazy preppers are several cards short of a full deck or setting out to destroy the country. Sure, FEMA recommends storing three days' worth of food and water, but we're already way beyond three days of our world changing.

The lights went out over a week ago. Even in our little community, people are running out of food.

"I think some probably have," Jake answers softly.

"What about the bombs? Did the bombs explode and kill people?" TJ asks.

"We have no way of knowing. We don't believe there have been any explosions nearby since there hasn't been any fallout. So right now, we're safe," I answer.

"But if there were bombs," Tony quickly interjects, "lots of people died?"

"Yes, Tony. If there were bombs then probably a lot of people died," I quietly respond.

His eyes fill with tears again, but he doesn't fully cry. "Do you think my dad is safe? Were there bombs where he is working?"

"I'm sorry, Tony," Jake says tenderly. "We just don't know. We don't know where or if any bombs detonated. I wish . . . " He lets out a heavy sigh. "I wish I could answer you, but we just don't know."

"Okay," Tony says so quietly we barely hear him.

I watch as Malcolm reaches out and touches Tony's shoulder, giving him a slight smile.

Tony nods at Malcolm, then says, "Mr. Caldwell, Malcolm told us earlier you usually read before bed. Will you read tonight?"

"I'd be happy too. I found a book of short stories in the rec room, thought one of those might be good. You guys ready?"

"Yes, but I was wondering," Malcolm says, "do you think Mom can read the Bible story first? The one she read during Bible study tonight? Mom?"

"Sure. Psalm 91, sometimes called the Soldier's Psalm, it's been helping me a lot lately."

"It helped you get home when you were lost in the woods, right?" Tony asks, elaborating a bit on the information I shared at Bible study.

"Well, I wasn't exactly lost. I knew where I was, but I was overwhelmed and tired. Plus, I wasn't feeling too good from my bonk on the head." I make a funny face, which they all three smile at. "But, yes, the passage helped me get home."

Jake holds the light while I read the Psalm. Then I hold it for him while he reads the story he picked out. Jake reads for only a few minutes when we begin to hear rhythmic breaths of sleep and soft snores.

"They didn't last long," I whisper.

"Stressful day. It wiped them out. Wiped me out too. You comfortable?"

"Sure. My foot hurts, but the blanket rolled up under it helps. See you in the morning."

"Love you, honey."

Even though I'm tired, I struggle with relaxing enough to sleep. I usually read to fall asleep, but with my eReader in the Faraday cage, just in case we get hit with an additional EMP, my attempts to relax fail. I thought about using a lantern and reading a paper book, but the cot is too skinny and my foot hurts too much to contort with a book and lantern. Instead, I'm replaying the last few days in my head. It's like a bad movie.

I think of today, watching Sarah with baby Andy, Sissy, and their older brother, Marc. The children were so scared; she was so good with them. And I suddenly remember, I'm a grandma again.

Sarah and Tate have been wanting this baby for so long. I do a mental inventory of the baby stuff we've collected as part of our preparedness efforts. We should be set up pretty well, even though we took a minimalistic approach, copying the Finnish with a Baby Box. Everything the baby needs is together in one box, and the box is baby's first bed.

For clothing, we took a page from the past and went with old-fashioned baby dresses, for both sexes—not only a few readymade dresses but fabric and patterns to make additional. Even with my minimal sewing skills, this is a project I can handle.

We did buy a few cute onesies that I couldn't pass up. They have sayings like "Grandma Loves Me" and "Grandpa's Little Helper." I love how the baby boxes came together, and I can't wait to give one to Sarah when the time is right.

I never did talk with Jake today—never shared my secret. There was just so much going on; the time never seemed right. Maybe tomorrow. Or maybe not. I've kept this quiet for so long now, surely there's no reason to be in a rush.

Chapter 29

Lindsey

Tuesday, Day 13
Underground Culvert, Tahoe National Forest
Near Sierra City, California

Dear diary,

Today, like yesterday, I'm bored out of my mind. So bored I thought I'd scribble out a note to myself on an old receipt I found in the bottom of my purse. This is my letter to the world. But now I'm out of space, so I guess I'll go back to being bored.

Sincerely,

Lindsey Maverick

"Hey, Linds, what are you doing over there with the flashlight?"

"Uh . . . nothing. Just making myself a note." I click off the light. I shouldn't be wasting the battery anyway.

"Okay . . . have something important you want to remember?"

"No, Logan. I'm just tired of being holed up down here. It's so damp, I'm always chilly, the water is terrible, and it is starting to stink in here. No, not stink . . . reek. It reeks. And I reek. I can barely stand my own stench."

"Agreed. On all points. Uh . . . not you reeking but me reeking. But there isn't much we can do about it right now. I don't think it's safe for us to leave. I really think the fine dust we noticed on things is fallout. Don't you?"

"Probably? I don't know. The only thing I remember from my classes was someone calling it radioactive dust. We've talked about this already."

"Yep, I know. I'm just reminding you."

"Okay. I think it was smart to put a piece of plastic sack out. The last piece was still clear when you checked it?"

"I didn't see any new dust. Hasn't been any new since yesterday morning . . . or what we assume was yesterday morning. It's getting hard to keep track of time. I still think we should aim for three days from when the fallout stopped. So not tomorrow but the next day, provided there isn't any new dust on the bag. Agreed?"

"Yeah. Then we ride like the wind and try to put some distance between us and the blasts."

"That sounds like a plan. But I do agree with you. We should avoid places likely to be targets. We were already going around Reno. We'll also avoid Salt Lake, Boise . . . where else?"

"Any military bases."

"Right."

"What do you think the chances of a shower, once we get out of here, will be?"

"Gosh, Linds. I'm not sure. You know showers were a challenge before the bombs, ever since the power went out. I don't think that would've changed while we've been holed up down here."

"I sure wish I could have cleaned up a little when camped the morning before the bombs. At least I'd have two less days of grime on me. The sponge baths we were taking at home weren't great, but they were something."

We sit quietly for a few minutes. "Do you think, when you went outside to check for fallout . . ."

"I'll be fine, Lindsey. We agreed it's smart to monitor it. We did it as safely as we could think of by you moving to the far end so you were safe, then me making as small of an opening as possible."

"I'm not worried about me, Logan. What about you? You went out there." I motion to the end of the culvert. "Did you get radiated?"

"Hey, hey. Let's not worry about that today. I took precautions. Made sure to cover myself with one of your emergency blankets. I'm sure it'll be fine. I'll be fine."

I want to argue. I'm not sure he'll be fine. And he reused the blanket. Did he get the dust on him when he covered himself with it the second time he went out? But he's right, I can't really worry about it today. "I guess I'm going to go back to sleep for a while."

"Might as well. At least we'll be well rested when we start our trip again."

"I guess. We'll need the rest since we'll be walking."

"Maybe not. I have a small hope I can get the bikes going. The kick-starters are such simple mechanisms, it's possible they weren't damaged."

"We'll see."

Chapter 30

Sylvia

Tuesday, Day 13
Railroad Tunnel
Between Shoshoni and Thermopolis, Wyoming

"Do we get to leave today? Do we get to leave today? Do we get to leave today?" Naomi asks, bouncing up and down.

"Naomi, enough," Rey cautions. "Yes, we've told you, we're going to leave today. We think it's safe now to start walking again."

"Good, Daddy. I'm ready to walk. It's boring and dark in this tunnel. Walking will be much better. You think, if we walk today and maybe tomorrow, we'll get to your friend's house?"

"No, munchkin. I don't think we'll be there tomorrow. We'll have to walk for many days. My friend's house is a long way. We'll even need to keep walking after Sylvia and Sabrina get to their mom's house."

"Okay, at least we get to leave today."

Though the rest of us contain it a little better, we're all excited to get out of here. The tunnel long ago lost its novelty, and since we don't have an outhouse nearby, it's really starting to smell in here. Seriously nasty.

We probably could've left yesterday. Our little fallout tester plate hasn't shown us anything indicating nuclear fallout. But to be safe, we stayed an extra day. We know there's at least one more tunnel on the tracks, visible from the mouth of the tunnel. After that, we're not sure. There may be some rock alcoves, which wouldn't provide nearly the protection we have in our dark, dank tunnel.

Within the hour, we've eaten, packed, and are on our way. We start off strong, but it doesn't last. Two days of inactivity haven't done us any good. And the Hoffmanns spent a couple of additional days at the campground before we met them.

Our goal today . . . well, we don't really have one. Just putting one foot in front of the other and working our way toward the town of Thermopolis is all we're trying for. We talked about it, and we think it's likely going to be two days before we get there—or two nights would be more accurate. I think Kim has a little hope life will be normal in Thermopolis and she'll be able to find a hotel and get a bath. Maybe even enjoy some time at the hot springs.

I have to admit, I too hope the state park is open and the hot springs are available. That would be heavenly. I suspect, though, the power outages took that offline. And now, with our concern over an EMP, things could be really bad. I could be wrong, maybe it's some sort of gravity-fed system and will be working. And maybe there wasn't an EMP or whatever. Maybe our phones are just dead. A couple of days and we'll find out.

Chapter 31

Mollie

Tuesday, Day 13
Bakerville, Wyoming

We've dodged a bullet. Two days since the alerts, and what we're now sure was an electromagnetic pulse, but no fallout. We've tested with the little keychain nuke alerts, the homemade Kearney Fallout Meters Malcolm and I made, and the strange Geiger counter thing.

We freaked out a little when the Geiger counter needle moved. But reading the instructions, we're confident it was for background radiation only—the kind always around.

Getting out of the basement is today's big event. We're ready—more than ready. There were several times having so many people in close quarters became an issue. Lots of little spats and snide comments were heard, especially among families.

There was also some wonderful camaraderie. We played cards and board games, sang songs, David Hammer led a daily Bible study, and there were even several rousing games of charades.

It wasn't all fun and games. We continued to work on our necessary projects. We waxed the cheese Jake bought on his crazy shopping trips. It's now stored in the root cellar. Since there wasn't fallout, Deanne spearheaded food preservation and continued to can and dehydrate using the outdoor kitchen. Because of my difficulties with stairs, I wasn't able to help with any of the aboveground duties, but I still found things to keep myself busy.

Yesterday, even with the fear of possible fallout, a trip was made to Lydia and the children's house. Leo was right; there was a treasure trove of booze and assorted drugs, along with several other things that may be useful to the community. We inventoried and stored it, after they made a quick stop to talk with Deputy Fred about what was found. The items in the house leave little doubt of a burglary ring. But it doesn't look like a second gang.

"So . . . Mollie," Evan says while we're having a small group meeting, "tell me again the names of the guys with Dan Morse."

"The ones who attacked us?" I ask, even though I'm sure it's who he means.

"Yeah, those guys. Can you remember?"

Can I remember? I'll never forget. I still see and hear them in my dreams. Even though Morse tends to morph into someone else—Brad Quinton, a man from my past who recently contacted me again—the other two always stay the same.

"Yes, I remember. Dan Morse called them Bo and Sanders."

Evan nods, Bill and Jake both shake their head, and Leo says, "You were right, Evan."

"What's going on?" I ask. "Evan's right about what?"

"Seems Lydia may have been involved with Dan Morse and his crew," Jake says quietly. "Evan noticed some similarities with the stuff at her place compared to the stuff at Dan's place. Leo talked with Lydia's oldest boy. Several guys would come around with his Uncle Brandon. Uncle Brandon fits the description you gave of Bo, the one you called 'the dirty hippy.' Leo asked the boy and he said they call him Uncle Brandon, but his friends call him a different name . . . to go with his last name Bowman. They call him Bo."

I can feel the color draining from my face. "Oh. Are we . . . does Lydia know?"

Everyone shakes their head, as Jake says, "As far as we know, Lydia and the children don't know about the . . . incident."

"The incident. You mean when they attacked us? When my girls and I fought for our lives? And my daughter was shot in the process?" I say between clenched teeth.

Evan clears his throat. "Right. We don't think they know about it. Lydia—she's not really coherent for us to talk with. And we have no intention of telling her anyway. As far as I'm concerned, she doesn't need to know now. Maybe at a future time when she's sober."

I shake my head. Great. Who would've thought quiet Bakerville could be the headquarters of a criminal enterprise? And those poor kids, to be living in the conditions they were and to be surrounded by that.

"What does Deputy Fred plan to do with Lydia?" I ask.

"Nothing right now. Someone will talk to her when she sobers up."

"Someone?"

"Yeah, he's deputizing a few former LEOs in Bakerville. We'll have a small force until things can straighten out."

"You?"

"He asked. I passed."

"I passed also," Bill volunteers.

"Really? Why's that?"

A look passes between them, one I can't decipher. Evan shrugs and says, "Fred found a couple of good guys. We weren't needed. Anyway, we thought you should know about Lydia. Everyone's excited to go home today. Doris is ready to be out of the safe room and sleeping in our own bed tonight. Not that she isn't, that we aren't, incredibly grateful to have been able to stay here while we had the threat of attack, but . . . "

His stammering makes me smile. "I totally get it, Evan. A fold-out bunk in a little room isn't the same as a comfy king bed. She'll probably heal much faster at home."

"Yes, that's what she says. Thanks for the wheelchair. It'll make things much easier for her."

"Sure. I'm glad we had it. My dad only used it for a couple of months before he passed. What's our cutoff time again?"

"3:00 pm," Jake answers. "No evidence of fallout by then, and everyone will disperse . . . except Belinda's family. They'll stay to help with Lydia and make sure Katie's okay. Tammy's going to head out and check on things at the community center and pick up stuff from their house. Bill and I are going to ride along."

Jake gives me a look telling me not to argue. We've already discussed it, and even though I don't like it, I know he wants to go with her. Me . . . I just want him to stay here.

Please, Lord, please help me to be strong. You are my refuge, my fortress. Your faithfulness is my shield, my rampart.

I give a slight nod and attempt a smile. "Sure, sounds like a plan."

"You going to hang out down here until we're ready for lunch?" Jake asks.

"I suppose. I know you'd like me to wait until closer to our deadline before going upstairs."

"I would, honey. We're probably definitely past the crisis, but you're still moving pretty slow, so . . ."

"Sure, I get it."

"I'll help you get things ready," Bill says to Jake. "Then, if you'd like, I'll come back down and escort Mollie upstairs."

"Oh . . . escort, huh?" I laugh. "It's a date, Grandmaster Shane."

Jake and Evan both shake their heads, and Leo gives a shrug as they head up the stairs. I hobble back to the storage section where I have a chair by the shelves. I'm able to sit and organize the lower shelving while I'm still confined to the basement. Only a few more hours and I'll be set free.

Once the neighbors head home, we'll move the livestock out of the shop and back to their regular housing this evening. The mystery cow I noticed the day we were coming underground turned out to be a newly purchased addition for David Hammer's place.

He was able to do a little trading with a small dairyman nearby and was bringing her home the morning of the alert. She's only a week or so from calving. I agreed to help them learn how to milk—even though I've only milked a cow one time, over forty years ago, when visiting a relative of my dad's. Hopefully, it'll be similar to milking goats. Only bigger. I sure hope she's an easy milker. Some of my goats . . . they're on the wild side.

While the rest of our guests are already upstairs or outside, Doris is still in the sick room, along with Madison and Katie. Belinda insisted they wait until the appointed time to be released. Three o'clock is when everyone has agreed to disperse, but we're having a pizza party at 1:30—a celebration of sorts.

Madison and Emma will be staying at our place, joining Keith, Lois, and Karen in the bunkhouse. Lois and Karen are tickled to have baby Emma to help care for while Madison regains her strength. Keith . . . not so much. His son, Tate, reminded him it'd be good practice for when our shared grandchild arrives after the New Year.

Katie's doing much better. While she still has a long road ahead of her, we're confident she's going to make a full recovery. Belinda has her up, taking short walks, and things are looking good. She'll be moving back to her downstairs bedroom.

Chatting earlier, Belinda brought up Lydia and her children. When Jake and the guys found her, she was drunk out of her mind and had OD'd on what was believed to be prescription pain pills combined with alcohol. Belinda isn't sure she would've survived if her son hadn't flagged them down. I shudder to think of those three children alone.

Lydia's doing better but not great. She's still pretty much out of it, spending most of her time sleeping.

"So, Mollie, you know there's little doubt Lydia's an addict, right?"

"I figured, from what you've said."

"Mm-hmm." Belinda nods. "She's still a little lethargic from the overdose and all, but I suspect to start seeing some serious signs of withdrawal at any time. I'm concerned, if things get bad . . . well, one of the things my mom's bringing back is . . . well, it's something like a straitjacket."

Chapter 32

Mollie

Tuesday, Day 13
Bakerville, Wyoming

My eyes must have bugged out of my head at the mention of a straitjacket.

"Yeah, Mollie, it sounds extreme . . . and it is. But she could be a danger to herself and others. My mom is also going to talk with Kelley. Kelley has more experience with this than I do. We might want to see if she could handle Lydia at her house. In the meantime, we'll keep her in the safe room. Mom and I will switch off caring for her, and Leo might take the occasional shift also. I was hoping you would help us as needed with Katie."

"Yes, of course. Maybe Kelley will have some good suggestions if she can't take Lydia."

"She might. She may also have medication to help ease her symptoms. That's not something I stocked."

"But you stocked a straitjacket?" I say with a laugh.

"Hey . . . a girl has to have her priorities." She winks.

What circumstance, other than the one we're faced with, would Belinda decide she should stock a straitjacket in her medical preps? Because of her late husband and his addiction and abuse issues? I wonder what Belinda will think about the newest information of Lydia being involved with Dan Morse and his gang of thieves.

"How are you, Belinda?" I ask.

"Oh . . . I'm okay, I guess. Mom and I have been talking with Madison. That helps, we're all hurting. Doris, she's hurting too . . . you know, not knowing about her children. She figures her daughter in Germany is fine, but Lindsey, the one living in California . . . " Belinda shakes her head. "I know Doris fears the worst. In some ways, she has it worse than we do—than Mom, Madison, or I. At least we know. We know our husbands are dead, my dad is dead."

I nod. While all of my children are here—*thank you, Jesus*—Jake's parents are worried about their younger son. Robert, his wife, and two children live in California. We pray they're doing okay, but not knowing is hard.

After a moment or two, Belinda says, "I guess, losing Terry, it probably seems like I should be glad he's dead. He wasn't much of a husband with cheating and drinking and the abuse. But it's still hard. Hard not to think about the good times, when he was sober. When he worked at being sober . . . not just being sober but trying to change, trying to make a good life for us. Those are the times I miss. Anyway, Mom and I will be fine. We'll give TJ as good of a life as we can under these new circumstances. We're all he has left, you know, so . . . we'll be fine."

"We're praying for you. All of us. I know you haven't been able to join the services David's done the last few days, but we lift you up in prayer."

Belinda shrugs and goes back to the safe room.

While I'm working on the shelving and cabinets—never the most exciting job—I spend a lot of time thinking about our plight. The new information about Lydia, will this cause new troubles? She had to know what they were up to, based on the stuff found in her house. Those poor kids. How long have they been living in this situation?

"Hey," Master Shane interrupts my pondering. "Jake says the fire's going, if you're ready to do your thing. Are you ready for our exciting date of walking up the stairs?"

"Thank you, Master. I think I'm about ready to ditch these crutches. Sure wish Belinda would agree." I stand up too fast, and my stomach and head suddenly revolt. I reach out for the shelving to get my balance.

It's been over a week since I got my mild concussion. The headaches are better, but I still have trouble with dizziness and my stomach not being quite right. Belinda thinks it should only be another day or two and I'll be fine. Good thing.

"You okay?"

"Mm-hmm. Just stood up too fast. Do you mind knocking on the safe room door? Belinda said to let her know when it was time for lunch. Can you tell her it'll be half an hour or so? She's going to release Madison and Doris to join us."

"Sure. Is Lydia in there with them?"

"Yes, now that she's cleaned up and not vomiting. Belinda moved her in there when everyone else was spreading out today."

Bill has a hard look on his face. I guess we both think the situation with Lydia might be trouble. He knocks on the door and updates Belinda before walking back over to me, then we start our trek up the stairs.

"So, Mollie, a pizza party is a good idea. You wouldn't believe how excited everyone is over it."

"I think what they're excited over is getting out of the basement. The pizza is just a bonus."

"Still, good idea."

"You all getting settled into your new lodging?"

"Yes, everything that needs to go in there is in the trailer, and Jake's putting some of the other stuff I brought in different spots. Art seems like a nice guy. He even offered me the bedroom since he gets up so early to do chores. Said he doesn't mind turning the dining room table into a bed every night," Bill says with a laugh. "I finally convinced him I'd be getting up early also. He's taking the bottom bunk, and I'm taking the top."

Art's staying in the nineteen-foot travel trailer Leo purchased when they were on a supply run. The trailer has a bedroom, of sorts, at the back with a double bed on bottom and a single on top. A curtain separates the small area from the rest of the small space.

Inside the bedroom, there's just enough room to walk and get into the beds. I hope Bill remembers where he is and doesn't sit up too quickly and bonk his head.

"Art has really taken to farm life," I say with a smile. "He wasn't always so . . . ambitious. I hate to say this, but the end of the world has been good for him."

"He pretty much told me the same thing. Aaron's happy with his space too. He and Leo really seem to get along, so he's okay rooming with him. Smart of Leo to buy the motorhome and travel trailer. Of course, I half think Aaron will be looking for the preacher before too long. He and Laurie, they've known each other forever. Only makes sense for them to get married."

"I heard they met at Taekwondo, that right?"

"Yep. She was in a few years before Aaron started. He was . . . eleven, I guess. She was fifteen and an upper green belt. He was a scrawny little thing, and she took a special interest in him. Not a romantic interest, but just to help him out. There wasn't even a hint they might be more than friends until after he finished high school. The plan was to wait until she finished college. She's got one more year to go. She worked for a few years as a dental assistant before heading to the university. But now . . . don't think they'll wait much longer."

"I noticed they wear matching rings. Promise rings?"

"Something like that. Kind of a cross between promise rings and purity rings."

"Ah, I wondered. I thought she was staying with him while she's here for the summer?"

"No, she was staying with his parents. He was at his apartment. They both stayed in Wesley when the rest of the family went to Wisconsin. I know Aaron's concerned with the family being separated while all this is happening. At least Aaron's folks are probably okay at his sister's house. So it's good you had the bunkhouse space available for her."

"Yes, she seems happy with staying in the bunkhouse loft, even with the baby in there and having to climb a ladder to get to her bed."

"I don't think she minds. Did she tell you about the trouble she had in Wesley?"

"No . . ."

"Well, I'm sure she will. Let's just say, you and her have things in common. Thankfully, you both have training to defend yourself. Well, here you are. Looks like your kitchen's already going full bore. You probably could've stayed downstairs and let everyone else handle it."

He's right. The kitchen is full. Two of my daughters and their in-laws are working away. As I step into the great room, Angela and Gavin are just walking in from outside.

"Hey, Mom. You look like you could use a chair. Let me help you get up on one of the bar stools. You can supervise from there," Angela says with a laugh. "Gavin, you want to sit by GrandMo and help her supervise?"

The pizza for today's festivities consists of both store-bought and homemade pizzas. Yesterday, Jake was able to get our small pulley-style generator running and charge the freezers for a while. Likewise, each of the neighbors with a generator and freezers still holding food went home and took care of theirs.

Generators and other backup systems are fairly common in Bakerville. Our community often finds itself without power due to winter storms or something happening with the lines. Earlier in the spring we had daily outages, which the power company attributed to pelicans flying into the lines. I know, Wyoming isn't a state people think of as having pelicans. We do.

The American white pelican summers here, and apparently, when they're sleeping on the river, the coyotes scare them into flight, causing the outages. At least that's the electric company's story, and they stuck with it.

The buddy system was employed, with no one going alone to check on their homes and everyone carrying a nuke alert. Even so, the pizzas and a few other things were starting to look less than stellar. Last night Jake inventoried what food we have needing to be used, so we're making another half dozen pizzas from scratch and adding in things from Tate's Schwan's truck acquisition, a deal he made when trading some of our goods for an almost full truck. And for dessert we're having ice cream treats, also from the Schwan's truck and in desperate need of needing to be consumed.

Even though we know the small generator works, we haven't tried the larger one or any of the solar systems. Jake thinks it'll be fine. Malcolm made a point of saying he's sure it won't work. I'm torn. Maybe we'll try it tomorrow.

Chapter 33

Lindsey

Thursday, Day 15
California

We're finally crawling out of our hole! Today is Independence Day. I don't think I've ever had a greater feeling of freedom. Goodbye, stinky rathole.

Logan pulled the motorcycles out. Under his strict orders, I'm still inside the pigsty, watching as he tries the bikes.

I let out a hoot when his starts up. "You were right!"

He gives me a smile as he moves to my bike. It sputters but won't catch.

"Not good," I say, shaking my head, doing my best not to cry.

Logan chews his lip and tries again. No dice.

"We're going to have to leave so much stuff behind if we have to share a bike." I'm still gulping back a sob.

"Let me work on it." Logan rolls the bike back into the culvert.

"In here?" I ask, stepping aside so he and the bike can get in.

"Radiation."

"Oh, yeah. Good thinking."

Before he starts on the bike, he moves our toilet buckets. With one end of the culvert open and the buckets out, it smells slightly better. Not much, but marginally.

After twenty tense minutes, Logan says, "I don't know, Lindsey. I just can't figure out what's wrong with it . . . well, other than thinking the EMP fried it. I guess that must be it."

"I hate to lose all our stuff, but I guess we can scrounge things up along the way. It'll be better than walking."

"Yeah. I wonder . . . " He stops talking and has "the look," the one he gets when he's processing something. I think of this as his

169

computer look. The data is flowing through his brain, and he's getting ready to spit out the results. I wait it out.

"Maybe the old truck will run. We could take it."

"The old truck?"

"You know." He points up to the old Toyota parked above us.

"Ick. Do you remember the inside of the truck? Nasty. Plus, should I remind you, that *taking* a truck is called stealing?"

"You'd rather walk? Or leave our few supplies behind?"

"No." I sigh. "I don't want to walk, and we need everything we have. We're already low on food. Why do you think it'll start? One of the things I know about EMPs is they take out cars."

"One of the things we *think* we know about EMPs is they take out cars. Do you know for sure? Besides, the truck is older than dirt. It should be about as low tech as our bikes."

"You mean, as low tech as the bike that doesn't run?"

"Touché, darling. Wait here while I go check it out," he says, grabbing a fuel can to take along.

In less than five minutes, the truck fires up and Logan lets out a whoop. Even though I don't want to ride in that filthy thing, I can't help but smile. Minutes later, he's popping his head back in our shelter.

"Your chariot awaits."

"Well done, my prince. So, we just going to leave the bikes here?"

"Uh . . . no. I'm going to take the front wheel off your bike and strap it down in the bed of the pickup. It's a full-size bed, so it should fit. Might have to leave the tailgate down. My bike will ride in the trailer, no problem."

"You have straps?"

"We'll use the stuff the guy had holding his garbage in place. And I have a few bungees. I think it'll be okay. Give me a little bit to get it all together, and we'll get started. You mind unloading your bike?"

Twenty minutes later, we're in this classy Toyota. Both bikes fit okay, but Logan has wished several times for a better way to secure them. They're bouncing around more than he likes. We have enough fuel salvaged for the bikes to be able to keep going until we find some vehicles we can vandalize and take fuel from. I don't think I'll ever get used to the thieving.

Leaving our shelter, there's a fine dust all around. Radiation. How much have our bodies absorbed? After about an hour on the road, the dust seems to disappear. We think we're out of the fallout area now—

hopefully we won't go back into it. We have no idea where the bombs hit. Were other cities targeted? Surely they must have been, but where?

Even though we think traveling at night might be safer so we avoid people, we decide traveling during the daytime will help us look for fallout. We know it's not a foolproof plan, the fallout could be so light we wouldn't see it, but it's the best option we have.

"Ready to call it a day, Linds?"

"I am. Sitting around not doing anything has made me tired."

"Let's start looking for a place to spend the night. Grab the map out of the glove box and see if you can find something that looks good."

The extremely well-used map is tattered with a hole in the middle. I get my bearings and look ahead.

"How about a state park?"

"Sounds almost decadent after our last accommodations."

"No kidding. It's not far. Maybe fifteen miles. Goose Lake State Park on the Oregon–California state line."

We ride in silence until he says, "We almost there?"

I take a look at the map. "Should be the next left road, 1-19. Then it's down a mile or so."

We reach the road and he slows for the left turn.

"Shouldn't there be a sign or something?" I ask.

He shrugs. "Good thing we have a map."

"Yeah. Take a right on the next road."

Logan makes the turn and comes to a complete stop.

"I guess it's closed," he says, while we both stare at the row of tree stumps blocking the road.

"Maybe we can move them and go in?"

He gives me a look and a smile. "Turning into quite the anarchist, aren't you?"

"No. I just— "

"Stop your vehicle. You are surrounded. Put your hands where we can see them," a loud voice bellows, very reminiscent of my trainer at the academy.

Logan whispers an expletive while shifting the battered truck into reverse.

"What should we do? Can you get us out of here?"

"Don't think so. Backing up with this trailer . . . I don't know. I can do it, but we'll be sitting ducks. Let's be ready."

Logan has both hands on the steering wheel. I glance at the shotgun sitting next to my left leg. The rifle is on my right side, tucked between the seat and the door. Both are at the ready. Our backpacks, now filled with items we've decided we need to survive, are in the cab with us. We each have a pistol on our hip and one on our ankle, plus I have my little S&W revolver in a pocket holster nestled on the seat. Two more handguns are in our backpacks. We have firepower. Can we fight our way out?

I put my hands on the dash . . . for now.

"All right. Now turn it off. Remember, you are surrounded, so nothing funny. We're more than happy to just shoot you."

"Not yet, Lindsey," Logan says, apparently reading my mind. "Maybe they just want to know who we are. Let me do the talking. Keep your ball cap on. I don't want them to know you are . . . you, yet."

He doesn't want them to know I'm a female. I understand. Human trafficking was an issue before things went crazy in our world. I have little doubt it hasn't gone away, and it's likely worse now. People who may have been law abiding before, for fear of being caught, now have little reason not to act on their depraved impulses.

"We're sorry if we've bothered you," Logan says. "We'll be happy to just back out of here and leave you be. Okay?"

"Why are you here?"

"Just looking for a place to camp . . . my . . . brother and I . . . that's all. We can find someplace down the road."

No answer for several moments, then a new voice says, "Where'd you come from?"

"We lived in San Jose. We left there on . . . uh, Saturday." Logan looks at me for confirmation. I give a slight nod, as he continues, "Yeah, Saturday morning. There was a fire. It looked like a bad one, so we got out."

"Any bombs there?"

"We don't know where the bombs went off. We were up in the wilderness a couple of hours outside Sac. We saw . . . " Logan chokes up a bit, then gathers his composure. "We saw two flashes of light, then two clouds. Mushroom clouds. We don't know for sure but think it was San Francisco and Sacramento. We've been holed up until this morning. We just want to get to our family's place."

"Can't say I'm surprised. Frisco and Sac both hit . . . yeah, sounds about right. I'd guess LA and San Diego too. Oh, and Seattle, they'd be targeted for sure. Plus lots of places back east, I'd suspect."

"Doesn't sound like they want to kill us, at least," I whisper to Logan.

He gives me a hopeful look and is opening his mouth to speak when the first guy says, "Why don't you two step on out so we can take a look at you. If you're armed, you should leave those things in your truck."

"Oops, maybe I was wrong," I whisper.

"Yeah, we're not unarming," Logan whispers back. To them, he says, "I'd love to meet you folks properly, but we're not unarming. How about you just let us back out of here? We won't bother you. Like I said, we just wanted to rest a bit and then get to our family. I'm going to start my truck up and back out. We'd appreciate it if you'd just let us go."

My hands are still on the dash; Logan's are on the steering wheel. He doesn't make any movement, giving them a moment to respond. I'm thinking through my actions if things start going bad. Without moving my head, I've been searching for the guys. There's a large tree on the right and a berm of some sort to the left with trees behind it.

"Logan," I whisper, "I'm pretty sure they're together and to my left, behind the slight knoll."

"Seems they might be. What do you think? Take off?"

Before I can answer, a new female voice says, "Oh, for Pete's sake. Just let them get out and we'll introduce ourselves like normal people. If they were a threat, do you think they'd just drive up here? Nope, they'd sneak around and . . . well, anyway."

Suddenly, there she is, to the right of the truck, rifle held across her arms in a nonthreatening manner. She's maybe in her midforties, wearing a brown and white patterned bandana as a headband to hold back her frizzy brown hair. She's a big woman. Not necessarily tall, but overweight. She's not exactly smiling but not scowling either.

"C'mon, guys. Step on out so they can see you. And you folks in the truck, go ahead and get out. You don't have to unarm but . . . well, let's be smart about this."

"Let's do it," I whisper to Logan.
"You sure?"
"Yeah, I trust her."

Chapter 34

Mollie

Tuesday, Day 15
Bakerville, Wyoming

Living back aboveground is great. I treasure waking up to the sun streaming in our bedroom window. Such a treat after sleeping in the dark storage room.

Malcolm, Tony, and TJ made a point of declaring, *"We are no longer hobbits,"* and then dancing around . . . looking very much like hobbits.

I hate to complain. I know how blessed we were only needing to stay downstairs for a couple of days as a precaution. No fallout means we can all get on with . . . well, with the business of surviving. Even without having radiation, things aren't all sunshine and roses on our homestead.

Many times, both day and night, Lydia will let out blood curdling screams. Our basement is nearly soundproof, but we'll still hear her wail if conditions are right. Poor Katie, back in her basement bedroom, hears it all. Lydia's in the straitjacket more often than not, secured in the safe room.

Tammy, Belinda, and even Kelley Hudson take turns staying with her. It was decided Leo wouldn't take shifts caring for Lydia. He started a shift, but she was behaving inappropriately toward him; grabbing him, trying to kiss him, even flashing her bare breasts at him. He ended up having Belinda take over.

Kelley believes Lydia has more issues than just detoxing. She may have a mental illness of some sort. She plans to spend time trying to diagnose her after the detoxing is completed.

Belinda, TJ, and Tammy are using the recreation room as a small apartment. The location works for caring for Lydia and Katie.

Unfortunately, it means TJ hears all of Lydia's outbursts. While his things are in the rec room, he's now sleeping on a camping cot upstairs in Malcolm's room.

Katie's healing well. I spend as much time with her as I can. Each day, a little more of my energetic and vibrant girl returns.

"Hey, Mom," Sarah says, setting little Andy on the ground. "Sissy, Lily, why don't you two take Andy into the office and play with the toys? You know, the box we set in there for you?"

"Okay, Sarah," Sissy says, giving her a sweet smile. From the first day, Andy and Sissy have really bonded with Sarah, choosing to follow her everywhere. Lily will sometimes join the little group, but only if Dodie isn't available. Lily loves my mother-in-law, even calling her grandma.

"Are they getting things done?" I ask Sarah, gesturing outside toward her camp trailer.

"Almost. It seemed kind of absurd to buy the camp trailer the morning after the airplane attacks. But now, I'm so glad we did. We've decided, once Lydia is well enough, we'll give her the bedroom and we'll take the futon in the living room."

"You think?" I ask.

"We do. It makes sense. The children are settling in, and Marc loves the top bunk, especially after we put the privacy curtain up. And with the railing Tate and Leo built, it's safe for him. Right now, Andy and Sissy are sleeping foot to foot in the bottom bunk. But one of them could sleep with Lydia in the queen-sized bed."

"And you think there will be enough privacy for you and Tate out in the living room?"

Sarah sighs. "Maybe not. Maybe we'll try it for a few days, and if it doesn't work, then we'll let Lydia and the children have the camp trailer. We'll find another space."

"There's still some time. Belinda thinks it'll be a while before Lydia's ready for anything other than short visits with the children. How'd the wall turn out?"

"Oh, it's nice! It was such a great idea. So smart of Tate," she says adoringly. "I never even considered adding a divider wall at the foot of the bed. I was worried it'd make the room too small, but it doesn't at all. It's more like a really large footboard. And it does give us a modicum of privacy."

"Kind of like Marc's curtain," I say.

"Exactly. Tony said Jake is bringing a bunk bed from someone's house?"

"Yes, the Styles. They were on vacation when this all started. They have the house next to Tony and Lily's house . . . or where their house was before it burned to the ground."

"So you're going to set the bunk bed in the loft room?"

"That's what we're thinking. I had a friend when I was in middle school and her brothers shared a room. The bunk bed was set up in the middle of the room and plywood was used to divide the space. They used it on one side of the bottom bunk and on the other side of the top bunk, giving each child a little privacy—or the feeling of privacy, anyway."

"I think it's a good idea, Mom. Tony doesn't really want to be too far from Lily right now anyway. Maybe later . . ."

"Yeah." I nod. "While they're grieving, it makes sense."

"And not just grieving for their mom, but for their dad also. I know . . . I guess we all suspect he won't make it back to them."

I change the subject. "Want some tea?"

"Peppermint?"

"Sure."

While I busy myself with putting the water on, Sarah says, "I'm so glad the solar system's working. When Jake first hooked it up and nothing happened, all I could think about was how rough things will be. We were spoiled coming here the day the power first went out. I was really scared to think . . . well, that we'd have to live like almost everyone else. I'm glad Jake only missed a wire. Do you think . . . does that make me selfish?"

"If you are, so am I. I thought the same things. Those were some tense moments for sure. Even though it's not a very large system, it'll make a huge difference in our comfort level. It is a bummer the large generator didn't survive the pulse. It was so convenient, having it set up to come on if the solar ran too low. We always assumed it would be affected by an EMP, but I still held out a little hope. We can get by without it, by using the small pull-start generators when needed. Thankfully, all of the solar systems survived except the one in the milking shed. So weird how it was affected, even smelling like burned wire, and the others were fine."

"And the washing machine. Losing it is a disappointment," Sarah says.

I stifle a sigh. "I know. At least the smaller, RV-style machines are still working. It does make washing more labor-intensive than my large machine, but it'll be a cake walk compared to washing everything by hand."

"But the machines are so small, Mom. Like you said, too small for washing jeans or bedding. So we'll still have to do those by hand. I'm not looking forward to using wash tubs and plunger-style agitators. I'm glad you bought them so we don't have to rub our clothes on rocks or something, but still."

I give a small laugh. "Yes, at least we don't have to take everything down to the creek and wash in cold water."

"You think others are doing that?"

"I . . . I'm not sure. Possibly."

We're both quiet for many minutes, lost in our own thoughts. Yes, we do have it very good here.

"Art said he thinks one of the hens wants to sit on eggs," Sarah says, changing the subject. "Jake told him how to mark some with a pencil. She's one of the small chickens, what do you call them?"

"Bantams."

"Yeah, the cute dark brown one with the furry feet."

"Clove. Her name is Clove. She hatches out chicks every year. Did Jake tell Art to give her six eggs and make her a nest in the dirt-floored shed?"

"Yes. And if a full-size one wants to sit— "

"Goes broody."

"Uh-huh, that. Then give the full-size up to fifteen, depending on how big she is. Doesn't sound like much of an exact science."

"Not too much," I agree. "But we'll welcome the new chicks. We'd like to try to get chickens or ducks set up at every house currently without poultry. That'll be a huge help on the food front."

As the tea kettle whistles, I limp over to the stove.

"What's Belinda say about your foot?"

"She's happy with it. The infection scare seems to have passed."

"Yeah, believe me, I heard about it."

"I'm sure you did." I give her a small smile. Belinda was less than happy with me a few days ago.

"She's hilarious, Mom. Going on about how she wanted to start you on some stronger antibiotics and you complaining about your stomach being a mess. Then you said, 'Let's slap some honey on it to heal it.' Oh, the way she says it, then follows with, 'Your mom is one of those weird hippie chicks,' it's just too funny."

I laugh a little at her impersonation of Belinda. "Yeah, but it worked. The Manuka honey made an almost immediate difference. Jake thought I was nuts, too, when I wanted to buy this crazy expensive honey from New Zealand as part of our medical supplies. When it arrived, he wanted to put it on his toast!"

"Tate would probably think the same. So it worked, but what now? You only have the one jar, right? Will local honey work as well?"

"We hope so. Several people in the community keep bees. I have quite a bit of research on local honey working as well as Manuka."

"Jake says there's a community meeting tonight and a dinner, in honor of the Fourth of July."

"Yes, Phil stopped by earlier to tell us. Deanne and Lois are making something to take."

"Should be fun," Sarah says with a slight smirk.

Chapter 35

Mollie

Thursday, Day 15
Bakerville, Wyoming

"Knock, knock." I lightly wrap on the doorframe of Katie's room. Katie is on the bed, dressed in sweats and a T-shirt, lounging on top of the covers. Leo is sitting on the chair beside her bed. He immediately stands when I step in.

"Leo, you can stay seated. I was just popping in to see if Katie needs anything or if she wanted to walk around. There's a dinner and community meeting this evening. Jake and I are going to go. You think you're up to it?"

"I'd like to, but I don't think so," she answers softly. "I'm glad you're here, though. We were . . . we were just talking about you."

"Oh?"

"Yeah . . . " Katie starts, but Leo puts his hand on her arm and says, "Uh . . . how about I go see if Jake's available? Katie and I wanted to talk with you two. Do you have a few minutes to wait?"

Hmm. Interesting. "Sure."

"I'll be right back."

"Here, Mom. Take the chair. Does Belinda know you're off your crutches?"

"Yes, I just have to be careful."

Katie nods, then starts asking me questions of no consequence about the homestead. I so want to ask what is going on but manage to hold my tongue. Patience is not my strong suit, so it's a definite struggle.

Leo soon returns, with Jake in tow. Questions mark Jake's face. I give a slight lift of my right shoulder as if to say, *I don't know, but I have my suspicions.* Jake gives a nod and tries to contain a smile.

Leo steps to the other side of the bed, then sits on the edge next to Katie.

"So, uh, thanks for joining us. We, uh . . . " Leo stammers.

"Leo, it's okay. I think they already know," Katie says quietly.

I try hard to look innocent.

"We don't really know," Jake says. "Go ahead, Leo."

"Yes . . . sir, uh, Jake. Mollie. I think you both know I love Katie more than anything. She's nothing short of amazing. And when I thought we might lose her . . . " He shakes his head, gulping in a breath. "But she's fine. She's going to make a full recovery. And I want, more than anything, for her to spend the rest of her life with me, as my wife. Can I . . . do I . . . will you give me your permission to marry her?"

The smile and love on Katie's face during Leo's stammering speech is adoring. Even now, looking from Jake to me, her entire face is lit up from the inside.

"Katie, this is what you want?" Jake asks.

"More than anything. I love him like cray-cray."

"Cray-cray . . . okay. Well, good then. Mollie? You look like you're about to bust wide open, so I guess you're on board."

I go to Katie for a hug. I'm crying; she's crying.

Finally, Jake says, "Yeah . . . Leo, welcome to the family."

Chapter 36

Mollie

Thursday, Day 15
Bakerville, Wyoming

While most of us go to the community center for the Fourth of July event, Leo, Alvin, and Dodie stay at the homestead with Katie. Tammy also stays to care for Lydia.

We quickly learn things in Bakerville vary from close to business as usual before the attacks, to desperate. We've had several deaths in our community, caused by lack of essential medications to suicides to a young boy dying from, what is believed to be, an allergic reaction, possibly from a bee sting. Without an autopsy, his family will never know what took his life.

Many people are now either out of or running low on food. Phil makes a point of welcoming everyone to the gathering, saying we're celebrating to acknowledge not only our good fortune of not having any radiation but also the Fourth of July, America's Independence. Even though we're cut off from the rest of the country, it's important to acknowledge we're still Americans.

There isn't a barbecue or fireworks, at least not the pyrotechnic kind. Still, there's a spectacular theatrical display.

We feast on pots of soup and loaves of homemade bread, brought by our family and a few others. I'm so glad we had food available because we discover just how bleak the situation is for some.

Before the nuke threat and the EMP was detonated, it was decided to empty the houses of people who were away when the attacks started—those who have little chance of making it back home. Whatever is found in the houses is inventoried and put toward the good of the community.

Deputy Fred put our friend Phil in charge of procuring—or as I think of it, stealing—these goods.

Fred agreed the useable items found in Lydia's house should go to the good of the community. There were a few things we set aside specifically for Lydia and her children, things that looked like heirlooms. We're not sure if they belong to Lydia or were part of the gang's booty. For now, we're erring on the side of caution. The one thing they didn't have much of at Lydia's house was food.

A few more families, including ours, were drafted to help in securing, storing, and inventorying the homes of community members who are gone and presumed unable to return anytime soon. Finding space for everything has been a challenge. Figuring out how to best meet the needs of everyone is the next challenge.

Bakerville isn't a town; we're a rural community. Our area, those who consider themselves part of the Bakerville community, is over forty square miles.

With the transportation issues, thanks to the EMP and a lack of fuel caused by the early attacks, it's a challenge to have one central location to meet and provide for people. Tonight's gathering has a turnout of about a tenth of the almost four hundred living in Bakerville. Well, we had almost four hundred before the attacks. I'm not sure how many are here now.

The low turnout is partly due to lack of communication and partly due to lack of transportation. Phil and a few others went around and invited people but couldn't get to everyone. Of the few attending, tempers are, understandably, frayed.

"Okay, people," Phil says, voice raised to try to contain the crowd. "That's enough. Let's bring it down a notch and make some plans."

"We need more than plans, Phil. We need food," one man cries out.

"I understand. Let's stick with the system we already have in place. If you need help today, go to Kelley. She'll keep track of it."

"She's going to write down on her little notepad how my family is starving? This soup and bread is the first meal we've had today. How do you think writing in a notebook is going to help?"

"Didn't she have your name on the list when this mess started? You said you were in good shape then but needed help wiring your generator to your well pump. Did she record the information and have someone there the next day?"

"Yeah, she did, but— "

"But you think this will be different? You think my wife is now unreliable?"

"That's not what I'm saying, Phil. We're just . . . we're hungry. My daughter is hungry. Do you know what it's like to have a hungry child?" With that, he breaks down, dropping his head as sobs wrack his body.

Phil goes to him and speaks quietly. The man soon nods and shakes Phil's hand.

Once again, Phil takes control of the meeting. "Friends, now is the time to come together. These last few days have been hard on many. With the threat of radiation passed, we can start making a difference. Okay, so let's follow the usual procedure. If you have an immediate need, see my wife. If you don't need anything and can offer to help others, see Sarah Garrett. If you need a little help but can offer assistance, see Mollie Caldwell."

I'm a new addition to this process. Originally, Doris was the one handling the people I now have. With Doris injured and immobile, I've taken over for her group. I don't expect my line to be very long, and Sarah's is likely to be even shorter. Kelley will have the bulk of the group.

"Phil, before we all had to hole up for the nuke strike that never happened . . . " A rumble goes through the crowd, relaying the general voice of "how ridiculous hiding out underground" had been. Yeah . . . I can't say I disagree, but you know, hindsight and all that.

Besides, we've heard a rumor from someone there were actual nuclear detonations. He heard it from someone else who heard it from someone else, so we don't really know.

"Anyhow, Phil . . . what about Mick Michaelson donating a cow? Is that still happening?"

"We're working on it. The problem is refrigeration. We need to figure out how we can get it processed and consumed before it spoils. If it were winter, we'd have a little leeway, but with summer . . . "

"How about a deer?" A female voice asks. "We could get a deer or two. They're not as big and we can take care of them before they spoil."

"My husband wanted to hunt," a lady I know from yoga at the community center says. "Phil told him to hold off. Said they had a plan and to wait on harvesting deer for now."

"That's right," Phil says with a nod. "We thought it would be smart to make sure we don't deplete the herds . . . you know, with the fawns still so young."

"How about a buck? They don't have fawns," someone scoffs, causing a spattering of laughter.

"True. And that's something to think about. Something else to think about is the issue with Chronic Wasting Disease."

"Zombie Deer? Who cares about that?" says the same guy who pointed out bucks don't have fawns. I look to see who it is. I can't see his face from where I am, but the voice is familiar. Maybe Jon Dawson, retired attorney and candidate for Prospector County Commissioner—at least, he was running before our world fell apart. I don't actually know him but do, of course, know *of* him.

"Right. That's what I thought too. Then I found out a little more about CWD. And frankly, Jon, it scared the bejesus out of me."

There's a new rumble through the crowd, displeased and mocking mainly, with a few people in agreement with Phil.

"As hungry as my family is," the man from before speaks up, "I have to agree with Phil on this one. I hunted the Thorofare last year, had my deer tested, and it came back positive. The CDC says not to eat deer testing positive, so the wife made me throw it all away."

"Sounds a little paranoid if you ask me," Jon Dawson says. "Just cook it really good and it won't be a problem. No problem at all."

Again, lots of responses and rumblings, mostly in agreement. Speaking very loudly, Phil says, "That's what I thought, too, but I recently found out that's not the case. Mollie? Kelley? Can you two tell us what you know about this?"

Oh, jeez. No. I don't want to speak to this crowd.

I look for Kelley. She's talking with a man and woman. She gives Phil a wave and shakes her head, returning to the lady she's speaking with. Jake nudges me and whispers, "Go on. They need to know."

Super.

"Uh, yeah. Sure," I raise my voice to be heard. "Phil's right. You can't kill this disease by cooking it out of the meat, can't freeze it out or use any chemicals on it either. That's one of the problems with Chronic Wasting Disease, there isn't a known way to fully eliminate it . . . which is why the recommendation from the CDC was to have your meat tested and dispose of it if it came back positive."

"Mollie, was it?" The way Dawson says my name makes me want to kick him in the teeth. *Oops.* That wasn't very nice of me.

I nod my response.

"Well, then, Mollie. Oh . . . *Mollie Caldwell*, I know who you are now." He smirks. "That might be all well and good to have deer tested and listen to the CDC, but I think we're a little beyond testing now, don't you?" He lets out a hearty, very fake chuckle. A few people join him.

I feel my face turning red.

I swallow hard and, with a quivering voice, say, "That is definitely a problem. We now don't have a way to test for Chronic Wasting Disease, so we won't know if a deer, elk, or moose we harvest is infected."

"So we eat a little tainted meat—big deal," the man standing next to Dawson says with a shrug. Dawson claps him on the back and physically turns away from me. He then says to Phil, "Move it on, Phil. This little girl's CWD is a nonissue."

What? Wait a minute. *Did he really just call me a little girl?*

Chapter 37

Mollie

Thursday, Day 15
Bakerville, Wyoming

I feel my eyes fill with tears. Jake's hand is suddenly warm on my shoulder. Supporting me? Or holding me back?

I blink rapidly and take a deep breath. I can't decide whether I'm angry or embarrassed. Anger suddenly wins out. I straighten my shoulders and pull myself up to my full five foot, two inches.

"Mr. Dawson," my voice comes out clear and strong, "Chronic Wasting Disease is not a nonissue. It has been found across our entire state. It's such a concern, Game and Fish was in the process of revising their management plan. I would think, as a candidate for County Commissioner, you'd be well aware of this threat to our wildlife."

He looks at me with fire in his eyes and starts to speak.

I talk over him, not yelling but loud enough to shut him up. "The reason the CDC recommended disposing of infected meat was because they don't know if Chronic Wasting Disease can jump to humans. You've heard of Mad Cow? Remember humans dying from it? It's pretty much the same disease. Personally, I'd rather not end up with a deadly brain disorder caused by eating infected meat, but that's just me.

"Maybe *you're* okay with the idea of not knowing who you are and needing your diapers changed. Totally your choice. And one more thing, Mr. Dawson, you may not be educated on CWD, but I am . . . this *little girl* is an amazing researcher. And if the thought of Chronic Wasting Disease doesn't concern you— " I shake my head " —that's fine. You're an adult and can make your own decisions."

The anger on his face doesn't carry to his voice. Instead, he's sickly sweet as he says, "Didn't mean to offend. I'm well aware of the irrational hype surrounding Chronic Wasting Disease. Most of us know it's just those PETA wackos and other antihunting groups trying to take our sport away with the media sensationalizing it all. But now, *Mollie*, we're not talking about a sport. We're talking about feeding hungry people."

Jake's hand tightens on my shoulder. PETA wackos . . . I don't even know what to say to this. It's not like Chronic Wasting and other prion diseases are some make believe ailments. Phil catches my eye and gives me a slight nod. *I'll take this*, he seems to be saying.

"Mollie is well aware of the need for food, Jon," Phil says in his rich, velvety smooth voice. "But she brings up a good point. There have not been cases of CWD jumping to humans, but if we were to start existing only on deer and they happened to be infected . . . well, we don't know what could happen. As she mentioned, Mad Cow is the cattle version of CWD, and humans did get it. People died from it. We're not saying don't harvest deer. We're saying, let's be smart about it. Let's put some guidelines into place before we start relying on venison. We have other options right now. Let's use those."

"Sure, sure, Phil," Jon uses his saccharine voice again. "I get what you're saying, what she's saying." He hooks a thumb in my direction.

I do my best not to glare at him.

"But hear me now, Hudson. It'll be a cold day before you or anyone else tries to tell me what I can do. I've played along with your little show of taking charge, but you try to push me on this and I'll . . . *we'll*— " he sweeps his arm to include a group standing near him " —make it clear you're not in control. The only reason you're the one facilitating anything is because I wasn't here for those early meetings. I'm a leader in this county, and there should be no doubt who people will choose to follow."

Phil smiles—sort of. A faint curve of the lips and the top row of teeth showing, while his eyes remain hard, unyielding.

"I have no problem with you taking things over, Jon. I didn't ask for this duty and am happy to pass it off to you or anyone else who wants it. Then I can focus on my wife, my family, and my close friends. No skin off my nose." He smiles larger, his white teeth a bold line against his black face. This time, it reaches his eyes. He begins to confidently move away.

There's a rumble throughout the crowd. The general consensus is Phil should continue as our de facto leader. Several people gather around him as he tries to make his way from the podium.

Even Jon Dawson's cronies seem to be opposed to Jon taking over. One of the guys standing closest to him whispers something, which Jon doesn't seem to agree with. The guy gives a hard jerk of his head. Jon, rather reluctantly in my opinion, nods.

"Now, Phil, there's no reason to be like that. We'll keep things as is . . . for now," Jon Dawson says loudly in the sickly sweet, condescending tone he seems so fond of.

Judge Isaiah Avery, now standing next to Phil, calls the group to order. I half wonder if he wishes he had his long-retired gavel to bang.

"All right, folks. I think we'll call it good for tonight. I understand tempers are a little short. We're all in a new situation, one which is causing all our nerves to fray. Let's meet up here again tomorrow, give everyone a chance to calm down. Let's also try to spread the word. Check on your neighbor and encourage them to come join the fun."

He pauses and dramatically raises his eyebrows and waves his arms. The tension is broken and several people chuckle.

"Seriously, we're going to have some announcements tomorrow night. Let's try to get the entire Bakerville community here. Carpool and conserve fuel. Ride your horse, your bicycle. We'll see you tomorrow at . . . " He turns to Phil and whispers something before finishing with, "See you at 5:00 pm. We'll share a meal again, then get on with business."

The group slowly disperses. Several people talk with Phil, and many make a point of talking to me, asking me more about CWD. The cronies continue to hang with Jon Dawson, who manages to look incredibly smug.

I want to punch him in the nose.

Whew. This anger. I'm so on edge today—the last several days. Dawson has just about pushed me over the brink.

I can finally break away to stand near Kelley and take down names for my group. Three people, that's what I have. Sarah has zero. Those who can help, already are.

We spend a few minutes assisting Kelley. There are several people out of food. Phil and Kelley make sure they go home with something to sustain their family until better plans can be made. Then we all head home.

As we're getting ready for bed, Jake and I are discussing the day—the meeting plus Katie and Leo's new engagement.

Out of the blue, Jake says, "Hey, Mollie. The day the missile alerts went off, before the alerts, you said you had something important you wanted to talk with me about. We never had a chance."

Oh . . . while I hadn't forgot—no way could I forget—I'd decided to let it go. At least for now. Obviously, in this new world we are living, I'm no longer receiving threatening phone calls from Brad Quinton, and the secrets of my past can stay a secret. Sure, I still feel a nagging in my conscience and know I'll need to confess. Someday. Not today. Not now when things are so difficult.

"We didn't. But it's okay. Things sort of . . . resolved."

"Okay." He looks skeptical. "So it wasn't something important?"

"It's fine, Jake. Truly."

"Fine—the type of fine meaning it's anything but fine?" His tone is serious but he gives me a wink, softening the delivery. I have a history of declaring things are fine but not meaning it. That was one of our issues during the time we nearly divorced. Learning how to communicate and sharing what is in my heart hasn't been easy.

I smile as best I can. "Not that kind of fine," a lie I try to deliver convincingly. "We're okay. I love you, Jake."

"I love you too. But you've been a little different since you got home. Thought maybe it was from what happened on the way, getting hurt and then having to kill those guys attacking Madison."

"Sure. That was bad— "

"I know, honey. Then, with Dan Morse attacking you all and having to kill them, you've been through a lot. The girls have been through a lot."

"You too. You were in the same situation when you rescued Angela and Doris. We don't really talk about it, about how we're feeling, to each other. We probably should."

"Yeah. Truthfully, my mind tells me I should feel worse about killing a guy. But I'd do it again. If it meant protecting Angela—any of you—I wouldn't hesitate."

"I feel the same. I just pray it's the end of it and we won't encounter that kind of violence again."

Please, Lord, make it so.

Chapter 38

Sylvia

Friday, Day 16
Thermopolis, Wyoming

Much to our disappointment, Thermopolis, just like Shoshoni, is nonfunctioning. And even worse, our fears have been confirmed. It is widely believed we've been hit by an electromagnetic pulse. No one really knows for sure, since there haven't been any announcements or confirmation from the government. But no one's phone will turn on, most cars won't start, and some people even lost their generators and solar systems.

Thermopolis is different from Shoshoni; they didn't escort us through town. Instead, they're letting us camp at the state park. And we've even been able to use the hot springs to clean up. Not in the soaking pools, unfortunately, but we were each allowed a gallon jug of the hot water and a private space for a sponge bath. It was pretty amazing.

In addition to the bathing water, we've been given fresh drinking water. They even asked us if we needed medical attention, which none of us are in need of. I was very happy to find a clothing exchange.

With all of the walking and our limited food, my pants aren't fitting right. Sabrina notched my belt so I could tighten it, but it's already in need of another. I guess walking across the state is a great weight-loss program. I exchanged my worn, dirty, size sixteen jeans for a slightly more worn but clean size twelve pair. They're a little tight, but after a few more days of walking, they'll probably be fine. I kept the sweats and shorts I have, since they each have a drawstring and work okay. Who would've thought I'd ever be on the end-of-the-world diet?

One thing we weren't offered was food.

They made it very clear we could camp here, overnight only, and clean up, but there would be no food available. Personally, I was very grateful for the hospitality. So was Sabrina. Kim . . . yeah, not so much. She didn't throw one of her famous fits, but she wasn't very gracious about it.

"It's beautiful here," Sabrina says with a sigh as we're all sitting and relaxing. "It's so much nicer camping on the lawn than the rocks and railroad track."

"For sure. We're fortunate they're letting us stay. I'm pretty impressed with how well they have things set up. It's kind of like a real campground."

"Yeah, at least it's not as crowded as the Boysen Reservoir campground."

I shrug. "Limiting how long people can stay probably keeps the numbers manageable."

"Sounds like they had a bit of a celebration yesterday, you know, for July Fourth. I can't believe we forgot about it. Not that we'd have been able to do much, but maybe we could have at least acknowledged it."

"Kim and Rey didn't seem too concerned when they realized we forgot," I say.

We're relaxing and enjoying the late afternoon. I'm having a cigarette, only my second one today. Kim hasn't asked for one since we entered the tunnel. I've opened up the carton and have two cigarettes left from the first pack in it. I did ask about buying cigarettes at the clothing exchange. The lady in charge said she didn't think there were any available.

Even with our location, in what is essentially a treed park on the edge of town, we have a nice view of the mountains in the distance. Like Sabrina, I'm looking forward to watching this evening's sunset. I was surprised when I found myself wishing to see it when we were in the canyon. Definitely not something I'd normally care about.

I've just ground out my cigarette and added it to my water bottle ashtray, a new one I've started after finding a trash can at the edge of camp for my previous bottle, when we hear, *"Hey, what do you think you're doing?"*

The yell, while not right near us, is loud enough to carry clearly.

The same voice says, *"Get back! You grab your friends and get back."*

"Hey, I don't know what you're talking about," a new voice says.

"You! I'm talking about you and your friends. Those two, circling around . . . what are you doing? Are you trying to flank me? Stop. Now. Put your hands where I can see them. Rodger! Rodger! I need help here!"

A shot rings out, followed by several more. I throw myself on to my stomach, pulling Nicole with me. Out of the corner of my eye, I detect Sabrina doing the same with little Naomi.

"On the ground," Rey hisses to Kim, while pulling Nate to him. "Kim, *now*. You know what to do."

Rey is belly crawling while dragging Nate toward a tree.

"Sabrina," I whisper, gesturing to Rey while starting the same procedure with Nicole. We're not all going to fit behind the tree, but if we can get the children back there . . .

More shots, more yelling. Pandemonium erupts as people are running, crying, screaming.

The tree is slightly elevated from where our tent is. Kim reaches it first and helps Nate.

"Keep going. Stay low. This hill will help as a barrier. Go to the trees over there," Kim instructs.

Rey turns and grabs for Naomi, dragging her the rest of the way. "Kim, take her. Go with Nate. Nicole, you're almost here—let's go. Okay, good. Keep going. Follow your mom. Sabrina, Sylvia . . . you good?"

Once we're over the slight incline, Sabrina pulls her sidearm. I follow suit.

"I'm good, Rey," Sabrina says. "Go with your family. I'm going to make it to the tree just over there, use it for cover, and protect our stuff . . . we wouldn't want someone to take advantage of the situation. Sylvia, can you do the same at this tree?"

How does Sabrina sound so calm? I let out a raggedy breath. "Okay, yes."

"Rey, you protect your family," Sabrina says, while handing him the gun from her ankle holster. We'd talked about letting him carry the .22 he used at the tunnel, but it just didn't feel quite right. He handled it fine and we trust him—it's Kim we aren't so sure about. After her original freak-out over our weapons, she hasn't said anything further. Still . . .

Rey takes the weapon, checks it, and nods, then makes his way toward his family.

Sabrina low crawls to the next tree. Man, she's quick. I guess all the exercising she does has paid off.

The shooting and yelling finally stops. But the crying out in fear and pain continues.

Sabrina motions me to stay put. Like I had any plans of moving.

"Rodger? You clear? Bennett's down," A new voice calls out.

"*I'm hit. Where's the medical team? Where's the sheriff?*"

"*On their way, buddy, on their way.*" Then louder, "*Civilians, Civilians, if you are camping, you are to remain where you are. The threat has been eliminated. You are safe. If you or a loved one requires medical care, sit tight. Help is on the way. If you are armed, holster your weapon or put it on the ground. I repeat. Holster your weapon immediately. An unholstered weapon will be considered a threat and will be responded to as such.*"

I catch Sabrina's attention and dramatically reholster my sidearm. She shakes her head. I motion again for her to do it. She finally nods and puts it away. I turn to look for Rey. He's crouched next to a tree a hundred yards away. He tucks the pistol into his pants and gives me a thumbs up, which I return.

From our slightly elevated vantage point, we're able to clearly see several people on horseback appear, followed by a horse pulling a dilapidated wooden wagon with a big red cross painted on the side. The ambulance?

It's nearly an hour later before the rescue crew gets to us. We're allowed back in our camp and asked about injuries. Naomi shows them her elbow and knee, both were scraped while crawling away. The very kind nurse gives her a Snoopy Band-Aid for each. We discover half a dozen are dead, including two deputy sheriffs—one was Rodger and the other Bennett, probably the first voice we heard who was trying to get the situation under control—and a bystander along with the three instigators. No one seems to know what started the altercation.

"So . . . you think we should stay here?" Rey asks after the rescue crew leaves.

"I'm wondering also. What do you all think?" I ask.

Kim, first to respond, says, "I don't think it's safe here. Too many people and now everyone's sure to be on edge."

"I agree," Rey says. "Unfortunately, we're coming up on dark. I don't think we have time to break camp, move to a new spot, and get set back up before dark. And where would that new spot be? Out of town? How many miles would we need to walk to find an area we can camp?"

"We'd have to walk several miles out of town," Sabrina says, pulling out one of the Wyoming Gazetteer pages. "Look. We're here. Here's the road we need to follow out of town. The first patch of BLM is at least six, seven miles."

"So let's just camp wherever we can once we're out of town," Kim says.

I shudder, remembering waking up to the farmer and his shotgun when we did that before. "Not a good idea."

"No. No way," Sabrina says at the same time.

"Why not?" Kim asks.

"Private property, honey," Rey says. "How'd you like someone camping in your yard?"

"Seriously? In times like these, people shouldn't be worrying about their own stuff, they should be helping take care of those less fortunate."

Rey shakes his head while Kim pouts. "So we're stuck here?"

"I think so, for tonight. We'll just need to continue our guard duty. I know we were all looking forward to an uninterrupted sleep tonight, but now . . . " Sabrina shrugs.

"Let's do it," Rey says. "What time do we want to leave? 6:30? So we'll do 9:00 to midnight, midnight to 3:00, and 3:00 to 6:00. I'll take midnight to 3:00. You two decide which shift you want, sound good?"

"You want first watch, Sylvia?" Sabrina asks.

"Yeah, sure."

"Okay, then. We should get to bed," Rey says. "Sabrina, you going to read to us tonight?"

I'm momentarily shocked he's asking. Since the night in the tunnel, Sabrina has read a Psalm each night. I didn't think anyone, other than Naomi, was showing much interest.

"I'd be happy to," Sabrina responds, pulling out her little travel Bible. "And I was thinking, now that we know for sure what day it is, I have an idea to help us keep track."

"Oh?" Rey asks.

"Mm-hmm. What if each morning, when we start walking, I read a Proverb? The book of Proverbs is divided into thirty-one chapters, so we could easily read one each day. Might help us keep track of the days better."

I roll my eyes. I'm pretty sure Kim does also.

"Are those as good as the ones you read now?" Naomi asks.

"They're a little different but still very good. The Proverbs are filled with wisdom. My grandma used to read a Proverb each day, corresponding with the day of the month. So since today is the fifth of the month, she'd read Proverbs 5. She said it was an old-time tradition."

"We can give it a try if you'd like," Rey offers with indifference.

Chapter 39

Mollie

Friday, Day 16
Bakerville, Wyoming

Since last night's excitement wasn't nearly enough, *ha*, this morning we have a gathering at the Snyders' house with the neighborhood watch leaders.

Many people going to this meeting were at last night's meeting, including Judge Isaiah Avery and Deputy Fred but, thankfully, not Jon Dawson. It seems when Phil first went to him about being a neighborhood leader, he declined. Said he wouldn't feel comfortable helping in that manner. So his next-door neighbor, recently appointed Sheriff Deputy Clark Thomas, is representing their neighborhood.

I wonder how Phil and Evan decided on zoning the neighborhoods? Some zones make sense. Our neighborhood, of which Jake is the official representative, has a natural division. We're mainly comprised of a new development, which used to be an old ranch.

When we first moved here, I told my boss's wife we were moving into a new subdivision. She visited us and laughed about my subdivision definition. She insists subdivisions don't often have thirty to one hundred plus acre parcels. True.

We're one of many named subdivisions in Bakerville consisting of large acreage. Those neighborhood zones make sense. But the outlying areas still operating large ranches were likely harder to group.

Neighborhood leaders who were not at last night's meeting got a visit early this morning. Phil, Evan, and Jake tried to make sure everyone knew. There's a surprising number of old cars and trucks here, still running after the EMP, along with ATVs and dirt bikes. Horses and bicycles are also being utilized for transportation.

The parade going by our house up to the Snyders' is keeping the children entertained for sure. Lily and Sissy especially enjoy seeing the horses go by. One horse was even pulling an old-fashioned buggy, refurbished and always popular in local parades and other events. Wyoming, *Forever West*, that's us.

The meeting starts with twenty-four people crammed into the Snyders' house. It soon becomes evident the close quarters, frazzled nerves, and lack of running water are not a good combination. I'm reminded of the gathering at the bar in Cooke City when I was trying to get home.

Evan wisely suggests we move to the back deck. The deck isn't large enough for all of us, but we make do. It's definitely better than being crammed inside.

I take a minute to search out Prospector Peak. Evan and Doris have an amazing view of the Peak. I glance around and notice I'm not the only one enjoying the landscape and fresh outdoor air.

The watch leader meeting starts off calmer than last night's event, deteriorates, and then returns to an even keel. Many of those in the lead positions aren't faring much better than some of last night's families.

The only good thing, if it can be called a good thing, is there aren't many children in Bakerville. We're a community of mainly retired people. Of the nearly four hundred community members, only about fifty are children. Sadly, the death of one little boy has lowered that number. Lydia's children, not community members before the events of late, are new additions to our community.

Is retired people starving better than children starving? I'm not so sure it is. No, definitely not.

A tentative plan is now in place for our community of Bakerville, a plan we hope will minimize our casualties. We're enacting measures like Cooke City put in place the day I found myself in their town. They were shutting it down. People could pass through, but they couldn't stay unless they belonged there. The road, a highway, would still be open, but an escort would be required to travel from Silver Gate to Colter Pass.

Bakerville sits off a main highway, with two paved roads accessing Bakerville proper. We'll leave the highway access alone and place a guard about half a mile off the highway on each road. These guards will be hidden from the highway, so we hope people will just pass on by. The single road sign pointing out Bakerville will be taken down.

There are two houses outside of the proposed guard stations. One family was gone when the attacks happened. Their house is already in the process of being inventoried and emptied. This family, a retired husband and wife I didn't know, had a couple of beehives.

The other hive keepers in Bakerville didn't want to add the new hives, said it'd be better to spread them out. Those three hives are now in our neighborhood, here at the Snyders' place.

A widow owns the second house outside the guard station. She's moving to Kelley and Phil's land and staying in a fifth wheel, belonging to a family who was away when the attacks happened. She was having a hard time alone anyway, so it made sense.

It is decided our family militia is being extended and will become part of the Bakerville militia. I'm not in favor of this, preferring our family unit stay close to home, providing local protection and minimizing the danger to my family, my children.

Food issues were also addressed. I have my doubts how well, or how long, these new plans will hold together. We'll see.

After the meeting wraps up and most everyone goes home, Jake and I, along with Phil and Kelley, stay to visit with Doris and Evan.

Doris is getting around fairly well in her wheelchair; she was in amazing condition before her injury and is determined to maintain her level of fitness. She's doing strength training and workouts from a chair. Evan even installed a pair of wooden rings off of their pull-up bar. He had a neighbor with a woodworking shop make them for Doris. Now that's true love.

Our men go outside to check on Evan's smoker, which is filled with wild game jerky, while Doris, Kelley, and I catch up. Doris shows us a holster she constructed to hang off her wheelchair. She modeled it after a bedside holster pattern she's made many times before.

It's nice and quilted and stiff enough she can draw quickly. Next to the holster is a pocket for her walkie-talkie, our community communication system. On her left side is a second bag, holding a pair of binoculars, a mean looking knife, duct tape, a pair of scissors, snacks, and a bottle of water.

Like Doris and her wheelchair accessory bag, I have my own bag, what people sometimes call an everyday carry bag, or EDC bag.

My EDC, outfitted similar to what each of us are now carrying in this new world, holds my radio and earbud, a folding knife, flashlight, small multitool, a length of paracord, and normal purse stuff. My EDC *is* my purse, after all. One thing I did stop carrying in my purse, at Evan's suggestion, was my driver's license. He said it'd be best in case I was captured. I give an involuntary shudder just thinking of being captured.

For years I've used a medium-sized crossbody bag, preferring it more than an over-the-shoulder bag because of the way it fits. Even though I've added a few gizmos to it, nothing much has changed. Jake, on the other hand, struggled with carrying a bag of any sort. He ended up using a multipocketed fishing vest, procured from one of our missing neighbor's homes, to hold his EDC items. Others are using fanny packs, small backpacks, or similar bags.

Evan made a point of saying he wished we would have discussed these types of things before our world fell apart. There's certain gear he would've liked us to have. According to Evan, simple things like tactical pants would come in handy.

Evan, Doris, Leo, and several others in the community have these multipocketed, quick-dry pants. Jake and I were terribly shortsighted on things like this. While we have rifles and shotguns for hunting, and we each have handguns, we didn't really plan for self-defense. So useful things, like tactical pants and utility belts, weren't something we focused on.

While we don't have actual tactical pants, we do have cargo pants and cargo shorts for hiking trips, and I bought each of us a utility belt for Christmas last year as part of our backpacking in bear country gear. But if we would've planned better, working in conjunction with Evan and his vast knowledge as a former SWAT member, things could be different. I have to wonder, if we would've made plans with Evan, would we have started a militia back then?

No. No way. Jake and I thought Bakerville was a safe area, a place where we'd be able to ride out any storms without incident. We were so naive.

"Wow, Doris," Kelley exclaims. "Did you quilt it by hand?"

"Sure. It's small, so it wasn't too hard. Besides, I can't get around to do much, so I spend a lot of time looking for handwork. I've been repairing clothes too. Please, bring me any sewing your families need done. With the help you two have been giving me, making sure someone is up here every day checking in and doing what needs done, your sewing is the least I can do."

"I might take you up on that," Kelley says.

"Me too," I add.

Besides for doing her best to remain physically fit, Doris is training for the militia by making sure she can shoot as well from her wheelchair as she could before. Not just with her handgun, but with *all* her weapons.

The sliding door to the back deck opens, and Evan pokes his head in. "We're going to take a walk and look at the beehives. Did you want to go along?"

"Well, honey, that sounds right nice," Doris says in a fake Southern Belle accent. "But I've got me a hitch in my giddy-up."

Evan shakes his head. "Yeah, I was going to say, if you'd like to go along, I could throw you over the back of the four-wheeler, carry you just like a sack of potatoes. Interested?"

Doris laughs. "You guys go on ahead. We're having a nice visit."

We chitchat about a variety of things, then Kelley asks me, "How's Katie doing?"

"Good. Very good. She's walking around, not alone yet, per Belinda's orders, but we get her up several times a day. Yesterday, I went in to check on her and Leo was with her. They both said they wanted to talk to Jake and me." I'm trying hard not to beam.

"Really?!" Doris gasps. "Was it what I think it was?"

"If you think they asked if we'd give our blessing to their marriage, it was."

"That's so wonderful," Kelley gushes. "Leo's a great guy. And Katie—she's amazing."

"I have to agree." I laugh.

"When's the wedding?" Doris asks.

"They'll set a date when she's a little better. Belinda seems happy with how she's progressing. Dr. Sam was over yesterday and agrees with Belinda's assessment."

"That's great. We were all so . . . " Kelley starts and then stops herself.

"Yeah, I know. None of you expected her to make it when she first arrived at Belinda's after the attack. Dr. Sam told me. He said, at first, you all thought just to keep her comfortable . . . but it was you who convinced them to try. Thank you for that, Kelley. You saved my little girl. I'll never be able to thank you enough."

Her brown eyes fill with a sheen of tears as she nods. "And soon she'll be getting married."

"You're so fortunate, Mollie," Doris says. "Not only is Katie okay, but you have all of your children here with you. It's so hard not knowing."

"I'm sorry, Doris. I can only imagine what you're feeling."

"It's hard. Very hard," Doris says, while Kelley nods. "At least with Jessica I can assume she's not affected by any of this. I mean, we think it's only a US problem, right? So I like to think she and my grandchildren are just fine. But Lindsey . . . when Evan spoke with her before the nuke alert, she and Logan were sheltering in place at their condo."

She visibly swallows as she attempts to compose herself. "Things were crazy in San Jose . . . too crazy for them to think it was even safe to leave. I'm so scared. If there was an actual nuclear attack in addition to the pulse we got, the West Coast would've been a target and they might have been . . . " Her voice fades off as she stares into space. She doesn't need to say they might have been close enough to a nuclear bomb to have been killed in the blast or the radiation following the blast.

"I know how you feel, Doris," Kelley says quietly. "Sabrina and Sylvia . . . I don't know where they are either."

"I'm sorry, Kelley. I'm feeling sorry for myself and forgot you're in the same boat. And, Mollie, please don't think I'm not incredibly happy for you that all of your girls made it here. I am. When they all arrived home, it was a party. Jake . . . he was ecstatic. Of course, you still being gone made it hard for everyone. You making it home, and David and Betty's children arriving from Texas, gives me hope that Lindsey can get here too. You feel the same, Kelley?"

"Absolutely. I know my girls. They'll do their best to get here or . . . " She doesn't finish her sentence—*or die trying.*

The worst part, if they don't show up—Sylvia, Sabrina, Lindsey and Lindsey's husband—their parents will never know what happened to them. Jake's brother and his family too. We'll never know. I'm reminded of stories from the pioneer days of families leaving from the east to never be heard from again. No one knew what became of their relatives. Our history is now our reality.

Doris gives a sad smile and a nod. "And you both heard about Deputy Fred? About his cousin showing up? Well, not his cousin, something happened to him, but the cousin's wife and children."

"I didn't hear about this. What happened to the cousin?"

"Where did they come from?" Kelley asks.

"Not sure where they're from. And I don't really know the story. I overheard him talking to the judge and Clark. Oh, should we call him Deputy Clark now?" she says with a smile.

Kelley and I both laugh. "No . . . I don't think so," I say. "Um, maybe I'm wrong, but I always thought they were kind of teasing Fred by adding *deputy* to the front. You know how he's kind of . . . "

"Like Barney Fife only not in a good way?" Kelley asks.

"Exactly." I nod.

"Kind of a slam to Barney Fife, if you ask me," Doris says.

We want to laugh, but we can't. Deputy Fred is . . . what's the word? Odd? Creepy? I'm not sure. Before, he wasn't someone I gave much thought to. He's always nice enough and not one to be concerned with, not like Dan Morse. Dan Morse was definitely odd and creepy, but also *off*. Fred is just different. The kind of person who tries a little too hard. I've heard someone refer to him as socially awkward. Maybe so. But I think of myself that way too, so . . .

And I definitely do know about odd and creepy. My life is so very different now than it once was. I certainly met my fair share of odd and creepy during that time. Brad Quinton was one. He seemed so great at first. Then I discovered he wasn't just odd and creepy, he was scary. Scary and ruthless.

"Yeah, so anyway," Doris continues, "I overheard him saying his cousin's wife and two kids are here, so he wants to make sure he gets some extra help to care for them. Seems they made contact those couple of days the phones came back on. They told him they were on their way. He'd been driving out looking for them every day and found them just down the road. The husband, his cousin, was killed in an attack, but the wife and children were fine. I guess they hid or something. So that's all I really know."

"Awful. They must be hurting terribly," Kelley says.

I start to agree when the rumble of an ATV reaches my ears . . . more than one . . . maybe three or four ATVs. Is someone coming up the hill from my house? Is there an emergency at home?

"Sounds like someone's coming," Doris says.

"One of yours?" Kelley asks me.

"Nope. Not coming up the hill," Doris answers abruptly as she pulls the walkie-talkie out of its designated pocket. "They're coming down the two-track from the wilderness."

I move near the window to peer out, keeping my body behind the wall. I catch a glimpse of a machine as it turns into a curve, three more four wheelers follow. They're still at least a half mile from the house.

"They'll probably just drive right on by," Kelley says with a bit of quiver to her voice, as she steps directly in front of the window.

I motion her to the side.

Doris shrugs and keys the mic on the radio. "Grandpa Ghost, you have your ears on?"

"What's up, Toots?" Evan's voice booms, not just through her radio but also through my own switched-on radio.

"Might have a fox in the hen house."

"At least four foxes," I say.

"Four foxes," Doris repeats into the radio.

"Confirmed?" Evan asks. He comes back immediately. "We hear them now. On our way."

"Might be nothing," Doris says.

"Or might be something," Evan answers. "We're at least five minutes out, all the way to the river."

All the way to the river? Way past where the hive's set up. They've been gone forty-five minutes at least. Doris and Evan's property, just over a hundred acres, connects to a piece of BLM land, which connects to a section of Wyoming state land. Someone, years ago, set up a fire pit on the state land, right next to the river. We've had several weenie roasts there. We usually take our Jeep to those parties. It's close to two miles on a winding road. No way can they be here in five minutes . . . more like fifteen—and that's if they run. And it's all uphill.

"I'll get back with you," Doris says.

"Affirmative."

"There they are," Kelley says, as quad number one crests the hill less than a quarter mile from Doris and Evan's house. If they drive by here, my house is just down the road. I pull out my own walkie-talkie to phone home.

Before I have it out, Doris's radio squelches. "Keep us in the loop," Leo says. "We're battening down here."

"Will do, Hollywood," Doris responds.

"Looks like they're slowing down," Kelley whispers.

Chapter 40

Mollie

Friday, Day 16
Bakerville, Wyoming

My breath catches. Not only are the guys on the ATVs slowing down, they're grouping up. The first one waits until the others catch up. Then they come to a complete stop, lined up. One of them points toward the house.

Doris rolls near the window, being careful not to silhouette in front of it. She has her binoculars up, looking over the situation.

"I don't recognize them," she says. "All men, armed with a sidearm and scabbards on their quads."

"Armed doesn't mean much." Kelley shrugs. "We're all armed. Could just be someone using the Jeep trail to get home. Seems smarter than taking the highway, with all of the troubles."

"Probably," Doris agrees.

The word *probably* is no sooner out of Doris's mouth, when the men move the quads into a single file line and shut them down.

"Uh-oh," I say. They each dismount and remove their rifles. The one on the front ATV begins to boldly stride our direction. The second one grabs his shirt to stop him, saying something, causing the striding guy to nod. We watch as they scatter and begin to walk slightly hunched. There's no trees or much cover in this wide-open space. They're not sneaking but are trying to make themselves smaller targets.

Doris is immediately on the radio. "They're not going by. Repeat, they have stopped and are approaching on foot. We are hot. Repeat, we are hot."

She clicks off the radio and fishes in the accessory bag on her wheelchair, pulling out an earbud. The earbuds are something we've made a point of collecting as houses are cleared out, a way to keep the noise level down when using our walkie-talkies. Some of the earbuds are designed to work with the handheld radios perfectly. Some only allow incoming audio.

My radio included an earbud with the most uncomfortable earpiece. I switched it out for a pair of cheap headphones, with incoming audio only. I dig around in my crossbody bag until I find the earbud in a small plastic case.

"Kelley, get the rifle out of the tub in the master bath," Doris says. "Put it on the bed for me and crack open the window. That's my station. Put the security bar under the front door and in the slider. Close the slider curtain. Do you have your radio with you?"

"I have it," she answers, moving quickly toward the master bedroom.

My radio is clipped on my belt, earbud in my ear. My pistol is out and by my leg. I make a conscious effort to index, keeping my finger well away from the trigger. I'm shaking. *Remember your training, Mollie.*

I take a deep breath. It's little help.

Kelley is back and securing the front door. The men have reached the driveway. It's still a fair distance from the house. One of them drops down, into the barrow ditch.

"He's going prone," I say, unnecessarily.

"Mollie, there's a carbine on the guest room bed. The screen is out of the window. That's your station. Kelley, I don't have another rifle out for you. The others are locked up in the gun room. You have your pistol, and there's another one on the table by the door. Take it also. Let's go." Doris is already wheeling toward her room, the strength in her upper body providing rapid propulsion.

"Let's hope it doesn't come to shooting. I'll call out to them, try to convince them to move along. Keep your radios on and be ready," she says over her shoulder as she enters the master bedroom. I'm halfway down the hall, in the opposite direction, on the way toward the guest room.

My heart is pounding. *Please, God. Please. Let them just be looking for directions, or water, or something.*

The blinds are down on both guest room windows. I move to the window nearest the bed, carefully lifting the blind enough to see out. Along the windowsill is a fabric draft stopper, the kind used at the bottom of a door to help keep the cold out. I pull it away; the window is opened slightly, enough I can get my fingers under to lift it higher. As promised, the screen is removed. The draft stopper must be working as a bug stopper.

I take a quick look. Only two guys are walking, moving slowly and cautiously toward the house. The one is still in the ditch. Where's the other one? I don't see him. I move to the rifle, a loaded AR-15—our militia has been training on these—along with two additional filled magazines. There's a green ammo box on the floor. I pop it open—more than half full. I shove one of the magazines into the unzipped outer pocket of my bag. The second, I sit on the floor by the window.

I check the AR, then make it ready. A trickle of sweat runs down my back. Kneeling at the side of the window, I slowly move the muzzle out through the small opening.

I'm barely in position when Doris hollers, in a much lower, huskier, voice than is her norm, "That's far enough."

The two guys stop and drop to a knee. The one in the ditch is hunkered down, at the ready. I still don't see the fourth guy.

I key the mic of my radio and quietly ask, "Where's the fourth?"

"Not sure," Doris responds.

"I've got him," Kelley stammers. "He made a run for the garage. He just disappeared around the corner."

Doris issues a single expletive. "Probably going to the back. Kelley, go to my craft room. Keep the back under surveillance."

The craft room is across the hall from the guest room I'm in. From there, she'll have a view of the back of the house, the garden, and Evan's large shop. From my window, I can see the entire front yard, driveway, up the hill—the one they just came down—and part of the garage.

The radio comes to life. "Where are you, Grandpa?" Doris asks.

"Not quite halfway back," Evan answers in a ragged breath.

Leo comes on, "Six of us at the creek. We'll be coming in from both sides of the road, three each side."

The land across the road from Doris and Evan's is bare ground, part of the acreage belonging to the house below. There's a large gulley, washed out from years of rainwater making its way downhill, which will provide excellent cover as Leo and his team approach from the other side of the road. Those coming on this side of the road, the house side, won't have the luxury of such cover.

The trespassers in the front yard have yet to respond to Doris. The two are still crouched low, using scraggly sagebrush as cover. The third is still in the ditch. I can see his head bob every so often, but the rest of his body is out of view.

The craft room door let's out a slight screech as Kelley opens it. A few seconds later, she says into the radio, "Got him. He is at the edge of the garden, using the burlap to hide behind."

"These guys move like they know what they're doing," Doris says to everyone listening. "Let's be smart."

"Understood," Leo says.

"Affirmative," Evan answers.

A third voice, maybe Tate, says, "Got it."

"Are we sure there are only four?" Leo asks.

Chapter 41

Mollie

Friday, Day 16
Bakerville, Wyoming

Oh no! *Could there be more?* Could these guys only be part of an invading force? Are there others stopped over one of the ridges, where we can't see them? It's hard to tell how many engines there were.

"We only have eyes on four," Doris responds. "Yes, there could be more if they're being sneaky. These guys could be the distraction."

My eyes are glued on the two in the front yard, watching for any movement, any little twitch. The one on the right lifts his hand slightly—a signal?—then calls out, "Hello in the house."

Doris waits a beat, and in the same overly gruff voice as before, responds, "Move along. You are not welcome."

"That's not very neighborly of you," he replies calmly, almost casually. "We're just looking for a place to rest a bit, fill up our water jugs, relax for a while."

"It looks like the guy at the garden is moving," Kelley says quietly, coming in clearly through my earbud. "He might be wanting to try the back door. I didn't check your utility door, Doris."

The utility door is in the laundry room, at the end of the hall with the rooms Kelley and I are in. The garage, while not connected to the home, is easily accessed from the utility room.

"The door is secured, but if he goes around . . ." She takes a deep breath. "Mollie, you'll need to move to the hall. That will put one of us watching each entrance."

"Go there now?" I ask.

"Not yet, wait until Kelley no longer has eyes on him."

"I still see him," Kelley says. "He's by the shop now, on the backside of it. Evan, if you guys are coming up, be cautious. If he turns, he could see you."

The mic keys three times, Evan's indication he understands. I wonder if they're so close he doesn't want to speak, or so winded from running he can't speak. I pray they're close and being cautious.

The guy on the right lifts his hand slightly. "So how about it, neighbor?"

Doris doesn't respond.

My heart is still beating much harder than it should. I've been in a similar position before, when I found Madison and her baby Emma on the road. I was so scared and nervous, I missed my first shot. In the end, it turned out okay. Those guys didn't know I was there, and I was able to catch them by surprise. But this time, the guys are ready. They know we're here. I can't imagine they haven't noticed the black muzzle of my rifle sticking out from the bedroom window.

The guy lifts his arm and lowers it. He and the other guy drop to a lower crouch and start moving. The guy in the ditch immediately fires on us while the two try to scurry away. Doris is firing, Kelley also.

I quickly sight in slightly ahead of the silent one, the one who didn't call out to us. I shot an antelope as it started to run last year. *Same thing, right?* Deep breath, let it halfway out, then three quick shots. He stumbles. I shoot again and miss.

Glass shatters somewhere in the house. *Please, God, let Doris and Kelley be okay.*

Another report from Doris's rifle—she's still firing; she must be okay. Silent bad guy goes down. His buddy, the talker, keeps moving toward the safety of the garage. Within a few seconds, he's firing on us. The silent bad guy who went down is crawling on his belly toward the garage while the other one provides cover fire.

I can't get either of them from this angle. I move to the far right of the window, a slightly better angle. If a piece of him sticks out just a little more, I'll have a shot.

Doris is still firing, the boom of her large caliber hunting rifle reverberating through the house, dwarfing the sound of Kelley's 9-millimeter pistol. The guy in the ditch is peppering the house with bullets. So is the guy in the backyard.

Into my radio, I say, "Two are using the garage as cover. Leo, your team, be alert."

"Roger," Tate, not Leo, answers in a barely audible whisper. "We're almost there, two minutes or so, coming in stealth." A perfect response from my former Air Force son-in-law.

"Doris? Kelley?" I ask.

Without the radio, Kelley yells, "I'm okay, but he's determined to get in. I can't hit him."

Through the radio, Doris says, "I'm okay. Trying for the shooter in the ditch."

Before I can respond, there's more glass breaking. With everything going on, I can't tell which window is out now.

"Utility door! That was the utility door," Kelley yells.

No!

"I'm on it," I yell back, not bothering with the radio. I grab the magazine off the floor, fumbling through a speed reload—something I've been practicing but need considerably more improvement to become proficient. Provided I make it through this day alive, I'll put in additional time to hone this skill.

New magazine in place, I scurry to the door, then drop down and peek around the frame down the hall. I can't see the utility room door or the invader. I cautiously work my way toward the door. I still can't see into the room, but I can hear the guy crashing around, trying to get the door open, cussing and ranting in hopes his words will magically slide the security bar out of the way and allow him entry.

Snugged up against the wall, I take a knee and a deep breath. My rifle is at the ready as I slide forward. He's hanging half in the shattered window, focusing on removing the security bar with his left hand, a pistol in his right, greasy hair hanging in his face. I have an immediate memory of Dan Morse and his criminal buddy, Bo—the one I think of as the dirty hippy, the one we think was probably Lydia's brother—before my girls and I killed him.

Shoot this guy or give him a verbal warning, an opportunity to surrender? *Another deep breath.* "Stop! Put your hands up!"

He drops his body behind the door and fires his pistol on his way down. The shots are wild and wide, booming through the small space. Several seconds pass, then he tries it again, raising his hand and shooting over the door. He's closer this time. I'm becoming a sitting duck.

I quickly run through my options.

Be ready to shoot his hand next time it pops over? That could briefly put him out of the fight, but if he's like some in our militia, he's capable of shooting lefthanded.

Shoot out the door? The door he's using for concealment, made of fiberglass, isn't going to provide much cover.

My problem with either option is I've had it drilled into me to never shoot without confirming the target; know what is in front, behind, and around it. Basically, I'd be firing blind in both instances. Could one of our guys, one of my family members, be in the line of fire, sneaking up behind the bad guy?

I key my radio mic and whisper, "Target at the utility room door, next to the garage. I am nearby and ready to fire."

"All clear," Tate answers.

"Affirmative," Evan says.

Seconds later, I catch a shadow, then his hand pops up. I let loose a series of shots into the door. He screams, then fires his handgun several times, wild and crazy shots coming back through the door. I shoot three more times, aiming lower this time. His shooting spree ends. I quickly change out to a full magazine. Yes, there's still ammo left in this one, but a full one sounds smarter.

Breathe in. Breathe out. I'm struggling with dizziness. The shots ringing in this room were almost too much for me. I've never been shot at before. Never been in an actual gunfight. Yes, I've killed before, but those times were very different.

"Mollie, report," Jake orders through my radio.

"I . . . I'm okay. I don't know his status. He . . . he's on the other side of the door."

"We're nearly there, Mollie," Tate says. "Found one guy lying against the garage, going around the building to check on your guy at the side door. Stay clear."

"Doris?" Evan asks.

"I'm good, got the interloper in the ditch. Eyes on Leo and his team. Looks like they're checking for other hostiles. Kelley?"

"Fine. Evan just . . . uh . . . eliminated the backyard threat."

"Mollie," Tate says, "utility room door is secure. I'm coming in."

"Stand down, ladies. We're coming in the back door," Evan says.

What feels like many minutes but is probably only seconds later, Jake is holding me, asking me over and over if I'm okay, telling me I did great.

I'm so dizzy from the ringing in my ears I can barely stand. Then my stomach revolts. I manage to make it to the bathroom before retching.

Leo and his team thoroughly check the surrounding area, not finding anyone else or evidence there was anyone other than the four. All of them had identification on them from Lewistown, Montana. Why they chose to attack us, we have no idea. Well, other than the obvious.

They wanted what we have.

It takes me some time before I begin to feel better. Kelley isn't in much better shape. Doris is pale and hurting, having managed to bang her leg during the firefight. Leo checks it and then calls Belinda to come up for a more thorough exam. A stern talking to follows the exam, with Belinda reminding Doris her ability to walk in the future depends on the leg healing as well as possible now. Of course, Belinda also realizes there was no option in this situation.

Doris and Evan lost half their windows and the utility room door in the shootout. Several other windows and the sliding patio door at the back of the house are cracked or spider webbed. The cleanup effort takes several hours. Plywood salvaged from empty homes is brought up to cover the windows.

Even with the efforts to secure the house today, I wonder how they can stay here long term. Will the plywood provide enough protection from the elements once winter hits? And will Doris be able to stand the lack of light? I know it'd drive me crazy. Maybe they can salvage windows from one of the other houses in the community.

Mollie Caldwell, I think with a gasp, *what is going on with you? In only a short time, you've become so used to stealing from your neighbors you're pondering how to dismantle homes?*

I try to go back, to amend my thinking. Those guys attacked us. They were willing to kill us to see what Doris and Evan have. We've been plunged into a world of chaos. A world where rules and ethics now mean little. Doris, Kelley, and I were also willing to kill, to protect our lives and the things we have.

I shudder, thinking what could've happened if we hadn't been successful in fending them off. One or all of us would be dead. We've already had our share of disaster and heartache in Bakerville.

Before, the perpetrator was one of our own: Dan Morse., who came completely unhinged with a vision that he should be the ruler of

Bakerville. When things didn't go the way he thought they should, he lashed out. He's no longer a threat—*because you killed him, Mollie*—but it's apparent our little community isn't immune to the possibility of attack.

The two-track road used by these aggressors is one of many similar roads coming out of the wilderness area. Off-roading on Jeep trails is a popular pastime around here. How can we monitor all of these routes? How can we keep our community safe when there are threats from nearly every direction?

Chapter 42

Sylvia

Wednesday, Day 21
Rest Area
Between Thermopolis and Meeteetse,
Wyoming

"Do you think they have an actual toilet we can flush?" Naomi asks, her voice dripping with awe.

"We'll see," Kim says patiently for the fifth or sixth time.

We've been able to see the rest area up ahead for quite some time. Since we told her what it was, Naomi has asked many questions about what we'll find once we reach it. At the time, we were giving her a goal to shoot for, just like we've been this entire leg of the walk. We'll see something up ahead and say, "See such and such? We'll keep walking until we reach it and then we'll stop for a break." Breaking the hike into smaller pieces has been helpful. Even so, Naomi and the other two children are very tired. I'm tired too.

The hike between Thermopolis and Meeteetse is brutal. It's hot, dry, and dusty, with the terrain covered in cactus and sagebrush, much like back at Boysen Reservoir, only without the beautiful lake nearby.

We've had trouble with water. The hot, dry climate combined with the walking makes us very thirsty, and we've run low a few times. It's been pretty stressful thinking we may run out of water.

We've been picking up bottles and jugs we find along the way, anything that can hold water. Not all of them have lids, but Sabrina has a few rubber bands in her backpack, so we've covered the tops with plastic and secured them with a rubber band. We make sure to keep those upright in the pockets of our backpacks. Containers with lids are being carried in my roller bag. We emptied it of food—we're running low on food also, which is stressing me out too—so it's now strictly for water storage.

Sabrina has a tarp we've used to collect rainwater during the storms by stretching it out over us as a shelter but making sure the front was slightly lower and dipped in the middle. She fills up the Hoffmanns' cooking pot first, then empties the water into the tea kettle and her little double broiler thing, then sets up the cooking pot to collect more.

Unfortunately, there's only been one rainstorm that filled the cooking pot more than one time. Even so, we were grateful for the water. As a precaution, we filtered the rainwater when we finished the collection process. Sabrina didn't think filtering was necessary, but the rest of us overrode her. We definitely don't need to get sick on this hike!

We finally reach the driveway to the rest area. Like Naomi, I'm excited about the prospect of an actual bathroom with running water. Fantasies of a sponge bath in the restroom sink are running through my head.

We've only started up the driveway when those fantasies come to a screeching halt. Wyoming rest areas tend to be one large, rather nice building with something resembling a lobby and the doors to the restrooms leading off the common area. It's obvious this one is out of service. We can see plywood covering the entire front where the door and windows should be, with large red letters saying, CLOSED.

"Does it say it's open, Mommy?"

"No, Naomi. Sorry, it's closed," Kim replies with a sigh. "Guess we should've known it was too good to be true."

"That's not good," Naomi says. "I thought I was going to get to flush the toilet." She says it like flushing the toilet is the equivalent to a ride at Disneyland. I'm both touched and saddened by her reaction. Has our world changed so much?

We keep walking toward the building. Naomi's the first to notice a spigot on the outside of the building.

"Can we get water from there?" she asks.

Nate looks it over and says, "There's no handle for the faucet."

With a pout, Naomi says, "I thought maybe I could play in the sprinkler."

"We don't have a sprinkler, silly," Nate says. Though he tries to hide it, he too looks plenty disappointed.

Sabrina looks over the spigot and says, "Let me try something," as she begins to rummage through her backpack.

After a few seconds, she pulls out what looks like a pocket-sized four-way lug wrench.

"What's that?" Nate asks, scooting closer to her so he can see.

"Ah," Rey says, "a sillcock key. Brilliant."

"A what?" I ask.

"It's a four-way water key," Sabrina says. "One of these ends should fit, and maybe we'll be able to turn on the water. If the water's still working, anyway. Sylvia, can you get a water bottle? As soon as I find the right fit, we'll give it a try."

"So it's a wrench?" Nate asks.

"Yeah, pretty much. There's four different sized square-shaped socket heads, and if I can find the right one . . ." She tries one end where the spigot handle should be, then shakes her head and tries a second. "I think it's this one." She spins the water key around. "Yep. Looks good. Sylvia, can you hold the bottle under the faucet?"

I move the bottle into position and realize I'm holding my breath. I exhale as Sylvia turns the key. The water flows freely from the faucet.

"Yay! You did it, Breena," Naomi yells, while jumping up and down.

Nicole and Nate high five each other, while Kim and Rey are pulling out more water bottles.

Once we have all of our empty containers and the cooking containers filled, Naomi asks, "Can we play in the sprinkler now?"

"Sorry, munchkin," Sabrina says. "I don't know how much more water there is, and we should save it for others to use. But I do think we have enough water we can wash up a bit, get some of the dust off. How would that be?"

"That'd be good, Breena."

We spend over an hour cleaning up and eating before getting back on the road. While it would've been nice to stop for the day, there are still several hours of daylight left. We're hopeful we can make it to Meeteetse tomorrow and then rest for a day or two. We need the rest.

Chapter 43

Lindsey

Thursday, Day 22
Backroads Wyoming

After those few tense minutes Logan and I experienced at Goose Lake State Park, things were fine. While we weren't exactly welcomed with open arms by the three families making the campground home, they let us stay the night.

I think the clincher was me being Logan's wife and not his brother. Even so, we slept in turns, just to be sure. And we left at first light.

That was almost a week ago. A lot has happened since then. The truck and trailer ended up being a near deathtrap. The confrontation at Goose Lake should've been our first clue to at least ditch the trailer due to lack of maneuverability.

We found ourselves in a worse pickle two days later in a ramshackle enclave in Nevada. This time, instead of talking to us, the thugs started shooting. I still don't know how we managed to get away. Logan drove the old truck and trailer backwards like he was Mario Andretti. We finally made it to safety. I stood watch while Logan checked out the truck; the radiator was shot up.

The day after we left the Goose Lake campground, Logan figured out why my bike wouldn't start. It seems the USB outlet he'd added for phone charging had been hit by the electromagnetic pulse, and it shorted something out. He did some stuff—I'm not sure what other than removing and cleaning up the battery—and got it going.

He seemed pretty surprised that would be a problem since the bike should've kickstarted even without the battery in place. He just kept saying, "Weird, makes no sense at all." Sense or no sense, he got it running. We're now back on the bikes. My bottom isn't too happy, but it beats walking. At least that's what I keep telling myself.

We were shot at again yesterday. It was a near miss, and I have the hole in the top my backpack, which I was wearing at the time, to prove it. As a police officer, we're trained to know we can be targets. But to have this happen as a civilian, driving down the road, minding our own business—no one's trained for that.

We're making terrible time. What would've been a two-day drive before the world fell apart, is now looking like a two-week drive. Partly because we're taking small roads, often no more than a goat trail, and partly because we've been ill.

It started the morning we left Goose Lake, with Logan sick to his stomach. He had to stop and throw up a few times. A couple of hours later, I was in the same boat. By the end of the day, we were sick from both ends. Never a good thing. And we were so tired, like we'd been up for days.

At first, we thought maybe it was the muddy water. Maybe the bleach didn't kill everything and we got some sort of bug. And who knows? It might be bad water—only I don't think bad water would cause the other things.

We have these rashes, almost like a sunburn, along with blisters in a few places. Logan had a bad nosebleed last night. And my hair seems to be falling out.

It's not terrible, but there's definitely more strands in my brush than there should be. And earlier, when I scratched my head, a clump of hair fell off. Just like that. I pulled back a tuft with the roots still attached. What I was scratching was a blister on my scalp. We're pretty sure it's radiation poisoning.

How bad? We don't know. We've yet to find any sort of operating medical center—no hospital, doctor's office, or FEMA camp in any of the towns we've gone through. We seem to be fully on our own.

We did meet a small family along the way. The man told us we should shower or bathe and wash our hair, but don't use conditioner. Something about the radioactive particles binding to the conditioner. We both took a sponge bath the evening we arrived at Goose Lake, which included washing and conditioning our hair. We made a point of repeating the process, sans conditioner this time.

The man also said we should get rid of the clothes we were wearing in our hideout and before we made it out of the fallout zone. We've done so. We decided our leathers should be fine with a good scrubbing, along with our leather saddlebags. We replaced all of our backpacks since they're permeable.

Will we be even sicker since we didn't do these things sooner?

Last night, we camped on public land outside of Cokeville, Wyoming. This morning, like every morning of late, we're slow getting going.

"Hey, Lindsey. You doing okay, babe?"

"I'm good. My body's a little sore from being back on the bike. You?"

"Yeah, same. How's your stomach today?"

"No diarrhea, so that's good."

"For sure. Wish I could say the same. What a way to lose a few pounds." He sighs.

I look him over; he's lost more than a few pounds. When this mess started, he was at least twenty pounds overweight, maybe a little more. Now, his leathers, which were too tight before, are fitting nicely. He can button the jacket from top to bottom, and he tightened the pants. They might even be a little loose.

I've lost weight too—weight I didn't really need to lose. I'm pretty physical, working out daily and keeping my weight at a level suitable for my extreme height. I like to think of myself as one of the mythical Amazon women—with all of my female body parts still intact—tall, blond, impressive, and not to be trifled with. My physical bearing has helped me immensely in my career.

"We're doing better, though," Logan says. "Making it into Wyoming is huge. Just crossing the state line yesterday made me feel like we're almost home."

"Are you ready to hit the road? Need to change your Depends before we go?" I bump him with my hip.

"Ha. I know you like to tease, but admit it, as terrible as it's been, those Depends have been helpful."

"Logan, I can't even talk to you about the fact, at thirty years old, we're wearing diapers. Never in my life did I think . . . " I shake my head. "I never thought I'd have diarrhea so bad I'd have to loot a pharmacy and steal adult diapers. Seriously. Stealing gas, stealing a truck, stealing diapers, stealing food, so much for being sworn to uphold the law."

"Hey, honey. I know this sucks. Right now, all I care about is making it to your folks. I want you safe. If we have to steal gas, food, and . . . diapers, then that's what we're going to do."

"Sir, yes, sir." I give a mock salute. He pulls me into a long embrace.

We've been on the road a couple of hours. Well . . . on and off the road, stopping as needed when nature calls. I'm still pretty good, just a little nauseous. Logan's not doing as well as I am. We went through the tiny town of Fronberg a few minutes ago, with a population sign indicating thirteen. We're on a small side road in order to avoid what, based on our less than detailed map, looks like a fairly long bridge. We've heard from a few people bandits are setting up on bridges and making roadblocks to rob and sometimes kill travelers.

We're finally making decent time; it's been many miles since Logan has needed to stop. As we come up an incline, we slow down—part of our safety procedure since we don't know what's on the other side of the hill. We've barely started the ascent of a medium-sized hill on this quiet sleepy road, when the hair on the back of my neck stands straight up.

For as long as I can remember, I've had . . . feelings. Nothing I can explain, but something like a sixth sense. It's helpful on the job, but it can also be annoying. My intuition isn't always right, but I do pay attention. I'm lead bike right now, so I slow to a stop. Logan follows suit.

"What's going on, Lindsey? Gotta go?" Logan practically shouts into my headset.

"Shh . . . " I motion by waving my hand at him, then quietly say, "I have the creeps."

"Got it," he answers. He's learned over the years it's best we follow my gut. I can point to the day when he pledged to always listen to my intuition.

About a year after we were married, he was working for a manufacturing company, setting them up to go to a fully paperless system. The company was participating in some sort of trade show and asked him to come along as an extra warm body.

We were living outside of Seattle then, and the event was at the large convention center in Portland. I tagged along for the trip—always nice to stay in a hotel room with the hubby. I was helping haul stuff in and out to set up their booth. Once they had it the way they wanted, his boss said he'd take us out for lunch, then we had to be back at 3:00 when people would start coming through.

They had a special piece on the table from a project they'd done and were rather proud of. It wasn't a large piece, maybe eight inches in diameter, but it was very heavy. The story accompanying the piece was what the owner was so proud of, it was a cutout from one of his earliest jobs and really put the company on the map. I suggested such a special piece be boxed up and hidden under the table, to bring it out only when someone was manning the booth.

The boss took a look around and said, "Nah, no need. There's no one here but other guys like us. The public won't be admitted for a couple of hours yet. We'll be back before then."

I had my creepy feeling over this piece, so I pushed it a bit. "You sure? From what you told me about this item, it's pretty special to you."

"Yep, I'm sure. No problem."

Wrong.

When we got back from lunch, the piece was gone. Security ended up being called in, surveillance tapes were reviewed, nearby booths were interviewed. The cutout wasn't recovered. The boss was so distraught he could barely make it through the event. Logan was a believer afterward.

"What's happening?" Logan asks.

"Not sure. Just feel like someone's watching us . . . or something."

I pull to a stop, looking around. There aren't many places close for someone to hide. We've been following a creek but have strayed from it a bit in this area of the road. The creek, a good quarter mile from where we're parked, is lined with trees and brush. That would make a good hiding spot . . . maybe someone's in there. The other side of the road is pretty bare, with only knee-high brush.

"Looks pretty empty, babe."

"Yeah, but you know how this land is. It can be deceiving. Plus, what's over the hill? Things change quickly here."

"Want to walk the bikes up?"

"Mmm. Maybe. I feel like a dope, but . . . yeah. Let's walk them. I could use a stretch anyway. You need to . . . go . . . before we go?"

He says nothing for a moment, likely evaluating the state of his bodily functions. "You know, I think I'm good—for now, anyway. Subject to change at any moment."

We both give a small laugh. It's good to have humor when you're afflicted with radiation sickness. *Are we going to die?*

We remove our helmets and have a drink of water before quietly starting up the hill with our bikes. My heart is pounding, not from the exertion of climbing the hill but from anticipation, or maybe fear. A shiver runs through my body. What's the phrase? Someone is walking over my grave?

About fifteen feet from the crest, I'm sweaty and shaky as my adrenalin peaks. "We need to stop, things are not . . . right," I whisper.

"What do you want to do?"

"Park the bikes and walk up. No. Not walk, sneak."

Logan nods. Once we have the bikes secured, we finish the hill in a low crouch. When we're within a few feet of the top, we drop to our stomachs, coming up the right side of the road. There's a large clump of sage and several boulders to use as concealment. We settle in and take a look.

Ah . . . okay. Thank you, gut feeling.

There's a camp at the bottom of the hill on the creek side. Nothing looks amiss, just a few tents and stuff around. Near the road, there's a couple of old pickup trucks and . . . what is that? Some funky looking car from a different time with large windows and rounded edges. In a way, it looks futuristic, but the faded yellow paint gives away its age.

Logan nudges me. Apparently, the first look was slightly deceiving. Barely visible, in something resembling a deer blind, is a guy standing watch. I take a second look over the area. There's a second guy on the other side of the road, also well concealed.

Then we hear the screams.

An angry male voice yells, "If you know what's good for you, you'll shut up now. The both of you." At least we think that's close to what he says; his words are slightly garbled from this distance. The screams, high pitched and desperate, are quite clear. And definitely more than one.

We carefully retreat, sliding back down the hill on our stomachs.

"That doesn't sound good. I guess we'll have to go back and take the main road and go over the bridge," Logan says quietly once we're several feet below the apex.

"What? We're not leaving without helping those women."

"Lindsey, no. We aren't sure exactly what's going on. There are at least three men—two we saw, one we heard. There's probably more. No. We're going around."

"No, Logan. The stealing and stuff . . . fine. But no way am I walking away from someone who needs help. I still have at least a little respect for my job, for my oath."

"We can't. Just the two of us? And as sick as we've been . . . how's that going to work, Lindsey?"

"I have no idea. Let's watch for a bit. But this time, let's separate. You stay on this side, and I'll go over to the left side. Gear up, rifles and extra mags at the ready."

"Lindsey, you know I love you, and I totally get you think you need to do this, but I don't like it. Not one bit."

He's right. I don't really like it either, but I don't think I could live with myself if we didn't at least try. "I understand what you're saying. Let's just . . . let's just watch. We'll be at the ready, in case they attack us, but we'll just watch. Let me assemble the rifles Winchester gave me. Maybe you could move the bikes? Take them down to the bottom of the hill, off the road, and try to hide them?"

"Hide them? In the sagebrush?"

"Maybe there's a gully or something. You know how deceiving this land can be. It might look board flat, but when you get up to it, it's not."

He shakes his head. I start removing the things we'll need from my bike so he can take it first. We'll keep our backpacks, knowing if we encounter trouble and have to run, we have the essentials. He returns a few moments later for his bike. I have the rifles together and everything organized and ready for . . . whatever . . . when he returns, carrying water bottles for each of us.

"Thanks, Logan. I didn't think about water. I know you're not completely on board with this. We'll just watch. Maybe things aren't what they seem and it's just a family squabble."

"Yeah, fine. You were right about finding a crevasse. From here, since we're elevated, we can still see the bikes, but at road level, they aren't noticeable. Took care of business while I was down there, so I'm good to sit for a while. Sure glad my stomach's a little better. You seem good. And I guess energetic enough in case things go bad?"

"Yep, I'm golden. But really, we'll just watch, see what we can find out . . . for now."

"Mm-hmm. It's the 'for now' I'm concerned about."

We decide I'll take my .308 and the .22 from Winchester along with my handguns—one on the hip, one on the ankle, and one on my appendix—and Logan has the AR-15 from Winchester and his shotgun along with a hip and ankle weapon. I'm suddenly wishing we would've brought both rifles. The second .308 rifle, with a scope and long-range capability, would be great if things went bad.

We settle in, making sure we're off the edge of the road and below the crest to help prevent us from silhouetting. We also make sure we can see each other. We'll watch for one hour—not that we know how long an hour is since we don't have anything to keep time, but we'll do our best to estimate. We'll then discuss what, if anything, we should do next. Unless something big happens before then.

The two hidden guys are still in their concealment, at least I assume it's the same guys. They could've swapped while we weren't watching. It's only a few minutes until a guy comes out of one of the larger tents. I take out a pair of small binoculars to get a better look.

He's big and dressed something like a lumberjack: a full, wild, gray beard, a fringe of longish hair that's bald on top, tan pants, and a red checkered shirt. Is that flannel? In June? I immediately think of him as Paul Bunyan.

Paul Bunyan walks over to a small pup tent. Within a minute, the tent unzips and another guy steps out. This guy's the opposite of Paul: short and scrawny, clean shaven with a funky haircut, looking like he should be on a skateboard. That makes four—deer blind guy number one, deer blind guy number two, Paul Bunyan, and Board Boy.

Paul and Board Boy are both well armed, just like us. While I want to assume these are bad guys based on the screams from earlier, it's possible we're misjudging the situation. Maybe they're just a group camping. Two guys keeping watch isn't a bad idea—smart, in fact. The screams . . . could it have just been an argument between spouses and our imagination is getting carried away? Is paranoia part of radiation poisoning?

Before the estimated hour is up, we have our answer.

Chapter 44

Lindsey

Thursday, Day 22
Backroads Wyoming

Logan scoots over near me, motioning me to move down fully out of sight. I'm glad he's here. With what I'm seeing . . . I guess, I'm not as tough as I like to think I am.

I've wanted to be a police officer since I was very young. My mom was Naval Reserve and had a job as a trainer for the federal government. She was gone a lot, either with her training job or her Reserve duties. I don't remember our dad. He was killed in a car accident when I was three and my sister, Jessica, was five.

Sometimes I think I have a memory, which may have been him, but I don't know for sure. It could just be all of the pictures Mom has of him playing tricks on my mind.

Jessica and I had a nanny, several nannies in fact. As part of my mom's work, we moved around a lot. My favorite nanny quit working with us so she could go to school. She said she was going to become a police officer. That was it for me. At the tender age of five, I wanted to be just like her. If she had her hair in a braid, I wanted a braid. If she was wearing a dress, I wanted to wear a dress. When she said she wanted to be a police officer, I wanted to be a police officer. Even after she left, the feeling didn't leave.

Jessica didn't get the same police officer desire I did. Instead, she grew up to be a nanny. Kind of funny when you think about it. She spent a summer in Germany between her junior and senior years of college, loved it, and went back after graduating. She signed up with an au pair agency and was placed within days. She met her husband, a German, and they now live there with their two small boys, my nephews. *Will I ever see them again?*

Our mom married Evan when I was fourteen, which pretty much sealed the deal on my desire to be a police officer. He was a deputy sheriff, not just a regular deputy either. He was part of the Special Operations Division, kind of a fancy way of saying SWAT team. One of Evan's specialties was protective overwatch, or as most people know the position: sniper.

When Evan learned about my interest in law enforcement, he nurtured it without being demanding. He was smart enough to know pushing me too hard would likely fail. Instead, he'd gently guided me. When I was older, we started training together. Being in excellent physical shape was a huge benefit in the academy. He also gave me in-depth firearms training on a variety of weapons. His armory is pretty amazing. Long-range shooting, his specialty, was also my favorite. Sure, handguns are great, but being able to make a shot at 800 plus yards is beyond amazing. It's now obvious this skill is going to be necessary.

"Lindsey, this is . . . terrible."

I nod. "I had a hope it was just a family squabble. I guess seeing half a dozen women roped together destroyed the hope."

"Definitely. And even though I wanted to before . . . I'm not okay with finding another way around. I don't think I'd ever sleep right again if we walked away from them without trying to help. But—" He lets out a huge sigh. "I don't want anything to happen to you. Maybe I could, you know, handle this and you can find a way around. We can look at the map and find a meet-up spot down the road."

"You're kidding, right?"

"No, I'm completely serious. Would you at least consider it?"

"No, I won't consider it. We're together on this, babe."

He gives a slow, sad nod. "I figured. So we for sure have four guys, two hidden and two watching the bound women. You think we ought to watch a little longer and see if any more appear?"

"Yeah. I kind of think they might be on some sort of a schedule. The women just finished relieving themselves and are now getting water. It's getting close to lunch time. Think they'll have the women start cooking?"

Logan shrugs. "Maybe. I'll go back to the other side. You nestle in. Be really careful, Lindsey. Don't let them see you. I'll scoot back over here in a bit, then we'll figure out what to do."

"That sounds like a good plan. Wait and watch. But, Logan, if they do anything rash, we might have to move without a plan. I wouldn't want to watch while one of those women was hurt."

"I know," he says, as he low walks to the other side of the road. I crawl back into my concealment. The women are still out, tied together, and do appear to be starting the lunch preparation. Maybe we'll be able to confirm the number of hostiles once lunch is served.

I estimate almost half an hour has passed when Board Boy goes over to one of the women and says something to her. She shakes her head, then he smacks her. I can't hear the sound of his hand connecting with her face, but I see the motion and watch her fall back, pulling the rope enough to also knock several of the other women off balance.

They quickly right themselves as Board Boy stomps off, gesturing wildly, leaving little doubt as to what his hands are saying. The women range in age, with the oldest looking to be around my mom's age and the youngest a child, maybe a young teenager. The one he smacked, I'd guess to be around my age. I'm sorely tempted to use the rifle and prevent Board Boy from doing anything like that again. I glance at Logan; he shakes his head at me. I sigh and reply with a nod.

Within a few minutes, Board Boy returns. The oldest lady gives him two plates. He saunters over to deer blind guy number one and then to number two, while Paul is given a plate. Board Boy returns for his own plate. The women move to a row of up-ended logs and sit down, none have food.

After a few minutes, Paul motions and they move as one to refill plates for him and Board Boy. The women return to the logs, still without eating. When Paul and Board Boy finish their second plates, they go to their respective tents and come out with rifles. Then each walk over to a deer blind. The guys in the blind come out and Paul and Board Boy take their places. So far, I'm still leaning toward only the four of them.

Deer blind guy number one is a slightly smaller version of Paul Bunyan—also bearded but with red hair instead of gray, wearing blue jeans, a ball cap, and a blue button-up shirt. Deer blind guy number two is just an average looking guy. The kind you'd see anywhere— the grocery store, a doctor's office, a school—midheight, brown hair, jeans, and a T-shirt . . . just average. Both have pistols on their hips and rifles slung over their shoulders, carrying their lunch plates.

I glance at the women; they're staring at the ground, unmoving. As the deer blind guys walk closer, they stand as one. Deer blind guy number one keeps walking toward one of the half dozen tents. Number two goes to one of the women, grabs her by the nape of the neck, yanks her head back, and kisses her. She doesn't fight back but doesn't return the kiss either. I feel a twitch in my eye, anger trying to escape.

Deer blind guy number one is still by the tent. Within a few seconds, a new guy stumbles out. Ugh . . . five guys. Make that six . . . one more is on the heels of number five.

Six . . . at least six. How can we possibly take on six? Four, maybe. With the element of surprise on our side, we might have been able to do it. But six? What about the other tents? Do they have guys in them? Hot tears flood my eyes. Are we going to have to just leave these women?

Logan whispers my name. I crawl down below the crest.

"Let's make this quick, Logan. I want to watch a little longer, then come up with a plan."

"We can't take on six men." His declaration sounds very final.

While I agree with him, I'm not ready to give up. "Let's just watch."

"Fine. But I'm staying over here with you. There's plenty of room for both of us."

He's right. A combination of boulders and brush makes this a fine spot for both of us to remain concealed. I nod.

"I need to use the bathroom, and we need food. I'll grab us something, then I'll be back, okay?"

"Yes, I'm going back up. I'll see you soon," I say, giving him a peck on the cheek. He pulls me in close and kisses me properly.

"You're a stubborn woman, Lindsey Maverick."

The new guys are eating. After they finish a second plate, the women eat. When they're finished, plates and pots are gathered up by the women. The two new guys escort them to the river . . . dishwashing time. The two original deer blind guys go to their tent. Logan's back with granola bars, a jar of peanuts, two sodas, and another water jug.

"I started some of the instant rice. I figure we might be here awhile, so it can soak and get soft for later."

"Thanks, Logan. Good thinking. How's your stomach?"

"You know, I think I'm pretty good. No problems lately. Maybe this . . . excitement . . . is keeping things at bay," he says, with a hint of a smile and a wink.

After a healthy length of time, the string of women and their captors return.

"I think the deer blind guys are sleeping," I whisper to Logan. "Or napping at least. They've been in the tent a while now. I think, if this is their routine—to swap guards after the meals, let the old guards sleep and then two guys take the women to clean up at the river—we might have an opportunity."

"What kind of opportunity?"

"Maybe one of us could surprise the guys at the river, take them out quietly. Then we'd just have the four."

"Take them out quietly? You mean like with a knife or something?"

"Yeah, that's what I was thinking."

Chapter 45

Lindsey

Thursday, Day 22
Backroads Wyoming

"Lindsey, I'm not Rambo. Neither are you. Did they teach you how to kill with a knife in the academy?"

"No. They taught us how to protect ourselves from a knife attack, but not how to attack. Evan trained me."

"Evan taught you how to attack with a knife? Oh . . . I guess that explains the giant knife you said was your seventeenth birthday present. Why the knives?"

"Because sometimes you have to neutralize a threat up close and personal. A gun isn't always an option. Haven't we discussed this before?"

"Well, Evan didn't teach me how to . . . to do *that*, and there's no way you're going to be up close and personal with those guys. If anyone is going to . . . what did you say? Take them out? It's going to be me."

We make our plan. It's a terrible plan. There's very little chance either of us will survive. We go over it again; what can we change? With a few tweaks, we decide it's as good as it's going to get. We snuggle close and hug each other tight.

"I'll be looking forward to some yummy rice when this is over," Logan says, kissing me.

"Me too. I love you, Logan Maverick."

"I love you, Lindsey Maverick. Even if you are a little cuckoo." He smiles and kisses me again. Then he scoots back down the hill. I quickly move to the other side of the road where Logan was originally hidden, the same side they've set up camp.

The women are sitting quietly on the stumps. The two new guys are in camp chairs, talking and paying little attention to the women. After several hours, the guys get the women up and let them go to the bathroom. Then they start the meal prep.

We're getting close. I'm nervous. Is Logan in place? Does he have a good view of what is happening, while also being hidden so they can't see him? Will he remember the couple of knife moves I showed him? While I do know basic knife attacks and counterattacks, they're not my forte.

Not only did Evan give me a great fixed-blade knife when I was seventeen, he gave me another one a few years ago, a Gerber Ghoststrike. It's nice and lightweight. Not legal to conceal carry in California, but fine to open carry. I don't carry it. It stayed in my nightstand drawer until we were packing up. Then it, along with my birthday knife and a Kershaw Speedsafe pocketknife—a gift from my mom last year when I went hunting with her—were freed from the nightstand and moved to the backpacks. The Kershaw is with me. Logan has the other two, along with his sidearms and the shotgun.

I've searched for Logan several times but have no idea where he is. Hiding, concealed somewhere in the brush. Waiting.

Nothing has changed with Paul Bunyan and Board Boy. They're still in their own deer-blind-style concealment.

Board Boy seems to be asleep, reclining against the trunk of a small tree, head flopped slightly to the side. Paul, on the other hand, is wide awake and taking his guard duty seriously. Seems to me it might be smarter to have guard duty immediately after sleeping, instead of watching the women then having guard duty. Of course, maybe they think the women are a bigger threat than someone coming down this quiet little road. Surprise, boys!

The meal preparation is complete, and the serving procedure used at lunch is repeated. One of the new guys takes plates to Paul and Board Boy, then the new guys eat. After they're done, they replace Paul and Board Boy as lookouts. No new guys have appeared, still only the six.

Paul and Board Boy get more food, then wake up the original deer blind guys. Paul wastes no time as he immediately heads to the large tent. Board Boy, after napping while on guard duty, spends a little time talking with deer blind guys while they eat.

When the women finally get to eat, Board Boy makes a point of harassing the same one from earlier. It's all I can do not to shoot him right then. He finally gives up and goes to his tent. A few minutes later, the women start to gather up the dirty dishes. The original deer blind guys reluctantly stand up.

One of them yells something to the women. I can't fully make it out, but it sounds like, "Let's hurry it up this time. I have better things to do than stand at the river while you women mess around."

Here we go. *Is Logan ready?*

It's been ten minutes. I know how long it's been because I'm counting. My hunting rifle is loaded and at the ready. It holds only five rounds. The 5.56 from Winchester is also ready. Without a scope, I won't be as accurate, but the semi-auto, compared to the bolt, might gain me a slight advantage. I sure wish the magazines were larger than ten . . . stupid "high-capacity" rules. Logan also left me the .22 in case I need it.

I'm focused on the guard on the opposite side of the road. I'm concentrating on my breathing, on staying calm. These help with the counting.

Every thirty seconds, I check for Logan. He should appear in a specific spot along the edge of the trees, positioned to remove the other guard. Where is he? Another minute passes.

A gunshot. Then a second. Please . . . not Logan. I immediately move on to plan B—take out the guards.

Deep breath in and hold it, gently squeeze the trigger. My shot is true. My guard falls. I swivel to the other guard, the one on this side of the road, to repeat the procedure. He's looking around, toward the tree line, trying to figure out what's happening. My shot isn't as accurate. He falls, but I've only winged him. A third shot rings out.

I shoot the second guard again; this one feels better. I scan to Board Boy's tent. It's shaking, like the zipper is stuck, but I don't see him. Paul Bunyan is quicker. The zipper on his tent is partially up, and I can see his hand sticking out. I'm glad they've positioned the doors so I can see what they're doing—very helpful, guys.

There's screaming. The women . . . please . . . please, let Logan be okay.

Paul—crouched low, pistol in hand—is in my sights. I send my last two .308 shots his way. The first one hits his left arm just below the shoulder, spinning him around. The second is a miss. I grab the semi-auto. He's kneeling, holding his arm, trying to pick up his gun with his left. A shot rings out, not mine. Not his.

I squeeze the trigger again, and again. Paul Bunyan is on the ground.

I look to Board Boy's tent. He's sprawled outside the tent. Another shot—a handgun, just like the last. Logan? It must be Logan . . . right? *Where is he?*

As overwatch, my job is to make sure the threats are eliminated, to keep Logan and the women safe. I put another bullet into each bad guy, starting with Board Boy and finishing with the new guys in the blinds.

Time slows down. There's no movement. No sound. The women are no longer screaming.

"Lima, Lima, your mama wears combat boots." Faint but I can hear it: the code for all is clear. If it would've been "code 4," the code everyone seems to know from television and Hollywood as all clear, I'd know he was under duress.

The code is good, but that wasn't Logan. It was a female. I stay quiet and watch the tree line. Very carefully, a woman steps out. Her hands are up. She's alone, not connected to the rope line, but it's clearly the oldest woman.

Again, I hear a yell, still faint for me at this distance, "Lima, Lima, your mama wears combat boots." She steps out farther, hands still clearly visible, then yells, "He told me you'd know what that means. Uh, Alpha, he's shot."

My heart drops. I yell the countercode, "What's the weather like?"

She turns her head. I can see her lips moving, talking into the tree line. She yells back, "It looks like snow but won't be a problem."

It's the right answer. "Everyone out from the trees," I call out. "Can Alpha walk? I want to see him."

I reload my hunting rifle while watching. In a matter of seconds, the youngest woman—the girl—joins the older lady, her hands clearly visible. Then Logan comes out, being supported by two of the women, followed by the last two behind them with their hands in the air.

All of the women are looking around, almost frantically . . . trying to find me? Or looking for their captors? The two helping Logan gently lower him to the ground. He searches me out. He's not likely to see me but knows where I should be. He gives me a thumbs up.

235

I grab my small binoculars to look him over. He's bloody. So bloody I can't exactly tell where he's been hit. Then I see a bandage on his arm and a second on his leg. He had a small first aid kit in his backpack, compliments of our raid on the pharmacy. I have a duplicate in mine.

He tries to call for me. I can see his mouth moving. "Lima, come on down," I think he says, but I can't hear him.

The woman shouts, "He's saying, 'Lima, come down.' It's hard for him to yell."

In the binos, I see Logan nod and smile. He gives me a thumbs up again along with the okay sign. I'm not going to get any further confirmation. Logan believes it's safe for me to join him. I look over the four dead guys again—just to make sure they really are dead guys.

The first guy, in the blind, was a headshot. No threat there. Second guy, on this side of the road in the blind, hasn't moved. Looks like there's even flies starting to do their job. Board Boy is definitely dead, as is Paul Bunyan. I can only assume Logan took care of the two guys at the river.

I feel a little sick. Not from the radiation this time, but from the killing. In the past few seconds, I killed four people. My total is now five. Five dead by my hand—Stanley James Parker in San Jose and these four evildoers. Of course, I can't really say I killed Board Boy. He was down from another shot, probably from Logan, but I made sure to finish him off. Each death was necessary, but still . . .

I shake my head to clear my thoughts. I need to stay focused. I can think about the killing later . . . or maybe not. Maybe I can just accept I did what I had to do and that is that. Right now, I need to get to Logan.

Three rifles—how can I handle three rifles while climbing down this slope? The .308 has a strap so it can go on my back. I'll carry the 5.56 and stash the .22. My hip weapon and backups are where they belong. I'm sure those ladies are going to love seeing me walking down, loaded for bear. I'll definitely look like the mythical Amazon woman; I just need a bow and arrow.

It takes me many minutes to reach them. I've barely let my eyes stray from the six women and Logan. The women continue to keep their hands visible and hardly move as I make my way toward them.

Once I'm within talking distance, Logan says huskily but with a small smile, "Pretty good plan, babe. Took you long enough to get down here. Barbara says we'd best be getting out of here. There are four more guys out looking for supplies. Might be back anytime."

Chapter 46

Lindsey

Thursday, Day 22
Backroads Wyoming

"I'm okay, Lindsey. I'm okay," Logan says, while I look him over. All I want to do is hold him, kiss him. But first, I need to make sure the bleeding's under control, make sure he'll be okay.

"Carlene," Logan says, motioning to one of the women, "she bandaged me up. The maxi pads were a good idea. I guess you knew what you were talking about when you said they were absorbent."

"Yeah, they do the job," I say, fretting over him. I don't want to remove what Carlene has put in place since the bleeding seems to be under control. The women have scattered, starting to gather things up so we can leave. Barbara, the oldest captive, is instrumental in getting the other ladies going. To say the group is shell shocked would be an understatement. Even so, they're very good about following orders.

"How'd you know?"

"How'd I know what? About the maxi pads?"

"Yeah, those."

"Seriously? I'm a girl." I wink and then say, "My mom told me. Said she read it in a book. I just remembered."

His left hand has a cut across the thumb, not bad but I'm sure it hurts.

"Got that while . . . you know."

I nod. "Both with the knife?"

He visibly pales as he says, "It went bad with the second. The first was perfect, like we planned. He walked off on his own. I literally caught him with his pants down. The second guy, I wasn't quiet enough. He must have heard me and moved at the last second.

238

"We fought, I lost the knife, and he pulled his pistol. I saw what was happening and managed to get into the brush. He winged me a couple of times in the process. The older woman saw what was happening and rammed into him . . . well, all of them rammed him since they were connected. But it was Barbara's instigating. Once I had a clear shot, I took it."

"So your arm and leg, that's where he shot you?"

"Yeah, but really, I don't think either is too terribly bad. The thigh is just a graze, not bad at all. The arm, it might be a little worse. He was firing wild, could've just as easily missed me."

Or just as easily have headshot you, I think to myself.

While loading up, Carlene gives us a quick overview of how they found themselves captives to Paul Bunyan and crew. Before the women were thrust together as captives, each was on a different path, going to stay with friends or family in an area they hoped was better than where they were coming from.

Carlene and her daughter, Aimie, were kidnapped from their home.

She let out a big sigh and said, "Eric and my husband, Richard, worked together."

"Eric?" I ask.

"Yeah. I think you called him Paul when you and your husband were talking . . . I'm not sure why. The one in the red flannel shirt."

"Oh. Mm-hmm. I know which one you mean." No sense mentioning why we call him Paul.

"Eric used to come around the house quite a bit, but last year we had to put a stop to his visits. It was . . . wrong . . . the way he'd look at Aimie. The day after the lights went out, he stopped by with another guy—he's out on a supply run right now. He said he was just checking on us. More like checking up on us. I think he was probably deciding then what he could do. When they came back, they had two more guys with them. Eric killed Richard when he opened the door. My sweet son, two years older than Aimie, was next. What they did to Aimie . . . to me . . . has been worse than the quick death my husband and son experienced."

Her shoulders shake slightly, but she doesn't cry while she shares her story. I don't have words of comfort to offer Carlene. "I'm sorry" sure doesn't cut it. I rest my hand on her arm for a moment. She looks up and meets my eyes, giving a small nod. "Thank you. The days ahead won't be easy, but we're out of the nightmare. I'm not sure what we'll do now. We can't go home. Eric set our house on fire."

Carlene and Aimie were the first of the prisoners. Barbara was next, found walking with her husband. He was killed outright. The additional three were added, one at a time, with their male walking partners murdered.

Carlene thinks it's likely new captives could be brought back with the four men who went out for supplies. Logan and I discuss setting up some sort of ambush to take them out and save any new hostages. We finally agree it's too dangerous, especially with Logan injured. While we don't think either injury is life-threatening, he won't be at full capacity. Barbara says they will fight, but as afflicted as they are, we can't risk it.

With Logan's injuries, we also can't ride the bikes. Aimie helps me retrieve both motorcycles and all our gear from where it was stowed. The other women pack up the things they want to take—which isn't much other than every available weapon, ammunition, and every crumb of food.

The women didn't want any of the set-up tents—too many bad memories. But there were a couple of tents, brought back on one of the expeditions, that haven't been used. We take those.

Somehow, we manage to get the bikes secured to an old Ford 250 flatbed pickup truck. Logan can't help much, but he gives excellent suggestions. Barbara must be in her midfifties but is amazingly fit and strong. I'm beyond impressed with what she's capable of, especially with the situation she's been in for the last couple of weeks.

A second Ford, a beat up 150 with a regular bed, is quickly loaded with the captives' gear. The third truck has a manual transmission, which none of the ladies can drive. I can drive it, but we decide it's best for me to be armed, riding shotgun. The funny looking car, which Logan informs me is an AMC Pacer, has an automatic transmission and tiny back seat. It becomes our third vehicle.

Where to go now, after being freed from their ordeal, is the question. One of the ladies, Samantha, has a friend near the tiny town of Pavillion, Wyoming, where she and her boyfriend were heading when she was captured. Not really out of our way to get to Bakerville, so we go there first.

"I'm sure Janet will let everyone stay for at least a few days. Then we can figure out where to go from there. I know Carlene and Aimie don't really have any place to go. Maybe you could stay? Janet's great. You'll really like her." Samantha's breathless when she finishes her rushed-on sentences.

Barbara gives her a slight squeeze. "I'm sure your friend is wonderful."

When we reach Janet's place, her home is a smoking pile of rubble, burned to the ground several days prior. There's no sign of Janet or her family.

At first, Samantha only stares, wide eyed and detached. Barbara reaches for her, but Samantha shakes her away.

"No. No. This can't be. Janet has to be here. Barbara, you said. You promised. You told me we'd find a way to escape and we'd come here. You promised."

"I know I did, Samantha," Barbara responds, barely above a whisper. "I'm so sorry."

"No. You're not sorry. You're a liar. Liar!"

With tears in her eyes, Barbara nods.

Samantha yells several obscenities, not exactly directed at Barbara but not sparing her feelings either. Then she crumples to the ground and begins to wail.

Logan, unsure how to respond to her keening, gives me a helpless look.

Barbara is the one who says to all of us, "Let's just give her a few minutes. She's had a rough time of it at the camp. The idea of coming here . . . it's what kept her going."

We give Samantha her space. As much as I'd like to get back on the road, we're pretty sure we're far enough away from the abductors camp and are safe from them. Of course, safe is relative these days.

After fifteen minutes or so, Samantha joins us. Her face is streaked with dirt and tears, and her eyes are rimmed red. "Any chance I could get a shower?" she asks.

"We have wet wipes," I offer.

"How about some of the water in a jug and a washcloth?" Barbara asks. "We could set up a sponge bath of sorts for you. I've done that while camping. It'll make you feel a whole world better."

"Could I do that also?" Aimie asks.

We spend another half hour at Janet's burned-out house while the ladies clean up. Thankfully, there's a small shed they use as a private washroom. By the time they're ready, Logan and I are both anxious to leave.

We're back to wondering where everyone will go. Barbara was on her way to a nephew of her husband's. A nephew she's never met in the ten years they were married, but she doesn't know where his house is. The other two women were in similar situations. And Carlene and Aimie are essentially homeless. Carlene has family in Kentucky but can't figure out a way to get there.

Without any other options, Logan and I suggest they continue with us until we can find a place for them. We don't know what we'll encounter in Bakerville, but I know Mom and Evan won't turn these women away. Plus, it might be good to have some extra help with my mom laid up. I don't mention this to them; no reason to get their hopes up.

Six more people to feed . . . at least we took the food their kidnappers had. From the raids they'd been out on, they had amassed quite a stockpile, enough to sustain the six women for at least a month with rationing. According to Barbara, they've been barely getting enough to survive now.

Before they started packing up the camp, she gave each woman a pouch of tuna. They've had several small snacks since then. I have no doubt they're all still hungry, but Barbara's smart to limit the amount given at one time.

It's only half an hour to the slightly larger town of Shoshoni. Logan and I hope for a safe place to spend the night. There's at least one motel in town; dare we hope they might be accepting reservations? There's also a pretty nice state campground just on the other side of Shoshoni on a large lake.

A few miles outside of town, we are met by a roadblock. I'm in the lead vehicle, the F150, and caught completely by surprise. I didn't get the creeps or anything before we were suddenly stopped. Samantha pulled herself together and is my silent driver.

The Pacer is a good hundred yards behind us. Logan's in the flatbed behind the Pacer, with Barbara driving.

Samantha crawls to a stop but leaves the pickup running.

"Where you folks heading?" the guard shouts from behind a car.

"Bakerville. To my parents' place," I answer.

"Okay. Well, good you have transportation. Shouldn't take you too terribly long to get there. I'd suggest you keep on driving and don't stop until you reach Thermopolis. They're letting people stay in the state park there."

"Sure. That'd be good. But we were thinking maybe we'd stay here."

"Sorry. We don't have any lodging options. You'll want to head on to Thermopolis."

"Maybe the campground before the tunnel?" I suggest. "We've had a long day already."

"Nope. You won't be able to stay there. They've had a few . . . incidents."

"Oh?"

"Uh, yeah. They had too many people at the campgrounds, and things went bad. Lots of deaths. Now, the people in the campgrounds, all of the campgrounds in Boysen State Park, are treating it as their own fort or something. They won't let you stay. But everything we hear tells us Thermop is still okay. They've got a pretty good setup there. Had a few problems, but they nipped them in the bud pretty quick. Heard they make improvements every day, to keep things running as smooth as possible."

"Okay, that's fine. It's only, what, thirty miles from here?"

"'Bout that. The canyon's a little iffy. You won't want to stop for people. Just drive like you mean it, and if someone's in the road . . . well, they should move for ya."

"Did he just tell me to run over people in the road?" Samantha whispers.

I give a one-shoulder shrug. Yeah, I think he did.

"You folks need some water? We can refill your jugs for you. We have a privy set up over there— " he motions to the south " —and another on the other side of town. Can't help you with anything else."

"Water, please. That'd be great," I answer.

"Okay. How about one of you gets out and collects jugs from everyone? Then we'll get you on your way."

I don't really like the idea of one of us getting out. I'm hesitating on my answer when he says, "Oh, uh, right." He steps out from behind the car, lays his rifle on the hood, and motions to his friend on the other side of the road to do the same.

"Sorry." He shrugs. "I guess I wouldn't feel too comfortable with a couple of guns on me either."

I slowly open my door and give a small wave back to the rest of our convoy. I want them to stay alert but not twitchy. Hopefully they'll understand that from my signal.

"I'm armed. I have a weapon on my belt," I say, before stepping from behind the door.

"Of course you do. Only smart to be armed these days. You're fine here, little lady. We have no plans of hurting you. We're just doing what's best for our own friends and family. You understand, right?"

I have three one-gallon jugs and a soda bottle in our truck. I decide that'll be good for now. Five minutes later, the water is filled. A third guy, who appeared out of nowhere riding a quad, escorts us through town. We regroup a few miles out of town where they have bathroom facilities set up. We all take care of business. Logan's stomach is acting up again. I'm not too bad.

I pass a new gallon jug of water to each of the vehicles and share the plan to drive like mad through the canyon. We switch things up and have Barbara and her larger truck as the lead vehicle—she seems a little less squeamish about the prospect of people jumping out in front of her and being forced to run them over. Only a little less squeamish . . .

The trip through the canyon is harrowing. Barbara sets the pace. We do have a few people jump out in front of us, but she never slows. There's one lady holding up a small baby. It's clear she's begging us to take the child . . . feed the child. My eyes immediately fill with tears.

We don't stop.

Chapter 47

Sylvia

Thursday, Day 22
Meeteetse, Wyoming

We're greeted by a welcome station—seriously, there's a big sign that says, "WELCOME STATION." Not check station or roadblock, which is what it is, but Welcome Station. The guy manning it gives us a nice smile and a lefthanded wave. His right hand is casually holding a shotgun. "Howdy, folks."

"Hi," Sabrina says with her own nice smile and wave. I don't have the energy to smile or wave. We're less than a half mile outside of Meeteetse. At the pace we're traveling, no more than fifteen walking days and we'll be in Bakerville.

"You folks passing through?"

"We'd like to stay a day or two," Rey says.

"Yep, okay. We have a city park people are camping in and around."

"There's a motel on the other side of the river. My mom stayed there before. Is it open by chance?" Sabrina asks.

Mom and Phil spent quite a bit of time in Meeteetse when they were on their cross-country trip in search of a retirement spot. They rented a cabin at the motel Sabrina's asking about. I know this because my mom points out the place each time we drive through this little town. She says pretty much the same thing every time, "*Oh, that little place is so nice. Right on the river and the perfect place to stay and explore the area. The owner, he was very good to us.*"

"You won't want to stay there," the roadblock guy says, with a look of panic on his face. "The owner, he didn't make it back after the attacks started. The young girl he had working as the manager, she took off when the power went out. She left the place in the hands of the guys working on the road crew. You saw that road work about fifteen miles back?"

"Uh . . . yeah. Maybe," Rey says, while the rest of us shrug. Fifteen miles back . . . was that yesterday or the day before? Who can remember?

"Well, anyway. I guess the crew bosses took off and left the workers at the hotel, just hightailed it out in the company vehicles. Can you believe it? So these guys are now mad at the world. They've got the motel, cabins, all of it as their dominion. So far, they're just causing a ruckus over there, but you mark my words—those are bad guys . . . bad dudes. They'll let you stay, for a cost. It used to be money they were taking. Then they moved on to beer and food. Now, I don't know what it might be. You all seem like nice folks, and with the kids, I don't think you ought to get messed up with that."

"Uh, right. We don't want any part of that," Rey says.

"Yep, between you and me, I don't even know if the manager really left. Far as I know . . . well, you catch my drift?"

We caught his drift. And bummer about the owner not making it back. According to Mom, he was a good guy. Hopefully, wherever he is, he's doing fine.

"Don't you have a police department in this town?" Kim challenges.

"Nope. We have—or I should say, *had*—two county sheriff deputies. One was away for training when this all went down. Her family's worried sick. The second, he was here, but we're not sure what happened to him. Don't know if he took off or met some unseemly end."

"What about his family?"

"Young guy. Lived alone. The town council's trying to scare up some protection for the city, you know, put something in place. We're manning a welcome station on each side of town and will start with more stuff. Not sure what all yet. Right now, we're doing okay. Just keep your distance from those guys."

"So, we can camp at the city park?" Sabrina asks.

"Yep. The other hotel is closed up. People are using the park and the vacant lot across the street. Those are pretty full, so we're letting people camp in the yard next door. That's old Agnes's place. She died last week, so guess it doesn't much matter if you use her yard. Mind you, we'd ask you be respectful and not use her house."

"Of course, we'll definitely be respectful, sir," Sabrina says quickly.

"And . . . uh . . . like I said, watch yourselves. So far, those guys are staying over at the motel, but you should keep aware and all. You folks probably know that if you've been on the road. We've heard some stuff from others."

We've run into travelers and have heard a couple of stories, but not much. When they see we have children, they clam up on the details and just tell us to be careful. We've also been hearing rumors there was more than just a high-altitude nuke detonated. We've met a few people who said they ran into people who saw mushroom clouds in Seattle. There are even rumors of people with radiation sickness. Sabrina says, if Seattle was bombed, it's likely other places were also. What kind of terrorists have bombs like that? Bombs causing a widespread EMP and destroying cities? Other than rumors, we don't really know what's happening in other places. And I have to wonder, does it really matter? At the moment, just getting to Mom's house seems like all that's important.

"Is there a place to get some food?" Kim asks.

"Sorry, no food. You can fish in the river if you'd like."

Kim makes a face.

"Thank you," Rey says to the gentleman, while offering his hand.

The walk to the park is easy and we're soon there. There are about three dozen tents set up in the lot, park, and what we assume is Agnes's place. We find a spot in Agnes's backyard, right near the river. There's another tent in the same area, a guy and gal, younger than Sabrina.

After the incident back in Thermopolis, we've been even more diligent. Rey's now carrying the 9-millimeter I had in my bag. The day after we left Thermopolis, we had target practice to make sure he knew what he was doing. Much to Kim's dismay, he made sure Nicole and Nate could also handle the weapon. He tried to persuade Kim to shoot, but she adamantly refused.

I was considerably impressed with Rey's ability to handle the pistol. Sabrina commented to me privately that he looked like he might have a lot more experience than he let on. Sabrina and I are still carrying our primary weapon on our hip and a secondary hidden weapon. The .22 revolver is holstered in Sabrina's backpack. The long guns have yet to make their way out of the shopping cart. As far as we know, Kim and Rey have no knowledge of these hidden weapons.

I'm glad they're letting us catch fish. We're rationing our food, but I think we'll run out before we reach Mom's house. When we were on the river, those early days after needing to hang out in the tunnel, we were able to catch fish to extend what we all brought along.

Rey's homemade pole combined with Sabrina's ultralight telescoping rod and reel combo—another item she was smart to pack—yielded half a dozen fish each day. Rey was getting pretty good at using his temporary set up. I really hated to leave the river; we've been landlocked since.

Sabrina set up a snare to try to get a rabbit, but we weren't successful. Maybe it's better we didn't get one. I seem to remember something about wild rabbits having flees or something during the summer. Ick.

There was an abundance of antelope between Thermopolis and Shoshoni. We thought about shooting one and staying put a few days to cook it up for traveling. Sabrina makes jerky in the oven or food dehydrator regularly, and she thinks making it over an open fire or setting up some kind of easy smokehouse would work for preserving the meat.

But we've decided against it, for now. Mainly because Kim made a big stink about how antelope aren't fit for eating. We'll see if she gets hungry enough to change her mind.

The Hoffmanns are out of everything, at least we think they are. Sometimes I wonder if Kim might be holding something back, a private food stash.

My new-to-me size twelve jeans I got in Thermopolis are now too large. The belt doesn't even help much. I found some twine and tied the belt loops together on each side. This at least keeps them up. Without a scale to jump on, I'm not sure how much weight I've lost. A lot. And way too fast.

Sabrina, who was very fit when we started out, is looking scrawny. Rey's and Kim's weight losses are also noticeable, but the poor children . . . they look terrible. Skinny and exhausted. All of us are using some sort of makeshift method to hold our pants up. Our shirts fit us like tents. A day or two off, especially if we can catch a few fish, might do wonders. I don't really want to put the weight I've lost back on, but the rest of them need a little more meat on them. Especially the children.

I'm down to only six packs of cigarettes. Some days I'm better at rationing than others. Just depends on the day. While the walking has been terribly monotonous, it isn't overly strenuous. There are a few small hills, but nothing extremely steep. Kim's attitude has been okay, but there's certainly something off about her. I truly can't figure her out.

Like Rey, even after all this time on the road, she still looks spectacular. She's no longer pink with a sunburn. Instead, she has a tropical look about her, tanned skin and her blond hair even brighter, bleached by the rays of the sun. Same with Rey—tan and gorgeous. He reminds me of the guy on the TV show *Lost*, the kind of bad guy. What was his name? Sawyer? Yeah, maybe. Wish I could pull up Netflix and find out. While I'm at wishing, I'd love to order a pizza and a six pack while I binge on *Lost* episodes.

Of course, after being on the road with Rey for almost two weeks, I no longer have any sort of crush on him. While he seems pleasant enough, like Kim, something's off. I can't put my finger on it, but I get the impression he's not very genuine. Just a pretty package.

"Sylvie, Breena, did you see the signs with the little animals on them?" Naomi asks, completely excited. "N'cole read to me, and it says they live here. They're like little dog things."

"Oh, yeah, sure. Black-footed ferrets," I answer. "Before . . . another time when I was driving through here with my mom, she took us to the museum. They had a big display about the ferrets. Did you know they thought this special ferret, the black-footed ferret, was extinct? Do you know what that word means?"

"No, I don't think I know that word."

"It means they thought they were all gone. Then, one day . . . gosh, I can't remember, I think maybe someone's dog was barking at one or something. Anyway, they found out these little guys aren't extinct. Now, they live around here and in a few other places. They're working to bring them back."

"Is that what's happening to us?"

"What do you mean, sweetie pie?" Sabrina asks.

"Are we going to go exited? Will we be all gone?"

"Exited? Extinct? You mean people?"

"Yeah. I know lots of people are dying. Are we going to be extinct like they thought the little animal was?" She starts crying as the last few words make their way out.

"Oh, no, honey," Sabrina says, pulling her close.

"Not at all," I say at the same time.

Sabrina hugs her tight, while I stand there looking on like a goofball. Sabrina's definitely the more affectionate of us. She seems to know when to give a hug or a kind word. I'm often late on even thinking about doing these things, then I feel like a heel.

"You sure?" Naomi hiccups.

"I'm sure. It's true some bad things have happened, but we're still here. And there's other people here. Soon, we'll get to my mom's house and you'll get nice and rested before you go on to your mom and dad's friend's place. Everything will be fine, you'll see."

"You promise?"

Sabrina pauses before saying, "I promise Sylvia and I, along with your mom and dad, are doing everything we can to get you where you need to be."

Naomi gives her a look, the kind of look that tells me she isn't buying it for a second. Her little shoulders slump. She screws up a face a few times and finally says only one word, "Okay."

Sabrina gives her a smile and asks, "Where's your sister?"

"Um . . . not sure. Thought she was behind me. Maybe she went with Mom and Dad?"

Rey found a new limb to turn into a fishing pole and took off down the river. Kim and Nate joined him while the girls were walking around the park.

"Let's go see," I say, thinking we should've seen her walk by.

Once we're on the bank of the river we see Rey, Kim, and Nate a little farther west. No Nicole.

"Where do you think she went?" I ask.

"Not sure," Sabrina says with a slight shrug. "It's really not like her to take off. How about I head down to where Rey and Kim are? Maybe she's with them and we just can't see her."

"Like lounging on the bank out of view? Yeah, that makes sense. While you do that, I'll walk back to the park, just to make sure. Naomi, you want to walk with me?"

"Okay, Sylvie. I'll show you the little animal picture."

"Sure, that sounds fine."

Less than ten minutes later, we're all back at camp. All except Nicole.

Naomi and I walked from the park down the main street in town. We saw the same guy, the one we talked to at the welcome station on the edge of town. He said he'd finished his shift for the day. He remembered Nicole from earlier but hasn't seen her since then. We asked a few other people if they'd seen anyone resembling Nicole. No dice.

Kim is near frantic as we form a plan to search for Nicole. It's decided Rey and Nate will walk the other side of the riverbank, and Sabrina and Naomi will walk around town again and try to enlist the help of others to search. Kim and I will walk this side of the riverbank, going in the opposite direction from where they were fishing. We'll estimate an hour and then come back to camp. Oh, how I wish for cell phones while we search.

We don't need an hour. Kim and I quickly discover what's become of Nicole.

Chapter 48

Sylvia

Thursday, Day 22
Meeteetse, Wyoming

Kim grabs my arm and motions me to be silent. Soft cries combined with mumbling voices—all feeling drains from my body. Nicole. *Someone is hurting Nicole.*

I glance at Kim. The look she gives me . . . it is hard to describe. Anger, pain, heartbreak, and hatred all in one. With her mouth right next to my ear, in a hauntingly calm voice, Kim says, "Give me your sidearm. Don't argue, don't discuss. Give it to me now. And, yes, I know how to use it."

I close my eyes. I can't argue with a mother wanting to protect her young daughter. I nod and oblige, handing her my Beretta. I then take my smaller Sig Sauer P238 out of my ankle holster.

Once again, mouth to my ear, Kim says, "I'll take the lead. Back me up. Make sure you don't shoot me."

I nod, hoping she knows what she's doing. This woman, who threw a fit about Sabrina and I being armed, is now—my thoughts are interrupted as she mouths, "Let's go," and she goes.

I'm right behind her, moving as quietly as I can, but not nearly as silent and deliberate as Kim moves. The thicket we're in makes everything difficult for me, but not Kim. She's like a butterfly flitting through the brush.

Entering a slight alcove, Kim drops to a knee. I follow suit. I catch a glimpse of a guy standing, watching. The glimpse is all I get before Kim fires and he goes down. She swivels and shoots again. Then she's moving, yelling, "Stay on the ground. Stay on the ground, and I might let you live."

I step forward slightly so I can see and back her up as she requested. The guy on the ground starts to get up. Kim is suddenly on him. Her body blocks my view as I hear a loud cracking sound. She stands up and turns to Nicole.

"You're okay, baby. You're okay," she calmly and quietly says to Nicole.

Then she turns to me and serenely says, "Sylvia, come help Nicole," as she steps to the first guy she shot and puts a bullet in his head. In the distance, we hear people yelling. I reholster my backup weapon and go to Nicole, glancing at the bad guy near her. He's a big guy, close to six foot, bordering on fat. He's bleeding from the arm and his . . . is his neck broken? Holy cow, I think it is. Necks don't bend that way.

Nicole's shirt is tattered, but her pants are still in place. *Thank you, Jesus.* Wait. Where did that thought come from? I stopped believing in divine intervention long ago. I stopped believing the night . . . the night I prayed and prayed for help and none arrived.

"You're okay. You're okay," I say, while unbuttoning the light shirt I'm wearing over a baggy tank top. "Here, let's get this on you."

I look around for Kim. She's doing something with the guy she shot in the head. She turns and catches me looking at her. "Good, glad you got her clothed. Sounds like we're going to have company. Uh . . ." She grabs my arm and pulls me away from Nicole, whispering, "Listen, you need to say you did the shooting, okay?"

"What? No. Why do I need to do that?"

"I'll explain once we get back to camp. I promise. Just do it," she says forcefully, thrusting my gun into my hand. I nod my agreement.

A man I don't recognize appears over the edge of the bank and slides down. He takes a look around, instantly understanding what has happened, and says, "Oh, no. Uh . . . let me help you with her."

As he reaches for Nicole, she lets out an ear-piercing shriek. "Don't touch her," Kim snaps. "We'll take care of her. You take care of these scum. Is this how the people of your town treat a young girl?"

"No . . . no, ma'am. I don't . . . they don't live here, at least I don't know them." There are now several other people around.

One guy says, "I think they're from across the river, staying at the motel."

I want to get Nicole away. "Can you all turn around? She doesn't need all of you here," I say.

There are many kind responses of, "Of course," "So sorry," "Didn't even think of it," as the gaggle of men and a few women turn and avert their eyes. Kim gives me a grateful look. Nicole, no longer screaming, whimpers as we help her stand. "Mommy. Mommy, I'm so sorry. I didn't see them." She breaks down in tears.

"You have nothing to be sorry for, baby," Kim says. "Can you walk?"

Nicole nods as we help her hobble away. After a few feet, one of the townspeople says, "Please, take this," and hands me a larger button shirt. I wrap it around Nicole, its length going to her knees. Hopefully the extra warmth will keep her from going into shock.

He then says, "Let me help you bring her up onto the bank. It'll be easier walking than along the river's edge."

I defer to Kim. She gives a slight nod and whispers to Nicole. Nicole now has a blank look and doesn't respond. The man makes sure not to touch Nicole, instead, bracing himself so he can help me and then Kim as we help Nicole. Once on the bank, Nicole completely collapses.

Chapter 49

Mollie

Thursday, Day 22
Bakerville, Wyoming

I'm hot. Miserably and uncomfortably hot. Several of us are using the outside kitchen to preserve food. I'd so much rather do this in the house with the air conditioner on full blast. But air conditioning is a thing of the past, and the pressure and water bath canners would just add to the already excessive heat inside.

While we can get some high temps during the summer, people are saying this summer is cooler. Not to me.

And without air conditioning, or at the very least fans—both drain the solar system too much to use—I'm miserable. We've been getting thunderstorms late afternoon. They arrive in time to help lift the oppressive heat. Looking to the mountains at the west, I can see a slight darkness. I pray it's the brewing of an afternoon storm.

We have a few small rechargeable fans, which are a slight help, but still. Even though it's been a couple of weeks since I was injured and got a bump on the head, I half wonder if this doesn't have my internal system messed up. I'm still sometimes dizzy and sick to my stomach.

"Are you okay, Mom?" Sarah asks.

"Oh, yes. Just feeling the heat."

"Your face is super red, Mollie," Lois says. "Can I get you some water?"

"No, no. I have water." I motion to my water jug. "I'm fine, really."

Sarah gives me a long look.

I give her a small smile and a nod. "Really, I'm okay."

"All right, Mom, if you're sure," she says as she rubs her tummy, caressing the babe growing inside. "Whew. This food preservation is hard work. It's no wonder you're so red faced. I feel like we never stop, and yet, I also worry we'll be done too soon and not have enough to get us through the winter."

"With the garden and livestock, along with what we've stored, we'll be fine," I say. "Plus, now that we're somewhat rationing, we can make it last."

"We're certainly blessed compared to others," Lois says. "With everything you and Jake have set up and Deanne's skills to plan the menus based on calories needed, we're in fine shape. It's even been an excellent weight-loss plan." She gives a chuckle. Lois has already lost several pounds, and we've only been rationing since the EMP hit. Of course, the extra physical activity also contributes to weight loss.

While we're still consuming plenty of calories, none of us are eating as much as we did before the attacks. The days of abundance are over. Deanne's used some of the research saved on a flash drive to put together menus to ensure we get enough calories, but not too much. While things are fine food-wise right now, with thirty-three people living here and under our care, it's already a consideration. Will we have enough to make it until the harvest next year?

Preserving this year's harvest and managing our livestock will be our main focus. With a somewhat short growing season, we need to make the most of it while we can.

Leo finished building a greenhouse, attached to our main house. It's a decent size and will not only help us extend the season but will also help warm the house by capturing extra heat. Jake bought three small greenhouse kits on one of his shopping trips, and they've been set up as well. We'll start planting in the greenhouses at the end of this month for a fall and, hopefully, winter garden.

Right now, we mainly have assorted greens, radishes, zucchini, and berries. We're pretty sure we're going to get a bit more fruit from our small orchard than last year, but not nearly as much as we need. The trees are still very young.

The number of berries we're getting is fairly impressive. We're enjoying our harvest fresh and also preserving it. Today, I'm pickling radishes in half-pint jars and pressure canning assorted greens, including the tops of the radishes. I also have additional greens and herbs on the drying screen.

Unfortunately, greens and berries, while tasty, don't provide a lot of calories. We'll be relying on the potatoes and winter squashes to beef things up, along with our livestock options and smart harvesting of deer, elk, and moose.

Deer have been severely affected by CWD, whether Jon Dawson thinks so or not, so we'll be very careful with these, using only the meat and avoiding the bones and organs. I hate that we'll have to leave so much behind, but we won't risk the possibility of CWD jumping to humans, *my humans.*

People like Dawson can do what they want, but on the Caldwell homestead, we're being cautious. Elk, which we have a small resident herd of in Bakerville, haven't been nearly as decimated by CWD as the deer. We'll still be cautious. The occasional moose around Bakerville should be fine; not many moose have tested positive.

We're only weeks away from harvesting our first batch of meat birds. We raise them on pasture in chicken tractors, open bottomed pens we move daily to new land. This is usually a cash crop for us. Each spring I take orders from previous customers and order the chicks in as day olds, which we pick up from the post office. Seven to nine weeks later, we butcher.

The first batch of 150 was four weeks old and on pasture when the attacks started. The second batch, 125 meat birds plus twenty-five layers, arrived the morning of the plane crashes. Obviously, there will be no third batch since shipping day-old chicks is now a thing of the past.

I wonder about things like commercial hatcheries. Were they able to salvage any of those birds to feed the people in the area? I doubt it. It's unlikely they'd have enough feed on hand to raise the chicks to butchering age. I suspect the large chicken houses are in the same boat. Not enough feed on hand. Same with pork producers and cattle feed lots. Did they turn them out? Will there soon be feral pigs and cows roaming the Midwest? I wonder if we'll ever know.

"Okay, Mom?" Sarah asks.

"I'm sorry?"

"I'm going to go check on the children, make sure they aren't driving Grandma Dodie crazy. Lois is going to the garden to see how Angela and Calley are doing."

"Oh, yeah. Sure."

"We'll be back shortly," Lois says with a smile.

After they've left, Deanne says, "You okay, Mollie? You seem preoccupied."

I stifle a sigh. *Jeez, these people.* "I'm okay. Just really warm."

"Katie sure looked good at breakfast this morning," Deanne says.

"She did. She looks better every day. I'm glad Belinda's still here, though, just in case."

"Sarah said Belinda's letting Katie walk around on her own now and even help a little bit."

"Yes, under strict orders to rest as soon as she's tired and to not push herself."

"They're starting her medical training again?"

"A little. Belinda's mostly quizzing her on what she knows."

"How are the wedding plans coming?"

"Good. She and Laurie both agree with what they want."

"It's wonderful to have a double wedding. The way I hear it, as soon as your friend Aaron heard about Leo and Katie's plans, he immediately proposed to Laurie."

"Yes. They'd been planning to get married after she finished college. But with everything . . . "

"Yeah. No reason not to go ahead with it." Deanne nods.

The wedding is two weeks from Sunday. It'll be a Bakerville-wide event held at the community center. Laurie's wearing a donated dress from one of our neighbors. The neighbor was married a few weeks ago, the Saturday after the attacks started. A time when we thought our world would quickly return to normal.

Katie's wearing my wedding dress from my marriage to Jake—a casual, light pink, sleeveless, floor-length dress in chiffon with a V-neck. The fit isn't perfect, but Doris is helping with alterations. They'll shorten it to knee length to update it and make it more Katie's style.

Katie couldn't wear the dress I wore to marry her dad. There was no dress, at least not a proper wedding dress. We took an afternoon off and got married at city hall. I wore a skirt and blouse, one of my work outfits as a receptionist. We'd only decided to marry a few days before. It was the right thing to do.

Katie does have the wedding and engagement ring I wore when married to her dad. Even though we didn't have a proper engagement, he bought me a simple diamond solitaire and gave it to me when he asked me to marry him. That was on a Friday. On Saturday, we went back to the jewelers and bought wedding bands. Not matching but both white gold.

Leo's parents were killed in a car accident a few weeks after he graduated high school. He had their wedding set, making sure he packed it when they left Manhattan in the early days of the attacks.

Originally, Leo wanted to offer his mom's ring set to Katie, but it was much too big. My old set was a perfect fit. Katie suggested Leo wear her dad's ring, but it was too small. Leo's dad's band—a titanium replacement to his original thin gold band that wore out—fits him fine and coordinates well with Katie's ring.

Katie offered her dad's ring to Laurie to give to Aaron. Leo offered his mom's set to Aaron to give to Laurie. Both were slightly large, but a community member was able to make slight alterations so they fit.

Truthfully, the rings aren't likely to be worn much. Most of the women on our homestead, me included, have stopped wearing their diamonds. Not only is there no reason, but with all of the food and garden work, they just get in the way. The guys working on the farm have the same issue.

Pastor Ralph stopped by last night and asked if it'd be okay to make it a triple wedding. Another couple, retired neighbors who've been dating for years, have decided to tie the knot.

Saturday, the day before the wedding, we'll have a small bridal shower. Mainly just the ladies living on our homestead and a few others in Bakerville we're close to. When my other girls were married, we did pampering sessions before the wedding. We went for pedicures and manicures, had lunch out, and celebrated the bride.

Nail salons are gone. Restaurants are gone. Those days are no more. While it won't be the same as the festivities leading up to Sarah, Angela, and Calley's weddings—and the wedding will also be much less elaborate—we'll have a wonderful time in this new world.

Deanne lowers her voice and asks, "What about Lydia?"

I shake my head. "Not great. She seems to be getting worse. Kelley thinks there's probably a psychological issue in addition to the detoxing. She's started sessions with her to try to reach a diagnosis."

"Does Kelley think this was something she was already dealing with? Or was it brought on by the detoxing?"

"She thinks she may have been taking some kind of prescribed psychotropic drug in the past. Leo didn't find anything in the house they were living in when cleaning it out. Kelley suspects she didn't like the way the prescribed medication made her feel and chose to self-medicate with booze and street drugs. She says that's pretty common."

"Yeah, I've heard of people doing that."

"Belinda has talked about taking Lydia back to the makeshift hospital they've set up at her mom's house, but felt our safe room and basement set up was better for the current circumstances."

"She still have her in the straitjacket?"

"Not always. She'll be fine sometimes, even asking to see the children and carrying on normal conversations. I think the straitjacket is more of the exception rather than the rule now."

Deanne nods. "You mind if I take a little break? I'd like to check on Sheila."

Sheila's having plenty of her own issues; likely the talk of Lydia and her troubles have spurred Deanne to concern. "Sure. I'll keep working on this and see you later."

Even with the excitement of the wedding, it's not exactly smooth sailing on the homestead. This new world we live in, even with our solar system, lacks most of the conveniences of our old lives. There's no running out for a quick bite to eat; everything is cooked at home. And with so many people living here, it takes some time.

Washing dishes and laundry for the masses is another daily chore requiring teamwork. There are building projects being worked on, salvaging, and so much more.

We're working hard to increase the production on the homestead, to take it from what was little more than a hobby farm to a sustaining farm, providing not only for us but to contribute toward the community coffers as well.

People who barely knew each other are now forced to live and work together. There are definitely some growing pains while we all adjust to our new life. And lots and lots of tears.

It's been just over a week since the shootout at Doris and Evan's house. The night it happened, I barely slept. Every time I closed my eyes, I was transported right back.

I'd feel the gentle recoil of the light rifle against my shoulder, hear the burst of the round, the muzzle blast, and the mechanical whine of the rifle cycling after each shot. The visual of the one guy stumbling after my shot grazed him, then taking a hard fall after the precision of Doris's rifle put him on the ground. The taste of gunpowder filling the utility room from the bad guy and me both firing.

And then the blood. It came later. Since I shot him through the door, I didn't see his blood. But I could smell it. I could even taste it.

I gasped as bile filled my throat. The alkaline burn caused my eyes to water. I spent the rest of the night in a chair, in hopes of not repeating the intense heartburn.

As I come to terms with this new killing, my sleep is finally starting to improve. Doris, Kelley, and I have talked a couple of times since the shooting. Doris is much more blasé about the event than Kelley or me. She knows it was them or us. Sure, I know this too—in my head—but the rest of me is struggling.

Kelley has done well at compartmentalizing the event, choosing to emotionally detach from the trauma. Oh, it's not that she's sweeping it under the rug, she's just not letting it consume her.

Me, I'm having a hard time. A few weeks ago, I was a mom, a wife, and a businesswoman. Today, I'm still a mom and a wife but currently unemployed. And I'm a killer . . . several times over.

Chapter 50

Mollie

Thursday, Day 22
Bakerville, Wyoming

"Hey, beautiful. What are you doing?" Jake interrupts my ruminating.

"Oh, I'm working on pickling radishes. But I kind of got sidetracked with thinking about . . . things."

Jake nods. "I just got back from meeting with Evan and Phil. Everything's almost ready for moving the meals from the community center to the local locations. What are we calling them? Terminals?"

"Stations, but it doesn't matter. Everyone will show up where they're supposed to, and that will be that. When will they be ready?"

"Couple of days."

"I'm glad Mick offered the use of the picnic area by his reservoir. I'm more comfortable with that than having everyone here every day. I'd feel like I was always . . . on. You know what I mean?"

Jake shrugs. "We're not entertaining, Mollie. These are meals for sustenance only. One decent meal per day, the use of the cooking facilities, and possibly something to take home for later."

"I know, Jake," I say, snippier than I should. "With our own lives and everything happening, I'm just happier people won't be coming here every day. That's all I'm saying."

"Mollie, these are our friends, our neighbors. How many times are we commanded to love our neighbor?"

I let out a large sigh. "You're right. I'm just . . . I'm in a foul mood. I've been thinking about our own food supply. Jake, maybe we should think about additional rationing. I'm worried we're going to run short. And we'll use extra food for the wedding. The garden we started this year was large enough for the three of us for eating fresh and preserving. Now how many of us are here? Ten times as many as our garden can sustain."

"True, Mollie. Which is why we've stockpiled things. We've always known the storage items were a Band-Aid while we were getting our garden and livestock up to speed to support everyone. With the change of doing the local stations, we'll send everyone down there for lunch, adding some of our storage goods and accepting some of the acquired goods as 'payment' for our efforts."

"Yeah, I'm not sure how I feel about that. I know I'm complaining we might not have enough food, but we're so much better off than most people. Feels like the salvaged items should be reserved for those who truly have nothing."

"Your concerns were noted," he says, exasperated. We've talked this to death, and he knows how I feel. "And they were quashed. Phil and Kelley are in good shape also, but they know accepting some of the salvaged goods is smart. It was agreed four meals per day is suitable payment for the salvaging, organizing, planning, and cooking involved. Deanne feels confident she can add enough of our own supplies to make it all even out. So she'll plan on adding supplies from our garden or storage, minus enough for four. Besides, it'll be easier than the way she's been doing it, with cooking a separate meal for the community every few days."

"I guess." I shrug. He knows this is really about stealing the food from our neighbors. Rationally, I know it should be used for those who need it today. If, and that is a big *if*, anyone missing makes it home, we can sort it out then.

"And for the wedding, since it's a community event with everyone invited, we'll use some of the community goods. Plus, Mick was great about offering a cull cow, saying it would be a wedding gift to the couples. And if the other couple joins them, it'll be fine. You talk of further rationing . . . I'm not sure we're to that point. I'm concerned, as physically active as we are, if we cut calories too much, people will get sick."

"I know. And I don't want the children to go without. Plus, Sarah needs enough food to support the baby. We might have to lighten up on the exercising so we can stretch the food."

"I don't think so, Mollie. The daily PT is important to get in better shape for the militia, especially now that we're not just planning a little neighborhood militia but a community-wide one. With so many people in Bakerville retired, our children have added quite a few younger people to the community."

Oh, of course he'd bring up the militia—another bone of contention between us. I struggle to keep my voice even, to respond kindly, *a soft answer turneth away wrath.* I give a small smile. "Sure, but as I've said before, many of the retirees are former police or military. And they retired fairly young. Shoot, Phil is our age. Evan's only a few years older. And at least a dozen others I can think of are still young. You know, fifty is the new forty. It shouldn't all fall on us."

"And as *I've* said before, it's not all falling on us. Look, honey— "

"Jake, don't honey me," I sharply interrupt. Oops, so much for my soft answer. "I hate it when you talk to me in that patronizing tone."

"I'm not patronizing you, *Mollie*. I know you're worried about our children being put in a dangerous situation. So am I. But remember, they're adults, and all of them are on board with being part of the militia. Even Sarah's doing it until she advances in her pregnancy."

I start to interrupt again; he raises his hand slightly to stop me.

"And you know, it's not just our family in the militia. Everyone able is participating. Take Doris for example, and shoot, that one guy—your husband's friend who uses a walker—he's even practicing his shooting. Said if nothing else, set him up somewhere with a long-range rifle and he'll keep any bad guys away. Plus, Belinda's training everyone on the militia and several other community members in first aid. Stop being so dramatic. It's not just us handling everything. I think things are still just not right with you. That bump on the head you took in Cooke City and the shooting the other day, maybe those things are affecting you more than you realize. None of this is like you."

"Fine, Jake. You seem to know everything. Just . . . fine. Look, I have things to do. How about you just give me some space and let me do it." I turn to move back toward my canning. Suddenly the world spins, my body is instantly hot, and my head swims.

"Mollie. Mollie, are you okay?" Jake's voice sounds very far away. I need to sit down; I bend my knees to bring myself closer to the ground as everything goes black.

Chapter 51

Sylvia

Thursday, Day 22
Meeteetse, Wyoming

Rey arrives a few seconds after we get Nicole up on the bank. He tenderly carries her back to our camp. The couple sharing our space realizes what happened and quickly tears down their camp, saying they'll move to the front of the house to give us some privacy. One of the townspeople, an older lady, shows up shortly afterward.

"I'm Bea. I have some medical training, used to work for the doc we had in town a dozen years ago. Would you like me to take a look at your girl?"

By this point, Nicole is nearly catatonic. She's no longer crying, just staring into the distance. She doesn't make eye contact with Bea. When Bea says something like "*raise your arm,*" Nicole complies in almost robot-like motions.

After a few minutes, Bea says, "Physically, she's fine. You saw the cut by her lip. There are a few scratches on her arms. He held her by the wrists, so they'll be marked. She might have a bruise across her jaw. It's a little red there now. From what I see, I think the, uh, attack was in the early stages. Doesn't look like he was able to . . ."

"She was still partially clothed when we found her," I say quickly.

"It's a miracle you found her when you did."

Absentmindedly, I say, "Yes, it is—a miracle."

"We brought some water, thought she might want to clean up. Let me just grab my friends, okay?"

"That's very kind," Kim says woodenly.

Bea nods and steps behind the line of lilacs. I've always loved lilacs. Now, I wonder if they'll remind me of Nicole and her terrible event. Or bring back the memories of my own dreadful event.

Five women step around the lilac hedge and into our little camp space. Bea is carrying a small hard-sided kiddy pool, each of the others has a five-gallon bucket.

"We can get you more water if needed. Our men carried these over for us, but we thought it best if we brought it the rest of the way. We have a couple of blankets and some rope, which might help with privacy, and a couple of towels." The women all say appropriate things and dismiss themselves.

We set the pool up between the tents and string the blankets. Nicole, still in her daze, allows Kim to help her bathe. After she's done, we dump the pool out and use the remaining water for the rest of us to take a sponge bath one at a time, with Sabrina and me helping Naomi.

"Is N'cole okay?" she asks.

"She's . . . she's not really okay, but she will be," Sabrina answers. She looks to me for confirmation. I blink rapidly to suppress my tears.

A little while later, the town mayor shows up. He quietly asks questions about what happened. Kim and I give very brief answers. Even though she's asked me to say I did the shooting, I don't volunteer this information.

"So, it looks like maybe when the one guy fell, he . . . um . . . hit the ground funny. Somehow, he broke his neck."

I say nothing; Kim says nothing. Sabrina looks shocked, while Rey's look is . . . I'm not sure. Knowing? Like he isn't at all surprised the guy could get shot in the arm and fall and bust his neck.

"Did either of you see what happened? Maybe . . . help explain how he could fall like that?" the mayor prompts.

I stay silent, as Kim says, "It was pretty slick in spots. A few of those rocks, you know, they had slime on them. Maybe he was on one when he went down?"

"Hmm. I suppose that could be what happened. It's the strangest thing for sure. Well, I'll let you folks be. I hope your girl will be okay. You're going to rest here a couple of days?"

"Yes, tomorrow and maybe the next day, if that's okay?"

"Of course. No problem at all. We've been working on a security force for . . . I guess, just in case. I didn't think we'd need them, but now . . . " He shrugs. "You folks can all get some rest tonight. My people are patrolling."

"Those guys, they from the motel?" Sabrina asks.

"We think so, but the motel folks aren't claiming them. Said they took off a few days ago because they didn't like the rules of staying at the motel. But . . . well, we don't really know." With that, he raises his hand in something resembling a wave and leaves.

Rey and Kim are whispering to each other. Sabrina motions, saying she wants to talk, so we take a walk around to the front of Agnes's house.

"What is going on?" Sabrina asks as soon as we're out of ear shot. "How did you shoot that guy and cause him to break his neck?"

I sigh and shake my head. "I didn't shoot him. Kim did."

Sabrina's eyes go wide. "What? Kim who hates guns? Where'd she even *get* a gun?"

"I gave her mine. As soon as we realized what was happening, she demanded it. She told me not to ask questions and just back her up. She shot both of them before I even knew what was happening. The one guy, he didn't break his neck when he fell. *She* broke it, snapped it like a twig."

"What? No. How?"

"I don't know. I couldn't see what she did, I just know she did. I think . . . I think there's more to Kim than they're telling us. And Rey, too, for that matter. You've seen how he gets. They both act all . . . I don't know, like stuck up yuppies, but then they do weird things that don't seem to fit."

"Great. That's just great. At least when we thought she was just a debutante we could deal with her. Now she's . . . she's snapping people's necks?" Sabrina's expressing more anger than I've seen from her in—gosh, I don't know if I've ever heard this kind of anger.

I shrug my response.

She takes a deep breath, momentarily closing her eyes, then much calmer says, "You think it was her mama bear coming out? That makes sense, right? People do anything to protect their children."

"Sure, I guess. But do you think our mom could snap someone's neck? And show absolutely zero remorse over it? Then, afterward, she said I needed to claim to be the shooter. Of course, you automatically thought I was. And seems the mayor and everyone else thought so, too, since I'm the only one with a gun. Kim made sure to give it back right away."

"Crazy stuff, Sylvia. Crazy. Let's go back. I'm going to ask them about this."

We start to walk, and she touches my arm. "How are you doing?"

I shrug. "Brings it back some. It was different for me, of course."

"Just because he didn't abduct you, doesn't make it any less than what happened to Nicole. He didn't beat you up and leave the cuts Nicole has, but if you remember, your wrists were bruised, just like hers."

"Of course I remember the bruises," I hiss. "You think I haven't spent the last four years remembering that night? You think a day goes by I don't think of it? You think the therapy sessions don't remind me of it? And then writing the check to the therapist each month. Do you know how tempted I am to write *rape treatment* on the memo? You think those nights I wake you up screaming are just . . . just for fun?" Tears are flowing down my cheeks. Yes. Yes, I know exactly how Nicole is feeling.

Softly, I say, "That night changed my life. Nothing has been the same since then. I only hope, since it was stopped, Nicole has an easier time of it than I've had."

"Maybe it's why we're with them," Sabrina says.

"So I can be reminded of the worst night of my life?"

"No. So you could be there to stop it from happening to Nicole."

"I didn't stop it. Kim did, remember?"

"Then maybe you're here so you can help Nicole through it. And maybe, just maybe, you can help yourself also."

"Oh really?" I snap. "You think it was God's plan for me to be raped so I can be there for some other poor girl?"

"No, Sylvia. The man who raped you was evil. I know you've tried to forget it, tried to pretend it didn't happen. You mention the therapy, but did you tell your therapist about it?"

"None of your business."

Sabrina tries to pull me into a hug; I resist. She pulls harder, but I stiffen and leave my arms at my side. She still hugs me tight.

As she finishes the embrace, she says, "You've tried to just move on, pretend it didn't happen. I know you wouldn't have told me either if you wouldn't have been such a mess afterward. And I know you're still angry at me for taking you to the hospital. But getting checked out, to make sure you weren't physically hurt, and having the 'Jane Doe' rape kit done was the right thing."

"Oh, but I know you think I was gutless for not going through with reporting it. But you forget, dear sister, I've seen the women who

268

do report it. No way was I going through that . . . " I suck in a breath to try to stop the tears, "that circus. No way."

Sabrina straightens her arms to look me in the face. "You are the bravest person I know. Don't ever think I've thought anything less of you. The Monday after it happened, you got up and went to work. You put one foot in front of the other each day. Would I have liked to have seen your attacker brought to justice? Yes. But don't ever think I thought you were a coward."

I nod, taking a deep breath again to control the tears but fail. I'm bawling. My knees are suddenly weak. Sabrina feels my body give way and gently ushers me to the ground. She holds me while I cry.

Sometime later, I ask, "Mom still doesn't know?"

"She doesn't know. I've kept my promise and haven't told anyone, not even Mom. But now . . . you have an opportunity to be there for Nicole. And maybe also for yourself."

I struggle out of her grasp. Pointing my finger, I say, "You don't know everything, Sabrina. You don't know what it's like, the way I feel. The way I wish I would've done things differently that night."

"You?" She asks quietly. "You did nothing wrong, Sylvia."

"Not true. I drank too much, you know that. I was tipsy and having a good time. I let myself go with him alone. I— "

"You did nothing wrong. Even if you were drinking, it was not your fault."

"Easy for you to say."

"Sylvia, we've talked about this. It wasn't your responsibility to prevent some guy from raping you. Do you think it was Nicole's fault those guys took her?"

"That's different."

"How?"

"She's just a young girl who was abducted. She didn't do anything wrong."

"Neither did you."

We sit in silence for a long time, watching the sun begin its descent.

"What time do you think it is?" I ask.

Sabrina lifts her hand up between the sun and the horizon. "Still more than an hour until sunset. We figure the sun is setting around 9:00 this time of year, so I'd guess 7:45 or so. You try it."

While estimating the time until sunset isn't difficult, just raise my hand and count how many fingers between the horizon and the sun,

269

each finger width is approximately fifteen minutes, it takes more energy than I want to expend. Besides, we both know she's right. She only suggested I try it to put my mind on a new subject. I let out a cleansing breath and lift my hand up. Why not?

"Yep, you're probably right." Then I surprise myself when I add, "What kind of colors do you think we'll see tonight?"

Sabrina gives me a smile. "I suspect it'll be a beautiful sunset. See the clouds well above the horizon? Should give us quite the show."

As much as I've groused about taking time to watch the sunset in the past, I've been sitting with her every night since we left Thermopolis to enjoy the end of the day. And we're up and packing things to hit the road when the sun rises. I'm starting to understand why Sabrina tries to see these each day. While I hate what's happened to our world, in many ways I'm finding a new appreciation I didn't have before.

Oh, I'd for sure turn back the clock to before the airplanes crashed if I could. So many people have died in the three weeks since then. And if there were actual bombs in addition to the EMP, I can't even imagine the death toll.

Please, God, be with the people who have lost so much, who are hurting.

The petition flows through, completely unbidden. I close my eyes, pushing back the prayer.

Back at camp, Nate and Naomi are sitting in the center of our space. He's drawing pictures for her. Rey and Kim are sitting close to each other on the edge of camp, whispering. They stop suddenly as we approach. Kim plasters a condescending smile on her face. I stiffen and open my mouth to say something . . . something like, *wipe that smile off your face before I wipe it off for you,* when Sabrina touches my arm.

"How's Nicole?" she asks. Naomi and Nate are a few feet away.

"We just checked on her," Rey says. "She's sleeping."

"Probably best," I say, giving Kim the side eye. "I'm going to go to bed early tonight also, right after we watch the sunset." I catch Sabrina's eye. She gives me a small smile and a nod.

"Will you read to us, Breena?" Naomi asks.

"I will, if you all would like me to," she answers.

After the Bible reading and prayer, we silently watch the setting sun. Sabrina was right, the colors tonight are amazing. As the sun dips behind the mountain, everything seems to intensify.

"Oh!" Naomi gasps. "That was beautiful. Did you see it, Nate?"

"Duh. I'm sitting right next to you."

"Nate," Rey warns.

He rolls his eyes at his dad, then turns to Naomi. "Yeah, squirt. I saw it. Definitely one of the better ones."

"Okay. Time for bed, you two," Kim says.

I start to get up also when Kim says, "Mind waiting a few minutes?"

"Can it wait? I'm tired."

"I'd rather it didn't. I'll be quick."

I stifle a sigh. Kim gets the children ready for bed. After they're in the tent, she returns and motions Rey, Sabrina, and I to move away from the tent area.

Once we're a fair distance away, Rey says, "Thanks so much for your help today, Sylvia. You also, Sabrina. Your quick thinking . . . well, it could've been much worse if she wouldn't have been found so soon."

I know he's right, but I've tried not to think about what their final plans might have been for poor Nicole. Likely not just rape. Murder. Could Sabrina be right? Could this be why she felt so strongly God was telling her to bring them with us? Ridiculous. If I thought that, I'd need to acknowledge God. Not going to happen.

At least, I'm pretty sure it's not going to happen.

Rey clears his throat. "I suppose you two might have a few questions."

Sabrina nods.

"You think?" I say.

"Uh . . . right," Kim says. "You see, when I was a girl growing up in Louisiana, my dad taught me, taught all of us, how to shoot and take care of ourselves. I'm not a fan of guns now, with my children, so I've given you two a hard time about your weapons. But I'm incredibly grateful you had them today. Thank you, Sylvia. And I'd still prefer my children not know I was the . . . that I know how to use a gun. Can you help keep my secret?"

"Doesn't Nicole know it was you?" I ask.

"She doesn't. She was so freaked out. She didn't really know what was going on. She thinks you saved her."

I sigh. Great.

"I thought you grew up in Florida?" Sabrina says quietly.

"Florida? Oh, uh . . . yes, that's correct. We lived in Florida too. We moved around some. My folks liked to, uh, see things."

"And the fact you broke his neck? Snapped the neck of a grown man considerably larger than you?" I ask between gritted teeth. "How'd that happen? Your dad have you wrestling alligators in Louisiana or Florida or wherever you may have lived?"

Kim smirks.

"Right, so . . . can you two help us out?" Rey asks. "Just keep it on the—what do people say? The down low? Do you mind, Sylvia? The children already think you're a hero. Can we stay with that?"

I look at Sabrina; she shrugs.

"I won't lie about it. If they ask, I won't make something up. But I guess, for now, we don't have to say anything more."

"Thank you, Sylvia. We appreciate it. Guess we can all get some sleep tonight. With the patrols, we should be safe."

"Yeah . . . seems so," Sabrina says.

"Well, good night, Sabrina, Sylvia," Rey says, while Kim gives a slight nod and heads to the little one-man tent. Rey stretches out under the stars. Sabrina shrugs and we head off to our tent. We whisper late into the night about what in the world is going on with Kim? It's obvious she's not exactly who she's led us to believe she is. And the story about her growing up doesn't match up at all.

I even sort of join in when Sabrina asks me to pray with her. She asks me to join hands with her, and I agree.

"Dear Heavenly Father, thank you for keeping Nicole safe today, for not letting anything worse happen to her. Thank you for Sylvia being there then, and also here for Nicole now. Sylvia knows better than anyone how Nicole is feeling. Please, if there is a way You can use the wretched thing done to Sylvia by an evil man for good, please do so. We pray these things in Jesus' name, amen."

I quietly chorus the amen.

Chapter 52

Lindsey

Thursday, Day 22
Thermopolis, Wyoming

A roadblock greets us as we enter Thermopolis. We're instructed to park in a community lot on the edge of Hot Springs State Park. We've no sooner stepped out of our vehicles when we're approached by a lady with a clipboard dressed in business attire, being escorted by a uniformed sheriff. The combination makes an impression—we mean business.

Logan and I share a look. I'm both impressed and slightly intimidated. Likely exactly the response intended.

After we're all out of our vehicles, the businesswoman politely but without much warmth says, "Hello, folks. Welcome. You need a night's rest?"

"Yes, that'd be great," Barbara answers quickly.

"Sure. We can make that happen. We can't let you stay but the one night. You can set up in the field. How many tents do you have?"

"We have two," Barbara responds to clipboard lady, then turns to me, "Do you and Logan have a tent?"

I nod. A tent was one of the things we acquired on an early pilfering expedition.

"Three, then," Barbara tells her.

"Oh, fine. Then definitely enough room here. Keep you nice and close to your vehicles. You can walk over the bridge and down the road to the State Bathhouse and get one gallon of warm water per person for cleaning up. We have some jugs you can use or you can take your own. And we have fresh water also. No food. And you can't fish in the river, sorry. Also, no open fires. If you have a camp stove, you can use it, or you can go to the community grilling station by the bathhouse to cook your meals. Sound good?"

We all respond it does. "Excellent. Looks like you could all use a stop in our medical tent also. Why don't you head there first? You can't miss it." She gestures across the bridge toward a blue tent with a red cross painted on each side. "One more thing, violence will not be tolerated. We'll treat you right, and we expect the same courtesy. If we have any trouble . . . well, it's shoot first and ask questions later. I noticed you're armed. That's fine, just keep them holstered."

"I know you said we could stay overnight . . . " Samantha says.

"Right. One night," clipboard lady quickly responds.

"Oh . . . okay. Is there any option to stay longer? I . . . most of us . . . we don't have anywhere to go." Samantha's voice cracks and she drops her eyes to the ground.

Clipboard lady softens her voice. "I'm sorry. Unless you know someone here and they'll take you in, we can't let you stay. We just don't have the resources to take in extra people."

Samantha's shoulders heave as she nods.

Barbara wraps her arm around her, whispering in her ear.

To change the subject, and because I'm desperate for information, I ask, "Is there any news out of DC?"

Clipboard lady and the deputy share a look. She gives a small shake of her head. "We haven't heard anything. There were a few Ham operators in town, but everyone lost their equipment in the pulse."

"So do we know if it's only the US that was affected?"

"We don't know. Rumors, that's all we have. Nothing concrete. As far as we know, World War III may have started." She drops her head for a moment, then pops it back up again and says, in a much too cheery voice, "Okay, then. Let's get you folks to the medical tent and get you checked out."

Our thanks are subdued. Clipboard lady and the deputy take their leave.

"Logan, you need to be looked at," I say. "Not just today's wounds but maybe the . . . uh . . . other thing."

"You mean the radiation poisoning?" Barbara asks.

Logan and I both look at her.

She shrugs. "You both have it, right? Saw a few others while I was on the road. Some looked a little worse than you, some a little better.

I suspect the ones who looked worse . . . " Her voice fades away and she gives another shrug.

"Uh, yeah. We think we probably have it," I stammer. "We were in California. We saw a couple of the bombs go off."

"We hoped there weren't really bombs," Aimie says. "We thought maybe it was a false alarm and then just the power going out and the cars stopping. When Barbara first told us she'd met people who had seen the bombs . . . well, I thought we were dead for sure. Of course, since Eric killed my dad and brother and took us . . . " She stares blankly as Carlene pulls her close.

Several hours later, after taking turns going to the medical tent and getting water, we have our camp set up and are resting comfortably. We've arranged things so the tents and the vehicles are in close proximity; we don't want to risk losing anything tonight. We know we should set up a guard schedule, but we're all so tired we decide to forfeit tonight's guard.

Logan and I do have radiation poisoning. He's a little worse than I am, and with today's injuries, he needs to be careful. The nurse—they don't have a doctor—said he'll probably heal slower than we think he should since his body was already weak. She told us to expect to feel better in a few days. Then, in a few weeks, we'll feel sick again, maybe even sicker than we are now. She doesn't tell us our chances of having cancer have now drastically increased. We already know this, and with the world we're now living in, I'm not sure it matters much at the moment.

She agrees the bullet wounds are minor and told us how fortunate we are to not be on foot. If we were on foot, she'd suggest we find someplace to hole up and let him heal. Of course, we're reminded it won't be where we are now. One night only, no matter what.

Each of the women are examined; they've had a rough time of it, and it shows. They all have bruising and Bobbi—the one I watched Board Boy shove to the ground—has a broken wrist. I'm instantly regretful, thinking I should've done something to stop him from pushing her, then Bobbi says the nurse told her it's been broken for days. It's wrapped in a bandage, and she's told to avoid using it, to try and let it heal. No promises are made that it'll be good as new.

I fall asleep quickly. Sometime later, the screaming jolts me awake.

Chapter 53

Lindsey

Friday, Day 23
Thermopolis, Wyoming

"You're okay, Gina. You're okay," Barbara croons. "We're safe now. We're safe."

"We're never going to be safe. Not in this world," Gina screeches.

"Hey, you all okay there?" A gruff male voice calls out.

"Yes, we're fine. Just a nightmare," Barbara answers.

"Yeah, thought so. It happens quite a bit," the voice modulates and softens as he walks closer to our camp. "You need some water or anything?"

I can hear Barbara whisper but can't make out the conversation, then hear her say, "No, I think we're okay. Sorry to disturb."

"It's fine, ma'am. Almost daylight now, so folks will be getting up soon anyhow. Besides, you're all down here in the parking lot, away from the walkers, doubt many heard you."

"Should we go ahead and get up?" Logan asks in a whisper.

"Can we lay here just a few more minutes?"

"Are you that comfortable you want to stay snuggled in?" he jokes.

"Mmm. Surprisingly, I think I slept better last night than I have since we left our condo."

We doze off for a while and finally get up when the sun's peeking over the mountain. Barbara, Gina, and Bobbi are already up. Their tent is put away, and they look ready to go. Carlene and Aimie are also up, but still moving slowly. No sign yet of Samantha.

"Good morning," I say quietly to the group. "You look like you're ready to get a move on. I'm going to run up to the bathroom. Be right back."

"Oh, hey, if you see Samantha up there, can you tell her we're going to take the tent down?" Carlene asks.

"Sure. No problem."

I'm back after a few minutes. "I didn't find Samantha at the bathroom. She make it back?"

"No . . . " Barbara says, with a flash of concern on her face. "Uh, maybe she went for a walk. Bobbi, you feel up to walking with me a bit to see if we can find her? She was mesmerized by the thermal features."

The rest of us break down camp and pack up. We have a cold breakfast of granola bars and candy bars from the food we pillaged from the kidnappers. Barbara and Bobbi reappear just as we have everything ready to go.

"Where's Samantha?" Aimie asks, her voice laced with concern.

"We couldn't find her," Bobbi answers, almost frantic. "We've looked everywhere. Where could she be?"

"We should let one of the deputies know," Gina says. "The one last night, he sounded nice. They've all been nice. They'll help us."

"Yes . . . " Barbara starts, then hesitates, "I'm concerned. She might be hiding so she can stay here. I know she was pretty upset when they told her she couldn't stay without knowing someone. She asked again in the medical tent, even tried to make a deal to work so she can stay."

"So what are you thinking? We should just go and leave her here?" Carlene asks quietly.

"No," I say firmly. "We can't. They've made it clear no one can stay. We don't want to abuse their hospitality."

"Oh? And why not?" Bobbi spews. "What do we care about hospitality? We're trying to survive. You might have someplace wonderful to go, but we don't. In fact, this is about the best place I've seen in weeks. Hot water, medical care, no one smacking me around and breaking my bones and . . . and . . . " She breaks down.

Logan and I say nothing. While we haven't had it easy, things have sure been better for us than for these women.

Barbara pats Bobbi's back and says, "Lindsey's right, honey. We can't stay here. They've set up a nice place for people to rest. That's all. We'll find someplace. I know we will. Right now, we need to find Samantha. I'm going to go to the medical tent and see if we can get some help looking for her."

I walk with Barbara. We file what is essentially an abbreviated missing person report. Within a few minutes, half a dozen people are ready to help us look. Bobbi stays with our vehicles in case she returns. The rest of us go out in pairs using a grid pattern devised by one of the deputies.

"Don't worry, folks," a man in a deputy uniform says. "We'll find her. We've had a few others who've wandered off. We have a good idea where to look."

"You won't hurt her," I say. A statement, not a question. "She's had a rough time and isn't thinking clearly."

"We completely understand, ma'am. We . . . uh, the nurse who treated you all, she told us to be gentle with your friend."

Oh, goodie. So they all know these women have been held captive by madmen for weeks. Well, maybe at least it'll buy Samantha some extra consideration.

After about an hour, Logan and I return to the cars, having completed our assigned area and ready to start another.

There's no need.

"Oh, Lindsey," Aimie cries. "It's so terrible. They found her. They found Samantha."

I make eye contact with the deputy standing nearby, looking like he'd rather be anywhere else.

He quietly says, "We found her near the river. There was no evidence of foul play."

At this, Aimie shrieks and cries out, "Why, Mama? Why? We've all . . . it happened to all of us. Why did she do that? We could've helped her."

Carlene gathers Aimie in her arms. "Shh, shh. I know. It's hard to understand. We're going to be okay, though. We're going to take care of each other, Aimie. You hear me? We're okay."

For several minutes, the only sounds are the river and the sobs of our group. Logan takes my hand. We're both teary eyed also but are doing our best to hold it together.

After several minutes, the deputy says, "We have a daily burial, if you'd like us to take care of her."

"A daily burial?"

"Yeah." He sighs. "We seem to have at least one death daily. Your friend, she's the third we've found today. One natural causes, the other . . . " He shakes his head. "Same as your friend."

"When?" Barbara asks.

"Three o'clock. We can't offer you a second night here, but you could move on to Meeteetse tonight. They have camping facilities. It's only an hour or so up the road."

"I'll get Samantha ready," Barbara says, wiping her tears.

"Let me help," Carlene offers, kissing her daughter on the head and whispering to her. Aimee nods and reaches for another hug from her mom.

While Barbara and Carlene prepare Samantha for burial, the rest of us are very solemn, finding ways to occupy the time by talking and crying, taking walks, napping, and playing cards—a deck provided by a different clipboard lady. Logan spends most of his time resting, which he very much needs.

The 3:00 pm service ends up including a fourth burial. It was done very quickly, yet tastefully. Even though Logan and I just met Samantha yesterday, it's still incredibly hard to lose her like this. We're on the road to Meeteetse by 4:00.

Chapter 54

Sylvia

Friday, Day 23
Meeteetse, Wyoming

Nicole, while not her usual self, is doing better today. There was even a bit of sparkle in her eyes when Bea and the other ladies from town delivered a cooler of food this morning. A quart of milk with a layer of cream on the top, half a dozen eggs, a loaf of homemade white bread and a loaf of pumpkin bread, along with a generous pat of butter, did a lot to raise all of our spirits. They even brought clothes for each of us, which are a better fit than what we've been wearing.

We spend the day resting. To pass the time, we play cards, thanks to the three decks packed by Sabrina; read, again thanks to a couple of paperback books Sabrina brought along; and sleep.

After our lunch of fish caught by Rey and Nate, along with thin slices of the pumpkin bread, Nicole asks if I'll escort her to the bathroom. Alone.

After she's finished, she says, "Can we walk a little?"

I nod and gesture toward the main street of town.

"No, down this side street." She points to the road in front of Agnes's house.

After a block or so, she says, "I wanted to thank you for coming for me. I know what they were planning to do, and if you wouldn't have got there when you did . . . " Her voice shudders to a stop. She sucks in a deep breath.

I suck in my own deep breath. Before I can say anything, she says, "It happened so fast. I didn't even hear them. The next thing I knew, there was a hand over my mouth. I tried to fight but couldn't. They pulled me into the bushes, then down the bank. The one with his hand over my mouth was breathing in my ear. The other one was giving directions, trying to keep us upright, I guess. Even so, the branches kept scraping at me and we stumbled a few times."

She pauses, staring into the distance. I remember reciting what happened to me in the same matter-of-fact tone at the hospital. Like Nicole, I was almost catatonic at first. Sabrina was there for me then, and also at the hospital when I was able to tell the story. She was quiet and just let me talk. I'll try to do the same thing for Nicole, even though it's hard to hear because all of my own memories are getting in the way.

"They told me what they were going to do, made a big deal about how great it'd be. The one who was dragging me, he was going to go first. I wanted to scream and yell, but they said if I did, they'd kill me and then they'd go and get Naomi and . . . and . . . you know. Since I messed up their plans, they'd have to grab her . . . and . . . she'd be my replacement."

I close my eyes. A quick death was more than those monsters deserved. Kim should've made them suffer.

"So I stayed quiet. Let them do . . . whatever. Then you and Mom showed up."

She stops and turns to look directly at me. "I don't think they would've let me live afterward. I thought about it, and it would've been better anyway. To die, I mean. I wouldn't want to live after that."

"You're right. You wouldn't," I say before I can stop myself. Her eyes widen. I touch her arm and quietly continue, "You wouldn't want to live, but you would. I'd make sure of it. Because I know. I know exactly how it feels . . . afterward."

"You know?" she whispers.

"I know," I answer quietly with a nod. "It was different for me. I wasn't dragged away by force, and there was only one man."

"What happened?"

I take a deep breath. I don't want to tell her, but at the same time, I do. Only Sabrina and those at the hospital know. Sabrina was right, I've never told my therapist. I gaze off into the distance.

"I was at a party, a dorm party. I was taking classes to finish up my degree. I didn't live on campus but was friends with some girls that did, so they invited me. I'd never been to something like that before. I was . . . " I give a little laugh. "I was a 'good girl.' Sure, I'd had a few drinks before but never to the point of getting drunk. This party was crazy—a couple of kegs, several types of punch with booze in them, and people falling down drunk. And the party was just getting started. The music was booming. There were so many people crammed in there, and it was terribly hot. I was instantly uncomfortable."

I look at her; she motions me to continue.

"The girls I arrived with, they scattered, going to talk to different people they knew. I was totally abandoned. I wanted to leave but didn't have a car. I thought about calling for a cab but wasn't even exactly sure where I was. I knew the general area but not the address. I decided to make the best of it. I made my way over to the punch table. At the time, I didn't realize it wasn't regular punch, but after my first sip, I could tell. I drank it anyway, then moved outside to the patio. It was at least a little quieter there.

"I was sitting on a little settee thing when this guy came over. I was a couple of years older than most of the people there and definitely an outcast, as far as I was concerned. He was cute and very friendly. He asked if he could sit by me. He didn't seem drunk like so many of the others. We chatted for a few minutes, then he pointed to the cross I was wearing. He said, 'Hey, are you a Christian?' When I said I was, he suggested we go to church together sometime."

"I didn't know you're a Christian," Nicole says. "Sabrina for sure, but you don't seem too enthusiastic when she reads or prays."

I give a soft, rueful laugh. "Yeah, I haven't been too enthusiastic. But before . . . before that night, I was a lot like Sabrina. Maybe not quite as devoted, but not . . . not how I am now."

"An atheist?"

"I don't think of myself as an atheist. I'm just not a believer." I shrug.

"So . . . " she prompts me to continue.

"I felt so flattered . . . this cute guy was talking to me. I was pretty dumpy. I've never been very pretty and have always been overweight."

"You don't think you're pretty? Sylvia, you're beautiful."

I'm shocked to hear this from Nicole—cute, blond, blue-eyed with drop-dead gorgeous parents. I stutter, "I've lost some weight."

"Even before, when we first met you at that awful campground. That's why my mom didn't like you and Sabrina at first. She's always threatened by pretty women she can't intimidate. And you two are beautiful and strong. My mom's used to being the prettiest and the star of the show. It took her a while to realize you two were just . . . nice."

"Nice, huh?" I'm surprised by this turn in the conversation. Never would I have thought someone like Kim would think anything of me. Sabrina, maybe. She's always been the prettier of the two of us, the more outgoing one. But me? No.

"What happened? I mean, if you want to tell me," Nicole says shyly.

"We talked for a little bit. He offered to get me another drink. He was so nice and easy to talk to. Then he asked if I wanted to go for a walk. He said the house was in a nice area with lots of different parks and walking paths. I didn't even think twice and agreed instantly. When I stood up, I felt a little off. Kind of woozy. I'd never drank enough to feel like that before. He grabbed me to steady me, then held my hand while we walked. I thought it was so sweet.

"We left the yard and walked a little bit. There were benches scattered along the path. It was very quiet, peaceful. These really pretty vintage looking lights were by the benches. We finally reached a bench where the light was out. It wasn't super dark since the glow from the other lights reached the area, but it was darker. Cozy. He asked if I wanted to sit for a bit. He started kissing me, then . . . touching me. I hadn't really . . . no one had ever . . . " I sigh. "I'd been kissed a few times but hadn't gone any farther. Remember how I said I was a good girl?"

"Yes."

I take another breath. "I was still a virgin. I wanted to remain one. Oh, not necessarily until I was married, but until I was in love. Until I found the right guy. And this guy, who I had only met a half hour before, was not him. I asked him to stop. He didn't. I demanded he stop. He put his hand over my mouth. Then I started praying—harder than I had ever prayed before. God would help me, I was sure. He'd intervene. He'd send someone to help. He'd strike the guy dead with a heart attack or . . . something. I was so sure He'd help me. The next thing I knew, my pants were down and . . . " I take a deep breath. "God didn't intervene."

Her mouth makes an *O* shape, and she drops her eyes. "I'm sorry, Sylvia."

My eyes fill with tears. I give a nod in response.

"Are you okay now?" she asks.

Am I okay now?

"To be honest, it depends on the day . . . sometimes the hour." I attempt a small laugh. "I'd like to tell you I've put it behind me, but I haven't. I don't think about it as much as I used to. It's still there but not such a big part of me, you know? Sometimes, I'll even go a few days without remembering . . . without it coming back to me. But then, something will happen and I'm reminded of it."

"I feel pretty awful today," Nicole says. "I feel sad and angry at the same time. And I'm not at all sad they're dead. Not at all."

"Whatever you are feeling today is fine. You're going to hurt, not just physically but emotionally. You went through a terrible thing. But, Nicole— " I wait until she looks at me " —you *are* going to be okay. You're an amazing young woman, and you're going to be fine."

"You promise?"

"I do."

Chapter 55

Mollie

Friday, Day 23
Bakerville, Wyoming

My collapse sure caused a ruckus. I guess I fainted, because the next thing I knew, I was in my bed and Belinda was checking me out. She doesn't seem to know why I passed out but has ordered me to rest. I'm confined to my bed.

After supper, I'm in bed with Jake sitting next to me, telling me how sorry he is for getting me so upset, when Kelley stops by. Seems Belinda thought it'd be a good idea for her to examine me also. I try not to think they're escalating this to something it's not. I'm not crazy, I just fainted. Why do I need to have a special talk with a psychiatric nurse practitioner?

I try not to show my irritation as she completes a nearly identical physical to the two Belinda has already given me since the episode. Episode. That's what both Kelley and Belinda call my passing out. An episode.

"Physically, you don't seem the worse for wear. You're looking much better than when you first returned home," she declares. "You've been sleeping okay?"

"Better than the first few days after . . . after Doris's house. We don't get to bed as early as we used to. There's so much to do, so we're taking advantage of the longer days."

"Yeah, I guess we're all doing that," she agrees. "It'll change when the sun starts setting earlier. We'll have reverted back in time, relying on natural light instead of artificial to do what we need to do. Of course, like you, we have a small backup system that survived the EMP. Lost our big generator, though, so we just have the wind turbine and the solar panels. Speaking of, I noticed the little wind machine on top of your place. When did you get it?"

"Oh, it was one of Jake's purchases during the early days of the attacks. Just got it up yesterday."

"That's good."

We're silent for several minutes as she looks in my ears, up my nose, pokes my forearm, and then finally says, "Kind of thought we were crazy. You know, before. Sometimes, I'd wonder why in the world we did the things we did—Phil and me. Why we stockpiled."

"Jake and I thought the same things. We stopped prepping a few times. Didn't get rid of anything but didn't add to our stuff. Then some event, somewhere, would happen and we'd be back at it. Now . . . now even with all we've done, it's blatantly obvious it wasn't enough."

"Seems that way, doesn't it? You start thinking about the situation, and even though things are fine today, all you can think about is how bad they're going to be in three months, or six months, or a year."

"Yes," I say quietly.

"You like things a certain way. I've recognized, over the years we've been getting to know each other, you crave consistency. When things start to fall apart, you fall apart. When your marriage took such a hard hit, after your friends died, things changed. You and Jake pulled away from each other. You didn't have the harmony you were used to. But you fought back, you started working on yourself and your marriage. You became stronger for it. I also noticed your personality has changed quite a bit."

"Oh?"

"You're not nearly as uptight as you used to be."

What? She thought I used to be uptight? I give a small laugh. "Okay?"

"Sure. It's not a surprise to you that you were, still are in many ways, the proverbial *Type A* personality. I'm that way too. Lots of people are. But for you, I think it was all encompassing. You always had to have your little ducks in a row, and so did the people around you. When things happened and your ducks were no longer lined up, you couldn't adapt. But then you got some help, and you're stronger for it. Jake too. I've seen the change in both of you."

"I thought we hid our troubles pretty well."

"Sure, you put on a brave face in public. I'm not just talking about when your friends died, though. The way you were before they died compared to who you are now, there's a difference. You and Jake are much stronger now than you were when we first became friends."

"You think?"

"Absolutely. You both seemed to be living in the present. While you still like your lists and your goals, you've lightened up. When a little thing goes wrong, it's not the end of the world to you . . . or at least it wasn't until the end of the world really happened." She gives a sad smile.

"Um, how do you know these things? I didn't think my . . . issues . . . were so obvious."

"Probably not to most people. It was little things. One time, we were over for dinner and you painstakingly arranged the vegetables you were roasting. The pieces were all uniform size and lined up perfectly on the baking sheet. That was my first clue. Another time, we were talking about something that happened weeks before, and you were still lamenting on it, analyzing it. I can't remember exactly what it was, it wasn't something you could change, but was still a burr in your side."

"Well, that sounds like me, both examples." I nod, slightly embarrassed.

"So, I think, maybe you're having panic attacks. You're no longer the totally uptight person you used to be, but you're not fully comfortable as the new person you were becoming, and things are wonky for you now."

"Wonky? Is that one of your big shrink words?"

"You know it. The bump on the head didn't do you any favors. But I really think it's more situation-related than anything. Things aren't the way they used to be. You need to adapt."

"So basically, stop being a whiney baby and buck up?"

"Not exactly what I'm saying. But we all need to buck up if we're going to make it. Those who don't . . . "

"They end up like Helen and the others," I say quietly. Helen was a neighbor who took her own life after her husband was murdered. She couldn't see a way to go on without him.

"Yes, we'll likely have more people like Helen."

Chapter 56

Mollie

Friday, Day 23
Bakerville, Wyoming

"Mom? Mom, are you awake?"

I lift my head toward the bedroom door. My girls—Sarah, Angela, Calley, and Katie—are all just inside the doorway. Calley's carrying a breakfast tray. There's several plates and a small bud vase with a single black-eyed Susan standing at attention.

"Are you hungry?" Calley asks with a smile.

"Time 'zit?" I ask groggily.

"About 9:00," Sarah says. "We know Jake brought you a cup of coffee and some toast earlier, but we thought you might like something more."

After yesterday's "episode," Belinda has ordered me to take it easy today. I tried to get up earlier, but Jake promptly sent me back to bed. I guess they all think I'm going to faint again.

Sarah's right, I would like something more. But with the rationing . . .

Angela must read my mind. "Don't worry, Mom. It's just some leftover oatmeal and a little sausage. You aren't taking food from anyone else."

I nod as I sit up and adjust my pillow.

"You need help?" Katie asks.

"No, I feel completely fine. Belinda's just being overly cautious."

The girls exchange a look, one I can't quite decipher.

"Enjoy your breakfast, Mom," Calley says. "I'll be back in a little bit to get your tray."

"Oh, I can bring it out," I say.

"Nope. Nopety, nope," Calley answers. "I'll take care of it. Then maybe you can move out to the couch and rest there. We'll be working in the kitchen, so we can visit with you. Belinda said either your bed or your couch until *she* decides you're well enough to get up."

I fight rolling my eyes and give a small nod. "Thank you for breakfast, ladies. I really appreciate it."

Calley gives me a kiss on the cheek and each girl moves in to follow suit before leaving the room.

The oatmeal's wonderfully creamy, topped with raisins, brown sugar, and goat milk. The small but delicious sausage patty is our own mix, using ground antelope, basil, and several other spices.

Jake and I had a long talk last night. He's probably right, I was being overly dramatic about the community militia and food situation. Definitely one of my faults and something I've worked on in recent months. I thought I was doing better about not ranting and raving. Guess not. Lately, I just feel so . . . wound up.

Maybe this is related to my minor head injury. Maybe it's related to the killing. It's not like me to be so . . . so . . . I can't really think of a good word. Catty? Malicious? Oh, I can think of an accurate one. Definitely *not* how I want to be.

Things bothering me now would've never bothered me before. In my mind, I know raiding the empty houses is the smart thing to do. I know using things from those homes, like finding new windows for the Snyders, is necessary. But when I think about it, I'm furious.

I know the militia is necessary. We're not completely safe here. We have proof of this. But again, it makes me angry when I think of it. Just thinking about thinking about these things gets my dander up!

Or maybe it's related to our world falling apart. I try to put on a brave face, to not complain about everything. And for the most part, I do okay. Most of the people living here think I'm handling things well. Cheery almost. But with Jake, I let my guard down. I don't hold back on my true feelings. As a result, he experiences the worst I have to offer.

I let out a huge sigh. *Please, God, please help me be a loving wife to Jake.*

As promised, Calley returns for my tray and escorts me to the couch—never mind I don't need an escort and feel perfectly fine.

They've done some rearranging of the furniture, having set up a card table and chairs near the couch and seating area. My girls, Deanne, and Sheila are all gathered around.

"What's this?" I ask.

"We figured we'd sit next to you and visit while we work on the processing," Deanne says with a shrug. Sheila nods and gives me a small smile, the first nonfrigid response I've seen from her since I've returned home. I return the smile.

"Sounds great. What are we working on?"

"We," Sarah says, motioning to everyone except Katie and me, "are working on the fermenting right now. We topped the turnips and are using the recipe in your book to make a lemon slaw with the turnip greens. The recipe called for spinach, but we figure this will work fine. You and Katie are relaxing on the couch."

Katie pats the seat next to her as I nod my agreement. The fermenting book, *The Complete Idiot's Guide to Fermenting Foods*, is a must-have for learning to preserve foods without heat or cold. Fermenting uses traditional methods, keeping enzymes, vitamins, and other beneficial probiotics. It's also a great method for preserving small batches since one jar can be processed at a time.

"We had radishes leftover from yesterday," Deanne says. "So those are being naturally pickled from the recipe in the book too. I'm pretty happy about not having to use the water bath or pressure canner today." She gives a fake wipe of her forehead with the back of her hand. "Whew."

"Will the radish pickles be ready in time for the wedding?" Katie asks.

"Yes, should be," I answer. "It takes them three days or so to process with the temperatures we are having. Once they're bubbly and softened, we'll move them to the root cellar to slow down the process."

"I don't really understand how this fermenting is safe," Sheila says. "What keeps the radishes and greens from rotting in the jar?"

"Good question," I say. "It's the addition of the salt and starter culture. The harmful bacteria can't tolerate the salt, so the starter culture begins the process and helps the healthy bacteria flourish. The good bacteria converts the sugar present in vegetables or fruit into lactic acid. Lactic acid is a preservative that helps keep away any bad bacteria, and also maintains the flavor and texture of food while keeping nutrients intact."

"I have no idea what you just said, Mom." Angela shakes her head. "But I guess it means fermenting won't kill us when we eat it."

"Exactly." I smile. "But remember, it's not the same thing as canning. Fermented foods aren't shelf-stable. They need to be kept cold, and they won't last as long as canned food. We'll get several months out of them, as opposed to canning foods which last for a year or longer."

While they work on the ferments, we visit. Sheila is surprisingly cheerful, chatting about the upcoming triple wedding—the older couple will be joining them—and the bridal shower we're planning for Katie and Laurie. She's asked if she can be in charge of decorations. Definitely a change from the mopey person she's been since I returned.

While I don't know Sheila well, I've been around her many times over the years. As Calley's maid of honor, she hosted her bridal shower and helped quite a lot with the wedding. We always had a good time together. It's nice to see at least a glimpse of the person I enjoyed being around.

Of course, I do know things are very different now for Sheila. Not only has society changed but she's also recently divorced. Rumor has it, Sheila's been a bit of a mess since her husband left. Maybe we have this in common. Both of us were a bit of a mess before the attacks and are needing to learn how to adjust in this new world. Shoot, I suspect pretty much everyone is in the same situation to varying degrees. None of us have truly adapted to our current circumstances.

A half hour or so into the work and conversation, Laurie joins us, carrying a large bowl covered with a dish towel.

"What do you have there?" I ask.

"Our latest experiment," she answers, carefully lifting the edge of the towel. "Cactus pads."

"Oh! Nice," I exclaim.

Angela makes a face; Sarah shakes her head.

"Kelley mentioned they're harvesting some of the cactus at their place," Laurie says. "I asked her for the details on how to do it and then what to do with the pads, so . . . " She shrugs. "I thought I'd give it a try. She said to harvest at midmorning—something about the acid being lowest then—and only take one-third of the pads from each plant so it can reproduce."

"You didn't get poked?" Katie asks.

"Oh, I did! Even though I was wearing long sleeves, gloves, and using a pair of tongs and a long knife. It's like they reached out and grabbed me."

"They seem to do that," I agree.

"Are you thinking we'll eat those?" Angela asks, the look of disgust still on her face.

"I'll need to take the spines off of them. Kelley said these are much smaller than the cactus used in recipes in the southwest and Mexico. And removing the thorns isn't easy. I'll wear dishwashing gloves and hopefully won't up with too many pokes. Thought I'd try using the flame from the stovetop to sear them. When they're cleaned, she suggests stewing them. So that's what we'll try first. I suspect they'll cook down quite a bit. This bowl will probably only give about a quarter cup per person when they're cooked."

"Should be perfect for an experiment, and it'll go well with tonight's dinner," Deanne says. "We're having an enchilada casserole."

"Sounds delicious," I say. "Perfect combination."

"If we like the cactus, we can harvest more. Kelley said each plant can be harvested several times per year. This bowl is only the tip of the iceberg for the harvest. I was only working in one section. And we can teach the rest of the community," Laurie says excitedly. I'm suddenly struck at the difference in her today than the first day she arrived at our homestead. Master Shane said she had a difficult time in Wesley. I haven't asked her about it, but it seems whatever it was isn't as much of a focus today as it was then. Time does help heal wounds.

Laurie moves to the kitchen to work on the cactus; Sheila offers to help. There are many yelps and laughs as they attempt to master the process. Our semi-open floorplan allows us to join in through their endeavor. I can't help but smile at the change in both of them.

Once they get into a rhythm and a quiet settles over the house, Katie brings up wedding plans.

"So, Pastor Ralph is bringing the other couple over tomorrow so we can meet. He's going to do their ceremony. Leo and I are still having David Hammer officiate ours." Katie raises her voice slightly to ensure she can be heard in the kitchen. "Laurie, have you and Aaron decided on Mr. Hammer or Pastor Ralph?"

"Mr. Hammer. We've enjoyed his services, even on the days it's not much more than a reading. His voice is so soothing. I feel like I am really hearing God's words come through him. Oh, he's so humble about it, of course. But . . . " Her voice fades off for a moment, then she says, "He's also been there to talk with me about things. It's been helpful. We liked Pastor Ralph fine, just feel a connection with David and his family, you know?"

I do know. Since the day of the missile alert, when we all holed up in our basement, David has conducted a daily service. The location of the meeting changes depending on the day. When our neighborhood is in charge of the Bakerville meal, it's held at the community center and tends to be a longer reading resembling a Bible study. Other days, it is a quick verse or two before group PT is started.

We've adopted Psalm 91, the Soldier's Psalm, as our promise, our guarantee. This verse helped me when I was trying to make my way home from Oregon. It was also my assurance when my girls and I were attacked, when Katie was almost killed. David shared with us a little about this Psalm and the belief many soldiers in World War I recited this Psalm daily. Not everyone's on board with the daily meetings. Sheila doesn't participate. My daughter Sarah and her husband Tate are also apathetic, having declared shortly before their marriage they're "free thinkers," which I guess is another way of saying nonbelievers.

Along with PT and militia training, we have all of our farm chores, cooking, gardening, food preservation, finishing the new lodging . . . the days just aren't long enough to get everything done.

Adding in the wedding celebration does create additional stress but is also becoming enjoyable. We're keeping the food plans for the wedding celebration somewhat loose. We're not sure what all will be available in the garden and what the looting teams might find to add to the supplies. We've put aside a few delicacies that have popped up— cans of shrimp and crab meat, hearts of palm, interesting pickles of all sorts, and several other unique and sometimes exotic specialty items in a can.

I had no idea some of those things even existed. And some, like the two cans of ox tongue, I'm not so sure about. I seriously doubt they'll make an appearance at the wedding feast.

Some of the more interesting items we found, and not just in the pantry, were at a nearby neighbors' house. They live in Bakerville part time, spending winters in Arizona, and were visiting their children on the East Coast when the disasters started.

Several days ago, I was helping Jake and a few others with the cleanout. We'd already emptied the cabinets and pantry. What a bonanza! Their large pantry was nearly full. Unfortunately, the freezer had also been full, and everything inside was lost.

As much as I hate pilfering from our neighbors, part of me thinks it should've been decided the day after the power went out. Then, maybe the freezers could've been salvaged with some kind of rotating generator schedule while the food was preserved.

While focused on the basement craft room, I was surprised to hear Jake say, "Woo wee. Welcome to Wyoming, consider everyone armed . . . and then some. Mollie, you have to see this."

He wasn't kidding. They have a gun room. Not a gun room like Jake and I have with a few hunting rifles and shotguns plus our personal pistols.

Nope.

Theirs is the size of a bedroom and more like a gun store. There must have been over fifty different rifles and carbines in every caliber and style you can imagine, almost as many shotguns, and even more handguns, along with several compound and crossbows.

"Um . . . what did he do for a living before he moved here?" I asked.

"No idea. I've only spoken to him to say hello. I'll ask David Hammer. He visited with him a few times. But I'm thinking either a gun dealer or he's the Godfather."

"Did the Godfather have a lot of guns? I've never seen the movie."

"It was a joke, Mollie. I was implying he was a hired killer for the mafia."

"Oh . . . Got it. Thanks for telling me it was a joke. I didn't know." Then I laughed like a crazy woman while Jake gaped at me like I was a loon.

"What are you going to do with them all?" I asked, after I finally got control of myself.

"Lock the room back up, talk to Evan, and go from there."

"You found a key?"

"Yep, it was on a hook in the furnace room."

"Sounds like a good plan."

The guns will come in handy with our new militia. Katie thinks Belinda's going to allow her to start doing more things—still no lifting but maybe easing into physical activities and allowing firearms practice.

She won't be a full member of the militia any time soon but can maybe be put in sentry rotation.

Of course, I'm banned from the militia for a few days, just like I'm banned from everything else.

"You feeling okay, Mom?" Sarah's voice jolts me back to the present.

I hesitate before answering. I don't feel too bad, but not great either. I sense the start of a headache coming on, probably from being forced to sit around. Maybe a nap is in order.

Chapter 57

Mollie

Friday, Day 23
Bakerville, Wyoming

"Hey, Mollie. How are you feeling?" Belinda asks.

It's been several hours since I excused myself from the food preservation festivities. I've had a short nap and am once again lying around. The headache never materialized, so maybe a rest was simply in order.

"Bored. Otherwise, I think I'm fine. It was probably just the heat."

"Yeah, you've said that before, only it wasn't really that warm yesterday. I want you to continue to take it easy. I just finished checking on Katie. She's resting in her bedroom. Like you, she tries to overdo it." Belinda gives an exasperated shake of her head. "Now it's your turn for a quick exam."

"Sure. Why not? You haven't poked and prodded me enough since yesterday. Maybe, after this time, you can release me to get up and do a few things?"

"We'll see." We both turn toward the bedroom window as we hear a loud squeal. At first, I think something nefarious has occurred but quickly realize it's Malcolm and one or two of the other boys.

"Do you know what they're doing?"

"Malcolm has TJ, Tony, and Marc doing sword practice," Belinda says with a wry smile. "He's convinced the militia group will decide to add swords as part of their weaponry, even after they said no at the last meeting."

I give a small laugh. Malcolm, Tony, and TJ join in on the militia meetings, even though they're not officially part of the militia, much to their dismay. Even so, they participate in meetings, PT, and some of the very basic training.

Everyone, except whoever's on rotating sentry duty, participates in physical training based on their current level of fitness. I lead a stretching and light activity group for the younger children and those needing a modified program. The workout is only fifteen to thirty minutes, early in the morning after chores but before breakfast, and focuses on movement. We also have daily self-defense training in the late afternoon—again, broken up by ability, with me leading the very young and those who are less physically inclined. Finding time in the day to get everything done is not easy. And for the next several days, Belinda's ordering me to let someone else lead the classes.

Aside from the PT and self-defense classes, part of the group—the ones who will be more involved in the community militia—has some sort of specific training, like in-depth hand-to-hand combat training, marksmanship of some sort, how to clear a building, and more.

At our last meeting, Malcolm spoke up. "I was thinking of a way the three of us— " he gestured to include Tony and TJ " —could help a little more. You know how I've been working on my sword training for a couple of years? I have my practice katana . . . a katana is a Japanese sword with a special blade and made to be held with two hands. It's— "

"You can tell us more about the katana later," Alvin gruffly interrupted.

"Okay, Grandpa, I'll tell you all about the history of it later. But anyway, I've been teaching Tony and TJ how to use the sword. I have the two katana practice swords since Dad and I used to practice together . . . before all of this happened. I also have a set of bamboo shinai for practicing kendo."

"That's fine, Malcolm. I know those are fun toys for you," Alvin said.

"But that's just it, Grandpa. They could be more than toys. What if we started working with them more to use in the militia? There might be times when someone can't use a gun, maybe they need to be quiet or they run out of bullets. If we had swords, we could still fight. You all carry the knives Evan's teaching you how to use."

"Malcolm might have a point," Bill Shane said. "I've worked with the shinai swords also. Wish I would've brought them along. While I fully agree with the truth of 'don't bring a knife to a gunfight,' it seems the more options we have for self-protection the better."

"I don't disagree," Leo said. "But I don't know if we have the time to add another training right now. We've already added in archery practice for the times we need to be stealthy and are trying to provide training on the variety of bows we've found. Plus, I'm not so sure there would be someone around to make swords. It's kind of a lost art."

Malcolm looked crestfallen as he nodded in agreement. "It's for sure a lost art. But there's lots of old people around here."

"Malcolm," I gasped, while everyone else in the group laughed.

"Sorry, Mom. But maybe someone will know. Maybe a blacksmith could do it. I think there are some blacksmiths around here, right?"

"Something to think about for the future, for sure," Alvin said. "Now, let's get back to the business at hand."

While Malcolm was mildly shot down at the meeting, he and the other boys have ramped up their own practice. They plan to be ready when we decide it's time to add swords to the militia.

"He doesn't give up easily," I say to Belinda.

She spends a few minutes doing her thing—looking in my eyes, having me lift my arms, and other exciting stuff.

"So, when was your last period?"

"Couple of months, I guess. I stopped being regular last year. I'm at that age, you know. Figured it would just stop one of these days. You think that's what's causing my problems? Menopause?"

"Maybe. Your doctor put you on estrogen replacement therapy?"

"Um, no. I've been using herbs to help with the symptoms. Those and acupuncture."

"Why am I not surprised by this?" She smiles. "With your honey for infection and the hippie commune you have going on here, I'd expect nothing less. So what are you using? Black cohosh?"

Hippie commune?

"No, wild yam, licorice root, and stinging nettle."

"Still taking those?"

"Not since before all of this started. I kind of thought I might be over the worst of it. The hot flashes eased up around the time my daughter Sarah moved to Billings . . . so early May. And my energy was a little better, which is what the stinging nettle seemed to help with, so I just kind of stopped taking things. I'll get back on it."

"Probably a good idea. Let's give you a pregnancy test first, just to make sure."

I break out laughing. "I don't think we'll need to do that. Seriously, I'm fifty years old, Belinda. And I've had perimenopause symptoms for about a year."

"Sure. And you've also been tired, irritable, and sick to your stomach for a few weeks. You know those are all signs of pregnancy in addition to being symptoms of menopause."

"Also signs of stress," I add, gesturing wildly to try to encompass this new, full-of-stress world.

She ignores me and soldiers on. "At your age, pregnancy is rare. Less than a 1 percent chance, but it can still happen. Jake have a vasectomy?"

"No, and I don't have my tubes tied."

"You've been using protection?"

"Belinda, did we not just cover the fact I'm fifty years old? Not a teenager. We use protection . . . " My voice fades away before I add, "Most of the time." Truthfully, we've become a little lax. After all, I'm in menopause.

"Fine." I sigh. "I'll pee on a stick. We have a couple of pregnancy tests in our supplies."

"I have one in my stuff. I'll get it and be right back."

I lie back in my bed, fluffing the pillows until I'm comfortable. I shake my head, thinking how absurd this is. In a way, I understand since menopause symptoms and pregnancy symptoms have some overlap. But really? I guess I can't fault Belinda for wanting to be thorough.

Belinda's gone for longer than I think she should be. I'm beginning to think she realized how preposterous the idea I'm pregnant is, when I hear banging and clomping on the steps. She's usually much quieter coming up the stairs.

I smile toward the doorway. It's not Belinda. It's Lydia.

And she's covered in blood.

Chapter 58

Mollie

Friday, Day 23
Bakerville, Wyoming

Lydia. Her clothing, her face, her hands . . . all soaked in blood. The metallic smell hits my nose. My stomach wants to revolt. I swallow hard.

In her right hand is a small knife of some sort, a scalpel maybe? Not the kind with a gentle curved cutting edge, but a pointed crescent-shape, sharpened along the inside edge. Blood drips from the tip, blemishing the hardwood. In her left hand is a pair of pointy scissors, also painted in blood.

Where's Katie? Belinda said she was downstairs resting in her bedroom. Is she safe? Does the blood spattering on my floor belong to her?

Belinda and Tammy, they're both in the basement. Katie . . .

I've been in and out of bed all day, so I don't have my firearm on my hip. It's locked in the nightstand. No way to get to it before she can get to me.

My instinct is to run. Can I get out of the bedroom and into my office before she is on me? Before she adds my blood to the splotches on the floor?

No. *Can I fight?*

"Lydia," I say as calmly as I can muster, while slowly moving toward the edge of the bed farthest from her. "Are you okay?"

"The vessels . . . empty." Eyes blank, she shakes her head.

"I can only imagine the concern you're feeling . . . over the, uh, vessels." My feet are now on the floor. I slowly stand and turn to fully face her.

"The vessels, they should be full, but . . . " She makes a slashing motion with the scissors. "The fork popped the vessels." She gives a sad shake of her head.

I'm inching my way toward the bedroom door.

There are voices coming from the kitchen or living room. My heart stops. It's Malcolm and TJ, talking about finding a snack. Lydia, staring at the scissors now, shaking her head, doesn't seem to hear them. I want to yell out, *Get back outside and stay away,* but I'm afraid this will cause her to snap.

Snap more. She's clearly already snapped.

I continue to carefully move toward the door—slow, miniscule movements. So small. Like silent stalking during hunting. I don't want to spook her by moving quickly. Slow. Quiet. Inconspicuous. If I do it right, maybe she'll just keep staring at the scissors and I can escape.

Katie. Is she . . . I can't think about her right now.

A small step with my right foot, making sure I'm fully balanced, then move my left. Right, left, step, step. Repeat. I'm halfway to the door.

"Hey, Mom. You feeling better?"

Lydia jerks up her head, raising the scalpel and snarling, showing yellowed, half-rotted teeth. Malcolm, a foot inside the bedroom, sees her and stops.

"Mom?" Concern, worry, and fear lace his voice.

"I'm okay, Buddy," I say as calmly as I can, eyes still locked on Lydia. "Step out of the room."

Out of the corner of my eye, I see his head move in my direction, confirming my status, making sure the blood covering her isn't mine. Then he turns back to Lydia.

She shakes her head.

"Step out," I say again, forcing myself to be cool as a cucumber. I want to scream, *Run!*

"No!" Lydia screeches. "The small vessel must not move. He must stay full. He cannot move."

Then she starts talking gibberish. The words tumble quickly, each stumbling over the first. Her enunciation is off, making her nearly inarticulate.

Malcolm and I both understand well enough. If he moves, she'll attack.

I give a quick glance in Malcolm's direction. I don't want to take my eyes off Lydia, but I have to see my boy.

Malcolm, he's standing tall in fighting stance, feet staggered about hip-width apart. He looks well balanced. The handle of his heavy plastic practice sword is in his left hand, and his right is resting midblade.

"Okay, Lydia," I say, as I take another small sideways step toward the door.

She notices my movement and bares her teeth again. This time, adding a hiss.

I try to smile. "You're okay, Lydia. We're going to make sure you're okay."

"Lydia is not okay. She emptied the vessels. Emptied them all." Her bottom lip sticks out in an exaggerated pout.

Emptied them all. Tammy . . . Belinda . . . Katie. My Katie. I suck in my breath. I want to cry. Not now. I can't.

"Lydia, Malcolm is just a little boy. Like your little boys, Marc and Andy. He's so young and innocent. Let him leave. You and I can talk."

She's ignoring us again, looking at the scissors and then the scalpel. I gently move my head backwards, hoping Malcolm will understand I want him to back out of the room.

He takes a very small, cautious step backwards. Lydia's head jerks up. She lifts the scalpel shoulder level and sweeps it downward, like Norman Bates in the *Psycho* shower scene. She's a dozen feet from Malcolm, so the stab doesn't connect with anything but air.

We're not talking our way out of this. I need Malcolm out of here so I can attack. I'm not waiting for her to be the aggressor. I'm going to tell him to run. He'll go for help while I subdue Lydia.

Before I can yell, *Run*, she springs, throwing herself toward Malcolm, blade slicing through the air.

I watch, as if in slow motion, as Malcolm steels himself, the heavy plastic practice sword moving as an extension of his left arm. He drives the sword hard into her stomach. The blunt plastic won't penetrate, but the force of the strike folds her, causing an *umph* to escape.

She squeals like she's been stuck, quickly recovers, then starts moving again.

Malcolm is between us, still in Lydia's line of fire.

"Run!" I yell.

He ignores me, swinging the katana again, this time connecting with her arm. The crack of bone sounds like thunder, her wail a siren. The scalpel hits the hardwood and clatters away.

"Mom," Malcolm says in a calm, steely voice, "you should go get Dad. I'll make sure she doesn't get up."

While I have no doubt he'd do just that, I'm not leaving my son. The evidence of what she's capable of is all over her bloody body.

"Give me the sword, Malcolm. I'll keep watch over her while you run and get your dad."

"Yeah, I suppose that's best since you're the mom and all. Where's your gun? You should probably get your gun since you aren't very good with a sword." That's the truth.

Lydia's still crying on the floor, curled up in a fetal position and cradling her right arm. The scalpel is several feet away. Where are the scissors? Her left hand is holding her right elbow. No scissors in sight.

"Okay, give me a second," I say, as I scramble over the bed. Seconds later, my gun's out of the small safe and I'm covering Lydia with it.

"Go now."

"I'll be right back, Mom. Shoot her if you have to."

Lydia sobs, like a little girl missing her favorite doll. So young, so innocent. The sounds don't match with the visual—the blood on her face, in her hair, covering her clothes.

Tammy's blood? Belinda's blood? *My Katie's blood?*

Chapter 59

Mollie

Friday, Day 23
Bakerville, Wyoming

"Mollie?" It's Jake, in my office, right outside my bedroom. He sounds so calm.

"I'm okay. Lydia's on the ground. I have her covered."

"Okay. Leo's at the back door. Can you tell him it's safe to enter?"

Seconds later, Jake and Leo are in the room. Lydia's moved from her spot on the floor to the rocket heater bench in our bedroom. I start for the basement.

"Wait." Jake swallows hard. "It probably isn't good."

"Katie?" Leo asks, immediately paling.

"In the basement, I think. I'm going." I shove down my emotions. I'm on the stairs when I hear Tate say he'll watch Lydia.

Leo and Jake are right behind me, blood droplets lead the way. Katie's bedroom door is open, splotches of bloody handprints covering the surface, the jamb, the knob. I hesitate a moment before looking in the room.

"Katie?" I say tentatively.

"Mom! Mom! By the safe room."

"Katie!"

Leo takes the lead, sprinting through the rec room into the storage section. Jake is on his heels; I'm right behind Jake.

There she is, kneeling with her back to me, her hands in front of her.

"Katie, I'll take over," Leo says.

"There's so much blood. I wanted to come up for help, but I didn't want to release pressure," Katie says, her hands and shirt covered in blood.

"Are you injured?" Jake asks.

"I'm fine. I was in my room when I heard noises. I came out to investigate and saw her. It was Lydia. She was bent over Belinda, st-stabbing her. She saw me and came after me. I locked myself in my room."

"Where's Tammy?" I ask.

"Safe room. I couldn't help her." Tears stream down Katie's face. "Belinda, she's still alive. Right, Leo? She's alive?"

"She's alive. Unconscious but alive. Jake, we need Dr. Sam. Can someone go after him? And Deputy Fred, better get him also."

"Tim called for Evan. He's on his way down. The walkie-talkie grapevine is active, and they're calling for Dr. Sam and Fred or one of the other deputies. I'll go upstairs and update them." Jake walks toward the rec room. "Be right back."

"Mollie," Leo says, "can you grab your trauma kit? The one you made for gunshot wounds."

After grabbing the kit, Katie and I help Leo as best we can. Belinda's a mess. I don't see how she can survive this, not with the amount of blood she's lost. As we're working on her, I notice a small box on the floor.

Digital Pregnancy Test—the reason she came to the basement. What happened? How did Lydia get the scalpel and scissors?

Leo's starts an IV and puts pressure bandages on the worst of the lacerations.

"She must have lost a lot of blood to be unconscious," I say.

"I think she was knocked out first, then stabbed. See the thermos over there on the ground?" He motions near the open door to the safe room. "It has blood on it. There's blood on the back of Belinda's head. I think she was getting something off the shelf, and Lydia conked her from behind."

Great, another head injury. I'm beginning to think our people need to start wearing hard hats.

"While she has lost a considerable amount of blood, I don't think it's up to the point of immediate death. I do still think she'll need blood, like Katie did. I'm not exactly sure how to do it, so we'll need to wait for the doc. I'm going to check on Tammy. You're okay staying with Belinda?"

"I'm sure I'm right about . . . you know," Katie whispers. "I'm sure she's dead."

He gives a solemn nod. "I'll be just a minute."

"What will happen to Lydia?" Katie whispers after Leo leaves.

"I don't know. I heard Deputy Fred is putting together some sort of jail, but . . . I don't know."

"I knew she wasn't well, but I had no idea . . . I don't think Belinda thought anything like this was possible. She wouldn't have kept her here with all of us if she thought something like this would happen. Was anyone else hurt?" Katie asks.

"No, we're all fine. Malcolm was able to stop her."

"Malcolm?"

"Yeah, with his practice katana."

"You're kidding. How?"

"Hit her with it. The heavy plastic broke her arm. I guess Leo should go take care of her."

Katie makes a face.

"There was nothing you could've done, Katie," Leo says softly. "It looks like one of the first wounds was fatal. Her brachial artery. She probably went quickly."

"Okay," Katie whispers, tears in her eyes.

Tammy is dead. Tammy, who was a retired labor and delivery nurse. Selfishly, I think of Sarah and her baby. Sarah took a lot of comfort in Tammy's familiarity with delivering babies.

I think of TJ, Belinda's son. He's had so much loss. First his dad, then his grandpa, and now his grandma . . . all violently killed—murdered—in the last few weeks since the attacks started.

Leo looks over Belinda, seeming satisfied for the moment. "I'm going to check on Lydia. Mollie, I'm taking your small trauma kit. If anything changes with Belinda, one of you come get me immediately."

Finally, after what seems like an eternity but is only a little over half an hour, Dr. Sam Mitchell arrives.

"Do you need me, Doctor? I need to go check on my son."

"Malcolm's your boy?" he asks, while checking Belinda. "Saw him upstairs, heard what he did. Amazing young man. Seems to be handling it okay, but I'm sure he'll want his mom."

"Where's Lydia?" I ask with an involuntary shudder.

"She's in one of your outbuildings. Jake said it's the one you use as a nursery. It had a stall we were able to secure."

"Yeah, for when the goats kid, gives them some privacy. They left her there alone?"

"One of your family members is watching her. She won't be going anywhere. I'll set her arm once I'm sure Belinda's okay. The deputy will be here soon. He was in the middle of something. Go on up to your son."

Dr. Mitchell was right, Malcolm was happy to see me and he was handling things well, mentioning many times how it was good he spends so much time practicing his sword play. I fully agree. He saved us.

Many of us living in the homestead are gathered in the kitchen, awaiting news of Belinda. Jake and a few others are downstairs. Jake wanted to take care of cleaning up the safe room, then he'll bring Tammy upstairs and we'll take her to her place to get her ready for burial. It'll likely be tomorrow. With no embalming, burying needs to happen sooner rather than later.

It's not long until Leo arrives to update us on Belinda's condition. Somehow, her injuries, while incredibly serious, are not immediately life-threatening. There were many cuts of varying degrees, and she lost a lot of blood, but no arteries were hit or even nicked. There is some concern about her left arm where a cut to the tendon, and possibly nerves, may have some lasting damage. Only time will tell.

"We know she's O negative," Leo says. "She knew her blood type and told us after Katie was injured. All of us on the original medical team know our type. So she's a universal donor, good for us if we need her blood, but she can only receive O negative. Tate's O negative, so we'll start with him."

"How do you know?" I ask.

"He was in the Air Force and knew his blood type. When he donated to Katie, he told me."

"Okay. Sorry, I can't help—B positive. Are we keeping Belinda here?"

"Yes, for now at least. Best not to move her. June Mitchell's with her now while Doc Sam sets Lydia's arm."

"And Tammy? Is she . . . about ready?"

"Jake, his dad, and Keith are finishing up. We'll bring her upstairs shortly."

"I'd like to take care of her," Lois says quietly. "We've become very close while they've been here. I'd like to do this final thing for my friend. I'll stay with her tonight."

Deanne reaches over and pats Lois on the arm, while Sarah goes to her and says, "I'm happy to help you, Mama."

"Thank you, Sarah. I'd appreciate it," Lois says, wiping her eyes.

So tomorrow we'll have another funeral. I've lost track of how many this will make since the attacks started. Too many, for sure.

Chapter 60

Sylvia

Friday, Day 23
Meeteetse, Wyoming

Sabrina is braiding Naomi's hair. Nicole, Nate, and I are playing cards while Kim and Rey watch. About midafternoon we have another visit from the town mayor.

"So, you folks look pretty good," he says. "Bea says she stopped by and brought a few things. I hope you know how, um, sorry we all are for the . . . troubles." He looks at Nicole as he says this; she quickly drops her eyes.

When none of us respond, he continues, "There's been some, uh, questions on what exactly happened. Oh, not *exactly*. I don't mean that at all. No, we know . . . anyway. The one guy, the one with the neck . . . problem . . . well, we just can't figure out how he slipped and broke his neck. It's just beyond our belief."

"Oh, that?" Kim says casually. "Does it really matter? Maybe the Lord works in mysterious ways. Maybe he sent us a miracle, which helped save my little girl from harm. I'm sure you believe in the Lord, right, Mayor?"

"Absolutely, yes. I absolutely do. Perhaps you're right. Maybe it was just a . . . miracle, as you say. Or a fluke. Something like that. Well, I'll let you folks get back to your day. Do you need anything? Maybe more hot water?"

"You're very kind." Saccharine Kim returns, now batting her eyelashes. "All of you are so nice to us. We can't tell you how much we appreciate the consideration. And Bea bringing us food and clothing, it's all very nice."

"Well, yes. Sure." He sounds flustered, which is likely Kim's intention. Wow, she can really work a guy.

Rey doesn't seem the least bit bothered by the way Kim's behaving.

"I'll, uh, see if maybe Bea or someone can bring over more water. Perhaps there's a little food to spare—you know, for the children also. When do you folks think . . . when are you . . . when do you plan . . ."

"To move on?" Kim asks, acting crestfallen. "Oh, Mayor, have we worn out our welcome?"

"No. No, not at all. Please, stay and rest up as long as you need. It's just . . . well, there's another family—a mom, three boys, and the mom's sister. The husband, he fell and broke his leg. Broke it bad. They were able to get him here, but he had a terrible infection. Bea tried, but she couldn't save him. They're trying to get home to Great Falls. At least I think it's Great Falls, somewhere up near there. We were wondering if they might be able to travel with you. You all seem to be able to take care of yourselves, but I think they'd be a good addition to your group."

"We're not going that far," Sabrina says quietly. "Sylvia and I are only going to Bakerville, Rey and Kim on to Bozeman."

"Right, right. I understand. But it'd get them closer. We've offered to let them stay here, but they're determined to make it home."

"I'm sure we don't have the resources to allow them to travel with us," Kim says haughtily. "We barely have enough to make it. In fact, I don't know how we'll make it once Sylvia and Sabrina leave us."

"We could take up a small collection to help with some of their needs," the mayor offers. "Enough to help a little at least."

"Do you mind if we think about it?" Rey asks.

"Not at all. I don't think they'd be much trouble. The children are teens. They were on a trip to check out colleges when things fell apart. Twin boys and a slightly younger brother. Those boys were able to make a travois and transport their dad. The mom and her sister are also pretty tough. I think they'd be an asset as opposed to a hindrance. You'd want to meet them, of course. After you discuss it a bit, if you lean toward taking them, we'll introduce you."

"I think we could certainly consider it, for the right negotiations." Flirty Kim returns, once again batting her eyelashes.

"Oh, yes. Of course. Negotiations." And with that, the mayor quickly steps through the lilac bushes.

Kim smiles triumphantly, as Rey quietly says, "Kim, that wasn't necessary."

"Maybe not, but it was fun," she cackles.

Weird.

Nicole and Nate both share a look, then shrug.

Kim . . . there's something definitely off about her. I mean, seriously—she broke a guy's neck. I think I'm being generous thinking there's something off. I think psycho might be the word I'm looking for.

"What do you think?" Rey asks Sabrina and me.

"No. Absolutely no," Kim says. "We don't need anyone else. I would like to see if we can get a little more food, though, so let's at least pretend to be in discussions and see what it'll buy us."

"You want to lead him on?" Sabrina asks.

"Sure." Kim shrugs. "A little. After all, they kind of owe us for what happened."

"Kim," Rey says stiffly, "they don't owe us. It wasn't the town's fault."

"I think we should take them along," Nicole blurts. "We need more protection. Dad and Nate are the only guys. All of us girls, we look like easy targets."

"We're not girls, Nicole. We're women," Kim snaps. "I haven't worked all my life at earning respect to be called a girl."

"Fine, Mom. Women. Even so, it sounds like they're strong guys and could make an impression."

Rey is nodding as he says, "Might be smart. Let's think about it. Sylvia? Sabrina? Sound okay to you?"

"I'm not opposed to it," Sabrina says. "We still have a week and a half or so before we reach Bakerville. Might make sense to have the help. And I do think Nicole is right about the show of force, especially when Sylvia and I are no longer with you."

My heart drops a little thinking of not being with the children, especially Nicole. I glance at Nicole; I think she feels the same.

"I agree, the right people could be helpful," I say. "But we do need to think about food and supplies, make sure they have what they need. And water containers, I think water will be scarce in places."

A while later, Kim and Rey ask if we can watch the children. They'd like to take a walk along the river, maybe try to catch a few more fish for dinner. We fileted the fish for lunch. We saved the bones and skin to make a soup chowder for dinner, using the rest of the milk

311

along with the bread. I can't even tell you how excited I am about soup and bread.

Shortly after Rey and Kim leave, we hear the rumble of engines. *Cars!*

What would've been a normal sound three weeks ago, catches us off guard. We've seen a few vehicles since we started walking, but they're few and far between, especially since the EMP. From the time we left the train tunnel until today, we've seen five cars. Now, we definitely hear more than one, and the sound is getting very close.

Naomi pops up and runs to the side of the house.

"Naomi, stay here," I say.

"I am, Sylvie. I'm just looking at the cars driving up."

Sabrina and I hustle to where she is, with Nicole and Nate trailing right behind. The five of us peer around the edge of the house, watching as a pickup truck with a flatbed loaded with motorcycles pulls up to the house. It's followed by a regular looking pickup and an old weird looking car . . . a car like I've never seen.

"That's a funny looking car," Naomi says. "It reminds me of my roller skates."

"Dork," Nate whispers, while Sabrina says with a laugh, "Your roller skates? Why does it remind you of those?"

"I don't know, but it does."

"It reminds me of a fishbowl," I say, causing Naomi to giggle.

"A fishbowl? That's almost as silly as roller skates," she says. "Oh, look. There's a girl about the same size as you, N'cole. Maybe she can be your friend and you won't be so sad."

Nicole looks at the girl and nods, as Naomi whispers, "Except the girl looks sad too. They all look sad. Maybe we don't want them here. They're too sad, and we don't need any more sad people."

Then, one of the ladies, a very tall blond around my age, sees us. She gives a small wave and a smile. Not a big toothy grin, but the kind of small smile that says, *Things are rough, but I'm friendly.*

We don't need more sadness, but I'm suddenly struck with a thought. We might need these people.

Chapter 61

Lindsey

Friday, Day 23
Meeteetse, Wyoming

I step out of the truck and survey the area, giving a small wave and attempting a smile for the two women and three children peeking at us around the corner of the house.

The little girl gives me a huge smile and waves back.

"You setting up camp?" One of the women smiles and asks.

At my nod, she asks, "Do you need some help?"

I look to Logan, who shrugs. "Sure, why not?" I answer, even though we don't really need help.

"I'm Sabrina. This is my sister, Sylvia, then Nicole, Nate, and this little munchkin— " she ruffles the smallest girl's hair " —is Naomi. We're set up behind the house. We've been traveling with the children and their parents since outside of Shoshoni."

"Where're the parents?" I ask.

"Went to try and catch some fish. They'll be back shortly."

"This is my husband, Logan, and our friends Barbara, Bobbi, Gina, Carlene, and Aimie."

"Aimie, you look to be about the same age as Nicole," the sister, Sylvia, says.

"I'm fourteen, almost fifteen," Aimie answers shyly.

"I'm sixteen, my birthday was the day before the planes crashed," Nicole says. "You been on the road long?"

Aimie looks at Carlene, who gives a slight nod, then she says, "We were . . . kidnapped. Lindsey and Logan rescued us yesterday."

"Oh," Nicole says quietly. "I'm sorry. I was kidnapped yesterday, too, but only for a little bit and . . . nothing super bad happened. But it was scary. Sylvia rescued me."

Nicole beams at Sylvia. Sylvia gives a small smile in return, looking embarrassed.

Carlene tells Aimie she can visit with Nicole while we all set up camp. They move over by a hedge of lilac bushes, with the younger girl joining them. A man and woman walk around from the back of the house.

Sabrina introduces us to Kim and Rey Hoffmann. Sylvia interjects, making a point his name is Rey, spelling it out for us. *Okay, then.*

Kim and Rey are both attractive. Very attractive. Even though it's obvious they've been on the road, they still have movie star looks. I suddenly feel terribly self-conscious.

I'm not ugly, but I know the last several weeks have been hard on me. I'm too skinny, and the radiation sickness is taking its toll. I lost another chunk of hair this morning, and my scalp is showing in places.

"You look very familiar," Kim says to me. "Do we know each other?"

She doesn't look familiar to me at all, but I spend several seconds searching my memory just in case. "I don't think so," I finally answer. "I live . . . *lived*, in San Jose. Before that, outside of Seattle. You?"

"I've visited both places but never lived there. We were living in Denver. Been there since shortly after Nate was born."

I shrug. "Maybe I just have one of those faces."

"Maybe so," she answers, unconvinced. "You just seem so familiar, it's almost strange."

Rey laughs. "Kim does this all the time. She says she never forgets a face, which is true, but she also sees other people in strangers. I've learned to live with it."

As we're finishing setting up camp, a man walks up.

Kim straightens and gets a huge, cloying smile. She turns on the charm as she says, "Hello, Mayor. Have you met our new neighbors?"

"No, not yet. Heard about them but haven't met them."

Kim takes care of introductions. Once those are completed, the mayor says, "So, Kim, have you folks had a chance to think about my suggestion?"

"Oh, we've barely had a minute to discuss it," she says sweetly. *Ugh. So fake.*

"We'd like to meet them," Rey says quickly. "At least, if it's okay with Sylvia and Sabrina. I think it's a good idea."

"I'm fine with it," Sabrina says.

"Me too," says Sylvia.

Kim rolls her eyes.

The mayor smiles broadly. "I'll go get them. I think Bea might have made a nice treat for you all for dessert. I'll see if she has enough for your new friends here also."

After the mayor leaves, I glance at Sabrina.

"There's a family here trying to get home," she says. "The dad was injured in an accident and passed away. The mayor asked if they could travel with us."

"Ah, makes sense. It's smart to travel in groups."

"For sure. We— " Sabrina points to herself and Sylvia " —don't have much farther to go. But Rey and Kim, they're going to Bozeman. The other family, even farther."

"Where you going?" I ask Sabrina.

"Home. To my mom's home anyway. She and her husband live in a little town near the Montana state line. Bakerville."

"What?" I blurt out, unable to contain my surprise. How can this be? "We're going to Bakerville too. My mom and stepdad live there."

"No way," Sylvia says.

Sabrina smiles. "That's amazing."

I look to Logan. He's also smiling as he says, "Small world."

I give him another look, imploring him to read my mind. He does, giving me a small nod before saying, "How big is the family the mayor wants to have you take along?"

"Two women, three teenage boys," Rey answers.

"And there's the seven of you? So twelve altogether?"

"Right."

"We could probably figure out a way to travel together, in the vehicles, if you all want. Give you a break from walking."

Sylvia and Sabrina hug each other, tears glistening in their eyes.

"Would you?" Sylvia asks breathlessly.

"Absolutely," I answer. "We're staying here tonight and will be in Bakerville tomorrow. It'll be tight traveling, and people will have to ride in the bed of the truck, but we can do it."

"Any of you know how to ride a bike?" Logan asks. "I can't ride my Harley with my injury, and it was easier for Lindsey just to ride in the truck. But we've got the two bikes and really need to use them to get everyone to fit."

"I ride," Rey answers.

"Good. Anyone else?" Logan asks.

"I never have," Sabrina says. "But can learn if you need me to."

"I'll ride the other bike," I say. "No reason for me not to."

"Let's get them off and ready, make any other adjustments needed so we can load up easily in the morning," Logan says.

A few minutes later, the mayor returns with the family of five and a good-sized plate of brownies.

The boys look like football players. Defensive linemen, in fact. Even though they're still in high school, they're all tall, several inches taller than my height of almost six foot, and husky.

The boys, seventeen-year-old twins and a fifteen-year-old, all have names beginning with A. I don't even try to remember what they are or which is which. I do catch their last name, Dosen. Their mom is a few inches shorter than me, about Logan's height. She's not really fat, but she's definitely not skinny. I think of her as husky also. Same with her sister. Their names are also a blur to me.

Maybe tomorrow I'll work on remembering their names. I suspect all five were heavier before—before this all started and food has become scarce for so many. I wonder how long it'll be before overweight becomes a thing of the past.

We visit with each other and share the brownies—I can't even begin to describe how amazing they taste. Yes, we'll all travel together. No one minds we'll be overcrowded on the drive to Bakerville. Two weeks less walking is well worth it. Logan and I, along with Sylvia and Sabrina, are confident the other two families will be able to stay a day or two in Bakerville before starting again.

The Dosens head off so they can get packed. We'll leave by 8:00 am. Logan and I learned from Sabrina and Sylvia about how things have been for them. Not good. Not as bad as what Barbara and the ladies we found have experienced. But not good.

Chapter 62

Sylvia

Friday, Day 23
Meeteetse, Wyoming

"So," Lindsey whispers conspiratorially, "what's the deal with Kim?"

We're sitting with Logan and Lindsey near their camp. Everyone else has dispersed and is resting or in groups visiting. I catch Sabrina's eye, then take a deep breath before whispering back, "Good question. How much time do you have?"

Sabrina gives me a slight smirk and a shake of her head, then says, "She's a little different, and we're not entirely sure what her deal is, but she's a great mom. And in the time we've known her, she's . . . changed."

"I'll say," I huff.

"Kim is very complex," Sabrina says.

"Ha. I'm not sure *complex* is the word I'd use to describe her," I say.

"What word would you use?" Logan asks.

"Crazy," I answer without hesitation.

Lindsey raises an eyebrow at me, only one—I'm always impressed with people who have that ability.

Logan's face immediately expresses concern.

Sabrina shakes her head. "Not crazy. She's not insane. She has all of her wits about her."

"Yeah, well, she's deranged. Isn't that part of being crazy?" I snap. As a freelance writer, Sabrina's a walking thesaurus and dictionary. Surely, she can't deny Kim is deranged.

Sabrina gives me a patient look before addressing Lindsey and Logan. "Kim has put Sylvia in an awkward position. Sylvia isn't . . . no, *we're* not quite sure what to do about it, if anything."

"Oh?" Lindsey asks.

Sabrina looks at me, willing me to explain.

I give a slight shake of my head. Nope, not doing it.

She lifts her chin at me.

Fine. Why not tell the entire world?

"You heard Nicole say she was kidnapped?"

"Yes, terrible thing. We didn't explain, but that's how we found the women with us . . . and Aimie. They were being held hostage. There was a sixth, Samantha, she . . ." Lindsey takes a deep breath. "She took her life yesterday."

Sabrina gasps, and I quietly say, "Oh." I'd be lying if I didn't admit to understanding why she would.

Logan wraps an arm protectively around Lindsey, then kisses her temple.

"I think Nicole's going to be okay," I say. "She didn't . . . the guys . . . they were stopped before . . ."

"That's good," Logan says quickly.

"Yes, very good. She's still very shook up and isn't without any injuries, but . . ." I shrug. "So here's the weird thing." I lean in to whisper. "Kim was a self-professed anti-gunner. She totally freaked out on us when she found out we conceal carry."

"Okay?" Lindsey says. "Lots of people are like that."

"Sure, but then do those people take someone's weapon and blast two guys without blinking an eye?"

"What?" Logan asks, while Lindsey does that single eyebrow thing again.

"Yep. She took my sidearm, killed one guy, shot the other in the arm, then get this—she broke his neck."

After my story, we spend some time discussing how Kim could've done those things. Sabrina still wants to believe it was Kim's mama bear instincts, but Lindsey says it sounds like there's much more to it.

"I'll admit," Sabrina says, "I don't really understand it. She doesn't even seem like the same person we met at the campground."

"Not at all," I agree. "She's . . . something is way different about her. Like a flip was switched." Saying that reminds me of a movie I watched a few years ago over at a friend's house, a movie about a female spy who lost her memory. Then, after a series of traumatic events, her memory starts to return and she finds out she's not just a spy but an assassin. I don't think Kim is suddenly regaining her memory, more like she's been hiding who she really is, and now . . . now what? It's the end of the world, so why bother faking it?

The four of us sit in companionable silence for several minutes when, to my own surprise, I blurt out, "How are the others handling their captivity?"

Lindsey gets a very sad look. "Not very well. They were . . . it was bad. They were kept for a couple of weeks. Not treated well at all. Carlene and Aimie, the mother and daughter, they were kidnapped from their home. They knew the guy who did it. He even killed Carlene's husband and her son—Aimie's dad and brother. And they weren't spared from the worst of it, like Nicole was. They have nightmares and . . . it's bad. Barbara, she's the most stoic of the group and seems to be keeping everyone together. But I think she's barely hanging on herself. I suspect she'll fall apart when given the chance."

"Maybe I can help them," I again surprise myself.

"You a counselor?"

"Nope. Paralegal. But I know a little about what they're going through. Not the abduction part but the . . . the rape part."

"I'm so sorry," Lindsey says, while Logan looks embarrassed.

Sabrina touches my arm and gives me a tender smile.

"Whenever they're ready, I'll be here for them." Tears fill my eyes. "And I'll be praying for them." I'm shocked to find I actually mean this.

Lord, use me for Your glory. Use me to help these women, these children, from what they've endured.

I'm shocked to find I actually mean this also.

Chapter 63

Lindsey

Friday, Day 23
Meeteetse, Wyoming

I'm not entirely sure what to think about the things Sylvia told us. Could someone without prior training break a guy's neck? I quizzed her extensively on what she saw, what she heard. She's convinced Kim did it, convinced she snapped his neck like the proverbial twig. Sylvia even stressed the guy was huge and that maybe, if it were a small, wimpy guy, she'd think it was possible. But not with such a big guy. Sabrina said the mayor even questioned how it could happen, and Kim blamed him slipping on a rock.

What kind of a person—what kind of woman—could break a guy's neck?

My mom. A woman like my mom could do it.

Not quite as tall as I am, but just as fit at almost sixty, my mom is impressive. She's like a combination G.I. Jane, Wonder Woman, and Marvel's character Black Widow.

Maybe more Black Widow than the other two. Black Widow wasn't born with superpowers like Wonder Woman. She developed them as a KGB agent. There were many times growing up when I half wondered if, instead of a government trainer, my mom had a more clandestine position with the government. I asked her about it once. She answered with a nonanswer, "*I go where my country needs me,*" then promptly changed the subject.

When I first started talking about not only joining the police force but possibly the FBI, my mom wasn't enthusiastic. She was okay with the police, with me being a cop, but not federal. She said I wouldn't like the politics. There's plenty of politics for city police too. Definitely not my favorite thing, but not too big of a deal.

Even with the abnormality surrounding Nicole's rescue, and having more questions than answers, Logan and I agree we'll still travel together to Bakerville. Not for Kim or Rey, but for their three children. They could use the rest, and hopefully my mom and Evan will let them regain some strength before traveling again. Those children are way too skinny.

I look down over my own way-too-skinny body. The nurse in Thermopolis said Logan and I would start putting weight on once the radiation symptoms passed. Good thing. Gaunt is not a good look on me.

We've found somewhat kindred spirits in the sisters. Both are well armed with several handguns and the small armory Sabrina has stashed in one of those little collapsible shopping carts city people use when walking to the grocery store. I'm duly impressed.

Of course, the terrible ordeal Sylvia experienced in her past probably has quite a bit to do with how they're dealing with this world we're now living in.

This trip has been such a long, drawn out ordeal. It's hard to believe we'll finally finish tomorrow. I hope my mom's doing well and is healing from her gunshot wound. When Evan told me about it, he tried to sound optimistic, but I could hear the fear in his voice.

Tomorrow. Tomorrow I'll be able to see for myself how she is.

Logan and I will build a new life in Wyoming. We'll rest up and recover from this trip, from the radiation poisoning, from all of the things we've been through these past weeks.

Maybe . . . maybe we'll even talk about having a child. That's not something I ever thought I wanted. Logan, the youngest of five, wanted to have children. When we were dating, he asked me about it, and I told him no, that it's not something I'm interested in. We even stopped seeing each other for a few weeks over it.

When we got back together, I made sure he knew being a mom wasn't for me. He agreed, and we haven't discussed it again. Oh, I see the way he looks sometimes. When my friend and her husband announced their pregnancy, I could tell he really does want a child. Not me. How can I be a SA with the FBI if I take time out for kids? They have age rules, and I'm pushing it now to make sure I'm in before I age out.

Now, the world has changed so much. The last thing I should be thinking about is a child. Our child. But I am.

It started almost as a whisper when we were in our culvert hole, attempting to avoid the fallout. I shut the whisper down pretty quickly. But it's kept returning, almost tormenting me. I guess the end of the world has given me baby fever. I wonder what Logan will think of this? Me changing my mind will surprise him.

Once we're settled and feeling better, we'll discuss it. I know he'll like the idea.

Chapter 64

Mollie

Saturday, Day 24
Bakerville, Wyoming

Malcolm stayed in our room last night, making a bed on our rocket heater bench. The cob bench is wonderfully cool in the summer. It's also hard and uncomfortable for sleeping on, so he added his camping mattress. Even though he put on a brave front for most of the day, by bedtime, he was pretty shook up.

We stayed up terribly late last night, just talking. Not only about Lydia, but everything—how much our lives have changed, the things he misses from before, and especially swords. His fascination with swords and swordplay started about a year and a half ago. He reminded us several times how good it is he likes swords. We wholeheartedly agree.

"I think God helped me," he said quietly. "He *knew* what was going to happen, and He made it so I could . . . so I could help you, Mom. I just wish . . ."

Jake and I both waited for him to finish his sentence. Finally, just above a whisper, he said, "I wish I didn't have to hurt her. I didn't like hurting her."

Then, for the first time since the incident—that's what we're calling it, *the incident*—he dissolved into tears.

Belinda regained consciousness around suppertime last night. Dr. Sam is confident she'll make a full recovery, but it'll take some time. Tammy hadn't been taken to her home yet, to get ready for the burial, when Belinda awoke. She asked to be able to see her, to say goodbye since Sam said she wouldn't be able to attend the burial.

Lois and Sarah, along with Keith and Tate as their escorts, took Tammy home. Sarah stayed and helped Lois prepare Tammy. Tate and

Keith made a simple casket out of scrap lumber. Sarah helped Lois with Tammy—finding a nice dress, fixing her hair, and doing her makeup. Even though it'll be a closed casket, they wanted her to look good.

Tate and Sarah came home so Lydia's children would have their usual nighttime routine. Lois and Keith stayed at Tammy's house; Lois didn't want to leave her there alone.

The burial will be at 2:00 this afternoon, followed by a community meal to replace our usual luncheon. Notification was sent out via the walkie-talkie grapevine and messenger.

Today was the day we were supposed to start our local meals. The stations were set up so people wouldn't have as far to go. Instead, each station manager will bring the meal to the community center.

It was discussed having the burial earlier, at our usual noon lunchtime, but with the rocks and hard ground, it'll take several hours to dig the grave. David Hammer and his boys offered to dig. They were able to get a few hours in yesterday as a head start.

The funerals before the EMP were much easier. Then, Mick Michaelson used his backhoe. Now, his backhoe and all the rest of his farm equipment are the equivalent of giant paperweights.

"Good morning, Mollie," Deanne, already working on today's meal, says as I walk into the kitchen. It's early, the sun isn't even fully up, but she's well into her cooking. She looks exhausted. Did she even sleep?

"Hello, Deanne. What time did you start?"

"Oh . . . I don't know, an hour or so ago. Didn't sleep well last night, so I figured I might as well get to it. I didn't wake you up, did I?"

"Not at all. I didn't even realize you were here. Jake's just getting ready. He'll be right out."

"Coffee's ready." She motions to a thermos on the counter.

"Ah, wonderful. Let me have a cup, then I'll start on today's bread."

"You've been cleared to be up and around today?"

No, but I'm not going to worry about it. Other than the slight headache yesterday, I had no other physical issues. I'm pretty sure I'm fine. I shrug my response to Deanne; she gives me an understanding nod.

"What are you making?" I ask, motioning to the ingredients spread in front of her.

"Pasta casseroles, something like a lasagna only not layered. Since we've salvaged a decent amount of pasta from the houses, seems smart to use it up. It's all different shapes, but I figure if I use one style per dish, it should cook evenly. I'm adding a little meat to most of them, a couple will only have cheese, and one will be vegan."

Even at the end of the world, we still have people on special diets. I silently wonder about the few people who were eating Paleo or low carb before the attacks. Will they eat the pasta casserole? I was one who watched my carbs before all of this; it helped with keeping my weight in check. Now, with counting our calories and the increased activity—as opposed to me sitting at a desk most of the day for work—carbs don't seem to be as much of a weight-adding issue. But I know at least one person in the community found limiting carbs to help with her arthritis symptoms. I wonder how she's faring. I'll search her out at the funeral service today and ask.

"Morning, honey," Jake says, giving me a quick peck. "Ready for me to start the bread oven?"

"In about an hour. Since I didn't start the sourdough loaves last night, I'll make the Cuban yeast bread."

"Sure, an hour it is. That should be right after breakfast, which I'm making this morning—you're still taking it easy."

"No need," Deanne interjects. "I have an oatmeal breakfast cake mixed up and ready for the oven. If you want to light the bread oven now, we can bake it and all of these casseroles out there also. No sense heating up the kitchen if we can avoid it."

"Sounds like a plan," Jake says as he heads out the door.

As I'm kneading the bread, I realize my stomach feels pretty good today. Maybe I'm finally getting back to normal. I think of Belinda. She went downstairs to get a pregnancy test for me to take, just to be sure. I never did take the test. Fifty-year-old women who've already started menopause rarely get pregnant. Even so, I feel like I should take the test, more than anything because Belinda wanted me to.

About midmorning, Deputy Fred arrives. I offer him the final cup of coffee from the thermos while Tony runs to find Jake.

"So, Fred, I hear your cousin's family is here."

"Uh, yep. Not my cousin, he didn't make it. Died just down the road. They were attacked. His wife and children managed to find a hiding place, which spared them. I'm broken up about losing my cuz, but at least his wife and girls are okay. I brought them home with me. They're in a pretty bad way." He gives an exaggerated frown.

"It's a miracle you were able to find them."

"That it is. I'd been out looking every day. I knew they should get here soon, so I was checking. You see, we were able to make contact when the phones were up and working, so I was expecting them."

I nod my response, as he says, "We've beefed up security after this. My cousin's death was only a few miles from here. Now we're making sure only authorized people get into Bakerville. We had a single person stationed at the main road before. We've doubled them up and added two people at the secondary road. You probably heard about this since your group's involved."

"A little, yes." No sense telling him how much I hate it. Hate isn't the right word . . . I want us to do our part for sure. I just don't like putting my family in danger.

Jake enters through the back door, saying, "Fred, sorry to keep you waiting."

"It's fine, Jake." Fred gives a wave of his hand. "I thought about calling you on the radio but decided this was best to tell in person."

With our grapevine system of communication, the walkie-talkie radios we're using to communicate are anything but private. For Fred to call us, his message would be relayed by six to eight people before a radio near enough had put out a call we would be able to receive.

A few people in the community had Ham radios. All but one are known to be fried. The final one, we don't yet know about. The owner took down the antenna and disconnected everything as soon as the alert arrived. He even moved the parts to his root cellar. He says when we reach day thirty post-electromagnetic-pulse, he'll then start thinking about putting it back together. Until then, it stays stowed away. He fears a secondary attack.

Most of us agree additional attacks are unlikely, but we understand his concern. I'm anxious for him to set it up so we can get news from the outside. We hear rumors but don't have concrete info. Was the US hit by nukes? Is there even still a US? As far as I'm concerned, yes. We even have a small hope we might be able to find out news of Jake's brother and his family. Surely, someone nearby Robert's home in California will have an amateur radio system.

"Okay, Fred. What's going on?" Jake asks.

"That Lydia chick offed herself," he says casually.

I gasp, while Jake shakes his head.

Fred continues with, "Yep. Used her pants and the doorknob. Can't say I'm overly upset about it. Saves me having to house her until we could decide what to do with her."

He looks pleased as he nods his head. "I know Kelley Hudson isn't going to be very happy about it. She made a big deal of telling me the lady was mentally ill. Yeah, well, no kidding. She also killed an important member of our community. Tammy was worth a dozen people like her."

While I don't completely disagree with him, it's still hard to hear him talk about her like she's nothing.

"So," he continues, "Jon Dawson's talking to Judge Avery right now, but you should be able to keep the children with no problem."

Oh, so that's how it is.

Jake catches my eye. We're very fond of Lydia's children, and Sarah's especially fond of them, but we already have Tony and Lily. Do we have the resources to care for three more?

Of course not, but no one does.

Jake relays my thoughts perfectly. "We completely understand the children need to be cared for, Fred. And as far as we know, there isn't a father in the picture or any other relatives.

"Yep, true. Seems she was a bit of a— "

"We do already have Tony and Lily," Jake interrupts, "at least until their dad gets back. Do you think there might be someone else who would want to take Lydia's children?"

"Not a chance. 'Sides, Dawson says since you found them, you keep them." The laugh he gives lacks all humor.

Jake gives a single grim nod. I guess I've known Lydia and her children would likely be with us from the day they carried her in on the stretcher. I thought she'd eventually recover and could be a mom to her children, though.

"We'll happily keep them," I say.

"Knew we could count on you, Mollie. We're going to bury Lydia as soon as we can get the digging done. Didn't figure we'd need a community meal since she isn't really a part of us. You want some kind of graveside service for the kids?"

"It'd be the right thing to do," Jake says. "Where are you burying her?"

"Same place as the ones your wife killed—our own little potter's field."

Ouch. What he said is technically true. I did kill them . . . well, one of them. My girls killed the other two while fighting for their lives. But the way he says it, it sounds terrible.

"We'll take her," I say. "We'll bury her on our land. If we're going to raise her children here . . . "

"It's only right," Jake finishes for me.

"Suit yourself." He shrugs. "We haven't started the digging yet. You want to send someone for her body?"

"Yep. Be right there. Uh, Fred, where is she?" Jake asks. "I don't know where you set up the jail."

"Not much of a jail. It's just a shed I reinforced at my place. It has a big sign on it. You won't be able to miss it. She's inside. Better hurry before she starts stinking up the place. Don't need that mess to deal with. And don't go to the house. My relatives are still in mourning."

"Of course. I'll be there in a few minutes."

After Deputy Fred leaves, Jake pulls me into his arms. "Well, I guess it only makes sense for us to take them."

"Yes, but not us. Sarah and Tate."

"You think? What about their baby?"

"They already stay with them. And it's not like she doesn't have all of us here to help. We need to talk to them. The children need to know before you bring her remains home."

Chapter 65

Lindsey

Saturday, Day 24
Meeteetse, Wyoming

"Good morning, sunshine." Logan wakes me with a kiss.

"Hey." My voice is hoarse with sleep. I clear my throat. "Is it time?"

"Think so. I hear people moving around, talking. Sounds like we might be the only ones still in bed."

"Yeah, okay. The sooner we get going, the sooner we get there. Finally." I sit up and expel a huge breath.

"Maybe, before you go greet our new friends," Logan says with a smile, "you might want to spend a little time with your toothbrush."

"Oh, really? Right back at you, Mr. Maverick." I pinch my nose and make a face of mock disgust.

Logan laughs and grabs me into a quick hug.

"I'm so glad we'll be there today. It's been such a . . . " I search for the word. Hard? Difficult? Nightmarish?

"I know," Logan says, his lips right by my ear. "But we've made it. And we've made a difference. You were right, insisting we help Barbara and the others. And taking everyone to Bakerville with us, it's the right thing to do."

"The time is always right to do what is right."

He gives me a look. "Ghandi?"

"No . . . but I can't remember who. Gosh, I know this too. Maybe when I wake up a little more I'll remember. Right now, I have a date with my toothbrush."

Shortly after 7:00, the mayor, the Dosen family, and a neighborhood lady who Sylvia called Bea arrive. Bea brought homemade bread, two quarts of milk, and two small plastic containers—one had butter, the other a soft, creamy cheese. I almost drool at the sight of the feast.

"Thought you should have a little breakfast before you leave," she says.

"Yes, yes. Before you leave," the mayor parrots. "What can I do to help you get on your way?"

Jeez. He seems terribly anxious for us to go. Logan and Rey ask him to help move a few final items, and he readily agrees.

We're pulling out of Meeteetse at 7:45, fifteen minutes ahead of our 8:00 goal. Everyone is, understandably, jubilant. We've all be traveling for so long, getting to Bakerville was starting to feel like a pipe dream. The Hoffmanns and Dosens will stay a few days before continuing on. While the Dosens don't need the rest, the Hoffmanns most certainly do.

After taking the bikes off the Ford flatbed, we moved and secured the gear and supplies from the F150 to the flatbed. The only way our large group could all fit was by enlisting the bed of the F150 for people hauling.

Barbara and Logan are leading our convoy in the large flatbed, with Barbara at the wheel and Logan riding shotgun—holding his shotgun. Rey is next on Logan's Harley. I think I saw a little tear in Logan's eye as he watched Rey mount up. No doubt, he'd much rather be riding than inside the cab of the truck.

The F150 follows, driven by Carlene. Sabrina is in the passenger's seat, pulling out a pump 20 gauge from the sisters' shopping cart after seeing Logan with his shotgun. Sylvia and the older children—Nicole, Aimie, the three Dosen brothers—plus the brothers' mom and aunt, are piled into the bed of the truck.

The Pacer is next. Gina is driving with Bobbi in the passenger seat. Kim, Nate, and Naomi are in the back seat. Nate wasn't at all happy about riding in the car; he wanted to ride in the pickup. Kim put the kibosh on it, saying she needed him in the car with her to help with Naomi.

I'm on my bike, finishing up the procession. Our plan is slow and easy. Logan and I have definitely learned a steady, safe pace is the best way to go.

As we pass the bridge over the Greybull River to leave Meeteetse, several men are standing on the side of the road in front of a motel and campground. The men who, according to Sylvia, may have been behind Nicole's abduction. One catches my eye; a chill runs through me as he stares me down. Soon, they're in my mirror as we travel the highway, with farmland on either side.

At our sedate pace, it takes an hour and a half to reach a large, lately well-known ranch ten miles outside of Cody. The ranch made headlines when it was purchased by husband and wife celebrities. There were rumors Cody was on its way to becoming the next Jackson. Not now, of course. Now, celebrity or not, we're all just trying to survive. Nothing like an EMP to even out the societal field.

We skirt Cody, choosing to travel by the airport and avoid the bulk of town, before finding the road that continues north to Prospect. We're close to our turnoff when I hear gunfire. Barbara suddenly increases her speed, and we all follow suit. The people in the back of the pickup hit the deck, making themselves almost invisible. At a turnoff on the highway, the big Ford pulls over. Once everyone is parked, I step off my bike.

Logan is out of the truck. "Everyone okay?" he asks.

"What happened?" I ask. "I heard the shots but didn't see anyone."

"They were on top of a roof," Barbara says, looking terribly pale. "Logan saw them right before the first shot rang out. I thought for sure . . ." Her voice fades away.

Logan's walking around the big Ford, then goes to the F150. He stops at the back bumper. "Looks like a shot took out the taillight."

Sylvia, who was sitting only a foot from there, blanches.

Sabrina touches her arm and quietly asks, "You're okay? You weren't hit?"

"I'm fine," Sylvia whispers.

"You sure it was hit?" I ask. "You know, this truck is pretty banged up. Wasn't the taillight already out?"

"Not this one. The other one was."

I nod. "Well, looks like we're okay other than that. Should we get back on the road?"

"Bathroom break first?" Barbara asks, motioning to taller, scrubby sagebrush along the side of the road. No trees in sight, so this will have to do for privacy.

An hour later, we're at the edge of Prospect, once again skirting the town. This time, we make it through the populated area without event. Again, we find a pullout after the town to regroup.

"Whew. I'm sure glad we're riding instead of walking, but my body isn't used to that position," Rey says, stumbling off the bike.

"I hear ya, man. When we were riding, those early days were hard. I had calluses where people shouldn't have calluses. Right, Lindsey?"

"Logan!" I admonish, with a shake of my head and a slight smile. He pulls me close into a hug.

Chapter 66

Sylvia

Saturday, Day 24
Outside of Prospect, Wyoming

I watch as Logan and Lindsey embrace. It's wonderful to see the love these two share. Maybe someday I can have a relationship, a marriage, full of love. Of course, my chances of it might be over. Not a lot of men my age in the retirement community of Bakerville.

I catch Sabrina's eye. She gives me a slight nod. I know she wants love, marriage, and children. No use worrying about this today. Today is the day we'll finally end our trek, and that's cause for celebration. I can worry about what the future may bring another day.

Sabrina signals me to move over to the side. Once I'm there, she quietly says, "They make a cute couple. Very much in love."

I nod but say nothing.

"Do not worry about tomorrow, for tomorrow will worry about itself. Each day has enough trouble of its own."

Scripture. Out of habit, I want to roll my eyes, call it hogwash. Instead, I say, "How is it you always know what I'm thinking?"

She makes a motion with her index finger, touching her temple and then pointing toward mine. "I get you, girl. You know that."

I can't help but laugh. She does get me.

"You doing okay?"

"Still a little freaked out by bullets hitting so close to me," I admit.

"Yeah. Freaked me out too." She gives me a small smile and taps my arm.

"Everyone ready to go?" Barbara asks, walking back to the flatbed Ford. "I'd like to get where we're going and be done traveling for a bit."

"Agreed," Sabrina and I say in unison.

Riding in the back of a pickup truck isn't something I've ever done before today. I have to admit, I love it. I love the feeling of the wind in my hair. Of course, it's not at all comfortable. Sabrina suggested putting our sleeping mats out to provide a little cushion. Unfortunately, the mats are only large enough for two people each. I gave mine to Nicole and Aimie. The Dosen sisters are using Sabrina's mat. The teenage boys and I are toughing it out. I should've spread out my sleeping bag. It would've at least provided a little cushion.

Even with the breeze, it's still hot. The sun is relentless, beating down on us and reflecting off the metal of the truck. I feel a trickle of sweat at my midback.

We're making good time, maybe going a little faster than before. The big Ford, still in the lead, crests a small hill. Rey is at the base of the hill as the Ford goes over the top. Before Rey makes it to the pinnacle, the air is filled with the crunch of metal, the breaking of glass. A torrent of gunfire follows. I again throw myself to the bottom of the bed, as Carlene swerves the truck to the side of the road, flinging me about like a rag doll.

"Everyone, get down," Sabrina commands.

I peek up, looking through the back window and out the windshield. Rey has stopped the bike and is creeping up the hill. Behind us, the Pacer and Lindsey have also stopped.

Seconds later, Lindsey is by the side of the truck, rifle in hand. She has a frantic look about her, understandable considering the truck her husband was in . . . well, we don't really know what's happening with it. But it went over the hill before the commotion started. My gut is screaming *danger, danger.*

"Sylvia, can you keep everyone here? I'm going to see what's happening. Let's get everyone hidden in the ditch," Lindsey orders.

"Okay, yes."

"You want me to go with you?" Sabrina asks.

"Please."

Sabrina takes the shotgun and they sprint toward Rey, now hiding behind a boulder near the top of the hill.

I hustle to get everyone into a secured position. Not that I really have a clue what I'm doing, but I try to think about what would be safe. Should I get the rifles out of the shopping cart? We might need them.

"Sylvie, I thought we'd be safe in cars," Naomi quietly says.
"I know, sweetie, me too."

Chapter 67

Lindsey

Saturday, Day 24
Near Bakerville, Wyoming

I can barely breathe. *Logan!* Please be okay. Please be okay. The gunfire has dropped off, instead of a steady bombardment, it's an occasional discharge.

"You ready?" I ask Sabrina.

"Ready."

We trot up the hill to where Rey is cowering behind a boulder. Large boulders and sagebrush dot the side of the road. I get an overwhelming sense of déjà vu; the landscape is so much like the area we found Barbara and the others. Only then, Logan was with me—by my side. Now, Logan . . .

He's fine. He has to be fine. He's probably on the floor of the truck, protected by the engine block. He'll be smart about staying concealed, behind cover. He has his pistol on his hip, his backup on his ankle, and a shotgun. He can protect himself and Barbara. They'll be fine. *Fine.*

As I reach the crest of the hill, the déjà vu intensifies. Sabrina and I walk in a crouch to Rey; he hears us and turns. The sadness on his face is evident.

"What do we have?" I ask in my cop voice, keeping my tone low. Stay professional. Logan is fine. He's fine.

"It's not good," Rey whispers.

I shift my gaze downhill. It's a steeper slope than most on this road. The climb up was abrupt, and so is the descent—a good place for an ambush. Our truck, the truck Logan is in, is in the ditch, leaning precariously. The front tire is gone, laying fifty feet away. The blue pickup shows many glints of silver. Bullet holes. Riddled with bullet holes. I suck in a breath.

He's fine. Logan is fine. He's hiding behind the engine block.

In front of the truck is a blockade of cars and railroad ties. The ties have been piled like a wall.

"There," Sabrina says, pointing to movement behind the barricade.

"There's several people," Rey says. "I've counted five, maybe six. They're all dressed similar, so it's hard to keep track."

I notice a slight accent to his voice, something I hadn't heard last night. British maybe? Sabrina gives him a strange look. He clears his throat. "So what are you thinking?"

"I'm going to . . . " I hesitate as I adjust my weapon. "I'm going to provide cover so Logan and Barbara can get out and get to safety."

A look passes between Rey and Sabrina. I want to scream at them, *Logan is fine. He's fine.* I hold my tongue.

"My shotgun isn't going to be much good at this distance," Sabrina says.

"True. You can be my spotter. We'll see if we can even the odds a bit, then we'll really let loose so Logan can get out of the truck. You and Rey can use your handguns. We'll make lots of noise."

"Should we have Sylvia come up?"

I think about it a second. "No. You and Rey for now. They're safer back there. Sylvia will make sure of it."

I take only a moment to access the situation and find a comfortable, yet concealed, perch. Within a few seconds, one of the attackers moves, lifting his head above the railroad ties. I don't hesitate. There's a pink spray before I hear the report of my rifle.

"G-good shot," Sabrina says.

My good shot receives a huge response from the other side. We're fired upon. We scrunch low.

"Be right back," Rey says, as he races down the hill.

Great. Run and hide. We didn't need his help anyway.

Sabrina and I stay down, out of the line off fire. I want to try another shot from here, then we'll probably have to move.

Once the salvo stops, I scour the blockade.

"Far right," Sabrina says. "I just saw movement."

I take a deep breath, waiting for my next target to show. *Hang on, Logan. I'm getting you out of there.*

Chapter 68

Sylvia

Saturday, Day 24
Near Bakerville, Wyoming

We've moved the pickup and Pacer slightly to give us a little extra protection as we hide in the ditch. Even though Lindsey thought I should get everyone organized and protected, Kim takes over. And she's amazing. It was her idea to move the cars.

Where I'm sitting, I can see Sabrina. She, Lindsey, and Rey are behind a small rock outcropping. Lindsey shot her rifle, and got a huge response from the others, the ones I think of as the bad guys. What else could they be?

Rey runs back down the hill toward us, moving fast but carefully, pistol against his leg, muzzle pointing toward the ground. As he gets closer, I can tell it's not the handgun Sabrina loaned him to carry. It's still in the holster. Maybe Lindsey gave him one?

He moves into our hiding area, looks at Kim, and says, "Your skills are needed. There's at least a half dozen of them. Well, one less, thanks to Lindsey."

Kim shakes her head and says, "No getting around this?"

"Doesn't look like it. The gig is up. You're on."

"Let's set up a backup perimeter," she says, in a strong and fully professional voice. The flighty, flirty Kim is no more. "Who here can shoot?"

I start to raise my hand when she says, "You're my spotter, Sylvia. You have those cute little binoculars for watching birds? Get them out. Might as well give me the AR-15 you two have been hiding in your shopping cart. Not what I'd prefer, but don't suppose you have a Barrett hidden away, do you?"

"A Barrett? No . . . just the shotgun Sabrina was using, a .22, and the AR."

She rolls her eyes. "I'll make do with the AR, but you bring the .22 in case we need it. I assume you have plenty of ammo for each."

"Plenty? We have some. I guess it depends on how well you can shoot as to whether there's plenty," I chide.

"Don't worry about me," she says with a wink. "Nicole, you stay back here with your brother and sister. Keep them safe. You can shoot the handgun your dad's been training you on?"

"Y-yes," Nicole stutters.

"Good. Watch your muzzle and handle it properly."

"I'm a decent shot," Carlene says. Turning to her daughter, she commands, "Aimie, stay with Nicole."

When it's all said and done, one of the twin brothers and his aunt, armed with my Beretta and my ankle pistol, along with the injured lady from Lindsey's group—incapacitated with a broken wrist—stay behind with Kim's children and Aimie. The rest of us slink up the hill. We've passed out all of the available weapons.

Kim directs where everyone will be, finding other rock formations to use as cover. She stations the other two Dosen boys on the hillside facing the Pacer and F150. "You two are to watch for any threats from the south. Protect our children. No scopes on the rifles, but they'll have to do. And you're both sure you can shoot?"

"Yes, ma'am. The older of the boys says. I'll use the .223, and he'll use the .22. We've both shot weapons like this many times . . . maybe not quite as nice as this one," he gestures, looking a little embarrassed.

Kim points to where she wants them and has the rest of us on the move. She points where she wants Carlene, the twins' mom, and the other girl from Carlene's group—Gina, I think was her name—positioned slightly down from the crest, able to see our vehicles and also the other side of the hill. "One of you behind each rock," Kim barks. "Keep your head down. You're here only as a precaution. Don't want you getting shot. Glance back toward our kids every once in a while. Keep an eye out."

"Rey, find a spot. Sylvia, we're going right there. The primo location."

Kim moves us to a slight depression on the left side of the small highway. We don't have any nice rock outcroppings like the others.

We have sagebrush and medium-sized boulders. Definitely not what I'd consider a primo location. I'd prefer something to hide behind.

Once we're in position, I have my first glimpse of the carnage. The flatbed is halfway down the hill in the ditch. From my angle, I can see the front end is crunched and the back window is broken out. I can't see Logan or Barbara. I can't imagine I want to see either of them. It can't be good.

Kim quickly lies flat, prone. I glance over at Lindsey. She's on also her stomach, focused on whatever she sees through her scope. As I'm watching, her rifle barks. The bad guys return fire. I'm flat on my stomach in the hole in the ground, trying to make myself as small as possible. I turn my head to the left to where Carlene and the others are. They're each scrunched low, making sure no part of their body can be a target.

As soon as the shooting stops, Kim says, "All right. Help me find a target. You know what to do?"

I look at her. Is she crazy? How would I know what to do?

She rolls her eyes. "Just tell me if you see anyone moving and where they are. Then, when I shoot, if I miss them, you need to tell me which way to adjust. Got it?"

"If you shoot and the shot goes too far left, I tell you?"

"Yeah. Then give me the distance of how far I was off. Who even knows if this rifle you've been clanking around in a metal cage all over Wyoming can shoot straight. We're at a definite disadvantage. Guess it'll have to do. Oh, hey. There's a head," she says as she fires. I barely have time to register what's happening, let alone watch where the shot lands.

"Where was it?" she growls, as they return fire.

"I . . . I'm not sure. I wasn't ready."

"You're going to have to stay on the ball. As soon as they stop shooting, I'm going again. There's a guy right in the middle. He'll be my target. Be ready this time."

I'm still on my stomach, trying to stay low. I position the binoculars so I can watch. My heart is pounding. Being shot at, being yelled at by Kim . . . I'm shutting down, getting tunnel vision. I take a deep breath through my nose and forcefully exhale through my mouth. I inhale again. *Lord, be with us.* The involuntary petition accompanies my breath. My exhale is calming and cleansing.

True to her word, no sooner does their volley stop, Kim whispers, "Now," as she retaliates with one single shot. Somehow, I'm ready and watch as she shoots.

"You caught his shoulder. His right shoulder," I say, as they shoot at us again. This is quickly getting old. How much ammo can they have? This time, the shooting ends almost as soon as it starts, perhaps giving me an answer to my question.

"Hmm. That should give him something to think about," Kim says. We watch as a person to the left rises up just slightly. Lindsey takes advantage of his appearance, firing her weapon. She doesn't miss.

Kim's immediately ready and lines up another shot.

"There," I whisper.

She takes an audible breath, then fires. A spray of blood.

I feel like puking but hold myself together.

Kim is almost gleeful as she says, "Just like riding a bicycle."

Did her dad teach her how to be a sniper too?

The bad guys return fire. When they stop firing, Lindsey shoots. Someone cries out and flops into view. Kim shoots. The back and forth continues.

It's a waiting game. The bad guys shoot every so often, but not nearly as much as I'd expect. Conserving ammo? We keep waiting for movement so we can zero in on them. I try to help Kim, but often she sees them first. Sometimes, she shoots before I even realize what's happening. The dust kicks up nearby as they attempt to return fire.

Rey found new concealment after a very close call. One of the ladies from Lindsey's group couldn't handle being in the line of fire and is now down where the children are.

From the little Lindsey shared about what the women had gone through, I understand. Carlene, who has also been through a lot, sticks it out. When we've been fired upon, she's even fired back. Kim told her to knock it off and leave the sniping to the pros.

Okay, then.

"So, that's six," Kim says sometime later. "Might mean something if we knew for sure how many we started with."

Kim motions to Rey. It takes a few seconds before she catches his attention and he slides over.

"What do you think?" he asks, a slight accent to his voice I've never noticed before. *British? German?* I can't quite place it.

"I'm done with this. It's way too hot and exposed up on this hill. Let's wrap it up. You want to be the bait?"

"Not really, but I guess it's time. I think, between the two of you, you got six." His voice has returned to normal. Maybe I was hearing things.

"Right. You catch any movement, Sylvia?"

"No, nothing since the last person. I think it might have been a woman."

"Yeah, well. Too bad for her," Kim says. "Rey, you want to go over and tell Lindsey the plan? Make sure she's ready? Not that I think she won't be. Looks like she has nerves of steel."

I glance over at Lindsey. She does look very determined. My guess, she's just holding it together, doing what she has to do, going through the motions. Kim, however, the woman is a cyborg through and through. My mom would probably diagnose her with all kinds of things.

Rey starts to scoot over toward Lindsey when I catch movement from behind the barricade.

"Kim, far left."

"Darn. I wasn't ready," she says. "Not like me to not be paying attention. I was thinking about how much I'm looking forward to getting to your folks' place. What do you think the chances of them having a juicy steak ready to barbecue would be?"

"Uh . . . slim would be my guess."

"Seriously? Isn't this cattle country?"

"I guess. It freaks me out you're talking about food when we're . . ." I motion to encompass what we are doing.

"Oh, yeah. I guess it would. Sorry."

"There. A shadow about the same spot," I say. "Oh, wait. It's a flag. A white fla— "

The word isn't even out of my mouth before Kim shoots. As the person falls, the white flag catches a slight breeze and drifts higher.

"Kim! A white flag means surrender," I sputter.

"Oops. Oh well, it's not like we can take a prisoner along with us. Probably the last one, realized he was in a no-win situation. Rey can do his thing, but we're probably done here." She signals to Rey, who shakes his head at her before starting to make his way along the edge to the roadblock, handgun at the ready.

It's many minutes, with no movement other than Rey, before he cautiously approaches Logan's truck. He spends only a few seconds at the truck before moving on. *That doesn't bode well.*

Rey disappears into the ditch. I'm starting to wonder where he went when I catch movement far on the other side of the roadblock. Pretty impressive the way he wormed his way around it. I have no idea how he did it, but it's impressive. These two are certainly much more than they've let on. Like the movie with Brad Pitt and Angelina Jolie . . . what was it?

"There he is," Kim says proudly. "He'll signal if there are any left."

Mr. and Mrs. Smith. That's who they are. Spies. Secret Agents. Assassins. Mercenaries. Great. Just what we need in Bakerville. I hope they at least work for the good guys.

Finally, Rey gives a signal. Kim says loudly so all on the hilltop can hear, "That's it. This mess is finished. Got them all."

I quickly look to Lindsey and Sabrina. Lindsey's shoulders droop, her chin falls to her chest. Sabrina puts her arm around her. I watch as her body convulses, wracked with sobs.

Chapter 69

Mollie

Saturday, Day 24
Bakerville, Wyoming

Jake and I find Sarah in the garden. Lydia's three children and Lily are with her. She's attempting to teach them the difference between weeds and plants.

"Where's Tate?" I ask.

"Up at the Snyders'. They're doing some kind of drills for the militia. From there, he's going up to work on the tractors."

"I'm going to see if Evan wants to go with me," Jake says. "I'll talk with Tate while I'm up there."

I nod as Jake kisses me goodbye.

"Can I talk to you for a minute, Sarah? Outside the garden?"

Her look is full of questions. I motion with my head to the other side of the fence. She nods and turns to Marc, Lydia's oldest. "Can you play with the younger children, Marc? Over on the edge where you won't hurt any of the plants. Remember, these are our food. We depend on this food."

"I'll take care of them, Sarah. You can count on me." He gives her a huge heart-melting smile, which Sarah returns.

"He's so sweet," she says as soon as we're on the other side of the fence. "They all are. It's hard to believe they can be so wonderful with the life we think they've had. And now, with what Lydia's done . . ."

"She killed herself," I whisper.

"What?"

"Deputy Fred was just here. Told us she hung herself."

"Oh, no. The children?"

I give her an imploring look and a slight shrug.

"Me? Mom, can they be . . . " Tears fill her eyes. "Oh, I love them so much already. You think, even though I'm going to have a baby, they can stay with us and . . . be mine? Ours? Tate loves them too. We talk about it. I've been praying for a big family. Do you think . . . do you think this is my answer?"

"You've been praying?"

She sighs. "Yes, a little. At first, it wasn't really a prayer, just a hope. We've wanted children, and after losing our first baby . . . I guess what I've been doing is praying. I never really thought God would answer. After all, I've turned my back on him, so why would he answer? And when we lost the baby, it was further proof to me God didn't exist. And if He did, He certainly wasn't interested in me. But lately, things feel different. I catch myself talking, petitioning, *praying*. Not just for my baby but for a family, for our safety, for so much."

I pull her into a hug.

When we release, she says, "I'm not saying I'm a believer again. But maybe I'm . . . interested. The sermons David Hammer gives are compelling. They make me want to learn more." She shrugs. "So what do we need to do? Will there be a formal arrangement? An adoption?"

"Fred said the lawyer and the judge want our family to keep them. Jake and I . . . " I shake my head. "They love you. I don't know about an adoption. I can't imagine there's anything legal set up now. We'll just have to take it day by day. It's not going to be easy. Things will probably come up as they get older, and we'll have to tell them about their mom. Jake's going to get her, and we'll bury her here."

"I'll tell them. You think Jake was going to have Tate come back here? I should wait for him. We'll tell them together."

When Jake finally returns, he and Evan take Lydia's remains to our icehouse. Built out of rocks and stones, it's a double-walled building with an insulated space between the two walls. We've never used it as an icehouse, other than testing it one winter. Building it was one of "those crazy things" we did when planning our retreat. *Ha, who's crazy now?*

Even without ice right now, the construction of the icehouse will make it cool enough to keep Lydia until she can be buried. While Jake was gone, a few of our other men asked me to point them to the cemetery. This was something Jake and I had discussed early in our property planning, an option for home burial.

We have a lot of rocks in our area, which made building an icehouse out of rocks a smart move. It also makes digging things by hand difficult. Surprisingly, there are a few sections on our land with amazing soil and fewer than average rocks—still a lot of rocks by many standards, but less by our standards.

One of the areas is where our large garden is located. The second area, a much smaller section near the far western edge of our property, is what we determined would be our graveyard, should the need arise. I walked Leo, Mike, and Tim to the location, and they got to work.

After Jake and Evan finish in the icehouse, they both join me in the kitchen.

"Everything go okay?" I ask.

They glance at each other before Jake says, "Yeah, it was fine."

"You were gone longer than I expected, so I wasn't sure. Sarah talked with the children. Deanne and I will get her, uh, ready. They may want to see her. I don't know if they should, but Sarah thought they might."

"Don't think they should," Evan says. "Let them remember her from before. They had a few nice visits with her on days she was lucid, right?"

"Yes, there were times she was fine and would ask for them."

"Best to leave it at that, then."

"Okay, sure."

"Um, Mollie," Jake says quietly, "did you or Malcolm hit her yesterday?"

"Well, yes. That's how her arm was broken, remember?"

"No. I mean, in the face?"

I stop to think. Did we? Malcolm hit her with the practice sword in the gut and then the arm. I never touched her, just held her at gunpoint until Jake and Leo showed up. "No, just the stomach and the arm."

"It's possible she was hit during the struggle with either Tammy or Belinda," Evan says with a nod.

"I guess," I agree. "None of us know what happened then. What's going on?"

"She has a lot of bruising to her face and . . ." Jake and Evan share the look again.

"And?" I ask.

They both shrug. "Things just don't quite add up. That's all," Jake says. "We're late because we went up to Jesse Richardson's place, you know him?"

"Maybe? His wife is the retired florist?"

Jake looks at Evan for confirmation. He shakes his head and shrugs.

"Don't know, but Jesse's a retired police detective from New York," Jake says.

I'm waiting for more, but neither of them continues. "Okay . . . so?"

Even though no one else is in the kitchen, or even in the house, Jake whispers conspiratorially, "So he thinks things are a little odd. Jesse suggested Dr. Sam take a look at her before we bury her."

"Because of the bruises?"

Again, the shared look and a slight nod from both of them. What are they not telling me? "But— "

The door bursts open. Tony and Malcolm come rushing in.

"What's wrong?" Jake asks, both he and Evan instantly on full alert.

"Nothing," Malcolm says, while Tony shrugs.

"So why are you barging in here like your hair's on fire?" Evan asks.

"Oh . . . I guess, we didn't think. Sorry," Malcolm says, realizing we're always on edge these days. "We just wanted to see if TJ was still visiting his mom. We finished our job, and Art told us to go play, so we thought TJ might want to play too."

"If he's done visiting with his mom," Tony adds. "We know he's pretty upset about his mom being hurt and his grandma dying. Thought maybe we'd make him feel better." He gives a small smile.

"You boys are very thoughtful," I say. "Why don't you calmly walk down the stairs and ask if he wants to join you."

As they leave, I look to Jake to finish our conversation. Instead, he says, "We'll talk later. Deanne said, since she has the casseroles ready, she'll get Lydia ready. Do you have something she can wear?"

We dress Lydia in a skirt and blouse. Deanne does a nice job of preparing her. We add a scarf around her neck to cover the ligature marks. Once she's presentable, I let Sarah know so she can bring the children in.

"Marc decided against seeing her," she says. "He made the decision for all of them since he's the oldest. He thinks it'd be better for them to remember how she was when she was getting better, those few days when the detox was working before the mental illness took over. He says those were wonderful days, and she was the kind of mom he thought they should've always had."

"I think he's wise beyond his seven years," I say.

"Yeah, he's probably had to be the grownup around the place more often than not. I hope we can give him a childhood. At least more than he's had. I know we all have to work around here, but I plan to still make it fun and make sure they all know how much they're loved. He told me Sissy's real name, Jennifer. He asked if we should start calling her that. What do you think?"

"I don't know. I think, maybe, it should be up to her. She might think of herself as Sissy, at least right now. But when she's older, she might change her mind."

Chapter 70

Lindsey

Saturday, Day 24
Near Bakerville, Wyoming

He's dead. Logan's dead. Kind, sweet Logan. He didn't even have a chance; they executed him. He'll never know about my change of heart, how I want to have his baby. *His baby.* That can't happen now. Logan is dead.

Barbara's dead too. I've tried to piece together what happened. There was something in the road, some kind of homemade bomb maybe? The front wheel was blown off, causing them to crash. Then they were shot, many times. I don't think he suffered. I hope he didn't suffer.

Logan. My husband. He's dead.

"We're almost home," Sabrina says softly. "We can bury them when we get there. Sylvia and I have liners for our sleeping bags. We can wrap Logan and Barbara in those."

"That's very kind of you," I manage to choke out. "You sure you don't mind losing those?"

"Not at all. Uh, they're not clean. We've been using them since we left home three weeks ago. I'm sorry we don't have anything better."

I almost laugh at her concern of wrapping my dead husband in a dirty sheet. Instead, I'm back to crying.

Logan. We were supposed to grow old together.

Chapter 71

Sylvia

Saturday, Day 24
Near Bakerville, Wyoming

Logan's and Barbara's remains are in the bed of the F150. Lindsey wants to sit with him, take these final few miles to be by his side, so the Dosen boys' aunt offers to ride Lindsey's bike. She's ridden before, but it's been a few years.

With the remains in the pickup, we do some rearranging—not everyone is comfortable riding in the back with two dead bodies. I'm on one side of Lindsey, Sabrina the other. We're both trying to support her and be watchful. Carlene is driving, slowly, cautiously.

"We were so close. We made it through some terrible things . . . for Logan to be murdered so close to home . . . we were sure Bakerville would be safe."

I don't know what to say, so I pat her arm and nod.

"Of course, I guess I should know better. My mom was injured, shot while they were out on a supply run. Not in Bakerville, but not too far away."

Sabrina, once again, knows how to respond. She pulls Lindsey close and whispers to her. I can't hear but have no doubt it's all the right things.

I pay attention to the surroundings, glancing around, looking for danger. I think about Kim. Danger is nearby when she is. She, herself, is dangerous. She and Rey both. Beyond dangerous. They'll need to be on their way as soon as possible. I worry about the children. Sabrina and I have grown incredibly fond of them. Will Rey and Kim put the kids in danger?

The way Kim gunned down the last person, the one who was surrendering, makes me think she's fully unhinged. Part of me agrees with her assessment, we couldn't take a prisoner. But the other part of me feel like she violated something important, some kind of humanitarian law.

The children could end up in a dangerous situation because of her derangement. I need to talk to my mom. As a psych nurse, she'll know what to do.

Derangement . . . is that what it is? Maybe multiple personality is a better description. Both Kim and Rey. Or . . . maybe they really are spies. *Ha.*

After the shooting was done and Rey gave the all clear, after we found Logan and Barbara, there was a short discussion on what to do with the other bodies. Kim mentioned a bonfire, not practical. It was decided to stack them in the ditch. Rey offered to take care of it. Kim, almost gleefully, volunteered to assist. Death doesn't seem to bother her.

I stood watch while they performed the grisly task, making sure I was looking anywhere but at those empty faces. The one I thought was a woman was a teenage boy not even old enough to shave. I barely kept it together after realizing this.

Also standing watch, for a different purpose, were the scavenger birds. A murder of crows . . . or are they ravens? A group of ravens is an unkindness. Both names seem fitting, whether ravens or crows. Whatever they are, they were waiting to do the job they've been designed for. I wonder how long we were gone before they started their work. I shake my head to drive away the macabre thoughts.

Focus on the landscape.

Such a beautiful area, one of the reasons Mom and Phil picked this place. Mountain ranges in almost all directions, plus their large mountain standing alone, rising from the floor of the basin, Prospector Peak.

This spot we're in, where Logan and Barbara were murdered, casually referred to as the wasteland, definitely lives up to its name from the road—barren with scraggly, short sagebrush and numerous bare spots, with patches of prickly cactus. Besides the scavenger birds, antelope, mule deer, and the occasional elk also make their home in this desolate country. So do rattlesnakes.

While this desolate area appears to leave much to be desired, unless you're a wild animal or slither along the ground, it's beautiful from a distance, especially from the buttes of Bakerville.

Mom and Phil can't see it from their house, but while visiting with their friends for a barbecue when I was here last time, I was amazed. The sun was setting and hit Prospector Peak and the wasteland just right. The mountain and parched land lit up with gold and copper sparks, almost like a fireworks show.

Bakerville isn't very far from here and is like an oasis in the desert; set in the shadow of the mountains, on the edge of the wilderness. People think of Wyoming as flat and barren, and while many areas are, Bakerville is almost lush. Oh, there's still plenty of sagebrush and cactus and native grasses, but there's also more trees, thanks to four different creeks and a good-sized river coming out of the mountains.

Mom and Phil have a creek running through their property, creating an almost park-like setting. Their nearest neighbors have used the available water to create a virtually self-sustaining paradise. They've even taken their place a step further and set it up as some sort of homesteading school. I have to admit, I had no idea people would want to go to school to learn how to live like pioneers. When our world was whole, I thought it was ridiculous. Now . . .

"We're almost there." Sabrina leans toward Lindsey and me. "Once we cross the river, the road is just up ahead."

Even after the murders, the killing we did, I can't tamp down my enthusiasm. A wave of guilt passes over me. I catch Sabrina's eye and see she feels the same.

Lindsey, with tears in her eyes, says, "It's been such a long trip. I'm so glad it's almost over. Not the way I expected it to end, but at least we'll be there soon."

"This is the turn?" Carlene yells to us.

"Yes!" we three respond in unison.

She takes the turn and continues the slow forward motion. We go about half of a mile up over a small hill when we see it.

A roadblock.

Carlene comes to a complete stop.

"What should I do?" she asks out the open window.

"It's probably just like the other towns. Don't you think?" Sabrina asks.

Lindsey nods; I shrug. Before the ambush, I would've thought yes. Now, I'm scared.

"Nice and slow," Lindsey says. "They're probably just making sure we belong here, just like the other places. Do it just like we've done before."

"You sure, Lindsey? This isn't . . . "

"Yeah. I think, if it were an ambush, they'd be hidden. This looks like a checkpoint. I think we'll be okay."

Please, Lord, let it be true.

Chapter 72

Mollie

Saturday, Day 24
Bakerville, Wyoming

Tammy's graveside service is nice, as nice as a burial after a senseless murder can be. Pastor Ralph officiates, and even though Dr. Sam originally forbade Belinda from attending, as we were all getting ready to leave, he relented.

She's carried to the gravesite on Leo's rollup stretcher and then moved to a camping cot. She lies there for the service, with TJ sitting on the ground by her head.

After the service, TJ comes with us to the community dinner, while Sam takes Belinda back to our place. Art and Alvin stayed behind to safeguard the homestead during the service, so they'll help him get Belinda situated back in the safe room.

Each of the new food station cooks brings the meal they were planning for today. Seems Deanne wasn't the only one trying for something different to kick off the local stations.

Jake and I are visiting with the Snyders and Hudsons when Mick Michaelson comes over to us.

After the greetings and pleasantries are completed, Mick says, "This is quite a feast, but I did notice it's a little light on meat. Pretty creative of someone to use Vienna sausage in the rice dish, but . . . well, I guess we ought to talk about butchering a cow. With enough people, we should be able to process it before it spoils. We'll have more time once the weather cools, but I think we'll be okay. Barney Sanchez and I met earlier today and came up with a rotation schedule. We'll each pick one cull from our herd every week, maybe two. Bobby Noland has a few to cull also. He doesn't run the numbers we do, but he'll still help.

"We need to thin our herds down anyway. It's going to be hard to put up enough feed to get them through the winter without our machinery. "I'm not a fan of horses and don't have any, but Barney's willing to help me with haying by using his horse and wagon. Who would've thought something he kept around just for taking to parades would be something we'd need for survival?" He shakes his head.

"So we'll need to find some implements, scythes, I guess, so we can harvest hay by hand. The corn and barley too. It's all by hand this year, unless Noland's team can get something figured out with the old tractors."

Bobby Noland has a group of mechanics, including Alvin, Tate, Mike, and Aaron Ogden, trying to get a few ancient tractors running.

Alvin used to be a bus mechanic with a school district in Northern California before he retired twenty years ago. Tate was a wrench bender in the Air Force—or as he calls himself, a Crew Dog—turned diesel mechanic. Mike is a general backyard mechanic. Aaron worked at an auto shop in Wesley.

The group has a few prospects they're working on by cannibalizing other pieces. So far, one tractor is running and in the final stages of being put into service, with needed attachments being retrofitted.

They've also been working on getting Jake's truck running. A mid-2000s diesel, it was fried, along with all other newish vehicles, when the EMP hit. Tate has a theory about how he can bypass the computer parts and get it working. So far, he hasn't been fully successful, but the experiment has been encouraging.

If he can get Jake's truck running, he'll move on to Leo's diesel. He doesn't think he can do anything for the gas engines—don't ask me why—but he might be able to get some of the community's diesels going, maybe even some of the diesel farm equipment. Of course, it's still theoretical, and they only work on this in their spare time, of which there is little.

Food, security, and day-to-day survival take up the bulk of our time. Getting the tractors running is important for producing and harvesting food. The pickup trucks aren't essential, especially since we have only a finite amount of diesel. Jake did say having a truck able to tow a large trailer would be helpful for bringing home firewood for the community. Because of Jake and Malcolm's hard work, we're in good shape on wood—at least for the upcoming winter. Many in the community are not. There are plans in the works to remedy this.

"I understand they're getting close," Phil says. "They have one tractor running. They're just working on new tires. I'm not sure about an attachment for haying, though. You'll have to check with him."

"Yeah, he's looking for an old mowing implement, thinks he has something that'll work but the connection is wrong. We'll need workers. In exchange for helping feed the community, we can trade for field work."

"We have a couple of reel mowers," Jake offers. "My daughter used a manual mower on her small lawn in Portland. Mollie and I used ours on the patch of grass we had in Casper. Would they work for haying?"

"Not sure. Don't know if they'd be strong enough for the height of the hay, but we can give it a try."

"We'll figure out a schedule for workers," Phil says. "Truthfully, the ones who'd be the most likely to work in the fields will be the same ones on the militia. We have to figure out a way to rotate them so we always have people fresh for both needs."

"I know it's going to be tough," Mick says, sounding indignant, "but we don't have a choice but to work the fields."

"Absolutely," Phil says quickly. "We're with you on this."

"We'll need the hay for the cattle," Mick continues, barely acknowledging Phil. He's on a roll and wanting to speak his piece. "We also need corn for the pigs. I figure we'll all be eating it. Same with the barley. It won't be exciting eating, but it should be just enough to get our community through the winter. Of course, next winter . . ."

His voice fades away, none of us finish his sentence. Next winter will be a different story. Thankfully, people had their crops in before the attacks started. We've also been blessed with a wet spring, and we're still getting rain almost daily. Next year, the crops will go in by hand. We'll need to make sure we save enough for seed. Also, we don't know what the weather will give us next year. Will we have enough rain so we don't need supplemental watering? Because without power, additional water will be a huge challenge.

"Sure wish those Baker brothers would join with the rest of us," Mick says gruffly. "I'm pretty sure they have some old implements. They still have a considerable amount of stuff left behind by their homesteading relatives. That family never throws anything away."

"I could go visit them," Phil offers.

"Don't bother. They ran me and Barney off with a shotgun. Made it clear they have their family to care for and that is that. The rest of us are on our own."

"They do have quite a group living on their ranch," Jake says. "I can somewhat understand wanting to take care of their own."

"Probably don't have any more people at their place than you have at yours, Jake," Mick says. "I don't see you refusing to help."

The conversation stops at the sound of several motors pulling into the community center. It's our new deputy, Clark Thomas, riding one of the official sheriff four wheelers. Deputy Fred had a gold star painted on three four wheelers and an old pickup to signify the status of those vehicles.

Behind him is an old Ford pickup and an old car. A Pacer? I haven't seen one of those since high school.

The pickup isn't even at a full stop when someone bounces out of the bed. A vaguely familiar girl around the same age as my daughter Angela steps out. Her black hair is piled on top her head, and she's skinny.

"Is that . . . " Kelley says.

"Yes!" Phil shouts. "Yes, it is. Sylvia!"

She hears her name and gives a huge smile, saying something to the others in the pickup bed before sprinting toward Phil and Kelley. I watch as a second, nearly identical woman scampers over the side of the pickup, then darts toward Phil and Kelley. Sabrina. I've met both girls several times when they've visited Bakerville.

From her wheelchair, Doris lets out a yelp. "I can't believe it!"

Figuring Doris is simply excited with the rest of us over Kelley's children making their way here, I smile at her and see she's staring at the old Ford. A tall, blonde, very skinny woman is standing beside the truck. She gives a small wave. She looks familiar, too, but I can't quite place her.

My question is answered when Evan waves frantically and exclaims, "Lindsey, you've made it."

"She's made it," Doris cries. "Evan, she's here. I knew she'd make it."

Lindsey shuffles over to Doris. She isn't moving nearly as quick as Sylvia and Sabrina did. Her movement is with effort. Is she ill? Doris, impatient for Lindsey to reach her, is almost bouncing in her wheelchair.

As I'm watching Doris, Kelley, and Phil have their daughters in their arms, hugs, tears, and cries of delight fill the air. Everyone present is smiling.

"Momma, oh, Momma," Lindsey sobs, embracing Doris. "I'm so sorry you're hurt. We tried to get here as soon as we could so we could help you."

"I'm fine, and you're here now."

Lindsey let's go of her mom long enough to hug Evan, patiently waiting for his turn.

"You okay, Linds?"

"I'm . . . " She shakes her head and breaks down, the sobs wracking her body. "Logan . . . he . . . " she chokes.

"Logan didn't make it," Sabrina quietly says. "We were ambushed a few miles from here. Another lady was also killed. We have them in the bed of the truck."

"We were so close," Lindsey cries.

Deputy Clark Thomas taps me on the arm. "Mollie, I met Lindsey before so knew she would be welcomed. She vouched for Sabrina and Sylvia. Plus, they look just like Kelley. So I brought them back also, along with the others in their two cars— "

"Good," I interrupt him, "definitely good to bring them in. You've made a couple of moms very happy."

"Yes, well, there's another party. Showed up right before they did. They weren't traveling together, so they don't know each other."

"Okay. So you use the usual protocol. No one in unless they know someone or have a skill we can't do without." I shrug, starting to turn away, wondering why he's telling me about this.

"Yeah, well, the guy says he knows you. Said if you refuse him, I'm supposed to give this envelope to your husband."

Give an envelope to my husband? Surely it couldn't be . . . I feel the blood drain from my face. My heart is pounding in my ears.

"His name?" I ask quietly.

"Brad. Brad Quinton."

Brad. Not only have I tried to forget him, I've hoped to stay away from him. There's no room in my life for a person like him. I guess he thinks differently.

Last month, he called me on my work phone. I thought I'd convinced him to leave me be. Guess not, he called again on the day of the plane crashes. He told me he wasn't going away, wasn't going to let the matter drop. He said he was in Wyoming on business and he'd show up on my doorstep. With everything that's happened since, I never thought he would. *Why would he?*

Even in the end of the world, I can't get away from my slightly scandalous past.

Before I can say anything to Clark Thomas, Doris shouts, "What are you doing here?"

I look toward her as she's pulling her pistol from the special pocket holster she constructed on the wheelchair. She's pointing it at an exceptionally beautiful, very blond woman in her early to midthirties.

Barbie. She reminds me of a Barbie doll. No, that's not right. She has the beauty of a Barbie doll but is much too skinny. Her body is more of an underweight gymnast as opposed to Barbie.

"Well, Albatross. You are the last person I'd expect to see," the skinny Barbie says.

"Likewise, Peregrine. Now put your hands where I can see them and sit yourself down on that chair." She motions to a chair a dozen feet away. "I know full well what you're capable of, and I plan to put a bullet between your eyes if I even get an inkling you're deviating from what I tell you to do."

"Mom? What's going on?" Lindsey stammers.

"Who would've thought it?" Doris replies in an almost dreamlike tone. "It's the end of the world as we know it, and my past has returned to haunt me."

Thank you for spending your time with the people of Bakerville, Wyoming.

If you have five minutes, you'd make this writer very happy if you could write a short Amazon review.

I appreciate you!

Join my reader's club!

Receive a complimentary copy of *Wyoming Refuge: A Havoc in Wyoming Prequel*. As part of my reader's club, you'll be the first to know about new releases and specials. I also share info on books I'm reading, preparedness tips, and more.

Please sign up on my website:

MillieCopper.com

Now Available

Havoc in Wyoming

Part 1: Caldwell's Homestead

Jake and Mollie Caldwell started their small farm and homestead to be able to provide for an uncertain future for their family, friends, and community. They have tried to plan for everything, but they never imagined this would happen.

Part 2: Katie's Journey

Katie loves living on her own while finishing up her college degree, working her part-time jobs, and building a relationship with her boyfriend, Leo. When disaster strikes, being away from family isn't quite so nice, and home is over a thousand miles away. Will she make it home before the United States falls apart?

Part 3: Mollie's Quest

Two or three times a year, Mollie Caldwell travels for business. Being away from her Wyoming farmstead is both a fun time and a challenge. They started their farm to be able to provide for an uncertain future for their family, friends, and community. The farm keeps the entire family busy, meaning extra work for her husband while she's away. This time, while on her business trip, terrorists attack. Her weeklong business trip becomes much longer as she tries to make her way home.

Part 4: Shields and Ramparts

The United States, and the community of Bakerville, face a new threat... a threat that could change America forever. As the neighbors band together, all worry about friends and family members. Have they found safety from this latest danger?

Part 5: Fowler's Snare

Welcome to Bakerville, the sleepy Wyoming community Mollie and Jake Caldwell have chosen as their family retreat. At the edge of the wilderness, far away from the big city, they were so sure nothing bad could ever happen in such a protected place. They were wrong. Now, with the entire nation in peril, coming together as a community is the only way they can survive. But not everyone in the community has the people of Bakerville's best interest at heart.

Part 6: Pestilence in the Darkness

Surrounded by danger, they band together with the community of Bakerville to move to a new defensible location. But they weren't prepared to have to give up so much for the security they so desperately need. And they quickly learn trust must be earned, not freely given.

Part 7: My Refuge and Fortress

When Jake and a group of hunters return to Bakerville and find their former neighbors slaughtered, they realize there is a new, even more deadly threat. Will their reinforced location be secure enough? And what about the radio announcement from the president? Will his promise of help arrive in time?

Find these titles on Amazon:
www.amazon.com/author/milliecopper

Acknowledgments

Thanks to:

Ameryn Tucker my editor, beta reader, and daughter wrapped in one. I had a story I wanted to tell, and Ameryn encouraged me and helped me bring it to life.

My youngest daughter, Kes, graphic artist extraordinaire, who pulled out the vision in my head and brought it to life to create an amazing cover.

My husband who gave me the time and space I needed to complete this dream and was very patient as I'd tell him the same plot ideas over and over and over.

Two more daughters and a young son who willingly listened to me drone on and on about story lines and ideas while encouraging me to "keep going."

Wayne Stinnett, author (WayneStinnett.com). A few years ago, I was looking for tips on moving my nonfiction PDF books to a new platform. I read Mr. Stinnett's book *Blue Collar to No Collar*, and while there were useful tips for nonfiction, what I really discovered was, I had a story I wanted to tell. As long as I can remember, I'd start creating narratives in my head and, occasionally, move them to paper. *Blue Collar to No Collar*, and specifically Wayne's story, inspired me to move forward. Imagine my thrill and surprise when an email to him received a response and tips on how to proceed in my own publishing. Thank you, Mr. Stinnett! I'm also a fan of his fiction works, *Jesse McDermitt Caribbean Adventure Series* and *Charity Styles Novel Caribbean Thriller Series*—very fun reads!

My amazing Beta Readers! An extra special thanks to Tim M. for his expertise in firearms and all things that go boom, Joe I. for reminding me to keep it simple, and Judy S. for always saying, "I can't wait to find out what happens next!"

And to you, my readers, for spending your time with the people of Bakerville, Wyoming.

Notes on Shields and Ramparts

For the fictional Caldwells, preparedness is a lifestyle. Many times, a book like this will result in a wake-up to the need to become prepared. Or for those who are already preparedness-minded, the need to move on to the next level.

To help you with your "prepper" research, I've developed a Pinterest page full of information shared in Shields and Ramparts. Go to: https://www.pinterest.com/MillieCopper33/havoc-in-wyoming-part-4-shields-and-ramparts/

About the Author

Millie Copper, writer of Cozy Apocalyptic Fiction, was born in Nebraska but never lived there. Her parents fully embraced wanderlust and moved regularly, giving her an advantage of being from nowhere and everywhere.

As an adult, Millie is fully rooted in a solar-powered home in the wilds of Wyoming with her husband and young son, milking ornery goats and tending chickens on their small homestead. In their free time, they escape to the mountains for a hike or laze along the bank of the river to catch their dinner. Four adult daughters, three sons-in-law, and three grandchildren round out the family.

Since 2009, Millie has authored articles on traditional foods, alternative health, homesteading, and preparedness-many times all within the same piece. Millie has penned five nonfiction, traditional food focused books, sharing how, with a little creativity, anyone can transition to a real foods diet without overwhelming their food budget.

The twelve-installment *Havoc in Wyoming* Christian Post-Apocalyptic fiction series uses her homesteading, off-the-grid, and preparedness lifestyle as a guide. The adventure continues with the *Montana Mayhem* series, scheduled for release in the summer of 2021.

Find Millie at www.MillieCopper.com
Facebook: www.facebook.com/MillieCopperAuthor/
Amazon: www.amazon.com/author/milliecopper
BookBub: https://www.bookbub.com/authors/millie-copper

Made in the USA
Monee, IL
21 July 2022